Other Books by
Christina Dodd

CANDLE IN THE WINDOW
CASTLES IN THE AIR
THE GREATEST LOVER IN ALL ENGLAND
A KNIGHT TO REMEMBER
MOVE HEAVEN AND EARTH
ONCE A KNIGHT
OUTRAGEOUS
PRICELESS
RULES OF ENGAGEMENT
RULES OF SURRENDER
THE RUNAWAY PRINCESS
THAT SCANDALOUS EVENING
SOMEDAY MY PRINCE
TREASURE IN THE SUN
A WELL FAVORED GENTLEMAN
A WELL PLEASURED LADY

CHRISTINA DODD

Rules of Attraction

Book Three of the Governess Brides Series

AVON BOOKS

An Imprint of HarperCollinsPublishers

This is a work of fiction. Names, characters, places, and incidents are products of the author's imagination or are used fictitiously and are not to be construed as real. Any resemblance to actual events, locales, organizations, or persons, living or dead, is entirely coincidental.

AVON BOOKS
An Imprint of HarperCollins*Publishers*
10 East 53rd Street
New York, New York 10022-5299

Dedicated with love to the Hall Sisters,
great aunts and grandmothers
for an entire generation.
We sang Silver Bells.
We drank orangeade.
We danced the hokey~pokey.
We were a family.
Thank you. You created wonderful memories.

Miss Hannah Setterington,
Sole proprietress of

The Distinguished Academy of Governesses

Which for three years has offered
the finest in governesses, companions, and instructors,
would like to announce she has sold

The Distinguished Academy of Governesses

~~For a fine fortune, and intends to look into the problems~~

~~from her past which continue to haunt her~~

effective March 4, 1843

~~yesterday.~~

1

*A*t this moment, Miss Hannah Setterington could unequivocally state that she was alone. Completely, absolutely, bleakly alone. As she let her valise slide with a thud onto the wooden boards of the railway platform, she looked around in the Lancashire twilight. No building rose among the encroaching trees. No welcoming light beckoned through a shaded window, no human voices grumbled or laughed, and the faint city glow that surrounded London even on the darkest of nights was absent here in the depths of the country. Indeed, she could no longer see the outlines of the mountains that rose to the north. Night and fog were settling over the landscape, the train was nothing more than a departing rumble along the tracks, and right now, changing her mind about this position of caretaker to the marquess of Raeburn's elderly aunt seemed wise.

But to whom could she announce her decision? The servant she had assumed would meet her was nowhere to be seen along the rural road that wound over the hill, past the platform and out of sight.

And she had a mission herein. She had come here to fulfill her heart's desire, and she wouldn't leave until she had done so.

Although she knew it was impossible for her to have made a mistake, she fumbled in her reticule and brought forth the letter sent by the housekeeper who had hired her. Hannah squinted through the rapidly fading light and read in Mrs. Trenchard's beautiful penmanship: *Take the train to Presham Crossing, arriving there on March 5, 1843, and there depart it.*

Hannah knew the date to be March 5. She glanced up at the sign erected above the newly constructed platform. Proudly it proclaimed *Presham Crossing.*

I will send a coach to bring you to Raeburn Castle, where the master most anxiously desires your arrival.

Hannah considered the narrow road again. No coach. No servants. No anything. Tucking the letter back into her reticule, she sighed and wondered why this evidence of ineptitude surprised her. In her experience, efficiency was a commodity she possessed which most others did not. Indeed, it was her efficiency that had enabled her to run the Distinguished Academy of Governesses alone these past three years, and successfully enough that when she had gone to Adorna, Lady Bucknell, and asked for help in selling it, Adorna had bought it for herself. "I need something to occupy my time since Wynter took over the family business," she had said as she wrote out a check for a tidy sum.

Now, at the age of twenty-seven, Hannah found herself in the enviable position of never needing to work again.

Although she would, of course. From the time she could remember, she had always worked. Sewing, running errands, helping out as a maid. Even when she'd studied at school, she had labored to be the best . . . then there had been that brief, terrible, and wonderful time when she had not worked.

Pulling her cape closely against her neck, she looked again at the road, but it remained obstinately empty and the light was fading fast.

Lately she had all too often recalled those days when she had been useless, unnecessary, a possession. Although the clarity of her memories discomfited her, it failed to surprise her. Every time she came to a crossroads in her life, a time when everyday tasks failed to occupy each second, her mind drifted back to the past, and she wondered again. At moments such as these, standing alone while wisps of fog became drifts and banks, blotting out the stars and wrapping her in isolation, she pondered what would happen if she returned to Liverpool, where the past awaited her.

Yet always she rejected the idea. In the end, she was too much the coward to dare face the consequences of her youthful misdeeds—and too wise to brood about them now.

Tucking her chin into her wool muffler and her gloved hands under her arms, she turned her thoughts along a more useful path—what to do. The servant had failed her, the village was nowhere in sight, and the night grew frigid. She would certainly not give way to panic because she'd been abandoned.

At least she knew she hadn't been followed from London. One of the many reasons she'd taken this position was the recent suspicion that she was being watched. Either that, or one of the three very somber, identically clad gentlemen who had taken the house across the street visited the market when she did, attended the theater when she did, and even appeared in Surrey where she attended the baptism of Charlotte's second child and visited with Pamela.

And who cared enough about the humbly born owner of a London business to find her and observe her every movement?

Only one man . . . and in all fairness, how could he ever forget her?

So when a job request came in for a companion for an elderly lady in Lancashire, she had decreed it to be fate. She sold her business and slipped away from London. The ignorant might call this flight. She preferred to call it a sabbatical.

She nodded firmly. Yes, a sabbatical to consider her future. The future of Hannah Setterington.

Still no coach. No driver. She considered the ways she had taught student governesses to deal with such dilemmas—with good sense and without rancor. If no one appeared within the hour, she would step onto the road and start walking, and hope that whichever direction she chose would be toward Presham Crossing. From there she would hire someone to take her to Raeburn Castle. When she arrived, she would give Mrs. Trenchard, the housekeeper, a firm but thorough upbraiding. Gently bred women who took positions such as governess and caretaker were frequently abused by the servants below stairs. Hannah meant to start as she would go on, and that included demanding respect. If that wasn't possible, then she'd best know at once before she became attached to the elderly aunt who, she'd been assured in the exchange of letters, was a lovely lady, if occasionally a little confused.

Hannah smiled into her fur muff. She liked elderly ladies. She'd been Lady Temperly's companion for six years and with her she'd had the chance to travel the world, seeing the sights of which she had only dreamed. Indeed, traveling with Lady Temperly had been quite different from moving from place to place with her mother, being ignored or taunted by English yeomen and their righteous wives. The glories of the Continent had opened her eyes to another world. . . .

From out in the distance, off to her left, she heard a creak and a pitiful groan. She froze, and for one moment allowed herself to wonder what kind of wild animals roamed so close to the mountains.

Then a *clop*, first one and then another, then another creak . . . with a sigh of relief, she relaxed. She recognized those sounds. Someone in some kind of conveyance had topped the hill and was driving slowly toward her. Dismissing her momentary alarm as if it had never occurred, she walked to the edge of the platform and stood waiting, sure that whoever it was was coming for her. So what if it wasn't a coach; no one else would be out on such an increasingly vile evening.

Although she strained her eyes, she could see nothing. Then a glow formed in the fog, and a wooden cart rolled toward her and stopped. A lantern was hooked to the side, a scraggly-looking character held the reins of a swaybacked nag, and when he opened his mouth he let out a belch that smelled of ale even as far away as she stood. Presham Crossing must be down the road the way he'd come, for he'd obviously been visiting the tavern.

They stared at each other in mutual disgust. She observed a tall man in the height of maturity, but much given to drink and not overfond of cleanliness if the swollen size of his nose and the filthy state of his garments were anything to judge by. She only hoped that the sight of her, dressed in her becoming black traveling clothes and upright with moral conviction and infallible command, would be an inspiration for him.

At last he asked, "Ye Miss Setterington?"

"I am."

In his odd Lancashire accent, he said, "I'm supposed t' bring ye to Raeburn Castle."

She gazed at the cart with its two wooden wheels, its splintered sides and the moldering hay in the back, and judged how little her new employer thought of her. If she had been like most who had no choice but to accept such contempt, she would have been sorely perturbed. But she was Miss Setterington of the Distinguished Academy of Governesses. She could get a position anywhere in the country, and she had enough to money in an account in the Bank of England to leave this place in a huff.

Not that she planned to. Not after she'd searched out this little corner of Lancashire especially—but her employer didn't have to know that.

Tonight she just wanted a hot meal and a warm place to sleep. "Who are you?" she asked.

Her peremptory tone brought his head up. He peered through the gray-and-brown straggles of hair that overhung his forehead. "I'm Alfred."

"You're late." She stepped down the stairs. "My luggage is on the platform. There is a basket and a valise. Hurry and get them, and let's be on our way." He stared, openmouthed, until she snapped, "Look lively now!"

Alfred responded like any dog to a sharp command, lifting his lip in a brief defiant show of teeth, then slithering out of the cart in obedience. As the slump-shouldered driver dragged himself to the pile of bags, she lifted her skirt, pulled herself into the cart, and settled on the wooden board of a driver's seat. From behind the cart, she heard a piteous groan as Alfred hefted her valises onto the pile of hay. She hoped that no vermin resided therein and resolved to examine her clothing when she at last reached a bedchamber in Raeburn Castle. Which, as sluggishly as Alfred moved, might be never.

"Come on, man, you don't want to keep your master waiting," she said.

Her encouragement produced no detectable increase in his speed. She had time to adjust her skirt and perch herself carefully on the far edge of the seat before he hoisted himself up beside her, bringing with him a fresh wave of ale-smell and body odor. He filled more than his half of the seat, not with any corpulence but with deceptively wide shoulders. She noted his broad hands as he lifted the reins to slap the horse—a horse who projected as much discouraged weariness as her driver. The nag leaned into the bridle and pulled the cart forward, then started the slow *clip-clop* of the hooves.

Then, and only then, did Alfred say, "He's not me master."

"Excuse me?" Hannah realized he was responding to her earlier remark. "Do you not work for the earl of Raeburn?"

"I work at Raeburn Castle. Have me whole life. But th' master we have now is nawt th' master we started out wi', nor th' master we'll have in th' end."

She worked through his surly comment before replying, "I suppose on a hereditary estate that is always true."

"Fourth lord we've had in as many years."

"Good heavens." As they reached the top of the hill, a minuscule breeze touched her cheek, and for a second she could see the dark shapes of the trees leaning toward her. "What ill fortune has brought about so many changes?"

"Cursed."

The trees disappeared as the fog closed in again. "Who cursed?"

Alfred threw her a disgusted glance. "The family's cursed."

"Ah." She couldn't restrain a grin as she realized he must be one of those peculiar men who got pleasure from recounting silly yarns. "I'm familiar with such tales. The young ladies I used to teach were fond of telling them. So the family is cursed. By a gypsy? A witch? For what reason? Love thwarted? Revenge?"

"Ye're making fun, lady, but that doesn't change th' fact we lost two heirs t' th' estate ten years ago in a shipwreck off th' Scottish coast, then th' old lord died four years ago, then his cousin last year went off a cliff int' the ocean, then *his* brother from a fall down th' stairs, an' now we've got this blackguard who's no more than a distant relative an' who ain't even from Lancashire."

Hannah's amusement faded. She knew better than to believe any tale this ignominious servant reeled off, but if it were true, the tragedy could not be discounted. "You can't blame the current lord for the place of his upbringing," she said. "Rather judge him on his good works and care for the estate."

Alfred snorted. "Been here less than a year an' got things running shipshape—"

"There, you see?" she said encouragingly.

"— But what's that worth when he's a murderer of his own flesh an' kind?"

The wooden wheels hit the ruts so hard Hannah's teeth jammed together. Her rump hurt from the wooden bench. Wisps of fog moistened her cheeks. Worst of all, she couldn't find her common sense. But she kept her voice steady and disapproving as she said, "You should know better than to indulge in slanderous gossip about the man who carries the title of your hereditary lord."

"Not me gossip, miss. 'Twere th' gossip from his own personal servants, it 'twere." Alfred hunched his shoulders yet further and stared ahead sullenly as if seeing a road made invisible by the mist. "Years ago, it was, he married a young lady, pretty as ye please, who was always laughin' an' teasin' him t' distraction, an' when they weren't lovin', they were fightin'. Fightin', fightin', fightin'. Then they'd love an' then they'd fight some more. His lordship's coachman says after one really big row, she up an' disappeared."

"That doesn't mean his lordship killed his wife."

"A female body was found weeks later, savaged by beasts."

Still Hannah valiantly struggled to be the voice of logic. "But that was not proof."

"He went an' looked at th' body, said it weren't hers, but th' young wife's maid accused him t' his face o' killing her. He didn't deny it, just stared, grim as death, until she ran from him. He's nawt been th' same since. Never smiles, nawt a kind word t' anyone, an' he can't sleep. Rides th' estate at night, an' that's no gossip, miss. Saw him meself one night, his eyes burnin' an' fevered."

She supposed the nag was finding its way up the steep slope on its own, for the reins were slack in Alfred's hands. She sat, clutching her reticule in one hand and the seat with the other, fighting the temptation to look over her shoulder.

In premonitory tones, Alfred warned, "If I were ye, miss, I'd get out while I could. A man who'll kill once'll kill again."

How had Alfred recognized her as a prime candidate for this kind of spooking? Probably he was laughing to himself while she surreptitiously tried to ease the chill of goose bumps from her skin.

Well, she wouldn't give him the satisfaction of knowing he had succeeded. In as tart a tone as she could manage, she retorted, "Even if His Lordship were the bloody-minded killer you say, I doubt that I'm important enough to attract his notice."

"Can't stay out o' the way o' a confirmed killer."

"If I don't stay at Raeburn Castle, it won't be because I'm deterred by absurd rumors of murder, but because of the shabby treatment which I've received thus far."

Alfred shrugged. "It's yer funeral, miss."

Such a cheerful fellow! "How much longer until we're there?"

"We're at th' top o' th' tor." He pointed ahead as if she could actually see the landmark he showed her. "There's th' gatehouse. Th' moat's been filled in these two hundred years. We're in th' courtyard now."

The lights of the castle loomed out of the mist in shocking suddenness. The wooden wheels rattled as they rolled across paving stones and stopped in the middle of the drive. Tilting her head back, Hannah looked up as far as she could, stunned by the massive pile of granite that rose so abruptly out of the ground. Somehow she'd been transported back in time and even now drove up to a castle that looked no different than it had in medieval times, when the windows had been nothing more than slits and every feature had been designed with defense in mind.

"Almost seven hundred years old, parts o' it. Many a child born here, many a life snuffed." Alfred turned and looked at Hannah, and his rheumy eyes shone moist and morose. "Good fortune t' ye, miss."

A door opened and a large square of light shone out, and against it she saw silhouetted several shapes, four male, one female.

A woman's voice blending a faint Lancashire burr with gentility, called, "Did ye get her, Alfred?"

"Aye."

"About time. The master's been fretting this last hour."

The female and three of the males, two with lanterns, hurried toward the cart, the female burbling with speech. "Miss Setterington? I'm Mrs. Judith Trenchard, and I beg yer pardon for the mode of yer transport. There was a . . . misunderstanding."

A misunderstanding? How interesting.

"I hope ye haven't been inconvenienced," Mrs. Trenchard said.

"Not at all." A footman placed a step for Hannah and helped her from her seat and onto the ground. "But I would beg for a maid to brush out my clothing."

As the footmen lifted their lanterns, dismay showed on Mrs. Trenchard's plump, lined face. She carried perhaps sixty-five years, and she exuded an air of competence and energy that contrasted with her apologies and confession of error. "I'll certainly assign you a maid. Come in before the damp settles into your bones."

Too late, it appeared. As Hannah stepped across the threshold into a dim cavern, she shivered, then found she couldn't stop.

Mrs. Trenchard clucked. "Billie, bring Miss Setterington a blanket. Aye, miss, 'tis an evil night to be out. I don't know what those new-fashioned railroads are thinking, to deliver at such an hour. Mark my words, they'll never catch on in Lancashire if they continue with such wrong-headed behavior. Thank you, Billie." Wrapping Hannah in the warm, clean wool spread, she hurried her toward the stone stairs that wound upward. "The master's waiting for ye."

Mrs. Trenchard was taller than Hannah, an unusually great height for a woman, and heavy-boned and broad-beamed. She clattered as she walked, the iron ring at her belt full of the keys that were the badge of her station. In her clasp Hannah felt like a leaf swept along in a great and powerful wind. "I'd like to freshen up first," Hannah said.

"Ah, no. We don't keep the master waiting here." Mrs. Trenchard sounded quite stern. "He's not as dread as they say, but severe and likes his way. I don't cross him and ye're already past the time he expected ye."

Hannah wanted to point out that that wasn't her fault.

But Mrs. Trenchard talked on as she pushed Hannah up the stairs. "The master wants to change the entrance so that guests enter a foyer on the second level. The kitchen's no way for visitors to first see Raeburn, and this stairway is so old and worn 'tis easy to take a tumble. In fact, the previous lord . . . but no matter." Stopping in the middle of the stairway, she leaned against the wall and, grimacing, held her side.

Looking down the spiral of stone steps, Hannah was alarmed. Taking Mrs. Trenchard's arm, she asked, "Are you ill?"

"Nonsense." Mrs. Trenchard shook her off and pushed her along once more. "Never been ill a day in my life. Hardy stock, that's me. My mother passed on just five years ago at the great age of eighty-nine." She pointed toward the glow of light from above. "Now, once ye're out of the kitchens, it's a beautiful house."

Hannah nodded. Perhaps Mrs. Trenchard had just had a bad day. Certainly she seemed strong enough.

"After the old lord died, the next two masters started fixing up the place and the last master, rest his soul, even put in stoves that heat twice as well as a fireplace. This lord was busy when he got the title, but now he's restoring the tapestries and cleaning the woodwork and replacing all the old parts. It's grand. Ye'll see."

"I'm sure I will." Hannah didn't know if Mrs. Trenchard always spoke so freely or if she were nervous, but as they reached the top of the stairs she realized the housekeeper told the truth. The cruder part of the castle had been lacquered over with a combination of modern furnishings and beeswax. The arched corridor widened, then opened onto a large, beautiful, well-furnished room that blended the ancient with the modern. The ceiling soared so high the illumination of the flickering candles could not reach into its heights. Dark wood paneled the walls, and polished shields alternated with old-fashioned gold-and-scarlet tapestries. Yet the furnishings were both comfortable and new, and for the first time since she'd come to Lancashire, Hannah saw a bit of the current mode that ruled London.

"The great hall," Mrs. Trenchard announced with great pride.

"So handsome!" Hannah replied. Her teeth still chattered.

She hated that. At this, her first meeting with the staff, the master and the elderly aunt, she wanted to appear strong.

Mrs. Trenchard turned down a dim gallery. Paintings lined the walls, doors opened off its length and at its end, Hannah could see a broad stairway that disappeared in the gloom. Yet everything was luminous and well-cared-for, and one of the doors stood, not opened, but propped against the wall.

As they passed, Mrs. Trenchard gestured inside. "The master is having the library refitted with all new oak bookshelves painted a pale yellow. He says it'll lighten the room, and I say it's fine."

"It sounds lovely."

"Then there's some that say we should leave well enough alone. The old ways are the best, they say."

She sounded interested in Hannah's opinion, although Hannah thought herself too new here to venture one. So she tried to straddle the issue. "Of course it's necessary to preserve some of the old things, but I'm sure it's easier for you if the castle is new and shining."

Mrs. Trenchard rounded on Hannah. "Why?"

"Because you're the housekeeper and the older possessions are fragile and harder to clean?" Hannah ventured.

Mrs. Trenchard studied at her with a hint of suspicion. Her eyes were a light color, although Hannah couldn't see them clearly in this light, and although she wasn't as old as she'd first appeared, the perpetual lines of worry aged her.

"Ye might be right. I don't know yet." Still unmoving, Mrs. Trenchard said, "If ye don't mind me saying—I've worked in this castle my whole life, and I'm right fond of his lordship's aunt. All of us who work here are."

"I'm pleased to hear it." Pleased to hear her charge was congenial. Even pleased that the servants liked her enough to interrogate Hannah.

"If ye don't mind me asking—the lord says ye have experience minding elderly ladies."

"I spent six years caring for Lady Temperly."

"She liked ye?"

"There was a mutual respect between us, and she was very kind. She left me her house. In that house I was able to start the Distinguished Academy of Governesses. I will always remember Lady Temperly affectionately."

Mrs. Trenchard studied her for another minute, then nodded. "The master's picked a good one, then. There'll be no turning back now." She led the way to a dark, ornately carved wooden door. "Here ye go. The master's inside the drawing chamber. He frightens some, but he's ne'er been aught but polite to me. Ye'll get used to his abrupt manner soon enough. Chin up, now, and stop yer trembling. It'll be warm inside."

Mrs. Trenchard whisked the blanket out of Hannah's grip and looked her over. Apparently she found little of which to approve, for she muttered, "No time to do more." Opening the door, she stepped inside.

Hannah followed her in and with a brief glance took in the small, comfortable surroundings. A fire burned on the hearth. Fresh flowers nodded in vases. A few books were scattered on a table beside a large, green brocade armchair. Paintings in the newest soft and delicate style warmed the plaster walls—and a gentleman stood with his back to the room, gazing out of the shiny, glass-paned window where beyond only black night and endless fog were visible. He was tall, broad-shouldered, long-legged, wore stark black and white and clasped his hands behind his back. His black hair hung over his collar, and for all the notice he took of Mrs. Trenchard and Hannah, he might not have heard their entrance.

Certainly he did not turn when Mrs. Trenchard curtsied and announced, "Miss Hannah Setterington, my lord."

For one moment he stood stiffly, a lonely figure waiting for . . . something. Then in a low, deep voice he commanded, "Leave us."

Hannah's breath caught.

That voice. That tone.

Her heart gave a thud. Then another. Then another, marking each second, each excitement, each fear.

From the back he looked like . . . and the reflection in the glass seemed to be familiar.

But she knew how wrong she could be. When *he* dwelt in her thoughts, all men looked like him.

And yet . . . and yet . . .

Vaguely, she heard the door shut. Slowly, he turned to face her.

And the foreboding which had haunted her for nine years became reality.

This man had never killed his wife.

Because *she* was his wife.

2

Dougald. Dougald Pippard. Not the marquess of Raeburn. Plain Mr. Dougald Pippard, a wealthy Liverpool gentleman and entrepreneur.

But he stood with his back to the window, and there could be no doubt. This was her husband, for his vivid eyes glowed with triumph. He had always been a keen observer of human emotions; now, she knew, he marked the winds of recollection and shock that swept her.

Yet when she had caught her breath, he said only, "You're late."

Late. Yes, nine years late for a meeting with the man she had married. Married despite her misgivings, and only after she had run away for the first time. She had caught a train, he had caught her and . . . "You're not the earl of Raeburn." Her voice didn't sound like her own. Too deep, for one thing, and very steady, considering the circumstances. "You can't be."

His lips, the narrow, chiseled lips over which she had once loved to linger, moved in slow, precise enunciation. "I assure you, I am."

"How? But . . . how?" A shudder rattled her.

His eyes narrowed. "Come to the fire."

She didn't wait to be told twice. Her instinct might be to flee, but her good sense told her he had set this trap with care and guile, and he would relish the chance to do whatever a man did to his runaway wife. So she would not incite him.

Besides, she was cold.

But her defensive instinct could not be denied. She couldn't persuade herself to take her gaze off of him for even so long as it took her to walk to the fire. So she sidled toward the cluster of chairs and tables around the hearth, watching him endlessly.

The years had wrought changes. So many changes.

When Hannah had first come to live under his roof in Liverpool, her mother had gone to work as his housekeeper, and she had been a skinny, wide-eyed twelve-year-old. Yet even then she had been fascinated by his face: the bold, French cheekbones, the strong jaw, the plain, short nose and the large ears. His skin had been brown, but his eyes were a beautiful gold-speckled green that bespoke some Scottish ancestry. His lashes were long and black and silky. His hair was fine and black and shiny. And he had been so tall: To the youthful Hannah, he had been the essential mix of Viking and Celt and salt-of-the-earth English. His genteel family had lived in the Northlands for two thousand years. They had adapted and adopted every new wave of migration while retaining their own Celtic roots, and Dougald liked to boast he was related to every family north of London.

Now time and experience had refined his features, giving them a bleakness that matched the bare, grim rock of the castle he called his own. His skin seemed stretched thinly across his bones, his gaze chill with intent, and his hair . . . dear God, a streak of white iced each temple.

The past nine years had not been kind to . . . whatever title he called himself.

Yet beneath her fright and dismay, treacherous desire rose in her.

Did he want her still? Would he want her tonight?

And would she fight, or would she want him in return?

She tripped on the fringe of the carpet, and that brought her back to the here and now, to the reality of the predicament in which she found herself and to the relentless observation of . . . her husband. She wasn't really close enough for the fire to do her any good, but the scent of the burning wood filled her lungs with the promise of warmth. If she remained where she stood, she could keep an armchair between them. A feeble defense, but at least a defense. Clutching the upholstery in her trembling fingers, she asked, "Tell me. How can it be that you are the earl of Raeburn?"

"I was fifth in line for the title. Somehow, the others died, and here I am."

He had always smiled before. He'd always had charm and confidence. The confidence was still there, but the charm and smiles had disappeared as if they'd never been. She should know him, but seeing him was like facing a stranger . . . a stranger who held rights over her. A stranger who had watched her grow up and who knew *her* only too well.

But she wasn't an overly polite, tentative eighteen-year-old anymore, either. She held advantages of experience and composure he could scarcely guess at. Schooling her expression and her tone to match the one she used to interview prospective governesses, she said, "You were a cotton merchant."

"I still am."

"You invested in railways."

"A risk which paid off royally."

"You *weren't* in line for any title."

"Obviously I was." He gestured around him. "I'm also the fourth in line for a barony." He shrugged, his broad shoulders moving up and down in a gesture of disdain. "Yet I can't imagine anything more pathetic than a man who gets his self-respect by boasting of a distant, noble connection."

She could. During the time she'd run the Distinguished Academy of Governesses, she'd met plenty of men who thought an obscure connection to William the Conqueror made them respectable enough to do whatever they wanted with her girls—or with her. She had always disabused them—vain, selfish gentlemen that they were. Too bad this lord was forged from a different metal. A little vanity and selfishness made a man easier to handle.

"You're late," Dougald repeated his earlier complaint. "I expected you over an hour ago. And don't tell me the train was not on schedule. It always runs on schedule."

"Your man failed to meet me promptly." She shivered again, chilled by a sense of lingering cold and the frost emanating from Dougald.

"My man?"

"Alfred."

"Alfred met you?" His voice didn't rise, but his tone didn't bode well. "In his *cart*?"

She remembered only too well his temper, so she carefully explained, "Mrs. Trenchard said there was a misunderstanding."

"Yes, I would say there was." Ruddy color lit his cheeks.

For a moment Hannah thought he looked much as the young Dougald had before he flew into a rage, and she took comfort in sighting the man she had known so well.

Better the devil you know than the devil you don't know.

Then he took a moderating breath. "My fault. I've been here only a year, and Mrs. Trenchard doesn't yet know which of my comments she should disregard."

The man she had married seldom acknowledged fault. Now he accepted blame, yet the housekeeper feared him so much she'd abused a fellow employee. "What did you say to her . . . about me?" Hannah asked.

"The truth."

Uncomfortable, to know yourself discussed before your arrival. "Did you tell her I was your wife?"

"Haven't you heard? My wife is dead, murdered at my own hands." He held them up, fingers shaped as if they cupped her neck. "I wouldn't deprive the people hereabouts of the pleasure they gain in repeating the tale."

Gruesome, to hear her own death discussed in such an inimical tone. "Why . . . how did such a story start?"

Unmoving, he ignored her question while measuring her with his gaze. "Sit down."

"Dougald, how could you have let such horrible gossip spread?" she insisted.

"Take off your hat. Remove your gloves and your wrap. Sit down and make yourself comfortable. You'll be here for a long, long time."

Straightening her shoulders, lifting her chin, she said with chilly, preemptory precision, "I don't intend to stay."

His jaw hardened and he pressed his lips together. Abruptly, he strode across the room, taking huge steps, right toward her. Chills chased up her spine, but she held her ground. He halted in front of the chair, blocking out the fire's light. "You keep this chair between us like a shield that will protect you."

His large hand reached out to her. She watched it and schooled herself not to flinch as he touched her. Touched her for the first time in so many years.

He cupped her jaw, his blunt fingertips brushing her ear, his palm lifting her chin. He wasn't rough. He touched her as if she were still the tall, impressible girl he had married, and that one, meager contact brought her a pleasure as sharp as pain.

"You hide behind that chair, but if I wished, I could pick it up and fling it across the room. I could take you to the floor and have you now, darling, and all your cries would be of delight." His thumb slid up and caressed her lips, and for the first time he smiled, a rapierlike smile of pernicious resolve. "But that would be too easy, so have a seat."

3

Hannah felt the stroke of Dougald's fingers on her face and stared at his grim, savagely satisfied features. All trace of the youthful, charming pirate had disappeared, leaving her confronting a brute so intent on vengeance and so puffed with importance he threatened her with subjugation and tyranny.

But if he was no longer the smiling daredevil, neither was she the soft-spoken innocent.

Wrapping her fingers around his wrist, she moved his hand away. "Be polite and I'll sit. Threaten me again, and I'm off to find Mrs. Trenchard and my supper."

He blinked as if he'd not heard such a contemptuous response in a great many years.

"Step back," she repeated.

He did, one single short step away from the chair.

Interesting. During the whole time she had lived with him, he had never, ever done anything she suggested or demanded, not even step backward to give her some breathing room. As far as he was concerned, he was always right, and he had cajoled or kissed or ignored all of her appeals and complaints. Now she wondered . . . had he learned compromise? Was he humoring her? Or had she learned to speak with such a voice of command that he actually listened?

Although, truth to tell, he still stood too close. But she would be satisfied with even so small a gain. Lifting her arms, she pulled the long hat pin free. "It was a long trip, and I find I'm feeling peckish. Please call for a meal."

He watched her body greedily, as if her raised arms had allowed him to view her naked glories rather than the formidable black wool of her winter cloak. She wasn't shivering anymore, she noted; the rush of anger and the uncomfortable brush with ancient passions had warmed her, and she was glad to place the hat on the side table and set about making herself comfortable. She unwrapped her soft wool muffler and removed her gloves, and stacked them atop the hat. Then, one by one, she slid the buttons of the cloak free.

"A simple repast will suffice," she said pointedly.

Dougald didn't seem to hear, hadn't even moved. He stared at her bare hands, at her long neck, and most of all at her face, his gaze lingering as if to compare the memory of what she had been with what she had become.

About that, Hannah had no illusions. In her youth, Dougald had told her repeatedly how very much he loved the silky glide of her blond hair, the brown eyes with that startling slant and the smooth skin with that faint hint of toast. She looked, he had said, like an Egyptian goddess.

But it had been nine years since last he'd seen her, and the past three years of hard work had truly wrought changes. Two white hairs hid among the blond strands—she'd found them after a particularly difficult month which involved a seduced governess, an indignant lord, and a swift marriage. Despite the best efforts of her devoted cook, she had lost the plumpness that had given her face its sweet roundness. And as she strode from classroom to classroom, from market to town house, her lush, pampered form had grown sleek and wiry.

So when she slipped her coat off her shoulders, she held it and waited to see what he would say.

He said nothing. He just looked without expression.

Surprisingly enough, she found his indifference lowering. Not that she wanted to reanimate his fiery threat, but she had thought Dougald would always respond to her. Apparently, in some well-hidden part of her soul, she still nourished the hope that he meant his vows of eternal passion.

Tossing her coat across the back of a settle, she said, "As I eat, we can talk."

"About what do you wish to speak, dear wife?"

"You can tell me how you discovered my whereabouts. You can tell me what your life has been." Most important—"You can tell me what plans you have made for me."

He lifted his chin and looked at her with such arrogance, she might have thought him a lifelong lord. "I will tell you what I wish to tell you. No more."

How she hated that arrogance! How often she'd had to face it in her dealings with the aristocracy! So she treated him with the same impatience she had found effective against other, more insolent noblemen. "Piffle. What good will you achieve by hiding the truth from me?"

"What will I achieve? Why, my own satisfaction, of course." He bowed, walked to the door, and opened it. "Charles." He spoke the word with that faint slur the English used when pronouncing the French name. "Charles, Miss Setterington is hungry. Tell Mrs. Trenchard to bring food." He glanced back at Hannah. "Bring a lot of food."

So he had noted her spare figure. Shutting the door, he leaned against it and observed her once more. "Please." He indicated the chair. "Sit."

As long as he got his way, he would play the polite host. Very well; she would remember why she had taken a job in Lancashire. She in turn would play the polite guest and hope that this farce did not assume the proportions of a tragedy.

Seating herself, she rubbed her chilly fingers before the flames. "Charles is still with you."

"Of course." He strolled across the drawing room, but he took no pains to hide his vigilance. "Where else would he be?"

"In hell, one would hope," she said pensively. The valet had been devoted to his master, and as long as she made Dougald happy, she had been tolerated. But always Charles had made it clear that her demands for attention and respect were the rants of an immature child.

"You haven't changed a bit. You still cherish that unreasoning aversion to Charles."

She almost rose to the bait. Almost. Catching herself, she settled herself back into the comfort of the cushions and nodded to him. "As you say, my lord, but Charles knows my face. What explanation have you given him? That your murdered wife has risen from the grave?"

"Charles knows." Dougald loosened the buttons on his formal coat.

"Knows what?"

Slipping his arms free, he walked toward her. She flinched backward, and he stopped. He smiled down at her with a hearty display of white, even teeth. He flung his coat on the settle over the top of hers.

A plague upon him for frightening her, and the more fool she for allowing him to see her skittishness! Tightly, she smiled back at him and watched as he seated himself. The chair was too close, allowing only a few feet of separation between them, bringing into the air a sense of stifling intimacy. He could observe her in the firelight and candlelight; with very little effort he could reach out and touch her. If she weren't careful, he would touch her, and her skin would flush and her blood heat, and how long could she conceal her body's response from him? "Charles knows what?" she repeated.

"Everything."

"Of course," she said bitterly. "You would never keep a secret from Charles."

"Yes." He loosened the buttons on his black-silk waistcoat. "I would."

Alarm rioted through her veins. His white shirt was shut to his throat, his cravat and collar securely fastened, but the sight of him making himself comfortable recalled other times. Earlier times when she sat on his knee and opened his clothing and to his chest and dark curling hair, and he would have to lock the door to keep out any intruders . . . she took a shuddering breath. She never thought she would say such a thing, but thank God for Charles and the incoming meal!

Cautiously, she asked the first of her questions. "How did you find me?"

"The money."

She bit her lip. She had been afraid of that. "The money I sent to pay you back for my education?"

"For that reason, I am grateful for it." He didn't *look* grateful. He looked incensed. "As for the cash, it was given to charities."

"I didn't care what you did with it. I had sworn I would pay that debt somehow, and when I could, I did."

"And I told you a wife does not reimburse her husband as if he were a dependent."

"I owed you," she said stubbornly. "I was supposed to pay you with children and companionship, and I did not."

"Yet."

That one short word hung like a sword over her head. Did he imagine she had learned meekness in the years she'd been away? Or was he simply willing to call forth the fullness of the law to force her to return to him as his wife?

Moreover, no matter how she wished to, she couldn't board the train and ride away. Not just because he would stop her. He would, of course, but she had outwitted him before and although it would be more difficult this time, she could do it again.

No, she had a mission in Lancashire. She had to stay here until she'd found what she sought. So she sparred with Dougald and hoped that when she escaped him she would do so unscathed. "So that is your plan for me? That I should become your wife

once more and give you children and companionship?"

"My wife is dead, or so they say. How ever would
we explain that?"

He hadn't answered her question. Wretched man, he
was determined to make her wiggle like a worm on a
hook. "A great many things would have to change before I once again took my place as your wife."

"I agree, but I daresay what you think and what I
think should change are entirely different *things*."

"What you and I thought about anything was always
different, my lord. To that we can attribute the failure
of our marriage."

"Dougald Pippard does not fail."

"There." She pointed at him. "That's exactly what I
mean. To you, this marriage is yours and yours alone.
Never mind that I make up the other half of it."

Dougald observed the finger pointed at him, and
with a lazy flip of the hand, said, "You are quite correct. Better that I had said, 'Dougald Pippard and his
wife do not fail.' "

That was not better, and he knew it. "I am not simply a part of you, indistinguishable from your being,"
she said. "I have a name."

"Indeed you do. Mrs. Dougald Pippard. Or rather I
should say—Lady Raeburn."

"Hannah," she said through gritted teeth. "My name
is Hannah."

He ignored her. "In the eyes of the law, you are indistinguishable from me. Mine to do with as I wish."

A threat again. Not physical this time, but a threat
nonetheless. Always before, he had manipulated, ma-
neuvered and intimidated her into the place he wanted

her to occupy. Either he had decided subtlety was wasted on her, or the years had hardened him. "I was never yours to do with as you wished. If you for one moment imagined that, then I must again say it is no surprise that our marriage failed." She waited with what she thought was admirable calm for him to denounce her.

Instead, he said, "Lord Ruskin did warn me you had become a no-nonsense woman filled with resolution. It would appear he was right."

"Lord Ruskin!" Hannah blurted. "How . . . why . . . when did you speak to Lord Ruskin?"

"Which of your questions would you like me to answer first?"

Dougald had spoken to Lord Ruskin. Dougald had confessed . . . heaven only knew what, and now he sat like a great, vengeful lump, smiling at her with a disturbing twist in his smile. She leaned forward and glared. "You make me want to box your ears."

He opened his arms and waited for her to try. But she was not so foolish, and at last he allowed his arms to sink to his side. "I believe you went to your friend Lady Ruskin, told her that you had a payment you wished to make to a certain Dougald Pippard of Liverpool, and without explaining why, asked if she could do so to protect your identity."

He knew it all. Despite her best efforts, he had traced her through her friends—and, if she knew Dougald, he had made matters most unpleasant for Charlotte. But Charlotte was a woman of resolution. "Lady Ruskin is one of my dearest friends, and I do not believe for a second that you succeeded in intimidating her."

"Not at all. Charlotte . . . or rather, Lady Ruskin, is a most agreeable female."

His intimate use of her first name gave Hannah pause.

"In fact, she completely complied with your need for secrecy, and even funneled the monies through her mother-in-law, a certain Lady Bucknell."

"Lady Bucknell?" Hannah thought of the beauteous, gracious Adorna who had so readily agreed to buy the Distinguished Academy of Governesses. Had she been motivated by more than self-interest? "Lady Bucknell told you where I was?"

"No, no." He scoffed as if the conversation should be crystal-clear rather than a maze through which he deliberately led her. "I received the moneys. I traced your payment to Lord and Lady Bucknell's London account. I went to Lord Bucknell at once, thinking really rather vile things about the two of you."

Hannah winced.

"He was incredibly insulted."

Hannah thought of Adorna's proper, stiff-necked husband. "I have no doubt of that."

"But as soon as I explained that I was your husband—"

"My husband." Hannah clutched the material over her racing heart. "You told Lord Bucknell that you were my husband?"

"Of course." As he observed her distress, that smile again twisted Dougald's lips. "He traced the payment to Lady Ruskin, and so the two of us went to Lord Ruskin."

"Lord Ruskin knows we're married?" Hannah came to her feet. *This* was what she feared. "Charlotte knows."

Charlotte Darumple and Miss Pamela Lockhart had started the Governess school with her.

"Yes. Charlotte knows." He observed her as if he'd been anticipating the pleasure of telling her how well and truly he had her surrounded. "But she trusts you implicitly. She insisted there must be a reason for you to run away and not return. She defended you quite hotly."

"Of course she would. She's . . . how long have they known?"

"Several months."

"They knew when I went down to the baby's christening. They never said anything." She searched her mind for any hint of censure. Perhaps from Lord Ruskin, but he didn't approve of her independence. The man sincerely believed each woman should be wed, and of her friends he had been the one most determined to find her a suitable mate. It had taken Charlotte to rein him in. Charlotte, who allowed her husband to rule as king of his home and his business. Charlotte, who controlled him with the strong hand in a velvet glove. But Charlotte . . . when Hannah had seen her, she would have sworn Charlotte was her usual dear self. And she knew. All the time she knew. Heaven only knows what she had been thinking.

Hannah paced away from the fire. "They still told you where I was."

"Lord Ruskin told me where you were. He was quite appalled by our situation."

"Of course he was. He thinks men are God's gift to the feminine gender, that women should be appropriately grateful. If not for Charlotte, he would be insufferable." She stared down at Dougald as he lolled in his chair, then walked away. If she didn't, she truly would try to box his ears, and she was not so foolish as to think he would suffer such an insult without retaliation. "Charlotte will have told Pamela."

"Pamela would be Lady Kerrich, I presume."

She turned on him and her voice rose. "Is there no one in England you didn't confide in?"

"I believe it is only Lord and Lady Bucknell, Lord and Lady Ruskin, and Lord and Lady Kerrich who know the truth. That is not so many people when compared to the whole population of England." He pointed out the fact calmly, as if the knowledge would pacify her.

Pacing back to the fireplace, she gripped the mantel so hard the carved marble cut patterns into her palms. "Those are my friends."

"A close and loyal circle."

Her friends, especially the ladies Pamela and Charlotte, who now knew she hadn't confided the most significant facts of her life. No doubt they were confused, and perhaps hurt by her lack of faith in them. And . . . and she couldn't go to them for succor.

As if he read her mind, he said, "Even if you were to find some way to leave Raeburn Castle—and I assure you, that wouldn't be easy—to seek shelter with your friends would cause friction in their marriages. I don't think you want that."

Of course, he was right. "I shouldn't have sent you the money. No good deed goes unpunished."

"It wasn't a good deed," he said with deadpan composure. "You were taunting me with your still-undiscovered existence."

"No, I wasn't!"

"Lie to yourself if you must, Hannah, but you knew that money would set me on the trail. Even without your friends' help, I would have found you." He leaned back, steepled his fingers before his face. "How could I not? You started a school. A very successful school for governesses, teachers and companions."

"I hoped you wouldn't still be looking," she mumbled.

"Another lie. You knew I would never give up so easily."

All right. So she had known that sooner or later he would find her. And maybe in the depths of her mind she had thought it would be easier if she didn't have to take the initial steps. To find him, call on him, justify her escape from him, then try and justify her lengthy absence when she knew they had to somehow resolve the issue of their marriage. Her skin crawled at the thought of that interview, and yes, perhaps she had imagined the shock of seeing him without warning would offset the preliminary worry. But he . . . he didn't have to point that out in such a hateful manner. "I see my mistake now," she said coldly.

"Very much too late. You had disappeared so effectively I had found no trace of you for eight years." He showed her the number with his fingers. "Eight years, Hannah, and I didn't know if you were alive or dead."

"I sent word!"

"Once! I had a letter once from London telling me you were well and not to worry."

"If I had written you more, you would truly have traced me."

"You were my wife. Of course I would have traced you! Instead I paid through my nose to a detective to watch for you. Do you know how many times I rushed to London, hoping against hope you'd been found, only to be cruelly disappointed?"

She shook her head.

"Nine times." He changed the number of fingers, and Hannah noted they were steady as a rock. "Nine times I rode the train down to the City. I visited whore-houses looking for you, fearing you'd been forced into that dreadful life. In my torment, I imagined you'd become some man's mistress."

He would think that. "As always, my lord, you imagine me to be nothing but a lock of hair and a female form. I am more than that."

"Oh, yes, you remind me of the dress shops! I visited thirty dress shops, Hannah. I thought that certainly you would be working in a dress shop or at a milliner's. You weren't. You weren't anywhere."

"No, I was—"

"Abroad." He smiled, a showing of white teeth that mocked himself and his fruitless search. "Now I know. You worked as a companion for Lady Temperly, an inveterate traveler, and when she grew too ill and old, you returned to London and quietly cared for her until she died."

"Yes." Yes, he would know everything now. This was the Dougald she remembered—thorough, ruthless in his investigation, determined to know everything, for he always said knowledge was power.

"Then you started the Distinguished Academy of Governesses with your two friends. They married quickly, but you didn't." He crossed his legs and straightened the knife-sharp crease on his trousers. "Of course not, you were already married. How distressing for you."

She hated him like this, all withering sarcasm and

cold judgment. Flinging herself back into her chair, she said, "I didn't want to marry. Once was more than enough."

She had the satisfaction of seeing his hands spasm. Then he placed them on the arms of his chair and leaned forward, and in slow, deliberate tones, said, "Be careful what you say, my dear. There were parts of our marriage you enjoyed very much."

Heated color rose from her toes to her forehead. But she found herself glaring into his green eyes with defiance. "Apparently, pleasure wasn't enough for me, was it?"

"Apparently not. But it would be enough for me—now."

4

$\mathcal{I}$n the measured cadence of Dougald's speech, Hannah heard his warning and found herself pressing her spine tightly against the back of her chair. Her lips felt stiff as she said, "I do not appreciate threats."

"Then don't taunt me unless you wish a demonstration of my current state of carnal frustration."

Did that mean he hadn't been availing himself of the women on the estate? Or was it simply a threat to keep her in line? Because as a threat . . . it worked very well.

He concentrated on her, and she suspected that beneath his coat, his muscles were bunched, ready for action. Would he take her regardless of her protests . . . and how long did she think she could continue to protest? Seeing him brought back memories she had steadfastly ignored. Memories of nights when he had braced himself above her, his eyes hot with passion, his muscles rippling . . .

She took care to remain still, to barely breathe, until at last he relaxed back into his seat.

Then she swallowed and, intent on surviving this dreadful interview with her virtue intact, she said, "I sent the payment almost a year ago. So why . . . ?"

"I received your money at the same time I was told of my cousin's death. I had no choice. I came to Raeburn Castle and assumed the title, and did what I could to relieve the retainers' distress that another lord had died in such an untimely manner."

Now *this* was the Dougald she remembered, and she mocked him. "As always, duty came first."

His dark eyebrows lowered. "Be grateful that I did not have time to come for you at once, or I would have done you a violence."

Which, she surmised, meant he didn't intend to do her violence tonight.

"Instead, I sent Charles to the City to watch over you."

She went cold. "Charles spied on me?"

"Intermittently for the last ten months."

"Ten months." The tale grew worse.

A tap sounded on the door, and Dougald called, "Come."

It was Charles, of course, like an evil gnome responding to his name. He carried a silver tray in his withered, rheumatic hands, not trusting his master's food to anyone but himself. A footman hovered behind him, holding a bottle of wine and two glass goblets as if they might explode—obviously he had already been trained to fear Charles and his caustic tongue.

"Bring that table. Put it between the master and the"—Charles glanced at Hannah, his chilly gaze acknowledging her—"the lady."

Tucking the bottle beneath his arm and both glasses in one hand, the footman leaped to obey. While

Charles closed his eyes in displeasure at so gauche a behavior, the youth lugged the low, round table to the fire. He deposited the wine and the glasses on the edge, then bowed and backed away.

Charles set the tray down, and as he fussed about, uncovering the dishes, Hannah observed this man who had served the Pippard family for so many years. His limp had been acquired during the Peninsular Wars, when he'd been a wounded French soldier saved by Dougald's grandfather. That act had secured Charles's undying loyalty, and he held each and every proper member of the family in reverence.

But Hannah had not been a proper member of the family—or at least not by Charles's definition. Now he stood before her, the short, stooped man who had been her judge and gaoler. The years had not been unkind, but then, he had always been ill-favored by nature. He was not noticeably older, nor was his nose any longer, nor did the skin under his chin sag with any more wrinkles. Yet his eyes still darted about, scrutinizing everything critically, identifying every imperfection and ignoring the ideal. How it must grate on him to wait upon her once more. She who had been so imperfect.

Or perhaps he relished this, seeing her reduced to caretaker. She didn't know. She'd never understood him, and even now all she could do was wonder why he had assisted in her capture.

Perhaps it was nothing more than a just desire to see his master released from their wedding vows.

She looked into the flames.

Maybe *that* was why Dougald had brought her here. To secure a divorce—after he had sufficiently tormented her.

But a divorce was messy and expensive, and she

couldn't ever see Dougald giving up in so public a manner. So what *did* he intend to do with her?

Charles handed the covers to the footman and flipped his hand to indicate that the youth should go, which he did, scuttling away like someone who had barely escaped execution. Stepping back from the artistically arranged tray, Charles said in his nasal, French-slurred voice, "I had Cook prepare my own recipe of *coq au vin* with a *soupçon* of bread crumbs for the top. May I serve you both?"

Hannah's stomach betrayed her with a grumble she hoped no one heard. Certainly Charles seemed oblivious as he ladled her old favorite into a large bowl, sprinkled it with bread crumbs and fresh parsley, and placed it on the table by her side. With a crack of the wrist, he placed a snowy white napkin in her lap and brought the table around in front of her. He placed the well-polished spoon close by her right hand, then hovered as she took her first bite.

What could she do? The chicken was tender, the broth well seasoned with thyme, the stew tasty with a bite of red wine and the vegetables the best to be had so early in the spring. "It's delicious," she murmured without quite looking him. "Thank you."

Mouth pinched, he bowed.

"I like a woman with a good appetite," Dougald said. "I learned very early that a woman who has an appetite for good food will have a similar appetite for . . . other indulgences."

Her head jerked up, and she glared at him.

With a twist of the corkscrew, Charles popped the cork and poured her a sparkling goblet of burgundy.

She picked it up by the stem and carefully felt the edges of the cut glass. They were perfect; cut to catch the light, yet smooth to the touch of the finger. And they were real. They were now. They were not slick like a bottle of wine passed back and forth between a man and a girl.

Taking a sip, she smiled, tight-lipped, at Charles. "Thank you."

Whatever else she could say about the man, he had directed the kitchen with such tyrantlike qualities that the cooking had always been perfection. In fact, he directed the whole household that way, leaving her with nothing to do but sew a fine seam. That had been a good part of the problem. Not all of it, but much of it.

"Will you eat, also, my lord?" Charles asked. Dougald looked as if he might refuse, and Charles rushed on, "You have barely eaten today. You need sustenance, and you heard Madame say the stew is delicious."

She saw Dougald flash Charles such a glare as would have withered a lesser man, but Charles withstood it nobly.

She didn't even know why she said it, but the words were out before she had thought. "I would feel more comfortable if you joined me, Dougald."

Dougald grunted, and Charles took that as assent, rushing to pull the big table closer to his master, prepare a bowl, and pour a goblet to the brim.

As Charles served him, Dougald said, "Hannah was wondering why you were so assiduous in your surveillance of her in London."

Hannah closed her eyes. Damn Dougald for telling him that!

Yet she waited anxiously to hear the reply.

"How could I not, my lord?" In a voice devoid of interest, Charles added, "You wanted her."

Charles, she reflected, had always best been able to put her in her place.

"That will do, Charles," Dougald said. "I'll ring if I need anything else."

Charles backed out of the room as if Dougald were royalty, pausing only to adjust a flower in the arrangement by the door. Then with a final bow, he left.

The door barely shut when Hannah burst out, "Why did you tell him I thought he would lie to you about my identity? Now he has another reason to dislike me."

Dougald raised his eyebrows. "What do you care? Charles is only a servant."

She stared at him. It was true. Dougald had dismissed his valet politely, as had been his wont, but without the fraternal byplay she'd so often observed. Always before, they had been comrades-in-arms, men against the world, friends forever. Now Charles seemed to be . . . just Charles. Just a minion. "Have you had a falling-out?"

Dougald settled back in his chair, ignoring his meal. "His behavior has not always pleased me."

"Oh." She took another, thoughtful bite. "That doesn't sound like Charles. I always thought he would build your railroad by hand, should you wish it."

"No doubt he would, but he mistook his place in a very important matter and failed to redeem himself. He will not get another chance."

Appetite gone, she put her spoon down. If Dougald were so unforgiving of Charles, what must he be thinking of doing to her? Divorce seemed almost too good for a wife who had fled and left a man to face the suspicion of murder for so many years.

Not, she reminded herself, that he had had to allow

the whispers to continue. He could have told the world she'd left him . . .

"Why aren't you eating?" he asked. "You're too thin."

"Why aren't *you* eating?" she countered. "*You're* too thin."

He wasn't, really. A man so large-boned could carry a stone more or less without noticing, but she thought that constant, grim cast to his face might soften with a bit more weight . . . and besides, a hungry man was an irritable man.

What *he* thought, she didn't know. She couldn't read his face anymore, but she stared back as he stared at her, challenging him with the tilt of her chin and the set of her mouth. Finally, he picked up the spoon and leaned over the table, and she realized she'd won.

She won one round. Perhaps she could win another. "Are you going to divorce me?"

He swallowed, glanced up at his long lost bride, and stared at her with the cold and still fury that marked all of his days. The mere fact she dared speak of divorce told him how utterly she misunderstood the situation. Divorce was difficult, expensive and a disgrace that followed one throughout the rest of one's life. As lord of these estates he would not jeopardize his new position by divorcing his wife, however erring she was. But that was not the real reason.

No, his plans for her were utterly different. In a tone as indifferent as he could make it, he said, "No divorce."

Her eyes widened. She searched his visage, frowning, worried, seeking the old Dougald, the man who had saved her from the depths of poverty, the man who had sheltered her in her youth and cherished her during their marriage.

He could have told her that man was dead, as dead as his wife was reputed to be. Killed by Hannah's own hand. But somehow he still protected her.

She turned her attention to her bowl. She ate silently, as did he, long enough for Hannah to fill her belly and empty the bowl.

As soon as she set her spoon down, he said, "You haven't changed. You can still eat, regardless of the situation."

"It's a trick I learned when I was little, and seldom knew where my next meal would come from." Cradling the goblet in one hand, she swirled the ruby liquid and watched as the firelight sparkled in the cut glass.

Avoiding his gaze, as she had sought to do all evening. So he would taunt her with those remembrances she so desperately sought to avoid. Dear God, how long he had waited to taunt her! "My dear, I asked especially that burgundy be served, since I know you like it so well. Is it . . . to your liking?"

She didn't look at him. She knew why he asked, but she clung to her pretense of ignorance like a shipwreck victim clings to the last vestige of the timbers. "The burgundy is excellent, but as I recall, your cellar was always superior."

If he remembered how to smile, he would have. Her evasion was masterful, but he knew it was only an evasion. That day on the train had changed her from a girl into a woman, and regardless of any misplaced effort she might make at modesty, he would remind her at every opportunity.

For he could never forget.

He grabbed the young street thief by the throat and shook him like a terrier with a rat. "Where is she?"

The lad clawed at Dougald's hands until Dougald loosened his grip. "There," he croaked. "She ran there."

He pointed at Liverpool's teeming train yard, confirming Dougald's worst fears. Young Hannah was leaving him the most direct way possible—the most dangerous way possible—on a train carrying freight to Birmingham. His betrothed was a little fool . . . The thief's struggles attracted his attention, and Dougald tightened his grip again. "Did you hurt her?"

"No, sir, I swear! Dressed like a lad, she was, an' carryin' a sissy pocketbook. I just laughed at 'er, an' she flung it at me!" The young thief swallowed. "No money in it, sir, but I didn't take no grudge. I wouldn't hurt th' lady, sir. I wouldn't hurt one o' th' touched ones." He pointed a grubbed finger toward his forehead.

Yes, the boy thought Hannah was insane. Perhaps everyone would think her insane and avoid her. Perhaps her own impetuosity would be her salvation.

Releasing the lad, Dougald raced through the crowds of men who worked loading American cotton onto English railcars. Occasionally one would glance at him, then grin and point further into the railyard, directing him after the girl who imagined herself in disguise. Each gesture confirmed Dougald's hope—his fear—that Hannah had not passed unnoticed. For while most of the men were hard-working, family men, some knaves would sneak away to take advantage of her plight. Dougald followed directions, hurrying, breathless, imagining the worst and fearing he would be too late. The men pointed him toward a train that puffed and chugged. Standing in the shadows, he hunted for her with his gaze as the train slowly pulled away.

And he saw her. Sitting in the open door of a car, dressed in one of his boyhood outfits, her feet swinging, her eyes wide and excited.

Beautiful, silly girl. He had sheltered her for five years, knowing she would be his one day, pleased with her intelligence, obedience, and femininity. Now the child had vanished, replaced by a woman whose curves no amount of schoolboy clothing could disguise. Errant strands of blonde hair dangled beside her face. A brilliant smile lifted her lips, as though the thought of escaping from him and from her obligations brought her joy.

Proof positive that she didn't comprehend the dangers that faced a young runaway.

Breaking into a run, he raced for the back of the train. He barely caught a handhold on the last car. He hefted himself up onto the platform. Balancing on the narrow, shaking boards, he studied his predicament. Hannah's car was the third from the end. The train was gaining speed. Metal rungs were fastened on the side of the car. He could climb up, crawl along the roof, jump between . . .

Standing there, he laughed aloud. He hadn't done anything so dangerous, so impetuous, in all the years since his father's death. These types of feats should have been performed by the much younger Dougald . . . he laughed again. Perhaps, after all, Hannah would prove his salvation.

The train rattled and puffed as he climbed the ladder straight up the side. The metal rungs jiggled in his palms and beneath his feet. Yet better the shaking rungs than the roof where he had no handholds . . . he crawled up onto the heated metal flat. The wind blew in his hair. The top of the car gave him a good view of Liverpool and the approaching countryside . . . and of his height about the ground.

He laughed again. Madness. This was madness.

Yet he couldn't let Hannah go. He had held her when she cried for her mother.

He crawled along the roof of the car, right down the center. At the junction between that end car and the next, he stood and eyed the distance between them. Below, the connector rattled and shook. The rails whisked away behind him.

He'd been a wild lad, and in those days he would have considered this a lark. Now he was a respectable businessman, and he understood consequences. If he missed this jump . . . Taking a breath, he leaped. He landed on all fours, the metal roof shuddering beneath his weight. But he made it.

Staying low, he raced like some primal beast toward the next jump.

Yes, now he understood consequences, even if Hannah didn't. Perils lurked out here, and how would she avoid them? Her earlier life hadn't been easy, but since he had taken her under his wing, she'd had only the best. Food. Clothing. Education. Finishing school.

The train was going faster. The gap between the next cars seemed wider. But this time he barely allowed himself a breath before he jumped.

Then he looked around. This was it. Hannah's car. He was on top. She was inside. The door was open, and the only way in was a simple bit of acrobatics . . . which he hadn't performed in years.

This time he didn't laugh. He swore. He inched to-

ward the side. He peered over the edge. Hannah's feet no longer dangled outside. Apparently, as the train had gained speed, she had moved back. Wise girl. Wise . . . well, no. Not so wise. She didn't know not to challenge Dougald Pippard.

She might not realize it, but he had bound her to him, and with the most honorable of intentions. Now his duty—nay, his affection—demanded he protect her, even if he had to protect her from herself. He smiled. Yes, she was his. She just didn't know it yet.

Grasping the door sill, he steadied himself, then vaulted around and down—

Inclining his head, Dougald lifting his glass and toasted the memory of that wonderful day when youth and love and adventure had been theirs.

Hannah seemed unimpressed with his salute. "So Charles hired the men who followed me in London . . . they were yours, of course?"

His appetite faded, and he replaced his spoon. "Of course."

"You set a trap."

"As soon as the situation here had stabilized, I called Charles back and hired the detectives to . . . make you nervous. Then I offered a job which I knew would appeal to you. It was only a trap if you sprung it." Putting his foot against the table leg, he shoved it aside. The dishes rattled, the silverware shivered, but he cleared the space between them so he could see her without hindrance. See her, dressed in those plain black work clothes. Always she disguised herself . . . on the train in boy's garb, today in a caretaker's severity. Always her beauty shone through. Nothing could hide the translucent skin, soft as a child's, or the wealth of golden hair, or the lips which beckoned a man to kiss them. If a man looked beyond her countenance, he saw the curvaceous figure . . . oh, not as rounded as in earlier years, but increasingly alluring in its slender grace. She walked, she moved as she always had; as if the Almighty had created her for Dougald's pleasure, and used her to entice him away from sin and into holy wedlock. The Almighty's plan had worked almost too well, for when she left him, she took with her every delight. She left only darkness.

Luckily, he dwelt well in darkness. He plotted to overcome the past. He planned for the future. And every scheme had worked, for she sat before him now. "If I had a doubt, it was that I could frighten you into giving up your precious Distinguished Academy of Governesses. After all, it offered what our marriage did not—work, and more work."

"You dare." She viewed him as if he were a monster . . . wise woman, for the years of loneliness and disgrace had created a monster within him. "Dare to accuse me of your own sins. You also worked, my dear. Worked endlessly while expecting me to allow you to care for me."

"Like a wife!" The heat with which he answered surprised him. He hadn't indulged in such useless indignation for years.

"Like a feeble-minded incompetent," she shot back at him.

"Your mother spoiled you for leisure."

Her voice rose. "She worked all the time, and I wanted to help her!"

He shifted in his chair, wanting to demand she see matters his way, knowing the futility of ever having

Hannah see reason. "I know. Your desire was admirable. Your ability to adapt to my desires was not."

"Mother taught me that work is virtue. That truth did not change because my circumstances did."

"And you have spent your life chasing after virtue like a kitten after an elusive butterfly." Dougald leaned his head back and watched her through slitted eyes. "Yet you abandoned your marriage and disregarded your wedding vows. Where's the virtue in that?"

She twined her shaking fingers together. "No more virtue than seducing an eighteen-year-old girl."

"You were eighteen and leaving me. Seduction was the fastest way to get control of you."

"Ah. Seduction saved you the time you would have spent on courtship." She bit off the words. "An admirable shortcut, my lord."

He laughed, a brief, hard laugh, and used his knowledge to hurt her. "I didn't have to seduce you. I didn't have to be so kind. I had already bought you—from your mother. Remember?"

5

$\mathcal{D}$ougald had never been cruel before. He had been manipulative, unscrupulous, and thoughtless, but never had he taunted Hannah with the desperate events that had brought her to him. "My mother didn't sell me to you. She placed me with you. There is a distinction." Hannah took a breath, trying to ease the constriction in her chest. "I considered myself one of your philanthropic undertakings. You had so many."

He shrugged. He had never talked about the people he helped—the orphans he had placed with families, the women he had found jobs for, the men he had trained.

"Besides, what else was my mother to do?" Hannah's voice trembled as she remembered that dreadful time. "She was dying."

"Exactly. She did the best she could for you in the circumstances." He sat so still, watching her, weighing her reactions, seeing the sorrow the memory of her mother still brought her. "And you are wrong. She knew exactly what I wanted from you. She and Grandmama set it up between them."

She couldn't help but mock him. "But you, you poor little thing, didn't realize their plan."

"Indeed I did. They told me they had arranged a marriage for me with you. You were thirteen then, a pleasant child, handsome. Your mother was of good Lancastrian stock, and she assured us your father, also, had been healthy and of sound mind. Although the particulars of your birth were not savory, illegitimacy was not a great enough matter to disrupt our plans."

She had never heard the story of her betrothal. Not quite like this. Not explained so bluntly, so indifferently, without the patina of regard to ease the dose. "I still don't understand why an adult man would allow his grandmother to make a match for him."

"Arranged marriages are a tradition in the Pippard family. They are always successful." His mouth curled in self-derision. "Why should I have been any different?"

She knew it was stupid when she said it, but she had to. "Because people don't do that anymore."

"Nonsense, my dear, of course they do. You've been in society enough to know how ridiculous you sound. How young." He chuckled, a laugh rusty with disuse. "In some ways, at least, you haven't changed."

I have. She wanted to insist he acknowledge how much she had changed. But in this matter, at least, she still believed what he did not. "For a twenty-one-year-old man to agree to train and educate a thirteen-year-old girl for no other reason than to have a wife at hand when he chooses to wed—that is obscene."

He was still smiling, if you could call that arduous bend of the lips a smile.

"You must admit," he said, "that most marriages are forged of some ingredient other than mutual affection. Greed, usually, but occasionally expediency."

"Expediency would have been your motivation," she accused.

He tossed the accusation right back. "Yours, also. I doubt you would have enjoyed being thrown out in the street when your mother died."

"You and your grandmother were not the kind of people to pitch me out." Whatever Dougald and Mrs. Pippard had been or done, she knew that for certain. "But even if you were, I would have found a position somewhere doing something."

"You were always so convinced of your infallibility."

"Of my infallibility?" She was startled. "I don't think so. Of my competence, yes."

"Think about it. Think about it now, using what you've learned of the world. The best you could have done was become a maid, probably in the kitchen. You were pretty and refined. You wouldn't have been like the other maids, so they would have made fun of you. The men would have been after you. All the men, from the footmen to the master and his sons." His hard tone and rough-gravel voice could only come from a man repelled by the thought of such concupiscence. He pressed her for admission. "I saved you from all that."

"You're right, of course." She owned up to it freely. "So I thank you. But what you have never understood is that my gratitude to you for the education and the finishing school could have been repaid by the sweat of my brow, not with my body."

He stared at her body now, then flicked a glance at her expression of fierce intent. "You have never forgiven me for taking your virtue from you."

She hated that he talked about the day she had worked so hard to forget. "I was so young, Dougald, and you swept me away with your sweet words and your attentions." *Your kisses.*

"You had found out about the arrangement, and you were leaving me." His voice lowered to a whisper. "On the train. Remember the train . . ."

They were rumbling along, headed for Sankey viaduct, and she tilted the bottle of wine once more, tasting the flavors of grape and oak, thinking that Dougald hadn't had very much of it, she'd been so intent on filling her belly. But looking him over now, watching him munch his apple, she didn't think he appeared to be thirsty. In fact, he didn't appear to be missing anything; he was a good-looking man, tall, dark and handsome, and if a girl dreamed of a man, he would be the ideal man to dream of. But he was too old for her—what was he, twenty-six? And so damn complacent and self-assured. It was frustrating, that a man with so much presence, a man who could sweep any woman off her feet, should choose a girl that he did not have to exert himself with. Such a shame; it was probably a sign of some spiritual deficiency on his part.

"What kind of spiritual deficiency?" his warm, deep voice asked.

Hannah blinked. Had she spoken aloud? My heavens, she had had too much wine.

"Probably a little too much wine," he agreed. "What kind of spiritual deficiency do I suffer from?"

"Wanting to . . . marry someone without taking the energy to court her." His steady green gaze mesmerized her. "Why would you abandon the thrill of the chase?"

"I chased you, didn't I?" Dougald asked seriously.

"That's not the same, as you well know." She

frowned. "I've watched you conduct business. You're an aggressive, arrogant competitor, and opposition whets your appetite."

He inhaled, expanding his chest fully. "You're opposing me. You've fulfilled my fantasy."

"Oh." Hannah swigged a drink from the bottle and passed it to Dougald. "Quite unintentionally, I assure you."

He stuffed the remnants of their lunch in the sack, closing that subject for the moment. Stretching hugely, he unbuttoned his shirt and rubbed his chest with the flat of his hand.

She covered her eyes with her hands. "Mr. Pippard. Please, this is improper!"

With a lazy purr, he said, "Surely not so improper between a man and his betrothed."

Dropping her hands, she glared at him. "Yes, it is, and you cannot make it the contrary by decreeing it so."

"You would be surprised what I can decree. Did you bring a blanket?"

"No, but I wish I had. At least then you could decently cover yourself."

"If I wanted to cover myself, I'd button my shirt again." Standing, he pulled his shirt out of his waistband.

She wanted to cover her eyes again, but if she did there was no telling what he would dare remove next.

"I'm just looking for a pillow. Between the meal and the wine and the rocking of the train, I'm ready for my nap." He loosened the last of the buttons, walked over and collapsed in the loose pile of cotton. Propping his head on his rolled-up flannel shirt, he shuffled the cotton around to his satisfaction and closed his eyes. "As

you keep pointing out to me, I'm not as young as you are."

"You're going to spill that wine if you're not careful."

Hannah blinked. The goblet in her hand was indeed tilting; hastily she righted it. She wished now she hadn't finished that wine. She wished she hadn't drunk at all. While she was at it, she should wish for a thousand pounds sterling and a pony of her own—and wish that Dougald didn't wear that knowing expression. Banishing her reminiscences, she pretended she thought of nothing but their discussion, abandoned for the Lord knows how long while she wandered the lanes of her memory. She groped for conversation, anything to take his attention away from her and her flushed complexion, and landed back at the Governess School. "These last three years have proved that I could be successful, so your concern for my youthful abilities is unnecessary."

"Success as an impostor is no success at all."

His charge took her aback. "What do you mean, an impostor? I'm not an impostor. I lived abroad and in London as a companion of Lady Temperly for six years. I was a good administrator and a good attendant, and it was as such I advertised myself and the school."

"You didn't use your own surname."

Indignation rose in her. "Illegitimate children don't have a surname. *I* didn't have one, as you very well know."

Briefly, the curtain of constraint lifted, and she got a glimpse of the snarling beast beneath his calm. "Yes, you did. I gave you my name when we married."

"I was grateful," she said tersely. She *had* been grateful. Her mother had called herself a widow, but always the truth followed them. Then Hannah would hear the taunts and the laughter. The gift of Dougald's name had been one of the blessings of their marriage—and the first chain she had thrown off when she escaped him.

"I didn't want gratitude, I wanted—" As his voice rose, he stopped himself.

But her voice picked up where his left off. "I know what you wanted. Undying love and devotion."

"I gave you much in return."

"When the thought of me intruded, then yes, you did. As long as I did as I was told, then yes, you did. As long as I didn't want too much or expect you to remember the promises you made that day when you convinced me that you loved me . . . then yes, you did."

In their raised tones, she heard the echoes of the past.

She thought, by the way he glared, that he did, too.

She had to master herself. If she did not, he would have the upper hand—as he had always had. Instead she had to show him her maturity, let him know he could no longer manipulate her by playing on her emotions. She'd learned how to curb her temper; dear Lady Temperly had instructed her, and she had refined her methods teaching the young ladies at the Governess School.

Hannah took several long, slow breaths, noting the faint odor of woodsmoke and the leathery scent of the chair. She allowed her gaze to roam about the drawing chamber, seeing the wide, black windows framed by heavy brocade curtains and the emerald brocade wallpaper, obviously new, that covered the upper walls. This room had been remodeled for a master's comfort.

She risked a glance at him.

A master who obviously knew what he wanted and how to get it. As she had been glancing around and separating herself from her anger, he had been observing her.

Had he once taken his gaze off of her since she entered the room? She thought not. So she must behave with sensibility and calm, for to be anything else would grant Dougald a victory. In a polite, even tone, she said, "If I had used your surname or my mother's surname, that would have made my departure a mockery. You would have found me at once."

"And saved us a damned lot of trouble."

"Saved *you* a damned lot of trouble," she retorted. "I didn't leave until . . . until our marriage had failed completely. Until I knew we had no chance."

His lips barely moved as he retorted, "We always had a chance."

"Nonsense." She kept her voice reasonable, pretending to herself she was explaining a sample situation to a particularly obtuse student. "You never listened to me. You patted me on the head and told me you knew best. I might as well have gone out and shouted my discontent to the wind."

"I adored you."

"I didn't want adoration, I wanted a life of purpose."

"Most women—"

Most women would be happy to be idle. How many times had she heard that before? She held up her hand to stop him. "Please. Not the same old argument."

Irritation flashed over his features. "I was going to say—most women would be happy to be idle, but I should have known that you would be different."

What did he mean? Was he saying he'd been wrong all those years ago? She glanced at him, but he sat there, austere and expressionless. If he had actually changed so much he could admit fault . . . She glanced at him again.

Now he was staring at her breasts with such a penetrating gaze they might have been bare, rather than wrapped in layers of clothing.

No, he hadn't changed. If he *had* actually changed so much he could admit fault, he did so to hide an ulterior motive. She had to remember who he was. She had to remember the hard lessons she had learned.

People didn't change.

And men were like people, only worse.

And Dougald . . . she chuckled softly. He was the preeminent man. Confident to his bones. Domineering because he was right. Raised by his grandmother and father to believe that the long line of their ancestors had been successful because they were inherently superior, and that Dougald was the ultimate result of all those generations of breeding. No woman had a chance against that kind of indoctrination. Certainly not a woman who did not know the truth surrounding her birth. Who even yet didn't know her father's family name. She would do well to remember that, and to ignore Dougald's broad shoulders.

So she began the flagging conversation once more. "Once, I had lived in the village of Setterington with my mother. A fair place it was, so I took that name as my own."

"You lived everywhere with your mother for a while." He was talking to her breasts as if they could hear. "Why not call yourself York, or Bristol, or East Little Teignmouth? Why Setterington?"

"I chose Setterington because I didn't think you knew about my time there."

"No." His fist tightened. "I didn't."

Hannah wondered if this new frankness between them would lead to a better understanding—or to violence. She didn't know this Dougald. In his face she sought some semblance of his former character, but this confrontation felt like the clash between interrogator and prisoner—and she knew very well which role Dougald fancied he played.

In as crisp as tone as she could manage, she said, "If you are done complaining, I would like to meet your aunt now—always supposing there really is an aunt."

"My dear Hannah, I would not lie to you about such a great thing." He allowed her to change the subject without objection. Of course. He would view her action as retreat. "Great-aunt, twice removed."

"I don't recall any mention of you having such a relative."

"Of course not. We are so distantly connected I had scarcely ever heard mention of her myself. But Aunt Spring has lived at Raeburn Castle all of her life." He sighed as if much put upon. "Gathering companions."

"Companions?" Hannah questioned. "I wasn't informed of any companions."

"Ladies of an elderly bent and interfering nature whom I have inherited along with the castle."

"Ah." She understood completely. If he wished to win the goodwill of the people on the estate, he couldn't fling an old woman from the only home she'd ever known; nor could he remove her friends.

Hannah looked him over, observing the lines of bitterness deeply engraved around his mouth, the severity he exuded. "*I* am to care for all of them?" she asked.

"Aunt Spring is the great-aunt. She suffers from moments of vagueness and is fond of rocks."

"Rocks?"

He didn't expatiate. "The other ladies are fine. More than fine. They are healthy with the exception of some hearing loss—that would be Miss Isabel, who owns a telescope and views the stars."

"Stars."

"Miss Ethel grows flowers."

"Growing flowers seems a more typical activity for an elderly lady."

"Typical." He seemed to consider the word, then shook his head. "I wouldn't expect typical. Miss Minnie takes a faint spell occasionally, and sketches. They all sew." He tapped his fingertips together. "You don't mind taking care of four such ladies, do you?"

What was she supposed to say? "Not at all."

"After all, the more work you're given, the happier you are."

Forgetting to be cautious of this new Dougald, she snapped, "Absolutely correct. Thank you for thinking of me."

One corner of his grim mouth lifted. She'd risen to the bait. He'd annoyed her; she had responded. If they were playing a game, he had won. If they were at war, then she had just handed him a weapon with which to wound her. She had to be more careful. She had to remember that, at this moment, he controlled her. Her comings and goings, her work and her leisure. He was the master, she the servant, at least until she had somehow worked out a way to escape him.

Escape Dougald . . . it seemed that with every encounter, she was trying to run away from him. Looking at him now, running away didn't seem like a bad idea.

Yet she held her cool composure like armor, and said, "It's good of you to hire someone to care for them."

She thought she annoyed him with her serenity, but before she could verify it his brief flash of irritation disappeared.

"It's not good of me at all," he said. "They are four eccentric women who have been making trouble ever since I arrived. I want them contained."

"Trouble?" Hannah searched her mind. "There was no mention of trouble in your letter . . . but then, there wouldn't be, would there?"

"The last main earl—the one who managed to survive for thirty-odd years—was Aunt Spring's brother, and he allowed her to take in any stray she wished. Once the number had reached overwhelming proportions, they were ungovernable."

Hannah scarcely contained a grin to see him so disarmed. "I thought there were only four of them."

With excruciating leisure, Dougald stood. "Do you find me laughable?"

Humor faded, and she found herself rising to her feet to face him. "Not laughable, but you speak of these ladies as if they were a battering ram and you a long-suffering portal."

For the first time since Dougald had turned from the

window to face her, she was no longer fearing him, wondering about him, glaring at him; indeed, she feared she bathed him with a look too fond, for he was not mocking or glaring.

Oh, no. It was much worse than that.

He stared at her as if she were an unsuspecting fawn and he a ravaging wolf. Had he followed her into her mind and joined her in her memories? Or had he remembered other times, passionate times? Times when they had joined together despite the fights and the unhappiness, because their bodies demanded and they had no choice but to obey?

If he knew about the Distinguished Academy of Governesses, he knew at least of the tribulations and challenges she'd faced. He knew she was strong and tough, that she wasn't the innocent he had come so close to destroying before.

Only . . . only the way he looked at her had nothing to do with business, or the years they had been apart, or the changes in their bodies and their minds. He looked and she was bathed in pure, animal heat. He projected a package filled with memories . . . her faint moans, his desperate passion, their two bodies nude on a bed, on a table . . . on the train. Whatever trouble they'd had between them never mattered when they held each other in their arms.

Then his eyelids drooped, hiding his thoughts. Gracefully he slithered back into his chair, and in a voice rife with boredom, he said, "Of course you will care for the aunts. You didn't dream I brought you here to act as my wife—in any capacity?"

Blackguard. Knave, rascal, *devil*.

How dare he dismiss her imaginings when he'd led

her to think exactly that? He had baited her, dangling memories before her, leading her where he wished. Proving she still wanted him.

With an aggression that was perhaps ill-advised, but necessary, she said, "You will not divorce me."

"No. I will not be the first to bring such a disgrace on the Pippard family."

"So what recourse do I have?"

"I think you know the answer to that." His fingers stroked the smooth, carved wood of his chair arm. "We can go on as we have. I will never tell anyone who you are and I will never be able to remarry. I will be the last of the Pippards and the title of earl of Raeburn will pass to yet another branch of the family." He paused, waiting for comment.

She knew very well he would not willingly suffer such consequences. "What other options?"

His voice, deep and sweet as syrup, warmed her as he suggested, "We can reconcile."

She took a quick, shallow breath, and she found herself looking everywhere but at him.

"Or we have a third option."

A third option? She could think of no third option. "What is it?"

"Everyone already thinks my wife is dead. So I could kill you."

6

*H*annah couldn't catch her breath. She stared at Dougald, this angry, hostile lord who stroked his chin and looked so thoughtful. The old Dougald would never be so callous, yet this man spoke of her murder with a calm that froze her blood.

"Killing you would certainly solve all my problems. As long as I didn't get caught, I'd be no more notorious than I already am." Then he laughed. A husky, ill-used chuckle. "Of course, I mention it only as one of our options. I would never truly harm you in any way . . . my love."

Swine! To jest about her death now, tonight, the first time they'd seen each other in nine years! To mention a cold grave while the fog swirled outside and the only soul who knew her true identity and background was the very man who menaced her. If she wanted proof that he truly did not love her, had never loved her, his words, his laughter provided that proof.

Well. She would not sit here and allow him to torment her. She had had a difficult trip. Merely seeing him had been a horrible shock.

She'd had enough. Enough of his threats, his sneers, his taunts, his reminiscences. She wanted to rush at him, to shake her finger in his face, show him his mistake in thinking he could humiliate her. Her, the headmistress of the Distinguished Academy of Governesses and the businesswoman who had guided the school to success!

Enough of being afraid. *She* wasn't afraid of anyone. Certainly not a man, a coward! who stalked her, who threatened to make her perform her marital duties unwillingly, who found joy in intimidating her.

"I didn't dream about you at all." Striding over to him, she stood over the top of him and looked down at him. Tilting his head up, he looked back.

Handsome? No, not any longer, but intense, burning with . . . with some emotion. Ardor, maybe. Hatred, perhaps. She would probably never know. The passions that lived in him were now disciplined, allowed out only on a short tether.

Masculine? Yes, shadow and candlelight sculpted his features, leaving no kindness, no tenderness, no soft curve . . . except for his mouth. That mouth . . . the lips were buttery-soft, plush and downy, especially when they kissed her neck, her breast, her thigh.

Tall? Yes, but she was, too. When they married, they stood together in the reception line and people had told them how well they looked together. A few indiscreet and rather tipsy gentlemen had brayed about how they would make beautiful children together.

They hadn't; she had quite consciously left before a child tied her to the man who had manipulated her. Disappointed her. No, during the long years alone she wisely never imagined anything about him. She didn't like the weeping that would inevitably follow.

Yes, this was Dougald, and she would *not* be afraid of him. Wedging her knee on the seat between his thigh and the chair arm, she asked, "If you don't want me to be your wife, why did you bring me here?"

He observed her as he would observe a cat he had vexed—with caution, yet without worry. For how much damage can one little cat cause?

His mistake. She was strong. She could taunt and threaten and intimidate, too. Better, she could make him want her, and she could take command.

"I want you," he answered. "To care for my aunt."

"You could hired a local woman." Placing her hand on his shoulder, she leaned closer to him and had the great joy of feeling him draw back slightly. Her aggressive rush had at least puzzled him. "You went to a great deal of trouble to get me."

"Perhaps I've grown parsimonious in my old age. After all, I don't have to pay my wife."

His breath brushed her face, the heat of his body burned through his waistcoat. His hands rested on the arms of the chair, seemingly at rest, apparently uninterested in lifting toward the body so close above his own.

"Slave labor," she accused.

"Almost as good," he said. "The loving labor of a spouse."

Sarcastic creature! But she didn't fear to confront him. "Or perhaps you have some other plan . . . ?"

"Anything is possible." He sounded vaguely bored. "But what is definite is that you're going to stay, and you're going to work, and you're not going to know my plans until I want you to."

"Maybe." She leaned all the way down, close enough to look right into his eyes, close enough that their lips almost kissed. "Maybe not."

Then she closed the gap—and kissed him.

She tasted the surprise on his lips. Good! Good. She'd taken the smug swine unawares with her sudden move.

Taken herself unawares, too . . .

Her eyelids fluttered closed.

His lips were the same. Smooth, wide, sensual. As a young girl, she spent hours exploring his lips, trying to identify why his kisses so enchanted her. She had never succeeded, and now as she rested her lips on his, then slanted her head to fit them closer together, she wondered if she should actually taste him. Open her lips over his, invite him inside, and if he resisted, she would take the initiative, go deep into the wine-scented cavern and show him just how much his wife she really was. . . .

No, she shouldn't. That would lead them places she didn't want to go. Instead she would keep it light, re-member the impulse that had led her here and under-stand she strove to take the upper hand.

She would ignore her own quickened breathing, the faint sheen of perspiration this contact brought her, and just touch his face with her hand. Just touch him softly . . . he'd shaved his chin. He'd shaved not long before she had arrived, because his black beard was nothing but a velvet burr against her fingertips. A burr on that broad jaw. She spread her fingers, seeking to touch more, and she located his cheekbone. Her thumb slid across, once, twice. The skin there was always smooth, a pleasure to stroke. Her fingertips rubbed his ear, circling each ridge, holding the lobe, then lightly massaging it.

Beneath her other hand, his shoulder flexed. Yes. A caress on the ear had always disturbed him. Always brought his body surging toward hers.

She broke off the kiss and straightened up. Prudence. A chance to grasp at discretion.

He wasn't surging toward her. He hadn't moved at all. His hands still rested on the arms of the chair, his thigh still pressed against her knee, he still watched her . . . still watched her.

Her lips felt swollen when she asked, "Shall I stop?"

"No."

"This is insane."

With heartfelt sincerity, he said, "To hell with sanity."

Yes. Yes. Perhaps she was deranged, but this asylum imprisoned two. Here, between the two of them, uncontrollable emotions rose and tossed them on the seas of passion, and no matter how he wished it otherwise, he responded to her. In this matter, at least, his discipline was inadequate.

Her hand slid into his hair, along his temple and into the silky strands. She sifted them through her fingers. Streaks of white. Dear heavens, he had streaks of white mixed with the shiny black, and he was but thirty-six. Between her fingers, she fancied she could feel the difference in colors. Certainly she could feel pain, loneliness, worry.

Had he suffered? How she hoped so!

Stroking the hair away from his face, she bent toward him again. His lips . . . sweet. Remarkably sweet for such a bitter man. With her eyes and her lips closed, she could almost taste him through the faint brush of his breath. Almost taste him . . .

Almost wasn't enough.

Softly she opened her lips on his, showing him, coaxing his mouth open. He was an apt student, ready to follow her example, just as if he'd never done this before, never seduced her, never brought her to whimpering pleasure just so he could bend her to his will . . .

Damn him. Her fingers clenched in his hair. Her palm leaned hard against his shoulder. She pressed her tongue into his mouth, taking pleasure in overpowering him.

And he . . . Dougald wouldn't stand for that. Of course not. He answered in kind, thrusting his tongue into her mouth, fighting with her for mastery. His hands spanned her waist, holding her in place.

As if she would try to get away now! Now, when she had him just where she wanted him, beneath her, kissing on her command. She had taken the initiative. Let him try to wrest it from her—

A firm, chilly, disapproving voice broke through Hannah's stupor. "We are going to have to keep an eye on those two."

7

Dazed, Hannah broke the kiss. She looked into his eyes. For one unguarded moment she saw passion and fury. Then he blinked and . . .

Nothing. She could read nothing there; if he had experienced any emotion—*any* emotion—he hid it well.

Deliberately, she blanked expression from her face, cleared her mind, and looked toward the source of that voice.

In the doorway. Four elderly women of various sizes and shapes stood just inside, observing Dougald and Hannah with expressions ranging from disapproval to bright-eyed interest.

"What a relief!" one round-faced, swarthy darling loudly said. "Dear Dougald has been here almost a year and hasn't shown a speck of interest in women. I had begun to worry that he danced to a different tune."

"Isabel, I vow you are too blunt." A white-haired lady shook her head reprovingly.

"You wondered, too, Ethel!" In contrast, Aunt Isabel's hair was completely, suspiciously black.

"Yes, but I wouldn't say so."

"He probably didn't hear me."

"He would have to be deaf not to."

"Oh, pshaw!"

While they squabbled like children, Hannah pushed herself away from Dougald—in a cooler moment, her plot for revenge seemed ill-advised and to have gone sadly awry—and stood on her own two feet.

Dougald rose and without primping—his hair appeared to be quite mussed—said, "Good evening, ladies." He walked toward them, grave and tall and apparently not at all perturbed to be caught kissing a stranger.

"How are you, dear boy?" The diminutive, gray-haired lady stood on tiptoe. Dougald leaned down. She kissed him on the cheek and patted his head. "Have I told you how happy I am to have my nephew here at last?"

"Several times, Aunt Spring." Hannah recognized the deep repressive voice. This was the lady who had interrupted them. She sported beautifully styled white hair, and she towered over the diminutive Aunt Spring in both height and breadth. Not that she was fat, but she was big-boned and broad-shouldered, the kind of woman who would have done well caring for the bedridden.

"But Miss Minnie, she may tell me as often as she likes." Dougald bowed to them both. "It is a pleasure to be so precious to my kind great-aunt."

Miss Minnie gave a grunt.

Aunt Spring lightly punched her in the arm. "You see, dear? He is quite a dear boy."

"Yes. He is." Miss Minnie did not so much speak as

decree, and she entered the room like a frigate under full sail. "Good evening, Dougald."

Dougald bowed at her, then at the lady with twinkling eyes and a mouth made for smiling who had so loudly doubted his masculinity. "Good evening, Miss Isabel."

Her dark skin and spiny features made Hannah suspect she was Spanish or Italian, and indeed when she spoke Hannah heard the faintest of Latin accents in her low, smoky voice. "Dougald dear, I've told you. You must call me Aunt Isabel. Everyone does." Tweaking his ear, Aunt Isabel winked at Hannah. "You, too, dear."

Hannah contained the bubble of amusement that rose in her chest. They were either giving her time to regain her composure, or they were always overwhelming in their impetuosity.

The white-haired lady whipped about the room at the speed of lightning. Stopping at the vase that Charles had rearranged, she restored the flowers to their original position, talking all the time. "Dougald, did you see my rosebush? I told you if we moved it to that sunny corner it would bloom, and today, even in this wretched weather, there was a most handsome blossom of yellow."

"Good evening, Miss Ethel." Dougald bowed.

"Aunt Ethel, please. The petals are pointed, you know."

She seemed to require an answer to her botanic conversation, but Miss Minnie had already turned to Hannah, "Is this the gel who's supposed to take care of Spring?"

"She is," Dougald said. "Aunt Spring, Miss Hannah Setterington will be your new companion."

Hannah curtsied. "An honor to make your acquaintance, ma'am. All of your acquaintances."

Aunt Spring trotted over, her heels clicking on the hardwood. "My, you're a pretty thing."

"Thank you, ma'am," Hannah murmured.

"Call me Aunt Spring." She placed her hands on either side of Hannah's face, turning it down toward her. "Aren't you tall?"

"I am, ma'am." Almost a foot taller than Aunt Spring, two inches taller than Miss Minnie, and about five inches taller than the other ladies, and they were of average height.

"When I was a gel, I wanted nothing so much as to be willowy like you." Aunt Spring patted Hannah's cheeks. "But Lawrence loved me as I was, and he was quite a handsome man."

"Lawrence?" Hannah had assumed Aunt Spring was a maiden aunt, one of the legion of girls who grew up not blessed by a dowry, never plucked by a suitor.

"My dear love. He was killed in the Peninsular Wars before we could marry." Aunt Spring's cheery face dimmed. "It was a long time ago, but do you know I still miss him? I think I hear him call my name, and I turn around, but he isn't there."

"Stuff and nonsense," Miss Minnie said.

"No, it's not." Aunt Spring didn't hesitate to contradict her formidable friend. "He is with me always, I'm sure. I just can't see him. Isn't it amazing and wonderful to think that love can last forever?"

Hannah looked up at Dougald. Hard satisfaction bracketed his mouth as he watched her with Aunt Spring. "Some love lasts forever," Hannah corrected.

"Some love gets bruised and neglected and spoils like an apple."

"You're too young to be so cynical," Aunt Isabel drew near. "How'd you develop such a trait?"

"She's probably been married," Aunt Ethel said. "Women get cynical when they've been married."

"Men get cynical when they've been married, too." Dougald replied.

"What have you got to be cynical about?" Aunt Isabel asked. "You murdered your wife."

Shock rippled through Hannah. For the first time she heard the charges spoken—and she had never expected to hear that from such an inoffensive source. She looked at Dougald, but he appeared impassive. Had he been accused so many times he no longer cared? Did his stoicism hide a need to defend himself?

Had he threatened her because he had so many times been threatened?

"You have disconcerted Miss Setterington," Miss Minnie said.

"Besides, Isabel, dear, you know we decided it made a marvelous tale, but that he didn't do it." Aunt Spring patted Hannah on the arm. "You don't have to worry that you'll be murdered in your bed. It's really quite safe here with Dougald at the helm. All the killings happened before he came."

"The killings?" Hannah replied faintly.

"She's referring to the deaths of the previous lords," Dougald informed her.

With a Latin relish for the dramatic, Aunt Isabel ignored them. "You ladies are the ones who decided Dougald was innocent, not me. I think it's wonderfully mysterious that he killed his wife. It lends him an air of foreboding. Things are dull around here without a bit of danger." Her tone changed from ominous to matter-of-fact. "Anyway, he probably had reason. Heaven knows I wanted to slay the old dragon I married often enough." She turned to Hannah. "Never marry a man who will take you away from your family, for then he can do whatever he wishes to you and there is no one to stop him."

"I can safely promise I will not do that," Hannah said.

"My old dragon divorced me." Aunt Ethel's eyes swamped with tears. "Do you know how much trouble and money it takes to get a divorce? It's an act of Parliament you know."

"So I've heard," Hannah murmured.

"But he wanted to get rid of me so much that he gladly paid." The tears dried, and her eyes snapped. "Now he's living with that little miss who used to be my chambermaid. He'll probably die in bed, and the undertaker will never get the smile off his face."

Miss Minnie nodded and proclaimed, "No fool like an old fool, I always say."

"You ladies may rest assured I have never yet given in to murderous tendencies"—Dougald bent a glare on Hannah—"no matter how much the person I am dealing with deserves it."

"There you go, dear," Aunt Spring said comfortably. "He didn't do it."

"He wouldn't admit to murder, now, would he?" Aunt Isabel demanded.

Aunt Ethel viewed him thoughtfully. "He's never denied it before, and he really *looks* like a murderer."

The other ladies cried a denial.

Hannah remembered the amused cast to his features

when he had suggested he could kill her and solve his problems.

"Yes, he does," Aunt Ethel said stubbornly. "Just look at him brood. He's been brooding since the day he got here. Not that I'm complaining, of course, Dougald dear."

Dougald just nodded as if he'd heard it before.

The ladies talked in front of Dougald and Hannah as if they weren't there. It was as if the aunts had been fixtures in the castles for so long the usual graces and manners no longer applied to them. Or perhaps they considered the others nothing but short-lived interruptions in the long stretches of their lives. Certainly Dougald acted as if nothing were out of order; he seemed used to the overtalking and the contradicting and the absolutely appalling bluntness the old ladies employed.

"I'm a fool for a man who can brood really well," Aunt Ethel said. "He could come and brood in my bed-chamber any day."

"Ethel!" Miss Minnie sounded sincerely appalled.

Miss Minnie was the elder. For all of her impressive size and upright posture, she was probably ten years older than the others, and Hannah would judge Aunt Spring, Aunt Ethel and Aunt Isabel to be well into their sixties. The age difference set Miss Minnie apart, perhaps not just in years but because of outlook.

"Just because there's snow on the roof doesn't mean there isn't fire in the furnace!" Aunt Ethel retorted.

Hannah didn't know whether to giggle or faint, so she did neither, pretending that she was regularly party to such conversation.

"Yes, but you know these children don't want to hear that."

The old ladies paused and looked at Dougald and Hannah.

Apparently Dougald decided there had been demonstration enough of the challenges Hannah faced, for he leaped into the gap. In a deadpan tone, he said, "Miss Setterington has told me she used to design clothing."

Hannah glared at Dougald. She didn't like to think of that, to remember how her simple dream of owning a dress shop had been used as bait to trap her into marriage.

The train rumbled beneath her, and Hannah sat very straight on her seat, ignoring Dougald's recumbent, shirtless form. Hannah's memory replayed Miss Blackmoor's dire warnings about what happens to girls who relaxed in a man's presence, much less one that went so far as to lie down.

Which was very tempting, after the meal and the wine and the rocking of the train . . . When Hannah was twelve and had started her menses, her mother had calmly and explicitly told her all the dry facts of human reproduction. But Hannah could not remember hearing anything about this jumpy, nervous flush Dougald had induced with his sea-green eyes, deep voice and careless etiquette. Because she scorned girlish talk as silly, she had no real idea why she felt little chills crawling under her skin, why her chest was heavy and hard to lift, why she suddenly had the urge to bite every one of her well-manicured nails to the quick.

She was sure she didn't know.

Not that he was doing it deliberately. He just didn't realize how seductive his attention could be to a girl with no prior experience with men. He could not be such a swine as to seduce her on purpose. He wanted to marry her, and her mother had said all men wanted to marry females untouched by the baser instincts. So he couldn't be interested in luring Hannah closer to him, using her own curiosity and ignorance against her.

Why hadn't she thought to buy a blanket? Then Dougald would be using it for a pillow, and she wouldn't be vigorously studying the landscape to keep her traitor eyes from sliding over that chest, carved and shaped by work and exercise, and those lovely, broad shoulders. He was bare and brown and very, very tempting for a girl who had spent her childhood and adolescence deprived of all but the most basic affection.

Who, until thirty minutes ago, had laughed at irresistible temptation.

It was good, for her own peace of mind, that she did not see those treacherous eyes open just a slit to check her discomfiture, and then close with satisfaction. "What work is it you want to do?"

Hannah jumped and rubbed her sweaty palms against her pants. Mumbling, she answered, "I want to open a dress shop."

"What? I can't hear you." He was craning his neck, trying to catch the words she threw away.

"I said, I want to open a custom dress shop," she shouted, suddenly furious.

"Oh." He dropped his head back, and grumbled, "There's no need to yell. It isn't that spectacular an ambition. The way you were cringing I thought you wanted to design kilts for the bare-arsed Scottish laddies."

"Not enough demand," she snapped, though a second later she was appalled at her response.

He smiled, an attractive, crooked smile. "There would be if you were doing it."

Which was almost a compliment, she supposed.

"And here I thought your biggest ambition in life was to be part of a family."

She froze. "What do you know about that?"

"You were a quiet girl, but when you looked at the families sitting together in church, you had longing in your eyes."

She hated for him to know that. She hated for anyone to realize how deeply she desired parents, grandparents, siblings—anyone she could call her own. In her experience, people laughed at bastards who wanted the unattainable.

But Dougald wasn't laughing. His lethal green-and-gold eyes were closed, his muscles lax. He didn't act as if he thought it odd for her to dream of family. He patted the cotton beside him. "But I guess you really want a dress shop. Why don't you tell me about it?"

Her courage began to bubble again.

Crawling across the splintering boards, she sat cross-legged beside him—although not too close—and told him her plans. Faltering at first, then with greater strength she told him how good she was with all kinds of sewing. She could take wool from the sheep to the loom. She knew how to make or alter a pattern, how to mark and cut, how to sew the finest seam. She loved to do needlepoint and embroider, how to crochet and tat. The gowns she created, the stitchery she did: All were works of art, and she loved them.

She saw him relax, and she saw him grin. That couldn't be good.

"Would you come back with me if I let you get your shop?" he asked.

Placing her hands in her lap, she prepared to re-
pulse the devil. "I can work. I can save. I can get my
own shop . . . eventually. I don't need you for that."

"I'm a good businessman, and you've got the enthu-
siasm and knowledge to make a success of your en-
deavors. What if I gave you the money?"

She brightened and sat up straight. "Would you?
I'll pay you back with interest, I assure you."

"My wife does not need to pay me back, even if the
shop should fail."

She should have known that was the catch. She did
know that was the catch, but she had hoped she was
wrong. "My shop won't fail. I have contacts in my
classmates and their parents, and I'm such a proper
lady, they'll brag about coming to me. I have design
ability and a good business head." Fiercely, she fin-
ished, "But I will not prostitute myself for a dress
shop. I'm in debt over my head to you already."

"I'm not asking you to prostitute yourself. I'm ask-
ing you to marry me." Exasperation rasped in his
voice like a file.

"I'm not afraid of hard work. I know how to live on
almost nothing, and I will open my own shop. I see no
reason to compromise my principles for money."

A slight, sinister smile tilted up one corner of his
mobile mouth. "Don't you?"

Dougald made Hannah nervous, examining her
face, her chin that trembled with an attack of belated
caution, her fingers laced with a steady tremble. He
stared at her neck, at the flush that disfigured the clear
skin of her chest where her worsted shirt sagged unex-
pectedly low. He observed too well. She blurted, "I
don't want to marry you."

"Don't you?" he asked again. Holding her trapped

by his unhurried, unflagging regard, he sat up. He reached out, so slowly, and caught her upper arms in his cupped hands. Gently, slowly, he shifted her so she lay in the warm place in the cotton that he had just abandoned, so her head nestled in his shirt. Then slowly, slowly, he lay down, his chest on hers, his hip beside hers, his thigh thrown across her legs, his face close to hers.

"You've never been kissed," he said, his face so close she could feel his breath as he spoke.

How had this happened? It was those glorious jade eyes that mesmerized and beckoned and reassured. It was his way of moving, sure and cautious, never a sudden motion to startle her. No other man could have brought her from sitting to lying, from angry defiance to angry anticipation, from breathless fury to breathless curiosity.

Aunt Spring shook Hannah's arm lightly to get her attention. "Dear, are you good with a needle? Because we, I and my friends, have a lovely workroom. The west wing tower room where I promise no tragedies have taken place."

Hannah had no idea what she meant. "That's good, I'm sure."

"I would think so! The light's good there, too."

"Very important," Hannah said.

"Yes, I can't see half the time," Aunt Spring answered.

Miss Minnie sighed. "That's because you need to wear your eyeglasses."

Aunt Spring's eyes widened. "I don't wear eyeglasses."

No one said anything, then Dougald leaned forward

and lifted the eyeglasses that hung on a string around Aunt Spring's neck. "Here they are, Aunt."

With a vague expression of surprise, Aunt Spring took the frames between two fingers. "Oh, thank you, Dougald. I've been looking for them everywhere." She smiled at her nephew. "Have I told you how happy I am to have my nephew here at last?"

This, Hannah realized, was the vagueness that had sent Dougald in search of a companion for his aunt. Aunt Spring wasn't demented or even senile, but forgetful and perhaps capricious.

"Indeed, Aunt, I am happy to be here with you." Turning gracefully to Hannah, Dougald used her to distract attention from Aunt Spring. "I told the aunts that you were an expert seamstress."

How Hannah resented him when he used his knowledge of her to manipulate her. To Aunt Spring, she said, "I am good with a needle, ma'am, but I don't design clothing anymore." She sent a meaningful glare his way. "My main criterion for fashion is that I wear nothing that itches."

If the thought of her in plain clothing repelled him, he hid it—with an exquisite bow.

He truly needed to be taught a lesson. Several lessons. Lessons about women, about wives, about respect and philanthropy for its own sake.

But she disdained to enlighten him. No matter that she prided herself on teaching the unteachable, no matter that the concept of Dougald obeying her wisdom enraptured her, she would realize he was obdurate and not give in to the temptation to instruct him.

"That is so clever of you." Aunt Spring fastened her large brown eyes on Hannah. "Right now, I'm wearing garters with ruffles, and they itch abominably. And for what, I ask you? No man has looked on my stockings for thirty years."

A sputter of laughter caught Hannah by surprise.

"But I shouldn't tell you that, should I? I am a spinster, and my duty is to set a good example for you youngsters."

"But if you lied about your garters, that wouldn't be a good example, either, dear." Aunt Ethel's hands fluttered to her mouth. "Lying is a sin."

"Spring doesn't have to lie about her garters," Miss Minnie said. "She shouldn't speak of them at all."

"Yes, but dear, I was just making conversation with Miss Setterington. I have to say something to the dear girl to make her feel welcome."

"Miss Setterington shouldn't have mentioned scratchy clothes at all." Miss Minnie lifted her lorgnette and surveyed Hannah. "It's obvious her breeding is not the best."

Hannah flinched as the old wound was poked.

With a pronounced chill in his voice, Dougald said, "I assure you, Miss Minnie, I would only allow a gently-bred woman to care for my aunt."

"Of course," Aunt Spring agreed.

Hannah wondered if he thought she would be grateful for his defense, when in fact she would never have been so shockingly frank if he hadn't provoked her. But no—he stood aloof from the madness of the proceedings. He didn't care whether she was grateful. He simply didn't like his choice of companion questioned.

"Minnie, you always worry about the proper phrase and don't think about the hateful message." Aunt

Ethel's blue eyes snapped. "Miss Setterington seems to be a lovely woman, and she sews, which is of the utmost importance to us. You're just jealous because you suffer from those fainting spells and you can't continue ordering us about yourself."

Miss Minnie's complexion turned waxy, and she sank down in a chair.

"Look at that." Aunt Ethel became all solicitousness and bustled over. "You're having one right now."

As Aunt Ethel waved smelling salts beneath Miss Minnie's nose, Aunt Isabel smiled at Hannah and nodded. "I hate it when my garters slip down around my ankles, don't you?"

Aunt Spring brought a rug and placed it around Miss Minnie's shoulders. "If you'd just tie them as I taught you, Isabel, they wouldn't make that disgraceful popping noise and fall apart!"

"Ladies!" Miss Minnie said weakly. "At least remember there is a gentleman present!"

Hannah found herself forgetting her resentment of Dougald and glancing toward him in helpless mirth. He still stood, feet braced apart, observing the elderly ladies with wary fascination. No wonder he wanted help with this distant relative removed and her companions.

Hannah caught his eye, and for one moment it was just as it had been during the early days of their marriage. They shared silent amusement, and then . . . then she didn't know what happened. The din of the ladies' voices faded; the room dimmed. For her, nothing existed except the steady gaze of his eyes, the lonely soul she could see within, the twining of their beings . . .

In a rush, sound and heat and reality returned. She blinked and returned to the library to hear Aunt Spring say, "I believe you're right, Minnie. We are going to have to keep an eye on those two."

8

"*H*ere ye are, Miss Setterington. The bedchamber
was aired and dusted this morning, and clean linens
placed on the bed." Mrs. Trenchard fit a large iron key
into the lock and opened the door at the very end of the
wide, shadowy corridor in the east wing of Raeburn
Castle. She gestured for Hannah to precede her, then
bustled into the minuscule bedchamber behind her.
"Sally unpacked for ye and brushed out yer clothing
and hung it in the wardrobe. There's water in the
pitcher and should ye require more in the morning,
catch one of the upstairs maids and they will oblige
ye."

"Thank you. This will do nicely." The single candle
Mrs. Trenchard held barely lit the bedchamber, but
Hannah could see that it wasn't what she was used to.
She had been the mistress of her own home in London.
Her suite had been large and bright, with a stove that
heated the room, three long windows dressed in velvet
drapes, and a broad, high bed with three pillows all of
her own covered with ruffled slips. Through a door, her

sitting room had contained a small desk where she could write letters and tally accounts, if she wished for privacy, and a comfortable chair where she could curl up with a book, should she desire. She'd had little time for such dalliances, but the chance for indulgence, when it came, had been a treasured one.

This room was adequate for a servant, nothing more, a dark, chill, old-fashioned chamber filled with discarded furniture, the single window framed by faded drapes. The bed was narrow, the counterpane drooping with age and the single pillow flat. She supposed she should be grateful that she was not to sleep in the attic with the other servants.

As Mrs. Trenchard lit the branch of candles on the table beside the narrow bed, she said, "You're on the back side of the castle here, the old part of the castle."

Hannah shivered as the wind outside slapped the window, and the curtains billowed slightly.

"Filled with drafts, this place is." Perhaps Hannah's distaste showed, perhaps Mrs. Trenchard still wished to apologize for that trip through the fog. In any case, she said, "I assure ye, Miss Setterington, I've had the chimney cleaned, but the fireplace still smokes."

Hannah looked at the small pile of embers on the miniature hearth. As far as she could tell, they gave out no heat, and the thin wisp of smoke billowed out with every gust. "I'm sure you've done what you could."

"But in all fairness, most of the other fireplaces on this wing smoke, too, His Lordship's included."

Dougald slept close. Hannah's gaze slid to the door. A large key stuck out from the lock, and she would use it.

"No improvements here yet. He's done the dear old

ladies' rooms in the west wing so they're comfortable." Mrs. Trenchard shook her head. "I just can't imagine why he insisted ye stay here instead of there."

Hannah could have told Mrs. Trenchard why the master assigned her this chamber. He wanted her close to him where he could torment her. He wanted her miserable in any way possible. He wanted her to see that he had the master suite with the big double doors while she had the small, dark hovel.

"Of course, give the devil his due, he did say ye deserved to be away from Miss Spring and the ladies, at least at night." Mrs. Trenchard ran her finger along top of the headboard, then squinted at her finger. Her eyes narrowed. "I'll send Sally up tomorrow to finish the cleaning."

Hannah felt sorry for the unknown Sally, and sorrier for herself. Thinking of the long line of closed doors along the corridor, she asked, "Who else sleeps in this wing?"

"No one else. Just ye and His Lordship."

"And Charles."

Mrs. Trenchard lifted startled eyebrows. Had Hannah revealed too much knowledge of Dougald's private habits or too much interest in his valet?

"No, not Charles," Mrs. Trenchard said. "He sleeps in the west wing, too."

Hannah was startled in her turn. To be always close at hand, Charles had always slept in a chamber off of Dougald's bedroom. Hannah had hated it, afraid to make a noise or raise her voice, always aware that Charles was hovering,

Then Mrs. Trenchard said, "Ah . . ." in a knowing voice. "Now, Miss Setterington, don't ye worry. M'lord is not the kind to make a move on one of his servants. Been here a year, and there's not been a single fuss about him among my girls."

"What a relief," Hannah said dryly. A relief to know he hadn't bothered the serving maids. A further relief to know Mrs. Trenchard hadn't realized the real source of Hannah's discomfort.

Another blast rattled the sash, and she went to the window and parted the drapes. The wind from the west had picked up, blowing the fog away. The stars glittered coldly in the black sky, the waning moon rode on the remnants of cloud, and she looked out over the shadowy hills and dales of Dougald's estate. The occasional tree reached its bare branches upward to scratch the heavens, the land rolled on to an empty horizon, and a road—the road that had brought her from the railway station in the opposite direction—wound away toward the unseen sea.

A gust rattled the aged casement, and Hannah shivered as a blast of cold air embraced her.

Mrs. Trenchard came to her side. " 'Tis a plunge from this window, so I'd not advise you to open it and lean out."

Looking straight down, Hannah could see the castle wall stretching straight down into the shadows. The ground seemed dark and too far away. Very far away. Dizzy with a rush of vertigo, she swayed forward, closed her eyes, then leaned back. "It is very high. There's the kitchen level, the main level right below us, I'm on the third level . . ."

"Don't forget the dungeons below the kitchen," Mrs. Trenchard advised. "They haven't got any windows and they haven't been used for a hundred years, but trust me, they're still there, dark and dank. I know it every spring when I send a crew down to clean them. Of course, we keep the wine down there."

"Of course," Hannah said, thinking how grateful she was *she* didn't have to go clean the dungeons. "Were they used a lot in the past?"

"The earls of Raeburn have had their ruthless moments," Mrs. Trenchard admitted. "Don't like to be crossed, not any of them. The first lord was a baron, came over with the Conqueror, and word is he took the land and made the dungeon and threw the Saxon lord right in there and left him to die."

"Lovely," Hannah muttered.

"By the time of the War of the Roses, the lords had won the title of viscount and the fourth viscount—he was not a pleasant man at all."

"Seems to be a trait of these lords." Although Hannah would not mention Dougald by name.

Mrs. Trenchard shrugged. "There's been the usual mix of good men and bad, but this one threw a Lancastrian into the dungeon and took his wife to use as leman. He would have lost the castle but when the king won all, His Lordship declared he had always been loyal and King Henry decided to believe him. Easier than trying to dislodge him, it was."

"Successful kings always decide on expediency," Hannah observed.

"I suppose. I don't know much about kings. I only know about the lords of Raeburn. My family's been serving them as long as there's been a Raeburn Castle, and even before, I suspect." Mrs. Trenchard twitched the drapes wider and pointed. "During Cromwell's reign, the lord was staunchly royal. See the crumbled remnants of the wall there?"

Hannah did. The wide, straight line of rocks and

moss rose and fell in a straight line behind the castle, black shadows of the past stretching across the fell.

"Cromwell and his men came with their cannon and battered the curtain wall right down. The lord barely escaped with his life. He fled to the Continent and came back with the Restoration, and his loyalty won him the title of earl."

"He sounds like a good man," Hannah said, "staunch and determined."

"Aye, a good man." Mrs. Trenchard scratched her chin. "A dreadful husband. He brought himself the prettiest little wife from France, and was so jealous of her that when she flirted with one of his retainers he hung the retainer and locked her into the east wing's tower."

"Not the dungeon?"

"He didn't want to kill her." Mrs. Trenchard sounded as if she were making excuses for the pitiless rotter. "He just wanted to be sure of her."

"I can't imagine she welcomed him into her bed after that."

"She threw herself out of the window."

Shocked, Hannah looked out to the ground below, and a wave of vertigo swept her again. She closed her eyes. "How dreadful."

"Most men don't want their wives making fools of them. His present lordship is no different in that matter, at least."

Mrs. Trenchard paused with such significance, Hannah opened her eyes. Mrs. Trenchard was dolefully staring out at the figure of the man on horseback, galloping away from the castle. Broad-shouldered and seething with energy, he leaned forward in the saddle and urged his tall, dark horse onward toward the sea.

His open coat flapped behind him, and the stark white moonlight shone on his bare, black hair where the distinctive silver streaks glowed.

Dougald, riding out at night, just as Alfred had said. But what was he fleeing tonight?

Mrs. Trenchard dropped the drape, cutting him off from Hannah's sight, and turned away from the window. "I suppose ye've heard the rumors about the current lord."

This, Hannah suspected, was the reason for Mrs. Trenchard's chattiness. "That he killed his wife?"

"Aye, that's the rumor. Does it make ye nervous?"

"No." Not when she knew it wasn't true—or, as Dougald would point out, it wasn't true *yet.*

Mrs. Trenchard smiled, obviously pleased. "When I first saw ye, I marked ye for a sensible soul. That man never killed anyone."

"How do you know?"

"When a soul has killed, there's a coldness within that shows—if ye know what ye're looking for. Them's that commit murder are damned, ye know, and they'll murder again, if driven to it, because what difference does it make? They know they're condemned to hell's fire when they die." Mrs. Trenchard's bleak, flat statement sounded like the sentence passed down from the most hard-hearted of magistrates. Then she clapped her hands and briskly rubbed them together. "Well, enough pleasantries. Ye're tired after yer trip, and ye'll want to rise early to see the sweet ladies. They're right excited to have ye here. 'Tis glad I am that ye'll be taking care of them. They're kind ladies, but a bit of a handful."

"I'm sure I'll enjoy whatever challenge they offer."

"Aye, miss. I'm sure ye will. After tonight, get to

bed no later than ten o' the clock. Those are all the candles ye'll get this week." Mrs. Trenchard frowned at the modest pile of books on Hannah's table. "Ye'll not get more just because ye've stayed awake reading. Remember, we servants aren't here to burn the master's coal and tallow. Also we have a curfew here. Nine o' the clock, and ye should be safe in yer bedchamber."

"Why?" Hannah foresaw some cold, dark, lonely nights spent huddled in her room.

"The servants feel better with a curfew. The deaths of the old lords have them jittery."

"Surely they don't think that Lord Raeburn . . . ?"

"They're a superstitious lot, they are." Mrs. Trenchard marched to the door, then paused, her hand on the frame. "Since tomorrow's yer first day, I'll tell Sally to stir the fire for ye when she comes up to clean."

Mrs. Trenchard pulled the door shut behind her, leaving Hannah alone in the barren bedchamber in her husband's home. Lifting the drapes, she looked again at the road, but Dougald was gone. Was he running from her? From the memories she invoked? From the passion that still existed between them?

Or was he running to escape his own desire to wrap his hands around her throat and murder her?

She dropped the curtain.

Heaven knew Hannah understood running. From him, from them. She had been eighteen the first time she ran from him and his plans. She had been a serious girl who scorned those schoolmates who believed in romance, who whispered about men and what they did in the dark. Everything Dougald had done on that train took her by surprise. Especially those kisses, not the dry pressing of lip to cheek, but that open, wet hotness . . . Dougald had been, and was, a magnificent kisser.

That didn't explain her own actions tonight. She didn't regret standing up to him. Nothing could ease her bone-deep uneasiness at seeing the changes in him, nor her anger that he dared threaten her, but she could only be so wary before her independent spirit re-asserted itself.

But to challenge him in such a way . . . she didn't even understand it herself. . . .

Whatever had possessed her to kiss him?

9

Whatever had possessed her to kiss him?

Dougald knew he shouldn't be riding tonight, but he couldn't retire to his bed. Not when, at last, his wife slept under his roof. The girl he had married was gone, swept away by years and experiences quite outside his own. In her place was the woman he had met tonight—unruffled, reserved, dignified. Composed until he pushed her too far. Then she retaliated with kisses.

Damned fine kisses.

His gaze swept the dim road before him and the tumbled hills around, and he felt, as always, a swell of pride. This was *his* estate. *His* lands. *His* title. The kind of honors that had for generations evaded his family, despite their best attempts. And now, because of a series of accidents—*accidents,* for he was not responsible for them, regardless of what the servants hinted—fate had handed all distinctions to him. And all Dougald could think about was Hannah, upstairs in the bedchamber not far from his.

He'd placed her there on purpose. He'd wanted her

close so he could threaten her with himself, keep her off guard, give her her share of sleepless nights. Now, ironically, *he* couldn't sleep.

Leaning into the saddle, he urged the stallion into a gallop. Trying to flee temptation, he supposed. Trying to avoid remembering her body, naked beneath his, and wondering what changes the years had wrought. Trying to escape the hovering notion that she should come to his bed . . . tonight.

She owed him an heir to inherit the estate, and she would give it to him—but not yet. He hadn't lived through the cold, lonely years, heard the whispers of "murderer," seen women flinch when he walked close, heard his business associates stammer excuses as to why they couldn't invite him to their homes, without developing a plan to deal with his errant wife. All that talk of alternatives had been just that—talk.

Divorce. She dared speak of divorce. There would be no divorce. No murder, either. No, that would be too easy.

But a reconciliation? Perhaps some would call it that. Certainly, he intended to keep her. Eventually, he would use her as his father had said a woman should be used. Without love, without passion, to procreate. And Hannah, earnest, emotional, enthusiastic Hannah, the girl who had dreamed of being part of a family— that Hannah would be miserable.

As miserable as he had been this last nine years.

He couldn't wait.

He had been so angry when, after they'd been wed for six months, she had run from him. Run from *him,* as if he were some kind of monster. He knew men who were worse husbands than he had ever been. Men who ignored their wives, who shouted at them, who beat them. And he, he who had been good to the girl—he was left to the laughter of his business comrades. Then . . . then he'd been accused of her murder.

The bitterness of it. That stupid maid of hers, claiming they had fought before Hannah disappeared.

Of course they had, but what of it? He would never have killed her. Never hurt her, never touched her in anger, no matter how much she tried his patience.

And she had. Always, she had, calling him a liar, demanding that he follow through on his promises. As if he would ever allow his wife to work. He had roared at her when he thought of the gossip that would cause.

Now he knew there were worse things than gossip.

The road wound toward Presham Crossing and beyond that the sea, and he followed it as he always did on those nights when memories and frustration drove him from his bed.

He never thought he would live under a cloud for so long. He had thought the slip of a girl he had married would be easily found, and he had feared only she would be hurt or, in her innocence, be taken advantage of. Instead she had vanished. Vanished except for a single letter.

He had worried. He had searched. He had hired detectives and raged at Charles. Nothing had yielded a single sign of her until . . . until that check had arrived. By then he had grown so used to having his servants and his colleagues cower from him he no longer cared. He was a loner, cold, disciplined . . . a man like his father.

More than anyone, he had realized the need to bait his trap carefully. He had feared to rush Hannah, to tip his hand, for if the girl without a pence or a friend could escape him, what could the woman do? She had her connections. He knew about them all. He knew that Queen Victoria favored the Distinguished Academy of Governesses with her approval. He knew everything about all of her friends, everything about her financial situation, the name of her dressmaker, and her shoe size. Because he wanted revenge.

Not because he cared for her. He *didn't* still care for her. Not like a husband. Not as if they were lovers. No, time and distance had accomplished their purpose. He grasped that when he'd received her money. He had stared at the check and realized this was it. The moment he'd plotted for for so many years. The moment that she delivered herself into his hands. And he'd been calm. No fury lit his fuse. No passion rioted through his veins. He had been calm. Absolutely calm. Calm.

Except at night. Except in his dreams. Except when his thoughts drove him from the bed to ride as he was riding now.

Damn the woman. Didn't she realize this was his chance to exact revenge? His chance, not hers. She had no right to kiss him, to torment him with the fragrance of her curvaceous body, the glint of her subdued, golden hair, the demands of her satiny lips. He was the one who had the right to torment.

But had he succeeded?

He held her in the palm of his hand, he knew it. She couldn't leave. No matter what he did or said, she wouldn't leave. Not until she'd discovered the truth about herself, about where she'd come from and who her people were. She'd been searching for that knowledge her whole life, and he had the power to give it to her.

But he wouldn't. Not yet. Not until he had what he wanted from her.

Which was revenge.

Surely she owed him that.

Sensing Dougald's abstraction, the stallion reached out with the bit. Dougald reined him in, controlling him with his knees and his gloved hands. The people on the estate expected the lord of Raeburn to ride like a damned centaur, and he hadn't disappointed them. In fact, he suspected he had exceeded their expectations, thank God. They'd already had enough shocks, with the last lord taking a tumble down the stairs and the one before that found at the bottom of a sea cliff.

Poor buggers. Couldn't hold their liquor, either one of them.

Anyway, a mere horse could not challenge Dougald's authority; for nine long years no one had challenged his authority. Grimly, Dougald lifted his gaze toward the black-velvet sky. Everyone knew him to be his wife's murderer, so they would never tell him *nay* for fear he would exact a dreadful retribution on them.

Only Hannah didn't cower from him. If she realized how carefully he planned her retrieval, how thoroughly he plotted his revenge, how the years had chilled his rage, she would cower.

Instead she kissed him.

His groin tightened at the memory. After all the hell she had put him through, and she dared to kiss him.

Dougald wanted to bellow. But that was no longer his way. Instead, he gave the stallion his head, and they galloped along the curving road toward the sea. The air cleared his head, the exercise brought his blood surging in his veins, but the demons that had driven him for so many years traveled with him. Always they were with him.

When he crested the hill above the Atlantic, he brought the horse back to a walk and rode the path that wound among the rocks on the beach and then back up into the meadows and windblown trees.

In his youth, the demons had held sway. He learned to fight in those years. He drank, he whored, he almost died.

But it wasn't him who died, it was his father.

Dougald had never again allowed his demons to be free.

Yet tonight Hannah, with her full breasts and upright figure and provocative poise, threatened to cut them loose. Damn her, it wasn't supposed to be this way.

His grandmother had picked her out, told him she would do well as his wife, and he had accepted that. Hannah had been but a girl, then. What difference had it made to him, when at the same time he was trying to learn his father's business and save it from the rivals who would have wrested it from him?

By the time Hannah was old enough to wed, he was used to the idea. He saw nothing wrong with the arrangement and, in fact, liked that he would have a wife who elicited no response from him except indifference. He thought, fool that he was, that Hannah would see the advantages to their union and accept it meekly.

Instead, she had challenged him.

My God, could he ever forget the first time she'd fled from him? Even better was what came after . . .

"You've never been kissed," Dougald told her. He didn't wonder, he knew. He could tell by Hannah's

amazement, by the way her large brown eyes glanced about the train car as if she could find answers there.

"I don't think that matters." She wet her lips. "I should sit up now."

Carefully, lovingly, as he smoothed his hands down her arms. She was such an innocent, politely suggesting that she be allowed to sit up when she should have been squalling like a banshee. She didn't understand that by running away she had brought herself to his attention and challenged his possessiveness. By the time she realized it, it would be far too late for her. "But I want to kiss you. I want to be the first." He slid his lips across both her eyes to close them. "You will let me do that, at least."

She shook her head no.

His lips crested her cheekbone and pressed one corner of her mouth, feathering light touches on and about her lips, teasing her, enticing her. She had skin like velvet, softer than any he'd ever touched, and he relished the sensation. Slanting his face, he pressed his lips to hers. He kept it tender, gentle, and she rewarded him when she relaxed with a sigh.

Sweet thing. Gentle. Soft. Yielding. She was perfect for him. He touched the crease of her mouth with his tongue. That surprised her. She jumped, and he touched her with his lips closed once more in reassurance. Forging ahead, he ran his tongue over her upper lip. Her eyes grew wide as if she didn't know what to think, and she put her hands on his shoulders and gave a push. Her fingers lingered, touching his bare skin, then she hastily dropped her hands away and turned her face to the side. "You should replace your shirt," she said severely.

"I will." Catching her chin, he turned her face back

toward his. *"When we're done."* He laved her lip again.

And she showed her defiant character by lifted her mouth to his and biting his lip.

He jerked back and dabbed at the damage. *"Witch!"*

She rose onto her elbow and scanned his face anxiously. *"Are you hurt?"*

"Yes." He leaned so close they were lip to lip. *"You'll have to kiss it better."*

Her gaze dropped, her dimples quivered, and she laughed.

He captured her mouth again and tumbled her back, and this time she let him kiss her without inhibition. Dougald moved slowly, touching her teeth, touching her tongue with tiny flicks of his, letting her taste him . . . If he could keep her distracted, move her from one sensual threshold to another, he could stay ahead of her morals and her doubts. His kiss so captivated her she was oblivious as he unlaced her shirt.

This was so easy, like taking comfits from a baby. And so difficult, for all he could think of was his own body's sudden drive to be inside her. Damn the woman, didn't she know what she was doing to him with her charming ineptitude?

No. No, of course she didn't.

She noticed what his restless hands had accomplished. She tried to push at him again. Again she broke contact in a flurry, acting as if the touch of his bare skin burned her.

He hoped they burned together.

Gazing into her velvet brown eyes, he did his best to mesmerize her with a gentle voice. *"I like you to touch me. Your touch is a pleasure. You stroke me and I purr . . . touch me as I touch you."* He opened her shirt wide, revealing her to the air and sunshine—and saw, for the first time, her perfect breasts.

She tried to scoot away, but he couldn't allow that. Not now. Throwing a leg over her, he kept her in place while he looked . . . and looked. Dear God, what breasts. They rose from her chest in sweet cream mounds, pale, delectable . . . his. Lightly he touched her, just the tip of her nipple with the tip of his finger.

In fierce and desperate earnest, she put her hands up to shove him away. *"Someone will see in!"*

"No." He let her hold him back. *"Look out. We're crossing Chat Moss. There's no one."*

It was true. They were passing over the vast peat bog that had caused the rail designers such trouble, and as far as he could see were shrubs and herbs and the occasional tree that reveled in the damp.

"We're safe." He caught her wrists. *"Now watch. Watch."*

Hoisting himself above her, he lowered himself. Her nipples touched first, nestling into the rough hair that covered his pectorals. His heart leaped with excitement. He wanted to overwhelm her, give her no choice . . . he wanted to crush her to him, take her now. His mind chanted encouragement. So he shook as their stomachs pressed together, and he fought every fierce, masculine instinct as he slowly flattened her breasts with his chest.

Overwhelm her, yes. Give her no choice, start this relationship as he meant to go on, yes. But he couldn't frighten or hurt her, and from the look on her face she was frightened.

He released Hannah's hands, and they sprang up to push ineffectively. She pushed and shoved until he slid *his arms around her, under her shoulders, and trailed his fingers through the hair at the base of her skull. Then she quieted, resting cradled in his arms, staring at his face as if some feature there fascinated her.*

Good. That was good. He couldn't help but smile and some of his triumph must have shown, for she dropped her gaze and squirmed as if she wanted to get away. He was taming her, gentling her to his hand, but he could see that she knew it and resented it.

"Sh," he whispered, although she'd made no sound.

"How do you do that?" she demanded belligerently.

He had thought her a girl, but obviously she was a woman, for she asked a question and expected an answer when he had no idea what she was talking about.

"How do you make my senses shut down?" she asked. "I can't hear, or see, or smell, when you touch me. I can only touch . . ."

Her voice trailed away, and he asked, "And feel?"

"Yes," she was whispering again. "And feel."

Focusing her eyes on his face, with a tentative finger she traced the accent line of his cheek, the scar beneath his eye, the velvet of his mouth.

"Have you got it worked out, now, sweetheart?" Dougald asked.

In a voice rife with tragedy, she said, "Yes. I'm a wanton."

"I can only hope," he teased.

A mistake. Immediately tears trembled on her lashes. He thought himself so clever, yet he had forgotten her mother had been disgraced by passion. That Hannah had lived with that disgrace every day of her life. Smoothing her hair from her forehead, he marveled at the soft texture of each strand. Keeping his voice low and persuasive, he said, "You're responsive, but that's nothing to be ashamed of. The release we find in passion is the closest we come to the soaring of the peregrine. You are so beautiful, you touch my heart, my mind. I've seen what damage a thoughtless husband does to a marriage. Won't you trust me? I'll give you all my attention, my wholehearted commitment. I'll not cheat you, not physically, not mentally. Marriage is forever, a vow spoken and meant to be kept. We'll be happy. You have many things you can share with me. Your charm, your diplomacy, your kindness—they will complete my life."

"What will you share with me?"

My God, her tone was plaintive! Was she thinking? Was she reasoning? Did she realize how painstakingly he planned each move, each word?

So he reached for her soul with a kiss. Their lips melded. He led her through a new dance, one she'd never performed before, and he reveled in her sensuousness. She moaned into his mouth, and tasted of autumn's apple and summer's rye, and of Hannah. Each touch of her tongue swirled him closer to bliss.

In one moment of sanity he thought that was wrong. He pulled away and stared down at her. At the doe-soft eye, the damp, full lips, the softly rounded cheeks. She couldn't lure him. He was older, he was the man. Yet if he weren't careful, she would ensnare him as surely as he sought to ensnare her. That would be awful. That would be . . . impossible. Men did not love. Not as women loved. Once he had captured Hannah's heart, he would hold her in the palm of his hand. That was the way it was supposed to be. That was the way he planned it.

She must have seen some of his consternation in his face, for she asked, "What's wrong?"

"Nothing." No, he was doing everything right. He couldn't fail.

The stars glittered. The harness jingled. The horse snorted. The lane curled up around a grove of trees.

Dougald *had* done everything right. Like any young, sweet, innocent girl, she had mistaken the passion between them for love. He had taken full advantage of her delusion, and carefully fostered her fantasy. Only after their marriage had she begun to suspect that he didn't love her. Perhaps, worse, she had begun to suspect she didn't love him.

But now he would make her love him again, and when she did—*Crack!*

Tree bark behind Dougald exploded in woody shards. What . . . ? Why? Could it be?

Dougald abruptly came back to the present. The stallion beneath him reared. Hell! Someone was shooting at him. During the brief moment it took to shake off past enchantment—

Crack!

A bullet tore through the air by Dougald's ear. Taking advantage of the animal's caprice, he tumbled out of the saddle and rolled away from the slashing hooves. Coming to his feet, he ran in a crouch, keeping his face down and his white shirt out of sight.

"Got 'im!" he heard a man shout.

As his stallion snorted and fought invisible demons, then raced toward Raeburn Castle, Dougald slipped into the small grove of trees beside the path. The salt-stunted trees were thin and windblown, the ground around them grassy, undulating meadow. Not far away the sea crashed against the shore, muffling any other sounds, but in the feeble light of the stars he saw two figures detach themselves from among the boulders and run to the place where he had fallen.

One tall, one short, neither held a pistol but both wore greatcoats with capacious pockets.

The streetfighter in Dougald knew he could take them.

The realist in Dougald recognized an ugly truth. Someone was shooting at him—at the lord of Raeburn. He'd scoffed when Charles said the servants whispered tales of sabotage and assassination. But he doubted this attack could be coincidence.

Someone was trying to kill the lord of Raeburn, and the lord of Raeburn . . . was he.

The men searched the ground with increasing indignation, coming ever closer to the trees.

Finally, one stood straight and exclaimed, " 'E's not here!"

Dougald smiled as he stepped out behind them. "Yes, he is."

As they scrambled to turn, he grabbed them by the hair and smashed their heads together. They howled as their skulls cracked. One went down. He grabbed the other by his rough coat and lifted him to his toes. "What the hell are you doing, shooting at me?"

And another man, unseen in the shadowy, jumbled landscape, struck him from the side. Dougald went down cursing as first the one, then the other, jumped him.

He should have remembered—always make sure of the odds before picking a fight.

10

*A*s Hannah descended the stairs toward the breakfast room, her muscles ached and her eyes felt gritty—the results of the previous long and eventful day. At least that was what she told herself. She didn't acknowledge a restless night spent chasing demons who turned into Dougald and in turn chased her while the flames of hell licked at their heels.

She had been so foolish—yesterday when she'd allowed herself to be trapped, and all those years ago when the girl Hannah had convinced herself she loved Dougald because he had seduced her—and because she had wanted him to.

Gripping the curve of banister, she frowned fiercely.

All the hard-won wisdom in the world didn't make a difference. It didn't matter what her mind told her, or that she looked back on the younger Hannah and pitied her belief that passion equaled love and that men fulfilled their promises, because when she was with Dougald—

"Oh, beauteous maiden who brings forth the morning!"

She gasped and almost tripped off the last stair as a dandy leaped lightly from his hiding place beneath the stairs. A gentleman of indeterminate years, dressed in the latest London fashions, he held a yellow rose he extended with a flourish.

Pressing her hand over her rapidly beating heart, she said in her frostiest tones, "Sir, I don't believe we've met."

"Of course not! I have presumed because I wished to verify that the report was true."

Who was this little fop who stood an inch shorter than she, wore higher heels on his shiny boots, and took such liberties with civility? "Report?"

"That the fairest lady in all the land had taken up residence beneath the noble roof of Raeburn Castle."

She stared at him. Did he think such flattery would turn her head? She knew very well how she looked this morning. She wore a subdued cotton gown of powder blue, its long sleeves trimmed with a cautious ripple of lace. She had pinned her plainest white collar close around her throat, and after a bit of inner debate, had tied a starched white apron around her waist. Silly to think such frumpish apparel would discourage Dougald, but she liked to think she had the good sense to dress with discretion.

"Ah, you wonder who I am. Could it be my new cousin did not even tell you of my existence?" The stranger flattened the back of his hand to his forehead. "I, who am his heir?"

This was Dougald's heir? She inspected him more closely. He wore checked wool trousers of brown and blue with a thin thread of yellow, a matched checked waistcoat, a large bow cravat and a gold-and-diamond collar pin. His brown frock coat sported velvet cuffs and collar of a most intense cobalt that matched his finest feature—beautifully lashed blue eyes that managed to hint at a melancholy that would have done Byron proud. Unfortunately, he did not have a Byronic coiffeur. Rather his brown hair grew long on one side and someone, probably his talented valet, carefully combed it over the top to hide the bald spot . . . which glistened in patches of pale skin from among the glutinous strands.

Hannah pretended not to notice. "You . . . live here?"

"Yes." He inspected the rose he still held, and she realized he had chosen it not for its beauty, but to match the yellow thread in his plaid waistcoat. "When I'm not in London, I make my home at Raeburn Castle."

"I apologize for my ignorance, sir." Hannah smirked. She was more and more aware of the trials afflicting Dougald in his new position. Although she feared she would be damned by her sentiments, she reveled in his calamity. He had always been so ambitious for himself and his family; in inheriting this estate, he must have thought he had achieved all his goals. But between the elderly ladies, the heir and his own wife, Dougald might have just bitten off more than he could chew. Not that Dougald could imagine such an instance, but she could—and had, many a time in her fondest dreams. "I'm afraid no one told me of your residence herein."

"If I could be so bold as to introduce myself—I am Seaton Brackner, Baron Onslow, the son of the twelfth earl's youngest brother and the current Lord Raeburn's fifth cousin once removed."

She curtsied. "Miss Hannah Setterington, sir. I have come to be a companion to His Lordship's aunt. And your aunt, also, I presume."

"So the report is true." He bowed and again extended the rose. "The fairest maiden *has* taken residence herein."

Solemnly, she accepted the blossom. "You flatter me, sir, but I am too sensible to allow you to turn my head. I will mark your interest as nothing more than a London-dweller's boredom in his current rural circumstances."

"You crush me." He offered his arm, and she placed her hand on his sleeve. "Rather, you would have crushed me, but I must believe you never look in the mirror or you would realize the sincerity of my adulation."

She amended her first judgment. Sir Onslow wasn't completely a little fop. Rather, he was a resplendent urbanite suffering in the ennui of the country, probably because of monetary concerns. He was also, she decided, her most likely source of distraction in *this* untenable situation. "Where are you taking me, sir?"

"My first thought was to the breakfast chamber, but if you prefer, fair maiden, I will summon my steed and toss you into the saddle, and carry you away from the drudgery of ordinary life."

She eyed the top of his head, which she could clearly see, and thought that the chance of him tossing her anywhere seemed unlikely. "The breakfast chamber sounds appealing." Although Dougald undoubtedly lurked therein.

Sir Onslow heaved a huge sigh. "Like so many young ladies, you lack imagination."

"I don't lack imagination. Rather I suffer from a strong streak of practicality." And the sure knowledge that if she tried to flee Raeburn Castle, Dougald would be after her in a flash. She wouldn't involve any man in the strife between her and her husband; someone would get hurt, and that someone would never be Dougald.

She and Sir Onslow strolled down the long, broad gallery that ran from the stairway toward the great hall.

"So you met the aunts," he said. "Or shall I say . . . Aunt Spring and her companions. By the way they scold me, they might as well all be my aunts."

His gloom made her smile. "I met them last night."

"What did you think?"

"They are lovely ladies, and I'm sure Aunt Spring will be a pleasure to care for."

"How discreet you are." He sounded woefully disappointed, but he brightened. "I always think the aunts are like a small pack of terrier dogs, circling and nipping, bounding and demanding."

She repressed a smile. "Not a pack, sir. They have quite distinctive personalities."

"Indeed! *Very* distinctive personalities, but taken as a whole, they are interfering, judgmental, benevolent know-it-alls."

"You seem . . . bitter."

"Not at all. I adore them, too. Who wouldn't?" He heaved a theatrically large sigh. "Only I do wish they had an ounce of discretion between them!"

From what she'd observed the previous night, she had to agree—the aunts said what was on their minds and what was on their minds frequently shouldn't be said. Their comments about her and Dougald had been discerning, their insight more so. She had been glad to leave Dougald last night and sit with the aunts in their drawing room where she smiled and nodded while they chatted, and at last pleaded exhaustion so that Mrs. Trenchard could escort her to her cramped, cold, shabby room.

To sleep badly and dream of Dougald.

The corridor looked quite different in the daytime, with sunlight coming in from a row of windows along one side. Hannah hadn't seen the windows the night before, nor did she understand how the castle bent inward to allow windows at such a place, but every ancient dwelling she'd ever visited displayed such eccentricies. "An interesting place, Raeburn Castle," she observed.

"A wretched old pile of rock," Sir Onslow said. "But it's *our* pile of rock, so we love it."

"Lord Raeburn is making improvements, I see." She indicated the door propped against the wall and heard the rumble of workers' voices.

"Lord Raeburn is a barbarian with no sense of history." Sir Onslow sniffed. "Worse, he won't improve my chambers until he's done his own. But what do you expect from a brute who killed his wife?" He peered at her intently, waiting to see her reaction.

Hannah was conscious of a strong desire to snap at him. Instead she stopped and used her firmest, most disapproving governess glare. "Do you know that or are you spreading unfounded rumors?"

"Rumors, of course!" Obviously, Sir Onslow was not the least repentant. "My dear Miss Setterington, I dine out on rumors. A man in my position is either a raconteur and a gossipmonger, or he is unwanted."

"Ah." Hannah relaxed her disapproval. He spoke the truth. When attending a dinner, she would prefer to be seated next to a man such as this than those eternally boring and endlessly proper gentlemen Lord Ruskin had deemed acceptable for an unmarried lady.

Well. She wouldn't ever have to worry about that again. "Nevertheless, sir, it seems ungracious of you to live off of Lord Raeburn's hospitality and malign him so viciously."

Sir Onslow smiled and primped. "I have done Dougald such a favor. Before he arrived here, only a small portion of England knew his story. What a ruffian he was in his youth. How he ran from his home because his father hated him. How he roamed the streets to loot and steal."

Hannah had heard that before, too, although that had been gossip whispered behind a young wife's back. And when she had attempted to question Dougald about the tales, he had distracted or ignored her.

Another part of his life she had not been allowed to share.

Sir Onslow continued, "I tell how Dougald reformed because he loved his young wife. How they fought and she threatened to leave him. How in a rage he declared if she wouldn't live with him, she would die."

A shiver chased up Hannah's spine. Sir Onslow's dramatics were a little too close to the truth.

"So he killed her and left her body to the wolves, and he's mourned her ever since." Sir Onslow blinked with delight. "I have spread the tale everywhere, and Dougald is now a man of mystery, fortune and passion from Scotland to Cornwall. He ought to be grateful. I've given him caché."

The scent of freshly baked wheaten bread drifted to her. "Is he grateful?"

"Probably not, but I told you he was a barbarian."

Hannah laughed. She couldn't help it. Sir Onslow's voice was droll, his wit refreshing after Dougald's oppressive desire for vengeance. Walking on, she asked, "Have you always spent time here?"

"Mother insisted. She said it was my heritage, and of course the lesser lights of the *ton* do find it impressive when I call myself Sir Onslow of Raeburn Castle." He smiled up at his ancestral paintings on the wall. "So I say it often."

Hannah twirled the rose as she chuckled at his self-deprecating tone.

Footsteps bounded down the steps behind them, and Hannah turned to see Charles, unshaven, disheveled, bloodshot eyes fixed on her, hurrying forward like a man with a mission. "*Madame,* if I might beg a word . . ."

"What unfashionable haste, my good man!" Sir Onslow pulled a handkerchief from his sleeve and flapped it in Charles's direction. "You bring a French wave of garlic with you."

Charles stopped, seeing for the first time her arm on Sir Onslow's sleeve. His already wrinkled lips pruned, and his head lowered. "*Madame . . .*"

"She is 'Miss Setterington' to you," Sir Onslow said.

Charles's mouth worked as he glared. He knew her name very well, he hated to be corrected, and he must especially hate being corrected when he knew himself to be right.

Hannah enjoyed seeing him discomfited.

Giving in with a huff, Charles said, "Miss Setterington, I had hoped you would accompany me to Lord Raeburn. He has a need of you."

Ah, so Dougald was not yet in the breakfast chamber. She didn't need to brace herself to see him. Not yet.

Charles had always been the servant who came in search of her when Dougald wanted her to tie his cravat, or sew on a button, or any of the other useless, silly tasks he had deemed acceptable for his wife to perform. The memory put her back up, and she sounded quite stuffy when she asked, "Did Lord Raeburn send for me?"

"Of course he didn't send for you!" Sir Onslow's indignation lifted him to his toes. "No gentleman would request a lady's presence before breakfast!"

Hannah ignored him. "Did he, Charles?"

Charles glared. "Not exactly, but I can't . . . he rather needs . . . I hope that you . . ."

Hannah didn't know what Charles hoped, but she listened as he stammered, searching for an explanation, and knowing he couldn't say what he wanted, which was, "It is not a woman's place to question her man's demands." Ah, to see Charles muffled could prove the greatest delight of this dreadful predicament.

"Thank you." She smiled at him and cast as strong a chill with that smile as Charles did with his glare. "I fear I must agree with Sir Onslow. If Lord Raeburn didn't 'exactly' send for me, then I shall wait until after breakfast to speak to him."

Charles stood, rigid and disbelieving, as Sir Onslow gestured toward the doorway, and said, "Right through here." As they passed Charles, Sir Onslow said, in a voice loud enough to carry, "Damn frogs put on airs and don't know a thing about manners."

Hannah didn't look at Charles, but she could imagine how a man who fancied himself the harbinger of French civilization in the wilderness of English society reacted to being called a frog. Her imaginings brought her immense pleasure.

She and Sir Onslow walked through a small, empty room containing little but a round, dainty dining table close to the window.

"This is the little dining room," he explained. "Meals are served here when four or fewer are eating. That is to say—never. Lord Raeburn's hospitality is quite . . . hospitable. Here we are, Miss Setterington, the breakfast chamber."

Hannah followed her nose through the next door. The rich, salty odor of bacon, sausage, and kippers wafted through the air, and beneath that was the toasty aroma of crumpets and muffins. Entering the darkly paneled dining chamber, she saw a long table that boasted seating for two dozen guests, dishes stood steaming on a sideboard, and the room was full of milling servants and elderly ladies eating a surprising amount of food.

"There they are," Aunt Spring said. "I told you they'd come down together." Then she squinted at Sir Onslow. "Well, not you, of course!"

"Thank you, Aunt." Sir Onslow indicated two empty settings between Miss Minnie and Aunt Ethel. He held the chair for Hannah as he asked, "Who were you expecting?"

"I believe she thought dear Dougald would bring Miss Setterington down." Aunt Ethel held her fork above a mound of scrambled eggs and kippers. "They appeared quite involved last night."

"Have you changed your interest?" Aunt Isabel asked Hannah. "Because you shouldn't. Seaton is a dear boy, but he's poor as a church mouse and his title is barely a generation old."

"Thank you, too, ma'am." On Sir Onslow's face Hannah saw the same beleaguered expression Dougald had worn when confronted with the aunts. Seating himself beside Hannah, he lifted a finger.

Mrs. Trenchard abandoned her station beside the side table and hurried over. "What can I do for you, Sir Onslow?"

He waved a negligent hand toward Hannah. "What would you like, Miss Setterington?"

"Hot chocolate, please, Mrs. Trenchard." Maybe that would cure the headache the mention of Dougald's name had caused.

"It's too early for liquor, so I'll have tea," Sir Onslow said.

Mrs. Trenchard smiled fondly on him and hurried away to give the order to a serving maid.

Sir Onslow leaned close to Hannah. "Now there's an interesting character."

Hannah followed his gaze. "Mrs. Trenchard?"

"Yes. Comes from an old family, devoted retainers. Aunt Spring's mother died in childbirth, so they brought in Mrs. Trenchard's mother as wet nurse, and she just never left. Until the day she died, she was at Aunt Spring's side, protecting her from every unpleasantry in life, and she raised Mrs. Trenchard to do the same. It's very odd to watch the two of them, with Aunt Spring so happy all the time and grim old Mrs. Trenchard racing up to check on her every chance she gets."

That explained the previous night's interrogation. "So I've been brought in to replace Mrs. Trenchard?"

"In a manner of speaking. She is the housekeeper, too, but she doesn't easily give up responsibilities."

Miss Minnie apparently decided there had been enough low-voiced conversation between them, for she bent a glare on them, and boomed, "The food's right there. Help yourself, Miss Setterington. We don't stand on ceremony in the morning."

"Thank you, ma'am. I find I have an appetite after my travels." Hannah went to the sideboard and observed such a variety of foods she wanted to rejoice. No one ever ate better than at an English country house, and she knew she could do justice to this repast—especially since Dougald was not present.

Sir Onslow joined her and rubbed his palms together in anticipation. That and the glint in his eyes when he gazed upon the fresh stack of scones explained the little pouch of belly that played havoc with the smooth line of his frock coat.

Picking up a serving fork, she began to place sausages on her plate.

In her sweet, carrying voice, Aunt Ethel declared, "If that young woman is going to flirt with every gentleman in the castle, we'll find her a husband very soon."

Hannah missed her sausage and the fork struck the porcelain with a *tink*.

Aunt Spring said, "Dear, she might have been flirting with Seaton—"

Hannah couldn't look at Sir Onslow.

"—But she was *kissing* Dougald."

"Already?" Sir Onslow sounded delighted—the raconteur with a new tidbit of gossip.

Hannah ignored him. He was the least of her problems.

Mrs. Trenchard shot her a scandalized glance and shooed the suddenly coughing servants from the room.

Matchmakers. The aunts were matchmakers. In Hannah's experience, matchmakers were trouble, for they manipulated their victims until they succeeded in their goal—marriage between two dupes.

Always before she'd walked a delicate line among the traps set for her and various gentlemen by the well-meaning matchmakers. She'd had to; matchmakers would not hesitate to trap her in a compromising situation, and more than one gentleman had indicated his willingness to be caught in that particular snare with her. But she had not been tempted.

Of course not. She was already married.

So what did she do now, when matchmakers not-so-subtly planned to set her up with her own husband?

"Perhaps she doesn't want to be married. Perhaps she simply wants a series of affairs. After being married to Irving, a series of affairs seems like a wise idea to me." In a reflective tone, Aunt Isabel said, "I wonder if I could interest any man in an affair."

"It would have to be several someones if you had a series of affairs," Aunt Ethel observed.

"Miss Setterington is as good as married to Dougald," Miss Minnie declared.

"Good morning." Dougald spoke just loudly enough to make himself heard over the din, but the silence that fell was instantaneous and uncomfortable. It was, Hannah thought, as if his black presence cast a pall over the frivolity.

Hannah didn't want to look at him, to remember her foolishness the night before—as if her kisses were more reprehensible than his threats and deception. But she quailed for only a moment before she stiffened her spine, turned and directed a clear glance his way.

And gasped.

11

It wasn't Dougald's black presence that accounted for the silence, but his appearance. One eye was purple and swollen shut, his lip was split and puffed up, he had a bruise on his cheek and a goose egg on his forehead.

Before anyone could remark, he said, "I fell off my horse."

A lie. Hannah had seen him look something like this before after a bout of fisticuffs that involved Midsummer's Night, too much ale and some old cronies from his days on the streets.

"Come here, young man," Miss Minnie directed in her severest tone.

He limped toward her, wincing with each step.

Hannah tore her appalled gaze from his face. She could do nothing for him. It wasn't her place. Glancing around, she saw the aunts shaking their heads in unison. Mrs. Trenchard stood wringing her hands. From the doorway, Charles glared at her as if his master's condition was her fault, and she understood now why he had sought her out. Perhaps he thought Dougald would listen to her and allow his wounds to be tended.

Dougald had never listened to her. Charles knew that.

Dougald didn't deserve all this sympathy. The stupid man had been fighting! She wanted to go up and shake her finger in his face and scold him, slap a bandage on his eye and tell him how his behavior was childish and ill-advised.

And why was Sir Onslow leaning against the sideboard and grinning like a buffoon at Dougald's limping figure? She didn't like that baron. She didn't know why she ever thought him amusing.

Taking his hands, Miss Minnie looked them over. "When you fell from your horse, Dougald, you seem to have landed on your knuckles."

Sir Onslow chortled.

Miss Minnie whipped her head toward him. "What are you laughing about, young man?"

Under the influence of her righteous indignation, he quickly sobered. "Nothing, ma'am."

"I thought not." Miss Minnie transferred her gaze to Mrs. Trenchard. "We need ointment and bandages from your medicine closet."

Mrs. Trenchard sorted through the keys on her belt. When she had found the right one, she curtsied, and said, "I'll get them at once, ma'am."

She scurried out, leaving a silence Aunt Spring rushed to fill. "How did dear Dougald scrape his knuckles falling off his horse?"

"He's been fighting, Spring, dear." Aunt Ethel shook her head, and her white curls bobbed. "I had thought the dear boy would be better with his fists."

Hannah straightened. Dougald *was* good with his fists. He'd told her so, and she'd seen him swaggering and proud after that brawl. So how had he managed to get himself so battered?

She looked at him with a little less heat and a little more thoughtfulness.

But he resolutely ignored her. Limping to the high, carved, armed chair at the head of the table, he seated himself with excruciating caution. "I couldn't be better." With his gaze, he challenged anyone to refute him.

Aunt Spring didn't notice. "Why were you fighting, Dougald? You've never fought before."

Dougald shook out his napkin and repeated, "I fell from my horse."

"You were fighting with your horse?" Aunt Isabel teased him.

He didn't return her smile. He probably couldn't. Not with that split lip. Hannah placed another crumpet on her plate—how had she thought to eat so much?— and started for her seat, when Mrs. Trenchard returned, hands full, almost at a run.

Charles started forward, but Miss Minnie boomed, "Give the bandages to Miss Setterington. We'll see whether she knows enough about nursing to care for dear Aunt Spring."

"*I* don't indulge in fisticuffs," Aunt Spring objected.

Charles began, "*Mademoiselle* Minnie, I already offered to tend the master's wounds, and he refused most vociferously. So if he—"

Hannah didn't wait to hear how that squabble would fall out, but strode toward Dougald armed with hard-won confidence—and a plate of food. She was a competent nurse, and her fingers itched to fix Dougald—in more ways than one. She gripped her fingers around his arm. "Let's go into the little dining room."

He looked down at her hand. "Miss Setterington, you are presumptuous."

She released her grip. "Very well." She turned her back and folded her arms, knowing very well what was to come.

"Dougald, dear, you look barbarous." Aunt Spring sounded distressed.

"Not delightful at all at the breakfast table," Aunt Isabel said reproachfully.

Aunt Ethel used one hand to shield her eyes. "The sight of blood makes me queasy."

Hannah heard Dougald's heavy breathing, and smiled. How she loved to see Dougald defeated by four frail old ladies.

"Damnation," Dougald muttered as he stood. "It was just a little fracas."

When Hannah looked back, Aunt Ethel winked at her.

Dougald began to limp out, but something caught his eye. Stopping, he stared at his heir. In a disgruntled tone, he said, "I've got a diamond collar pin just like that."

Seaton touched it with his finger. "Then I must compliment your good taste."

Dougald shook his head and moved on, and Hannah heard him mutter, "Gooseberry."

Mrs. Trenchard followed Hannah and Dougald. A footman hurried to pull out a chair at the small round table.

With ill grace Dougald seated himself. "I will remember this," he said to Hannah.

Mrs. Trenchard set the bandages and ointment beside him and a steaming cup close to Hannah. "Your hot chocolate, Miss Setterington."

"Thank you, Mrs. Trenchard. Lord Raeburn, you remember everything." Hannah placed her plate close to his right hand—she had learned a few things in her years of caring for the ill, and one was that they had to be on their deathbeds before they turned up their noses at food. "As do I."

They were at a standoff, at least with a footman at the door and Mrs. Trenchard hovering behind Hannah, ready to render assistance.

Dougald showed his teeth in an angry snarl. "*You* should eat. You're already too skinny."

"Thank you, my lord, for that fawning assessment. Your countenance could use improvement, also."

He gave a bark of laugh, then stopped as it pulled his lip. "Vixen," he said in appreciation.

"Eat. It'll keep your mouth busy." She smoothed his hair back.

He jerked back as if the touch of her burned him. "When did *you* learn anything about nursing?"

"I learned much when I tended Lady Temperly, and even more while directing the Distinguished Academy of Governesses." Moving slowly, she touched his chin. When he let her, she lifted it and looked him over. "Eighteen-year-old girls have a way of getting into mischief, and when the mischief is done, someone must bandage their wounds."

"You must have loved running your academy. All those girls doing what you told them. You could imagine they were your children." He paused. "That must have been almost as good as having your own family."

She wanted to slap him, but his face was worse than she'd first thought. When she slid her hands along his scalp, she found two more swellings the size of a hen's egg. He'd been soundly drubbed.

Right now, she was glad. "You really are a swine," she said conversationally.

Mrs. Trenchard said, "Miss Setterington!"

Hannah ignored her. Mrs. Trenchard had no part in this war between Dougald and Hannah. "My lord, do you suffer a headache?" Hannah asked.

"Of course," he snapped.

"Can you see clearly out of the good eye?"

He leered at her chest. "And a lovely view it is, too."

Mrs. Trenchard gasped. Apparently she wasn't used to hearing her master compliment women on their breasts.

Hannah took what comfort she could from that.

"He needs cold rags wrapped around his head and a cold slab of beef on this eye," she told the housekeeper.

Mrs. Trenchard gave instructions to the footman.

"How is he, Miss Setterington?" Aunt Ethel peered from the doorway at the stricken Dougald.

He reared back. "I'm fine, Aunt Ethel. Why is everyone talking about me like I can't hear? And why is everyone making such a fuss over a few cuts? I'm fine!"

"I suppose you are. Anytime a man is that cross, he's going to live." Aunt Ethel retreated, but Hannah heard her mutter, "More's the shame."

Charles appeared at Dougald's left shoulder and lifted his superior French nose toward her in challenge.

She didn't care, as long as he didn't interfere here. After all, he had helped Dougald get dressed. He'd had his chance to reassure himself of Dougald's health. She said, "I'll do his scrapes first."

Mrs. Trenchard twisted the top off a clay pot and extended it toward Hannah. "Comfrey mixed with lard," she said.

Hannah dabbed ointment on his lip and found the words bubbling from her unrestrained by propriety or eavesdroppers. In a furious undertone, she demanded, "What have you been doing, Dougald? Trying to get yourself killed? Never before were you so foolish as to take on a fight you couldn't win."

Dougald tried to jerk his head out of her grasp. "That stuff stinks."

"A penance for your sins." She spoke loudly enough for Mrs. Trenchard to hear, directed a quick smile her way, then smoothed the ointment across the scrapes on his chin and over the inflammation on his ear, and murmured, "Where did you go last night? To the pub with Alfred?"

"You're nagging," he said.

"Someone needs to." Her voice rose. "You came close to getting yourself killed."

Mrs. Trenchard flinched.

Both Dougald and Hannah looked at her.

In a choked voice, she said, "Just like the other lords."

Dougald snorted. "Yes, Mrs. Trenchard, but you've heard the rumors. *I* killed my wife, and I killed the other lords so I could have the title. I'm not going to kill *myself*."

"Yes, my lord." The jar Mrs. Trenchard held trembled. "I had forgotten that, my lord."

Hannah lifted his left hand. "Why were you limping?"

"Stepped in a hole. Twisted my ankle." His free fingers crept toward her plate and plucked up the crumpet.

He'd always liked crumpets.

She slathered his knuckles with ointment. "Sir Onslow says you're now a romantic figure in all of England."

"Sir Onslow." Dougald fixed his brooding gaze—or rather, half his brooding gaze—on her face. "You've been flirting with him."

She stopped smiling. "I don't flirt." Taking the strips of bandage, she wrapped each finger.

"You've been talking to him."

A footman arrived with towels floating in a basin of water. Another brought a cold piece of beef on a plate.

Hannah lifted a towel from the basin and wrung out the cold water. "I do talk."

"I don't want you talking to him."

Their voices were rising, but Hannah couldn't contain herself. "Don't be ridiculous."

"He's dangerous."

She slapped the towel on his head. "If I listened to rumors—so are you."

He caught her wrist.

She looked down at him.

Beneath the bruises and the scrapes, he was wearing his cold, angry face again, and his scowl very effectively conveyed a warning. "Don't listen to rumors. Believe it. I *am* dangerous."

He was threatening her again, in the broad light of day and after she'd been kind enough to bind his wounds. If he weren't already hurt, she would pummel him. Jerking herself free, she glanced at the servants. Mrs. Trenchard's stiff face proved she had heard at least part of their quarrel. The servingmen appeared to be straining to hear.

It didn't matter, though, did it? This whole situation was untenable, and Miss Hannah Setterington was not about to allow any man to intimidate her. Certainly not her own husband. "Piffle! I don't have to put up with such nonsense."

"What are you going to do about it?"

Lifting the beef, she placed it carefully over his bad eye and stepped back to survey the results. "You look incredibly silly." Stepping toward him, she leaned over, picked up her mug of now-tepid chocolate, and said softly and fiercely, "I'm catching the first train back to London."

As she turned to leave, he grabbed her skirt. "Mrs. Trenchard, ask Aunt Spring if she will attend me here."

Mrs. Trenchard curtsied and hurried into the breakfast room.

"What do you think you're doing?" Hannah asked. "You can't keep me here by force."

"Force?" He removed the meat, revealing his battered face. "No. I don't need force."

Observing the intensity of his one-eyed gaze, she thought that he was going to fling himself at her. She placed her cup on the table so she could defend herself.

Defend herself, or welcome him . . . what a conundrum!

She no longer knew which action she most wished to take. All the years she'd spent by herself had been chaste ones, and she'd been proud of her constraint. She had looked on men, handsome men, men who wooed her, men who attempted seduction with the sweetest phrases and the most forceful embraces, and she had disdained them. With her wit and the occasional sharp box to the ears, she had cut them down, reduced them to their true form—sulking boys or needy beasts. She had imagined herself as a buttress of righteousness, a fortress so strong mere charm and dapper virility could not assault it.

Now she realized that she had not been strong— merely she had not been challenged. Those men had not been Dougald. Nothing of their bodies or their souls had called to her passion or her loneliness, for none of those men had been the mate for whom Nature intended her.

Nature cared only that two bodies came together in passion to reproduce. Nature didn't comprehend that a woman might need to be more than a female propagating to increase the tribe.

Now as Hannah faced her mate, heard his threats, knew that he wished for . . . nay, had *plotted* her capture as if she were a pet who had run away, she still experienced the brief, sharp pain as her nipples pinched, and the warm, sluggish wanting settled in her belly.

She had to stop this. If he knew—and Dougald had always been acute where animal passions had been concerned—he would act in the way most likely to make her miserable and please himself. She had no doubt what that action might be, and it involved her long-buried emotions and two nude bodies.

She pulled away from that thought with the maidenly dismay never experienced by the younger Hannah. She had to bring this scene to an end. Somehow, she had to get out of this room before he tried to impose himself on her, or she too frankly told him what she thought of his younger self and his current despicable and much-stained soul.

Folding her arms over her chest, she glared down at Dougald. "I am Miss Hannah Setterington of the Distinguished Academy of Governesses. I do not tolerate threats."

In a tone as cold and firm as her own, Dougald answered, "I don't make threats."

They stared at each other, locked in a battle of wills, neither willing to turn away.

Aunt Spring appeared in the doorway. "I fear I'm not very good at bandaging wounds, dear boy. You're better off with Miss Setterington."

Hannah and Dougald broke eye contact.

"That's not why I begged that you attend me, Aunt Spring," Dougald said.

She hurried toward him. "Then what can I do for you?"

In a voice as fulsome as a traveling actor's, he asked, "Didn't you tell me you knew the Burroughs family?"

The name meant nothing to Hannah. She tried to yank her skirt free of his grasp.

Aunt Spring blinked at their tug-of-war. "Why, yes, dear. What's left of them. Only the old couple, and that's a shame." She turned to Miss Minnie, Aunt Isabel and Aunt Ethel who, led by curiosity, had followed her. "Dougald is asking about the Burroughses."

"We know them," Aunt Isabel boomed. "A pleasant couple, but rather stiff."

"Stiff?" Miss Minnie sniffed. "They are quite full of themselves."

Never one to allow the conversation to elude him, Sir Onslow appeared behind them. "Yes, ma'am, but the family has been in the district since before the Tudors. Some would say they have the right to be full of themselves."

"Well, they will die out now," Aunt Isabel stated. "They haven't anyone at all."

Dougald twisted Hannah's skirt in his bandaged fist.

"You said they had lost their son in his youth, not long after they'd refused him permission to marry a certain Miss Carola Thomlinson?"

Hannah stopped tugging so suddenly she fell back toward Dougald. She caught herself just before she would have tumbled into his lap. She whirled to face him.

He sat enthroned in his chair, bleak and hard, the man who knew her secrets. The man who knew how to pull her strings. The man who knew her mother's name—and who knew how desperately Hannah wished to discover what family she had left. He had known she would come to Lancashire and stay, regardless of what he did or said, for a chance to meet her grandparents. Probably he was the one who had subtly directed her inquiries to the correct place.

No wonder he was so confident.

"Burroughs." She tested out the name. "Burroughs." Her father's surname. She'd never known. Her mother had never told her. She had tried to ask, but her inquiries gave her mother such pain she had waited and waited—until it was too late, and her mother could no longer tell her.

Now Dougald knew the name of her grandparents. Her father's parents. She turned to Aunt Spring, unable to repress the kind of eager desperation only an orphan could understand. "Can you . . . will you tell me where they live?"

Aunt Spring smiled at her. "Do you know them, dear?"

"No. No, but I . . ."

"Family friends, no doubt," Aunt Ethel said.

"Yes." Hannah looked around to find herself the focus of every gaze. She hadn't thought of this. That she would have to explain herself to anyone. Why should she? She had imagined she could make discreet inquiries over an extended period of time. She hadn't thought that Dougald would be at Raeburn Castle, making it impossible for her to stay. Making it impossible for her to go. "I suppose you could say that, although it has been years . . . they probably don't know me."

In a voice rife with disingenuous, convivial surprise, Dougald said, "I have an idea, Aunt Spring. Why don't you invite them to visit in, say, a month? By then Miss Setterington will have settled into her position and we'll know more about her and her relationship with the Burroughses."

Aunt Spring clapped her hands. "A capital idea, Dougald! I shall write them at once."

"Keep her presence a surprise," he instructed. "We don't want to announce her too soon."

"It would be wonderful to see their faces," Aunt Spring agreed. "Will that be acceptable to you, too, Miss Setterington?"

Hannah stared at Aunt Spring's face, alight with anticipation. She saw the aunts, cheerful and awaiting her decision. She observed Sir Onslow observing her. She beheld Charles and Mrs. Trenchard, watching the scene as all dedicated servants do, trying to predict the course of their own future by the words of their masters.

And she glared at Dougald, smug, satisfied, bruised but unbeatable and as always, victorious.

Bowing to the inevitable, she said, "I would like that, Aunt Spring. I would like that very much."

12

Did she really think he would let her escape? Dougald watched as Hannah exited the dining room surrounded by the old ladies he had taken under his wing, and he chuckled softly. Bitterly.

Not long after Hannah had left him, he had set about discovering the identity of her grandparents. He had imagined presenting her with the knowledge like a gift, one that would prove to her that she had been right in returning to him. Only she'd never returned, and now, like a miser, he held the information tight in his fist. She'd pay him for these facts. Pay him any way he chose.

Vaguely he was aware of Seaton moving to sit at his right hand, but he gave him no attention. Let Seaton speak first. Let Dougald hear what he had to say.

After all, Dougald reasoned, Seaton had killed at least two earls of Raeburn, and he was trying to kill another.

Dougald had her trapped. Again. Completely. In every way possible.

As Hannah stood by the window of the aunts' large, sunny west wing tower workroom, she looked across at the tower that rose above the east wing. There, another Raeburn wife had been trapped, and she had freed herself with a suicidal leap.

Not that Dougald would ever actually lock her in, or that Hannah would ever jump to her death, but Dougald had her trapped just as neatly as if he'd turned a key. Her stomach churned. She'd never felt like this, not even when he'd threatened to murder her. That had been a vague menace, words meant to shock. And she had rallied because she didn't believe him capable of murder. He had been, after all, her lover. Their bodies had entwined, their passions had been as one, they had been as close in thought and breath as any two people could be.

At least . . . she had thought so. Perhaps their closeness, too, had been nothing but a chimera, brought on by a youthful imagination and her need to have someone, just one person, to love her. Because Dougald was now standing among the ribbons of her desires, using them to tie her up and tie her down.

Aunt Ethel's voice penetrated Hannah's gloom. "Go on, Aunt Spring, ask her."

Hannah cringed as she wondered what circumstance they wanted clarified.

High above the rest of the castle, the tower room caught the morning and evening sun and all the light in between. The aunts huddled over a long table strewn with proof of all their interests. One of Aunt Ethel's prize roses sat in a pot before Miss Minnie's sketch pad. A variety of polished stones, silver settings and jeweler's tools were placed neatly before Aunt Spring's chair. Aunt Isabel's telescope was pointed out the window toward the sky. Bits of needlework and pieces of tapestry were scattered about on every surface. The room appeared to be awash with brightly colored threads of royal blue and purple, crimson and pale peach. Facing each other by the largest window were four large looms.

Looms. What were the elderly ladies doing with looms?

"Ask her, Aunt Spring. You know we must know if she's the one."

Hannah looked out over the green, rolling hills of the estate, but she could distinctly hear Aunt Isabel's clarion tones. Indeed, she could hear them all, for they raised their voices to compensate for Aunt Isabel's loss of hearing. Clearly, there were no secrets residing in this chamber.

Hannah braced herself as Aunt Spring trotted over and asked, "Dear Miss Setterington, is it true?"

"That depends on what you're asking," Hannah said cautiously.

"We could only be interested in one thing." Aunt Spring blinked myopically at Hannah. "Is it true you know our dear Queen Victoria?"

Hannah stared into Aunt Spring's guileless eyes. That was not at all the question she expected. After that scene at breakfast, no doubt the whole castle buzzed with curiosity about Hannah's connection to Dougald. A plethora of rumors must be circulating about Hannah's relationship to Dougald. About her family background. About her legitimacy.

"You're asking me if I have made the acquaintance of Queen Victoria?" Hannah repeated in bewilderment.

"Yes! Yes, that's exactly it."

Why did Aunt Spring want to know? How should Hannah reply?

For Hannah did know Queen Victoria. She didn't wonder how Aunt Spring had obtained this information. That was obvious; Dougald had investigated Hannah. No depth of her life had been left unfathomed, no corner unexplored, and he had chosen to pass this particular bit of information along to his aunts. "I have met Her Majesty," Hannah admitted. "She has been a supporter of my academy."

Aunt Spring darted an excited glance toward the other ladies, and in a joyous tone, she cried, "It's true, girls!"

In an excited rush of bobbing curls and flapping skirts, Aunt Ethel rushed forward while Aunt Isabel followed, asking, "Did she say it was true?"

"Yes, Isabel, it's true." Miss Minnie spoke clearly and directly to Aunt Isabel, then hurried along with every evidence of excitation, her faded eyes sparkling.

"Now you must tell us all." Aunt Ethel wore gardening gloves and held clippers; before the aunts' conference she had been tending a variety of potted plants throughout the room. "Is Her Majesty as young and pretty as her portrait?"

"She is very pretty, and very young to have such an awesome responsibility." Actually, Hannah had often thanked her stars that she hadn't been born to the task of ruling England. Pomp and ceremony surrounded Her Majesty's every moment; the only time she seemed to have to herself were those times when she, her consort and children fled to Scotland for a respite.

"We have this picture of her." Aunt Isabel showed

Hannah a small canvas, a replica of the official coronation portrait. "Is this what she looks like?"

"That is very like her," Hannah said.

The aunts exchanged glances.

Why did they care so much?

"Have you seen her dear consort?" Aunt Spring
asked.

"Prince Albert?" Most people were interested when
they discovered Hannah had met the royal couple, but
she seemed to be fulfilling these ladies' dreams. "Yes,
I've been presented to them both."

"We have this portrait of him." Miss Minnie pulled a
yellowed newspaper clipping from within her capacious apron pocket. "It's not one of those vulgar lam-
poons, but a real portrait. Is that what he looks like?"

"Indeed it is." Hannah looked around at their eager
expressions. "Now you must tell me why you want to
know."

Aunt Ethel stripped off her gloves and placed them
beside her clippers.

Aunt Spring caught Hannah's hand. "Come and sit
down."

Hannah followed her to the sitting area. A cluster of
chairs and settees surrounded an iron stove, and even
though the windows were cracked enough to let in the
fresh air of a brisk March day, the stove glowed with
heat. The aunts crowded close; Hannah had noticed
that when ladies reached old age, their skin thinned,
their bones grew birdlike, and they sought heat like a
drug. Indeed, the curtains on the windows were thickly
lined to keep out the breezes that so battered Hannah's
bedchamber, and one whole wall was draped in magnificent purple velvet to cut down on the drafts.

So Hannah took the chair farthest from the stove,

pushed her sleeves up, and asked, "Why are you so interested in Queen Victoria?"

Aunt Spring glanced around at her companions.

"Go on, Aunt Spring." Miss Minnie nodded. "You should tell Miss Setterington what we have done."

"Yes." Aunt Spring sat down, then bounced up like a child wroth with excitement. "For years my brother was the earl here."

"Yes, so I understand." Although Hannah didn't know what this had to do with Queen Victoria.

"Rupert was always a cranky man. Very aware of his position. Always going on about the duties he faced. And tight as a tick with a tuppence." Aunt Spring shook her head. "I was born here, and I always lived here, but the way he acted you would have thought I stole the bread from his lips."

It was a sad story Aunt Spring told, often repeated among the unmarried ladies of England. "I imagine he made you uncomfortable," Hannah said gently.

Aunt Spring scrunched up her nose. "No . . . he wasn't a very forceful man. More of an impediment than anything, and he was the type of man who would have complained if he'd been hung with a silk rope. Why, even when dear Lawrence asked for my hand, Rupert complained about Lawrence's poverty. As if I wouldn't have been happier being a soldier's wife than Rupert's dependent!" She nodded until her curls bobbed. "If not for Rupert refusing his permission, I would have had the joy of living with Lawrence. He was killed on the Peninsula, you know, a hero to the last, and at least I would have had so many more memories . . ." She stared forward, mouth tucked down, eyes sorrowful and vague.

Silence filled the chamber. Hannah saw how Aunt

Spring's friends exchanged glances, then smiled sadly at each other.

Leaning over, Aunt Isabel patted Hannah's hand and her loud voice contrasted oddly with the delicate moment. "It's a melancholy thing to know that one of us could have been happily wed, if only for a short time, and so pedestrian a thing as funds impeded that union, and so dread an event as death put an end to love forever."

"Oh, no! I still love him, and he still loves me. Someday we'll all be together—he and I and dear little . . ." Aunt Spring touched her forehead as if she were in pain. Then in a rush of enthusiasm, she clapped her hands. "In the meantime, I have my friends to keep me happy. Lawrence was my true love, and a true lover wants happiness for the loved one, no matter how long the wait."

"What a lovely thought," Hannah said—while Hannah thought, *Another proof that Dougald had never loved her*—as if she needed such proof. He wanted her miserable, and he was doing a fine job of it. She sometimes felt the epithet "bastard" was branded on her forehead. That was why she had come to Lancashire. To discover whence she had come.

Dougald realized. Of course he did. Years ago she had explained how much she wished to know her background, and at that time he had decreed her longing to be nonsense. The manly donkeybrain had actually told her she should live for him. Any sensible person would have known she would rebel at this, but not Dougald. He had been oblivious . . . until now. Until he could use his knowledge as an ambush.

Her gaze rested on Aunt Spring. She was the key to Hannah's release. Aunt Spring knew Hannah's family—probably knew where they lived. What was to keep her from going to her grandparents by herself, introducing herself as their granddaughter, and having a nice visit?

She put her hand to her neck and felt her own rapid heart rate.

What, besides a fear of a brutal rebuff?

"Spring, dear," Aunt Ethel said, "You were going to tell Miss Setterington why we want Queen Victoria to come visit us."

Without knowing quite how, Hannah found herself on her feet. "You want to have Queen Victoria visit? Here?"

"Dear Miss Setterington, a lady does not shout." As she reproved Hannah, Miss Minnie leveled a black frown at Aunt Ethel.

"So sorry." Aunt Ethel looked apologetic and embarrassed. "I meant to let Aunt Spring tell the tale."

"Miss Setterington wasn't shouting. She simply spoke clearly for a change." Aunt Isabel tugged at Hannah's skirt. "Dear, you have a tendency to mumble."

"I'll do better," Hannah said numbly.

"Now, dear, sit down and let Aunt Spring explain everything."

Aghast, Hannah subsided into the chair. No matter what Aunt Spring said, it could never explain what Dougald had thought when he told the aunts that Hannah knew Her Majesty. Was she supposed to write the Queen and invite her to Raeburn Castle? Why? Did he think he would gain power from the Queen's visit? If so, he had quite underestimated her powers.

"When Rupert's wife died, I helped with his sons, and when his sons were almost grown and I was just wondering what I should do with my life"—she smiled at Miss Minnie—"when my dear friend of many years lost her brother and her home, and I realized we would be well suited as companions."

Miss Minnie watched Aunt Spring steadily, and Hannah thought the grim old woman's expression held affection as well as impatience with the rambling narrative.

Aunt Ethel piped up, "Then my husband's wandering eye got caught by that little hussy of a maid, and when I was at my lowest ebb, dear Minnie told dear Spring about me, and she offered me a refuge."

They all looked at Aunt Isabel, waiting for her story.

"My husband died, may the old goat rest in peace or at least rest. He didn't make a provision for me at all, but Spring said any friend of Ethel's and Minnie's is a friend of mine, and I . . . I really had no choice." Aunt Isabel added hastily, "Not that I'm not happy and grateful to be here, I just want to assure you I had a great need. I didn't come here only because of the good times the ladies enjoy."

Hannah said, "His Lordship the earl must have been . . ."

"Oh, yes, quite perturbed that I would share his largesse with my dear friends. He groaned and griped like a man with a worm in his bowels." Aunt Spring placed her fingers on her lips and stared out the window. "Hm. I never thought of that. Maybe he did have a worm."

"It's a moot point now," Miss Minnie pointed out.

Aunt Spring looked at her vaguely.

"He has passed on to his reward," Miss Minnie explained. "Or punishment."

"So he has." Aunt Spring nodded. "And as a Christian woman, I should mourn his death, but after the boys died—they were my nephews, you know, and his sons—he went from disagreeable to morose."

Aunt Ethel stood and clasped her hands, then unclasped them and clasped them again. "They were his children, dear. There's nothing quite as dreadful as having your children predecease you."

Another sad story, Hannah realized, one so sad Aunt Isabel drew her friend onto the settee beside her and patted her veined hand.

Aunt Spring's voice broke and her eyes filled with tears. "I know, Ethel. I do know."

"Perhaps we should not dwell on such a sad subject." Miss Minnie nodded significantly at Aunt Ethel. "Instead you should tell Miss Setterington why we want to see Queen Victoria."

"Yes, dear," Aunt Spring said. "I did."

"Perhaps you could clarify the reason for me," Hannah suggested.

Aunt Spring gestured toward the worktable. "We have something for her."

"For the Queen?"

"Yes, and we want you to write her and tell her she should come."

"But, with all due respect, the Queen will not come on my summons."

"But she must." Aunt Spring's voice rose in distress, and she touched her fingertips to her cheek. "You must write her and tell her to come so we can give her . . . give her . . . the thing."

At Aunt Spring's forgetfulness, a tension permeated the companions.

"The thing?" Hannah encouraged.

"That we've made her," Aunt Spring insisted. "Oh, I can't remember the word."

From the doorway, Mrs. Trenchard said, "The word doesn't matter, Miss Spring. You can show Miss Setterington what ye have done right after ye've had a spot of tea."

"Oh, yes!" Aunt Spring clapped her hands. "Dear Judy, did you bring cream cakes?"

"I did indeed, Miss Spring. I know how much you like them." Mrs. Trenchard wheeled in a white-tablecloth-covered cart filled with cakes of every kind, tiny crust-less sandwiches, and two steaming china pots. As she set out the cups and saucers, she asked, "So how do ye like yer new companion, ladies?"

Aunt Isabel turned to Aunt Ethel. "What did she say?"

"She wants to know if we like Miss Setterington," Aunt Ethel said loudly.

"Of course we like her." Aunt Isabel grinned at Hannah with a spark of wicked humor. "She knows the Queen."

Hannah grinned back at her.

"She's a lovely girl," Aunt Ethel said.

"She is so kind."

Aunt Spring's praise was predictable—Hannah suspected Aunt Spring seldom spoke ill of anyone—but it warmed Hannah's heart.

"She will do very well," Miss Minnie pronounced.

Miss Minnie's approval gave Hannah pride.

Mrs. Trenchard set out little plates. "Miss Setterington, it seems you have won them over, and so quickly, too."

Mrs. Trenchard's commendation seemed less than

sincere; probably she desired to be relieved of the arduous duties of caring for Aunt Spring, yet at the same didn't wish to be so easily replaced. Hannah could understand. Since she had sold the Distinguished Academy of Governesses, she had occasionally—and shamefacedly—hoped that Adorna's handling the transition of authority did not proceed too smoothly.

So Hannah said, "I was hoping to speak to you at your convenience, Mrs. Trenchard, to ask how I might better serve Miss Spring and her ladies."

"I'd be delighted to help you." Mrs. Trenchard smiled, obviously gratified by Hannah's deference. "Do you want me to stay and pour?"

"You're busy, dear Judy." Aunt Spring hugged the housekeeper's shoulders. "We'll serve ourselves, and you can return to your duties. I know how busy you are on laundry day!"

"Yes, thank you, Miss Spring." Mrs. Trenchard stood stiffly under Aunt Spring's embrace, yet she lingered, watching with apparent enjoyment as the aunts recommended first one cake, then another, to Hannah.

Miss Minnie poured the tea, and it was perfect: warm, richly amber, fragrant. The food was delicious, certainly worthy to serve the Queen . . . Hannah pulled herself up short. But it was madness to imagine Queen Victoria coming to shabby Raeburn Castle, especially for some bauble made by four eccentric old ladies. What *had* been Dougald's plan?

She sipped her tea. "When can I see what you've made the Queen?"

The aunts exchanged glances, then put down their cups.

"Now, if you like," Aunt Spring said.

Mrs. Trenchard was forgotten as they urged Hannah toward the long, purple-draped wall. The housekeeper cleaned up the tea, glancing toward Hannah and the aunts in a manner half-longing, half-relieved, and completely guilty. Then she wheeled the cart out of the door.

Aunt Ethel and Aunt Isabel each grasped a pull on the curtain and stood, quivering, waiting for instruction.

"Are you ready, Miss Setterington?" Aunt Spring asked.

Ready for what? Hannah nodded.

"Show her," Miss Minnie commanded.

Aunt Ethel and Aunt Isabel pulled the curtains back, dragging the heavy material along the rod, revealing a tapestry.

And not just any tapestry. A huge, magnificently conceived, ornately woven tapestry representing Her Majesty Queen Victoria dressed in her coronation robes, with Prince Albert at her side.

Hannah stared in awe, and when she collected herself enough to shut her mouth, she stared again. The work stretched fully ten feet tall and sixteen feet across, filling the wall, filling the eyes with artistry. This wasn't the Bayeux Tapestry, with its course of war and conquest. This was a tribute, a modern gift done with the forgotten skill of a past age. These ladies, these enfeebled, hard-of-hearing and neglected elderly, had accomplished their feat with four looms and their considerable talent.

Hannah stood in veneration of their skill and virtuosity.

The enfeebled, hard-of-hearing and neglected elderly were almost dancing with impatience.

"Tell us what you think," Aunt Isabel demanded.

"The detail . . . the creative precision . . ." The representation of Queen Victoria actually looked like Queen Victoria, and if Albert suffered from one cheek being higher than the other, no one would fault the originators of this endeavor. "It's splendid." Hannah spoke to Aunt Isabel, making sure she did not mumble.

"I told you it was good!" Aunt Isabel announced triumphantly.

"How long have you been working on it?" Hannah asked.

"Since her birth in 1819," Aunt Ethel told her.

"Twenty-four years . . ." And Hannah was amazed they had finished it in so short a time. "Her Majesty truly ought to—" she bit off her words. Queen Victoria truly ought to see this, but without Dougald's permission she dared not issue an invitation. "It is simply breathtaking."

"Look at the background. We used different symbols to indicate her sovereignty." Aunt Spring swept her hand wide to indicate the greater background. "Isabel placed the moon and the sun, and suggested the sprinkling of stars to indicate the Queen's majesty."

"The royal blue makes a most stunning framework." Hannah stepped back, amazed at the amount of labor and thought the aunts had put into the tapestry.

Aunt Ethel pointed to an open jewel chest. "Aunt Spring suggested the gems to represent the wealth of the nation."

"The colors are extraordinary." Hannah moved closer to admire them.

"Ethel suggested the roses—red and white to imply the sweep of British history, pink for Her Majesty's eternal youth, and the thorns . . . see the thorns?"—Miss Minnie indicated the brambles that coiled across the bottom of the montage—"to show that England defends her own and can never be conquered."

"So wise. So thoughtful." Hannah couldn't take her gaze from the harmonious tapestry, resplendent with symbolism and grandeur. "Who designed it?"

"Minnie did, dear. She did the sketches and when we had agreed on them, we divided them into panels. Each of us had two panels to weave. Then we matched them up and sewed them together . . ." Aunt Spring clasped her hands in excitement. "We did it all ourselves. We didn't let the sewing maids touch it. We wanted it to be our own tribute to Queen Victoria. So you like it?"

"Marvelous." Hannah was running out of adjectives, and the tapestry deserved them all.

"Is it worthy of Her Majesty?" Miss Minnie asked.

Hannah drew her breath, but she couldn't equivocate. "She would be honored to receive such a gift."

"So you will invite her to Raeburn Castle?" Aunt Ethel's blue eyes shone.

What could she say? How could she answer? Stalling for time, hoping for inspiration, Hannah said, "As you can imagine, Her Majesty's schedule is set up months in advance. After I write her, it could be months, even—"

"Are you telling us she won't come?" Miss Minnie asked.

Trust Miss Minnie to recognize Hannah's dubiety

and address it bluntly. Scrutinizing the tapestry again, Hannah was transfixed by Queen Victoria's direct, all-seeing gaze. Hannah couldn't lie to the aunts, nor could she give them anything but her best effort. They wanted this so much. They deserved to show the Queen their homage, just as the Queen deserved to see the results of their devotion. "You do understand, I cannot promise you anything. She may never come."

"We know. She's the Queen of England. But if we didn't ask her, she would never even know," Aunt Spring explained.

"What's the worst Her Majesty can do? Send her regrets?" Miss Minnie's hands trembled, and she sank into a chair. "We must try, or our endeavor is for naught. Anticipation, after all, is all that's been keeping us alive."

Seeing the parchment white of Miss Minnie's complexion, and the way the others rushed to pat her back and wave smelling salts under her nose, Hannah believed her. In fact, unless the Queen came soon, Miss Minnie might not be there to see their triumph. "Courtesy demands that I speak with Lord Raeburn before I issue the invitation." And speak she would, most forcefully.

"That is satisfactory." Miss Minnie pushed the smelling salts away. "So you think we'd have time to fix Albert's face? I'm quite accomplished with the sketch pad, but not so much so with the loom, and I'm still not satisfied with his uneven features."

"I agree, his features could be more symmetrical." Remembering Queen Victoria's devotion to her consort, Hannah added, "I assure you, there is time to reweave him."

"Good." Miss Minnie pointed at the tapestry. "Get the footmen in here to take it down. We'll take it apart and go to work immediately."

13

Charles shut the door of Dougald's Spartan office with his usual concern for his master's delicate sensibilities, but Dougald saw immediately that his faithful valet was disturbed. Disturbed, and Dougald knew why.

Hannah had arrived outside his door.

He paused, his quill hovering over the book of estate accounts. "Yes, Charles?"

"My lord, *Madame* is wishing to speak with you . . . again."

"Is she?" An unusual urge grew in Dougald. The urge to smile. He had been thwarting Hannah's wish for private conversation for almost a fortnight. He enjoyed it, and probably far too much, but he forgave himself the unrestrained emotion. Ignoring Hannah seemed such a small retaliation for so many years of worry and disrepute.

"She begs to speak to you, my lord." Charles imbued a great deal of Gallic histrionics in his plea.

Histrionics would do no good. "Begs?" Dougald snorted. "I doubt that."

"Perhaps that is not quite the term she used, but she sincerely wishes a moment of your time to ask a question."

Dougald didn't need to talk to Hannah to know what she wanted. She wanted to know about her family, or perhaps what he intended to do about their marriage. Neither of which he intended to tell her right now. She would know the answer to both those questions when he decided she would know, no sooner. "Tell her to go away. I don't have time to deal with a mere companion to my aunt." Once more, he lowered his head to the long column of numbers. Figuring the income and output of the Raeburn estate had proved to be a challenge, especially when so many different lords had had the keeping of the books these last few years.

Charles sighed. Charles did not approve of his master's torment of his estranged wife, although Dougald didn't understand why. After all, Charles had considered Hannah a dreadful nuisance and an unworthy wife, and he had been proud of his part in routing her from Dougald's life. He had interfered in their marriage. Then he had bragged to Dougald that he had rescued him from a wretched union. Bragged, when nothing was more wretched than the loneliness and apprehension that followed.

Dougald still felt a trickle of shame that he had allowed himself to be so misled. He had allowed his own pride and ignorance, and Charles's opinions, to destroy his marriage.

Shame, Dougald had discovered, only made him more ruthless in his handling of Hannah. "Charles!"

Charles brightened, if the slight lightening of his melancholy expression could be so labeled. "My lord?"

"Did you find out anything about the deaths of the last two lords?"

Charles's face fell back into its usual sagging lines. "*Oui*, my lord, I did, but I thought to discuss it with you when I had your full attention. Right now, *Madame*—"

"She can wait." Dougald wiped off his quill and placed it on the blotter. "Come. Sit down. Tell me if my suspicions are correct."

Unhappily, Charles glanced at the door. "But *Madame* is waiting. I should tell her—"

"*Miss Setterington*"—Dougald emphasized the lesser title—"is nothing but an employee. She may wait upon my indulgence for as long as it pleases me. Sit down and tell me the results of your investigation."

"As you wish, my lord." Ten years ago Charles would have been offended by Dougald's tone of voice, and he would have shown it. Now he obeyed with alacrity, knowing himself to be on eternal probation. He sat in the straight-backed chair and faced Dougald across the desk, an aging Frenchman dedicated to the well-being of Dougald's family. Folding his hands fussily in his lap, he said, "I first came to Raeburn Castle five years ago while, on your orders, I searched for *Madame's* . . . Miss Setterington's family. There was talk in the district then of the deaths of the noble young sons—definitely an accident, my lord, unless the killer somehow managed to cause a storm at sea."

Dougald nodded. He had heard enough to be satisfied with that explanation.

"I heard that the old lord was dying—again, the natural advance of age rather than any human cause—and I naturally knew of your connection to the title—"

Dougald steadily regarded Charles. "I had scarcely heard of it at that time. How did you?"

"Your father—"

"Of course. My father." Charles didn't need to say another word. Dougald well remembered his father's avaricious pursuit of nobility, respectability and wealth. All in the name of the Pippard family. Everything for the continued glory of the line. And he had made himself like his father.

Dougald's eyes closed for a moment, and he thought of Hannah outside his door, sitting, or pacing, or cursing him. She would be the mother of his child, the carrier of the Pippards' continued glory. He hoped she appreciated the honor done her, for he would make sure that she got damned little gratification from her position as wife to the lord.

Charles said, "I came back periodically—"

"Why?"

"I found myself fond of the area, and in those days when you so kindly granted me a holiday, I returned here."

Dougald stared at him. It wasn't true, of course. Charles never went on holiday without purpose. He had been returning to Lancashire to check on the title, hoping against hope that fate would favor his lord. As indeed it had.

Charles dropped his gaze away from Dougald's, and in a rapid voice, said, "If what I have discovered is true, my lord, then I must agree that the two previous lords were killed by some deliberate means."

"Pushed down the stairs. Helped off the cliff . . ." If Dougald didn't know better, he would say Charles had been behind those crimes. After all, Charles saw nothing wrong with serving the Pippard family in any way he could, and he might imagine inheriting the title would soften Dougald's displeasure with him. But Charles wouldn't have had Dougald shot, if for no reason other than the fact that his own fortunes would fall with his master's.

Dougald looked down at his fingers. One joint on his thumb was still slightly swollen, and it pained him to bend it. Cracked, he supposed, or the joint was jammed. He sported a fading bruise from cheekbone to forehead, and he liked to keep his ankle elevated. He'd never been beaten so badly, and if not for his street-fighting experience he wouldn't have escaped. As it was, he'd left two men unconscious and another with a broken arm. He had hurried back to Raeburn Castle as quickly as possible, hoping to send someone back for them. But only crazy Alfred had been awake and he refused to let Dougald in. The stupid drunk had kept shouting about the family curse and how the ghost had returned until Mrs. Trenchard had been roused by the clamor. She, of course, had set things right, rendered first aid, sent for Charles and dispatched men to search for Dougald's assailants. The attackers were gone, and no trace of them was found in the district.

Damn. Damn! If Dougald had just one of them, he'd find out who was behind this nefarious plot and he'd be swinging by a noose before the year was out. "Who do you think is doing this?"

Charles ducked his head. "I am a miserable failure, my lord, not worthy to wipe your shoes."

"Yes, yes, but you're the most intelligent agent I have working for me."

"But I was not able to find the assailant on either of the previous lords, or on you."

"Seaton," Dougald pronounced. "That squirrelly fop is the only one who has cause."

Charles's mouth twisted one way, then another—he was thinking of how not to offend. "With all due respect, my lord, for your superior intellect and vast experience in judging your countrymen—I don't think Sir Onslow has the stomach for it, my lord."

Dougald offended Charles on a regular basis, but in this case he was almost tactful. "That's why he hires thugs to do his dirty work. He's a nasty piece of work."

"Gossipmongering does not a murderer make."

Dougald eyed his valet. "What are you getting at?"

"You know about the falseness of assuming murder. You have been trapped in that injustice yourself." Charles sat forward, his hands clasped. "Think, my lord, how obviously Sir Onslow relishes the tales surrounding your supposed crimes. Think how obviously he courts *Madame*, even though you immediately made your interest clear."

Yes, on that first morning Dougald had been blatant in placing his claim on Hannah. He shouldn't have, but with the pain, he hadn't been himself. "Since then, I have kept my distance."

"Causing even more talk, my lord." Pressing his lips together, Charles flung up his hand to stop any of Dougald's protests. "But no, that is not the point. The point is, if you were killed, Sir Onslow would be the prime, indeed the only, suspect."

"Because he's the heir to the title and fortune."

"Because he spreads slanderous gossip about you. Any man who had killed the previous two lords would show more stealth in his handling of you."

Dougald leaned back in his chair. Charles had made his point. To have pursued a goal with such single-

minded determination, Seaton would have had to
scheme and plot for years—and for what? To allow his
greed and dislike to sabotage him so close to his goal?
Of course it was possible, but . . . "Why do you care so
much whether I suspect Seaton?"

"Because, my lord, if you are wrong—the person
who wishes you dead is still undetected."

"Yes . . ." Dougald caressed a still-tender bruise on
his forehead.

"At least entertain some doubt. You have Sir Onslow
under surveillance." Charles knew his master, so it
wasn't an inquiry.

"Yes." Dougald had not thought to rehire the three
detectives who had watched Hannah so soon, but he
had sent for them. They had arrived. They followed
Seaton, visiting where he visited, blending in with
their dark coats and their gentlemanly demeanor. They
were damned expensive, but Dougald couldn't depend
on anyone at Raeburn Castle. Not anyone.

"I do not know who the culprit is, but I will continue
to watch for him, and watch your back." As was his
wont, Charles struck a pose, fist on his chest. "You are
safe, my lord, as long as Charles is with you."

In the current circumstances, a little posturing was
admissible. "Thank you, Charles."

"Now, my lord, may I invite Miss Setterington to
join you?"

Posturing, but not manipulating. "No." Dougald
picked up his pen, dipped it in the inkwell.

"But Miss Setterington has been waiting—"

Dougald pointed the pen at Charles. "I don't want to
hear you say another word about Miss Setterington."

"But my lord—"

"Not a word." Dougald returned to work.

 *   *   *

Outside of Dougald's study, Hannah sat knees together, hands folded, mouth pursed, her exasperation swelling to unmanageable proportions. What was wrong with Dougald? She needed to talk to him about one thing. She needed his permission to invite Queen Victoria to Raeburn Castle. That would take approximately a minute, but she had not been given a minute. It was not appropriate to ask at dinner. Every day for a fortnight, she had traipsed down from the aunts' workroom, through the corridor, through the great hall, through the chapel, and to the dim, windowless anteroom outside Dougald's office. And every day she found Charles surrounded by candles, sitting at his desk, looking like the devil incarnate with his thin, white, wispily erect hair and his big, black, tormented eyes. She would state her desire to speak with Dougald. He would go into Dougald's office and shut the door. And he would be back almost immediately with the report that Dougald was too busy to see her.

Today he was taking longer.

She ought to give up and send a message through Charles, but she was stubborn. She had already lived through this same scene time and again during her married life, and she liked it even less now.

Standing, she paced through the anteroom and out into the chapel. This tiny chapel had been an original part of the castle, built when Saxons and Normans fought for preeminence. On the left side on one high wall, stained-glass windows depicted the life of Saint Martha and shed colored shards of light throughout the temple. A patina of age covered the ceiling's carved, vaulted rafters. Whitewashed plaster covered the walls above, intricately carved and polished wood below.

The pews gleamed, worn smooth by the hands and bodies of so many worshipers. A small door near the altar led into the vestry. Candles burned eternally in their iron sconces upon the altar, and a sense of peace pervaded the very walls of stone, plaster and wood.

If only Hannah could find that peace for herself.

"Charles, I need to speak to Dougald now!"

Charles stared down his nose at Hannah. "Monsieur Pippard is much too busy to be bothered by domestic matters during his workday. Take your pressing matter up with him tonight."

"I am his wife. I have the right to talk to him when I wish!"

"Better yet, don't bother him with your trifling concerns. A true woman makes her man comfortable when he returns from a busy day. She makes sure the house is tidy, she pretties herself, and she never complains."

"I don't need to be told how to care for my husband."

"Obviously you do, or you would not be here now."

The echoes of that miserable time still sounded in her ears. How dare Charles presume—then or now—to judge her need unimportant? And how dare Dougald ignore her in such a manner? She was the former proprietress of the Distinguished Academy of Governesses. Young ladies had quailed beneath her gimlet stare. And she couldn't even get into Dougald's office to stare at him in a gimlet-eyed manner!

Turning, she cast a dark look through the chapel at the closed office door. Charles had been in there for a very long time. Perhaps that meant Dougald had satisfied his childish need to make her wait and would at last speak to her.

"For God's sake, Hannah, do you have to go on

about that dress shop? I'm tired of hearing you whine."

"I'm not whining, I'm reminding you of your promise."

"Forget the promise! Don't I provide for you well? Don't you have servants to fulfill your every whim? Aren't you dressed in the finest clothing?"

Hannah could almost taste her despair. "Yes, yes, but that's not what I want. At least tell Charles to let me run my household. I have nothing to do!"

"Don't be silly. Most women would be happy to live as you do." Dougald frowned at her. "You must stop complaining about Charles and learn to get along with him. He is my most trusted servant, and I will not dismiss him on a girl's whim."

"You don't trust me as you do him."

"Darling, don't be silly." Dougald pulled her toward him and kissed her forehead. "You're my wife."

Which wasn't an answer. She had known it even then.

Her greatest fear was that Dougald believed she actually yearned to be with him now as she had yearned to be close to him during their brief time together.

She didn't. She saw Dougald every day during breakfast, and every day during dinner, and if she saw his remote, sardonic, demonic visage more frequently she would suffer nausea and perhaps hives. Not only did she see him during meals, but she had to be polite to him. She had to pretend respect for his position of lord of Raeburn, and not snort when he requested his daily update of her activities. She had to speak civilly to him, and if she took the opportunity to insinuate he should help her determine her correct duty, he also took the opportunity to insinuate he'd tell her when he was infernally good and ready.

She had to put up with his staring at her. He watched her endlessly, his green eyes relentless. He listened when she spoke. He made a general nuisance of himself with his inarticulate attentions, which she knew must be aimed at making his criticism clear. If only she could speak to him freely, without the gleeful eavesdropping of the aunts and Seaton. Then she would tell him she didn't give a damn about his attentions, and he could just stop trying to make her apprehensive because it just wasn't working.

Dougald and Hannah were performing a dance, one where she pursued and he evaded, and dammit! she didn't want to pursue him.

Struck once more by the injustice of the situation, she sank down in the front pew and stared forward. Did the Dougald she married no longer exist? Had he ever existed, or had he been a figment of her imagination? For she didn't recognize this difficult, brooding lord who seldom bothered to hide the dark corners of his soul. If she had just been introduced, if she didn't know the truth, she would easily believe that he had killed his wife.

Perhaps she would be wise to use caution when speaking to him.

If she ever got to speak to him.

There had to be a solution to this situation. Perhaps she could find it here. For all six hundred years, the altar had been the heart of the castle. The steps were worn with the tread of hundreds of feet shuffling forward to receive communion. The altar itself had been formed of oak, and cleaned and waxed diligently so that the pure golden grain still shone, and a shining white, crisply ironed, and embroidered cloth draped over its edges.

This chapel had seen birth and death, heard prayers and curses, and within its walls countless baptisms had been celebrated, countless funerals had been performed. Beside those life-changing events, Hannah's current adversity could not compare, but still she bowed her head and asked for guidance.

When she raised it again, she looked around eagerly, expecting to see a celestial solution presented before her. Instead she observed, in a gleam of blue light from the window, a rough place in the wall on the left side of the altar. It was near the floor—one of the carved panels looked as if it had rotted away from the wall.

She glanced toward Dougald's office. The door remained stubbornly closed, so she went to investigate the damaged plank. Kneeling, she saw that the panel had indeed been scarred with rot or—she rubbed at it when her fingertips—some sharp object had been used to gouge the edge until it separated from the plaster beneath.

What had happened here in some musty corner of history? Had a child carelessly done this with his toys? Had a resentful servant sought to destroy a piece of the lord's chapel?

Hannah caught the edge of the board with her fingernails. Yes, it was loose, and as she pulled it back, she saw, not plaster as she expected, but a shadowed cavity between the board and the stone castle wall. Perhaps something was hidden here—

She needed a candle to peer inside, but as she half rose, she hit her head. Hard. So hard she fell to her knees and for a moment, just a moment, saw nothing but swirling black and red.

When she recovered, her forehead rested on the floor and she heard Charles calling her.

"*Madame. Madame*! Are you ill?"

He was bending over her, and all she could think was that her head hurt and she felt silly. "I hit my head," she said.

Charles took her arm and helped her to her feet. "On . . . what?" He sounded amazingly skeptical.

She looked up to see, but blinked against the glare of light from the stained-glass window. "I don't know. I didn't even know I was under anything, but when I tried to stand . . ."

Charles helped her to the pew. "Sit, *s'il vous plait, Madame*, you look quite peaked."

"I tell you, I hit my head on something!"

"I believe you," he said in a soothing tone that irritated her yet more. He didn't seem concerned with her condition, he was too busy craning his head around, and just when she was ready to snap at him to leave her alone, he pointed toward the floor. "Look, that's what it was."

"What *what* was?"

Leaning over, he picked up a carved, wooden curlicue. "This must have fallen off one of the rafters."

Cautiously this time, she looked up and scanned the beams. "I don't see any place it could have come from."

"It's very dark up there, and the carving is old. I will tell my lord Raeburn that he should renovate the chapel soon before someone is hurt."

She glared at Charles.

"Hurt further," he amended. "May I suggest you go

upstairs to your chamber and sleep? I will explain to the aunts that you have taken ill, and have a repast sent up on a tray. You should rest after such a blow on the head."

Contrarily, his kindness made her testier—she knew very well what it meant. "Will his lordship speak to me?"

Charles actually managed to appear contrite, and even wrung his hands. "I'm sorry, *Madame*, he hasn't the time."

"I don't really *want* to see *him*. You know that, don't you?"

"I do understand that, *Madame*."

"I just have a single question which only he can answer."

"Perhaps if you told me the inquiry, I could pass it on to him . . ."

She hissed.

"Or perhaps not," he allowed.

"He's playing a game, and he's going to lose," she said.

"I fear you are right."

Charles was humoring her, and that made her even more irritable. Dougald *was* playing a game, but she didn't have a chance of winning, and she and Charles both knew it. "He isn't going to like what happens next."

Charles bowed. "Do your worst, *Madame*."

Infuriated by his civility—her head ached too badly to deal with an amicable Charles—she stood. Ragged bits of black crossed her vision, and for a few humiliating moments, nausea threatened.

"I think I should escort *Madame* to her bedchamber," Charles said.

"That won't be necessary, my dear man." She took deep breaths and steadied herself. "It will take more than a blow to the head to stop me."

"I see that."

She suspected sarcasm, but it was too much effort to respond. Slowly, carefully, she made her way out of the chapel, down the corridor, up the stairs and, after only a moment's hesitation in which she debated whether she should return to the aunts, she proceeded to her bedchamber. There she took out her portable secretary, sat down at the table by the narrow bed, and started a letter which began, "My dear and gracious sovereign, Queen Victoria . . ."

14

"𝓔thel, dear, I think this white yarn will be better for the dear prince's cravat." Aunt Isabel's voice echoed loud and clear in the aunts' workroom.

"No, dear, I want to weave a block with this darker thread because I'm starting the shadow." It was Aunt Ethel's turn at the loom, and she defended her choice fiercely.

"I think a few more white—"

"No, dear, that was the mistake we made the first time—"

Aunt Ethel and Aunt Isabel were in the best-lit area with the best ventilation—the area where the tapestry was constructed. Miss Minnie, Aunt Spring and Hannah sat by one of the large windows, catching the light of the westering sun on their handwork. Hannah ducked her head to her embroidery and smiled as she listened to the two ladies argue about Prince Albert's cravat. The four aunts were like children, eager to squabble, stubborn and determined on their own way. But one common goal united them; they wanted the

Queen's tapestry to be perfect, and they worked it one piece at a time.

Aunt Spring clucked her tongue as she polished one of the handsome stones she had collected from the creek bed. "I told Isabel not to go over there until Ethel had finished."

Miss Minnie put down her sketch pad and removed her spectacles. "I wish they wouldn't override my decisions. I plotted every color of thread to be used." Rubbing the bridge of her nose, she said, "I suppose I should go handle this."

Hannah covered Miss Minnie's hand. "Let me."

Miss Minnie relaxed back into her chair. "Would you, Miss Setterington? You have a diplomatic touch I seem to lack."

She seldom commended anyone, so Hannah glowed beneath the gruff praise. Rising, she walked where the two ladies debated the virtue of bleached white versus unbleached white. She interrupted them without remorse, for if left to themselves she would never get a word in edgewise. "The light is fading, but from what I can tell, the work is progressing well."

"I had hoped to finish this row before I quit," Aunt Ethel lamented.

Stepping back, Hannah viewed the whole panel of the tapestry. In the three weeks she had been at Raeburn Castle, they had taken the panel containing Prince Albert out of the tapestry, unwoven it from the top to his shoulders, and begun the painstaking process of recreating his visage and the background. Each block of color had to be separately woven and sewn to the next block; each mistake compounded itself, but the aunts' work was meticulous and painstaking. Hannah was the overseer. Miss Minnie was the artist. The other three aunts took turns working on the loom. Hannah had hoped to keep them busy at least until the following Christmas, but with their enthusiasm the tapestry would be finished again by autumn, or even late summer.

"Of course, Aunt Ethel, you must do what you wish, but in this light . . ." Hannah shook her head. "I fear such hurry is what caused the problem with Prince Albert the first time."

Aunt Ethel put down the bobbin. "I *was* straining my eyes."

"Come on, dear." Aunt Isabel hooked her arm through Aunt Ethel's and drew her to her feet. "Let's go see if Mrs. Trenchard is sending supper up to us, or whether we have to change to go down to the dining room."

They went off, amiable as always, and Hannah contemplated the letter she had posted to London over a week ago. If only Her Majesty would reply, how happy the aunts would be! It wouldn't be the same, of course, as having Queen Victoria view the tapestry in all its majestic glory, and sometimes Hannah dreamed of the scene with the Queen overcome by the honor done her, thanking the aunts in her own gracious manner, while Hannah stood beside the Queen and smirked at the incredulous Dougald.

Good sense always pulled her from those reveries and slammed her back into reality. A reality where Queen Victoria would never have time to make such a gesture. A reality populated by kind old women, a coxcomb of an heir, Charles, a variety of servants who didn't know exactly how to treat her—and a husband who had trapped her, threatened her, and now steadfastly ignored her.

A reality she couldn't leave because if she did before she met her grandparents, she would be eternally regretful. Even if in the end they rejected her.

"It is looking well, isn't it?" Aunt Spring stood by Hannah's side and lightly touched the tapestry.

"It's going to be perfect." Hannah gazed at the kind, short, graying lady beside her. Miss Minnie sat with her eyes closed, gathering her strength for the rest of the day, and this was Hannah's chance to ask, uninterrupted, the questions that had plagued her since her first morning here. If she wished to take matters into her own hands, this was the moment. "Aunt Spring, have you invited the Burroughses to visit?"

"Oh, dear, was I supposed to?"

Hannah bowed her head in a brief moment of heartache. This was why Aunt Spring needed a companion. Sometimes she forgot things. Little things, like speaking to Hannah about the Burroughses. Big things, like where her bedchamber was located. Everyone helped her. The other aunts, Hannah, Mrs. Trenchard, Sir Onslow, the servants . . . but she couldn't be left alone anymore, or she might lose herself in the corridors of Raeburn Castle.

"I can invite them if you like," Aunt Spring said. "Do you know them?"

"Not personally. I know of them."

"Perhaps your parents knew them?"

"Yes." *Oh, yes.* "My parents."

"The Burroughses are a lovely couple, a little older than I am." Aunt Spring moved a little closer to Hannah and whispered, "I don't like to gossip—"

All the aunts loved to gossip.

"—But they used to be quite high in the instep."

Hannah knew. She knew better than anyone. "Why?"

Aunt Spring shrugged, showing an earl's daughter's hint of haughtiness. "The usual. They've money, and their families have been here since the dawn of time. But they were both the last of their lines, and only had a single child, and he died without an heir. They are quite alone now." She sniffed. "I told them they shouldn't have chased that young woman away, but they didn't listen to me."

Hannah longed to hear the story from an outsider's viewpoint, to find out what really happened in that summer twenty-eight years ago. So she asked, "What young woman?"

"Miss Carola Tomlinson."

The name resonated with Hannah.

"She loved Henry so much."

"Henry." Hannah tasted the name. Her father's name was Henry.

"He loved her, too, but he was one of those young men who loved . . . without character." Aunt Spring fiddled with the frame of the loom. "She was so comely."

Hannah remembered watching her mother, thinking she was the prettiest lady she'd ever seen. Only when Hannah had grown older did she observe the lines of worry and the dark circles that too much work put under her eyes. "Yes."

"But she had no family. She was just a governess to a neighboring family."

Hannah flinched.

"So they sent her away, and he let them." Aunt Spring raised tear-filled eyes. "He sank into bad company, and died in a pub brawl not three months later."

"So he couldn't ever come after her." Hannah knew

he was dead; her mother had told her, although how she had discovered that Hannah never knew. But somehow it helped to think he had been unhappy with his decision, and to imagine that perhaps, if he had lived, he might have worked up the nerve to defy his parents and wed Miss Carola Tomlinson. As to whether he had known about Hannah's impending birth . . . that, she feared, would be a mystery, at least until she spoke with her grandparents.

Her grandparents. Perhaps they were cruel. Perhaps they were kind. Perhaps they deserved no forgiveness for the hideous fate they had wished upon their grand-child, and perhaps Hannah had no forgiveness to give them. But she had to know. She had to see them. She would take matters in her own hands.

Next week was her half day off. Filled with drastic resolution, she asked, "Where do the Burroughses live?"

15

Hannah had her information, the information she had come to Lancashire to find. Aunt Spring had provided it freely, without imagining how much it meant to Hannah or how chagrinned Dougald would be that she had obtained it. Furthermore, Hannah felt sure Aunt Spring would have provided her with the Burroughses' direction even if she had understood the situation.

So why did Hannah feel so guilty?

Probably because she had kept the facts from Aunt Spring and the others. They were such lovely ladies, taking her into their embrace, telling her all their secrets, making her job a pleasure. With the renovation of the tapestry proceeding so well, and the kindness of her charges, the only fly in the ointment was Dougald and his despicable superiority. If not for him, she would be perfectly happy. *Perfectly* happy.

To prove it, she hummed as she held her candle high and walked down the corridor to her bedchamber. The darkness did not bother her, nor did the hideous, shabby wallpaper, nor did the shadows that stretched and wavered in the candle flame, nor did the deep-set doors, closed and mysterious, and certainly not the absolute, wretched loneliness of her situation.

Mrs. Trenchard had told the truth when she said only Dougald and Hannah lived in this wing. The liveliness, the camaraderie, the brightness that characterized the aunts' wing was absent here. The servants came in the daylight to dust and wax, to replenish the water in the pitcher and take her laundry, but at night each step echoed on the polished wood floor and Hannah found herself fantasizing about Dougald and what she wanted to say to him—if she ever saw him.

Stopping opposite the double doors, she stared at the master's suite. Mayhap he was inside, and she could trap him and tell him . . . everything. How his evasive tactics were not breaking down her fortitude. That she was happy being his aunt's companion and nothing more. That she didn't care whether they ever again lived together as man and wife, and in fact she scarcely thought of what might happen if the two of them were alone together on a bed. Oh, and . . . that she'd invited Queen Victoria to visit Raeburn Castle.

Hannah chuckled softly. He had done everything in his power to prove he cared nothing for her, but she would wager he'd definitely care about that invitation.

She took a step closer to the doors. Truly, a valiant woman would knock on those doors and speak to her employer. It was foolish to refrain. More than that, it was cowardly, a mark that, despite her assurances to herself, his nerve-wracking tactics *were* working.

Reaching out her fist, she rapped on the panel. The thick wood muffled the noise, yet it sounded loud in the emptiness of the corridor. Compulsively, she glanced around. The corridor was still empty and dark. So she knocked again.

Nothing. He didn't answer. No light shone from beneath the door. Probably he wasn't inside.

So why did her hand reach out and close around the doorknob? The metal was cold in her palm; she paused and wondered at her insanity. Then she turned the knob. The latch clicked. The door opened.

She lingered on the threshold and peered into the Stygian gloom. If she stepped through, she would be thoroughly invading Dougald's privacy.

Not that he didn't deserve it. In London, he had had her watched, for heaven's sake.

But to sneak into her estranged husband's bedchamber seemed illogical and not at all like her.

Except that she'd had a healthy dose of curiosity when she was a girl. Look at her eagerness for new experiences. That curiosity had gotten her into Dougald's arms and into the unendurable marriage to begin with.

Which was a good reason not to go in.

But she wanted to know what his room looked like. So she set foot through the portal and, candle aloft, stepped cautiously into the middle of Dougald's sitting room.

A few coals glimmered in the fireplace, casting their feeble light over the furnishings and carpets. From here, his life as the master of Raeburn Castle wasn't much different than hers as the aunts' companion. His sitting room was large, his bedchamber larger, but the carpets were faded and dreary, the embroidery on the chair seats was frayed, the wallpaper might have been stylish once, but not for at least forty years and, as Mrs. Trenchard promised, the coals cast a pall of smoke into the room. The man who had worked so hard for the pleasures of life now worked, but ignored the pleasures.

"This is wretched." She smoothed the ugly, worn material on one of the chairs. "Really ugly. Who chose the fabric, the village blacksmith?"

The door slammed against the wall, and Dougald said, "Actually, I believe Aunt Spring's grandmother chose the fabric."

Hannah jumped and whirled. Hot wax splashed onto her hand, and she held on to the candle by instinct only.

Dougald watched, his green eyes gleaming. He stepped across the threshold. His broad shoulders blocked the door, his fists rested on his hips and made him appear yet larger. There was a message in his stance. She wasn't getting past him.

"What are you doing here?" Hannah demanded.

He lifted an eyebrow.

Of course. This was his suite. "You're wondering what *I'm* doing here. I was just . . . looking." She sounded guilty. That was bad. "I wanted to speak to you." There. That was firmly spoken. Better.

"The room was empty."

"I thought I might come in and wait."

"How . . . bold . . . of you," he drawled.

His mockery reminded her of her indignation, and she shed guilt as a duck does water. "If you had consented to speak to me when I requested it, I would not now be driven to such behavior."

With chilly detachment, he said, "I didn't wish to hear you nag."

"Nag?" About inviting the queen to Raeburn Castle? She narrowed her eyes. "About what?"

"Our marriage. Your family." He gestured toward

her, his palm broad, his fingers splayed. "Whatever it was that you wished to nag about."

He was insufferable, imagining he knew her thoughts. In a grand gesture of defiance, she told him, "I don't need to nag you about my family. I spoke to Aunt Spring."

She thought he would roar with fury. Instead he smiled a chilly smile. "I suspected you would."

Perhaps he didn't understand. "I now know not only my grandparents' names, I know where they live."

"I understand."

But how could he? He wasn't scowling or forbidding her. "I'm planning to go see them, Dougald. You can't keep me from it."

"Certainly. Go." He leaned negligently against a chair. "Let me know what the Burroughses say when you appear out of nowhere and claim to be their heir."

"Their heir," she said foolishly. "To what?"

"They have a tidy little fortune. A pleasant house. No descendants to inherit. So when you arrive and say you are their long-lost granddaughter, I would love to hear how they react."

He did understand. He understood better than she did. "I'm not interested in their money, and I'm sure the estate is entailed." At once she heard the feebleness of her protest. No one would believe that she, an orphan, a woman who worked for her living, didn't care about her grandparents' fortune.

"I've spoken to Mr. Burroughs. He's a tough old hawk, a former military man with few illusions and little patience with pretenders. He put me on the rack about my past and my background. Can you imagine what he will do when he meets you, Miss Hannah Setterington? A woman who doesn't even use her mother's last name?"

To have come so far! To have learned so much! And to have reached such an obstacle in her search for family! "I have no proof of my parentage," she said stiffly. "If what you say is true, then I can never convince them who I am."

"Maybe they'll see a resemblance between you and their son. Or maybe . . ." Dougald rubbed his chin in false thoughtfulness. "Maybe proof exists."

Taking a hard breath, she asked, "What proof?"

Dougald dropped his performance. "A packet of letters written from your father to your mother. Your mother left them with me. That will be the evidence they seek."

"Letters? From my father?" She could scarcely contain her joy. Evidence of her father's existence. Words he had written. Words she could read. Then she realized . . . the letters were nothing to Dougald. Nothing but leverage over her. With impetuous demand, she said, "Give them to me."

"No."

"You're a jackass."

"Such flattery will not win my patronage."

His black hair swept back from his forehead, lending a stark elegance to his features. The pale flicker of the single flame played across his face, showing the thrust of his cheekbones and angle of his jaw in sharp relief. Not a hint of a smile softened his lips. His large eyes didn't *watch* her; they performed a surveillance. Nothing she did, no nuance of thought or speech went unnoticed. His dark suit blended with the night that surrounded them, but still she saw and sensed every muscle in his body. The strength of his shoulders, the bulk of his chest, the narrow hips and mighty legs. Yes, he had lost weight since their wedding day, but she never doubted he could run her down and overpower her. In this light, in this place, he looked very much like the avenger who haunted her nightmares and not at all like the lover of her fantasies.

"What do I have to do to get those letters?" she asked.

"You know."

Did he mean . . . ? But of course he did. If he was trying to make her uncomfortable, he succeeded only too well. He said such terrible things to her. Hurtful things, with no hint of kindness or affection. Nevertheless, now, her heart beat with the rhythm of their haunting desire. Here, in this dark, smoky room with his gaze lingering on her, she again experienced that long-ago flush of excitement, of newness, of fascination. Her breath came too quickly—had Dougald noticed? Prudently, she pressed her knees together beneath her petticoats, but whether to eliminate the pressure and the dampness or to preserve the sensation of his imagined flesh, she didn't know. And she wished—la, how much she wished!—that she could ever believe in the future as she had that first day on the train when she believed he loved her . . . and she believed she loved him.

The darkness clung to him like a lover, and she wanted to retreat into that darkness. "Why don't you have a candle?" she demanded.

"I like to watch you walk past."

Shocked, she stared at him. He had been standing there when she walked past? Was it so dark and she so engrossed in her thoughts she had missed him?

And . . . and he had watched her on other nights, at other times? When she was singing or . . .

"You talk to yourself," Dougald said.

She couldn't deny it. She talked to herself when she was nervous or lonely, and as she traipsed down the corridor she was frequently both. Frantically she tried to recall how much she'd spoken. What she'd said.

His teeth gleamed in the dim light. "It's a nasty habit, one that leads to insanity . . . or does it mean you're already insane? I can't remember."

Why did he watch her? Did he dream of doing as he threatened? Did he plan to murder her? Or spring on her and take her? "You should be able to tell," she answered.

She knew Dougald. He wouldn't murder her, and if he wished to . . . well, he'd warn her before he did the deed. "So will you have me committed?" Testing him, she offered him an alternative. "I believe insanity will free you of unwanted wedding vows."

He rubbed his chin in false thoughtfulness. "I hadn't thought of that. Thank you for the suggestion."

"If you have me committed, you have to admit you never killed me, yet allowed the rumors of my death to circulate—to your detriment." She challenged him with her stance. "Who then will be considered the lunatic?"

"I would be, for not disciplining my wife."

"There's my Dougald. Always a brute." She turned her back on him—akin to the lion tamer who audaciously turns his back to his savage beast—and walked to the drapes. Lifting a tassel, she faced him again. He hadn't moved. "Brute or not, you don't have to live like this, with everything old and shabby. Whoever picked out this pattern should be shot."

Dougald flinched.

She stared at him. "You don't agree?"

"I hadn't noticed."

"Since when? You used to want the best."

"I used to care what others thought."

"We're talking about basic comforts."

"The chairs are old, the mattress is lumpy." He shrugged. "I don't sleep anyway."

"Maybe that's why you're so cross." Walking to the candelabra on the table, she lit the candles. The room looked no better illuminated by a dozen flames. Smoke had stained the drapes and wallpaper in uneven streaks, and the acrid odor permeated everything. As she looked around, she thought that he needed . . . well, he needed something. A softening influence, or some firm, reasonable discourse.

She'd never been able to talk sense into him, but her nemesis could. "What does Charles think of this?"

His eyes became slits of green ice. "I don't ask him."

Dougald's hostility didn't impress her. "He always liked his creature comforts even more than you."

"He has his creature comforts—elsewhere." Dougald took a step into the room. "Nothing about me is the same, Hannah. If you're trying to judge me by my past actions, you are doomed to failure."

"Then there are subjects we need to discuss."

"Not tonight. Not here. Not now."

"You said nothing about you was the same, but I'd have to say it is. You still want your own way. Of course—you are a man." Sitting down on one of the overstuffed chairs, she crossed her arms. "Tonight. Here. Now."

Still half-hidden by shadow, he leaned his shoulder

against the wall. For a moment, she caught a glimpse of the old Dougald in his half smile. "You are very bold for an erring wife."

"It is not I who erred, Dougald."

His smile disappeared, leaving the grim-faced stranger. "I know that. I have punished the other culprits."

What did he mean? Of whom was he speaking? Charles? *Himself?*

"No one defies me, Hannah. Remember that."

No, he didn't punish himself. He was too conceited for that. "*I* did."

"Nor does anyone force my hand," he continued. "I will not have a scene tonight. We will talk when I choose, and no sooner."

She pounced on that. "You admit we will talk?"

"Actually . . . when I deem the time is right, I will talk and you will listen."

Blast the man and his everlasting impassability! He drove her to fury as no one else could. Coming to her feet, she rushed toward him. He didn't step away from her—why should he? She couldn't harm him. He let her grab him by his lapels. "You haven't changed a bit. You are still the same old Dougald, dictating and ordering and deciding. You haven't learned anything. But"—she shook him—"you don't seem to realize. I am different."

"You're older. You're thinner."

"I'm richer." She looked up at him, her chin jutting out. "I don't have to put up with your nonsense, Dougald. I have enough resources to support myself."

"Money?" He touched her under the chin in slow, light, sweeping strokes. "You have money?"

She ignored his caress. After all, she was very

much in earnest. She wanted him to hear her, to know she had succeeded without him. "I've been accumulating money since the first time Lady Temperly paid me. I didn't have much at first, but I saved every spare tuppence."

He nodded. "In an account in the Bank of England."

"Yes. Finally, when I sold the Distinguished Academy of Governesses, I deposited all the profit. I don't need your job. I can get a train ticket. I can hire a carriage. I can go somewhere and live like a lady, and you can't stop me."

"Not even if I explain to the constable that you are my wife?"

His words halted her rush of words as water extinguishes a flame. But the way he said it, the way he looked at her, and the artistry of his fingers along her jawline and down her throat—ah, she wasn't chilled. Not now. He looked down at her as if he owned her, and recognized his possession. Acknowledged his ownership. She whispered, "Why would you do that?"

"Do you really imagine I would let you go to the train station? Let you leave me again?" He laughed, brief and harsh. "When in truth you are my spouse, and a man has the right to control everything about his wayward, fickle, heedless wife?"

Love, or the illusion of love, wasn't enough. It had never been enough. The golden hours were long gone, the hope was dead and the passion . . . well, if the passion was not completely vanquished, that simply meant she should stiffen her spine, lift her chin and call on her defenses to sustain her.

"I would find a way to escape you, Dougald. You know that. I did it before."

"But if you do, my darling, you will be as you were

before. Without resources, without friends who can help you, and you're really quite a well-known figure around England now." He cupped her chin and held it still. "I would find you."

At his words, laced with lambent amusement, a chill snaked down her spine. "What do you mean, without resources?"

"Your account at the Bank of England? The one where your savings are deposited? I have closed it. Everything a woman owns is under the control of her husband." Smiling down into her appalled eyes, he placed his hands on her waist. "What is yours . . . is mine."

Like an inept dancer, she moved stiffly, her knees locked, her feet stumbling, as he twirled her out of the door and into the corridor.

"Sleep well, my darling." He kissed her on the lips, stepped into his suite and shut the door in her dazed face.

Hidden by the shadows of the corridor, a figure observed as Hannah backed away from the door.

This development bore watching.

16

$\mathcal{H}$annah drove the pony cart through the cool April sunshine up the road toward Burroughs Hall. She had dressed in her best day costume: a chestnut-colored satin gown with full, tiered and embroidered skirt, a black-velvet jacket and her matching chestnut bonnet with ruched ribbon trim. Her black-leather gloves were steady on the reins, and to the onlooker, she knew she appeared to be calm. A calm belied by the number of times she had changed her clothing that morning, and by her heart, which insisted on thumping in a disturbing and unsteady beat.

But as the pony moved steadily toward the black-metal fencing that surrounded her grandparents' estate, Hannah practiced speaking the unspeakable. *Sir and madam, I don't know if you are aware of my existence, but I'm the daughter of Miss Carola Tomlinson and your son, Henry.*

Or—*Mr. and Mrs. Burroughs, twenty-eight years ago, your son Henry loved my mother, Miss Carola Tomlinson, and I am the result.*

Or—*No doubt you've dreaded this day . . .*

That was it, really. If her grandparents knew of her impending birth and had still sent her mother away without a shred of mercy, then they would not now want her in their lives. And even if they did, would she want them? Could she forgive them the misery of her early life and the sorrow of her mother's early death? Mama had been only thirty-one when she died. Hannah was almost that now, and to think of death when she felt herself to be just reaching the peak of power, knowledge and strength—that would a bitterness beyond hope.

The main gate stood open, the house visible through the trees. Somewhere in the vicinity of her heart, a pressure built. A breathlessness and an ache of dread. And just before Hannah would have entered, would have taken that final, irrevocable step to fulfill her dream, she pulled the reins to the left and swung onto the side of the road. Stopping the pony, she climbed out of the cart onto the grass, damp with the previous day's showers. Holding the reins in her hands, she stepped forward until her face was pressed between the metal bars.

She stared at the brick house, built in the Palladian style of the last century, mellow with ivy and crisp with white trim. It wasn't too large, perhaps twenty rooms, the home of a well-to-do country family. The scythed lawns and mature trees framed the building, and like trim on a package, blooming roses climbed on arbors around the grounds. Burroughs Hall was beautiful, every orphan child's fantasy.

Hannah couldn't bring herself to drive forward, climb the stairs and lift the knocker. Her fingers tightened on the cool bars. Her parents had met there. They had fallen in love there. She had probably been conceived in one of those rooms close against the roof. But she didn't belong. How could she? Her grandparents had driven her off before she had first seen day's light.

The front door opened, and Hannah tensed. Who would it be? A man in an old-fashioned blue-satin livery and a powdered wig stepped onto the portico.

Hannah relaxed. A footman. He lifted his hand, and from the back came the jingle of tack and the clop of horses' hooves. An open carriage drove up to the stairs, a young coachman in the driver's seat. The footman and the coachman spoke. Hannah was too far away to hear even a whisper of their conversation, but she thought . . . surely this meant . . . yes, there he was, an upright old gentleman bristling with mustache and eyebrows, dressed in a brown suit. He walked out of the house, licked his finger and raised it to the wind. He nodded as if pleased, then pulled a silver watch from his pocket, opened it, and turned impatiently toward the door. In a deep, impatient voice, he called, "Alice, do you always have to make us late?"

A stooped lady dressed in maroon silk with a feathered bonnet joined him. Her feathers shook in a constant tremor. Hannah could see her lips moving, but she spoke like a lady should, quietly, and Hannah couldn't hear a word.

Her throat dried as she stared, for the first time, on her only relatives in this world.

She didn't think to move, to go forward or to go back. She could only stand and stare as the footmen placed the steps beside the coach and assisted first the elderly lady, then the old gentleman into the vehicle. The footmen shut the door, and only then did Hannah realize she should—no, she must—conceal herself. Quickly she led the pony and cart into the bushes, and the branches still rustled behind her as the carriage passed on the road.

Then, like the cowardly fool she was, she rushed back out and stood on the road, watching them ride away.

Her grandmother and grandfather, and she couldn't even find the courage to show herself to them.

That night, as Hannah trudged to her bedchamber, the floorboards creaked wearily beneath her feet, and the corridor smelled of ancient grievances. The candle she held burned fearfully, afraid to light the corners or reach to the towering ceiling, and her loneliness weighed on her as never before.

"Because the loneliness has been compounded by cowardice," she said aloud. She could blame Dougald for frightening her too much to go on, but that wasn't the whole truth. Throughout the years, whenever she imagined meeting her family, terror had always mixed with the anticipation. Perhaps he had heightened the terror with his well-placed barbs, but if she were brave, she would have gone forward anyway. She opened the door to her room. "Don't let me hear you whining about your desolation anymore, Hannah Alice." In her inner eye rose the vision of her grandparents as they stepped into their carriage. "Not when you let such a golden opportunity slip away from you."

Her vision disappeared when the single, rickety chair inside creaked, and a dark figure rose.

Hannah gave a squeak of fright.

In a low, furious tone, Dougald asked, "What in hell

did you think you were doing, inviting Her Majesty to Raeburn Castle?"

"*Must* you sneak up on me like that?" She laid her palm flat over her pounding heart. Then, lifting the candle high, she illuminated him, his perennial scowl and his black, close-fitting, conservative suit in all its formality. He was such a handsome man, but she had no patience with his endless brooding and his skulking—his appearance now gave her no pleasure.

"Answer me. Why didn't you tell me you invited the Queen?"

"You might have asked me to attend you downstairs. Besides,"—she mimicked him, "I don't want to hear you nag."

"Just answer the question. What in hell did you think you were doing, inviting Her Majesty to Raeburn Castle?"

He ground the question out from between clenched teeth—an interesting phenomenon, and one she'd like to view more of. But for the first time since she'd arrived, she faced the former Dougald, the one with a temper. The former Dougald had never done more than shout at her, but then, he had not been branded as a murderer at that time, either. So she answered with cool civility. "You told the aunts that *I* knew Her Majesty, but you wouldn't speak to *me* to tell *me* what you wanted done about their desire to meet her."

"I didn't expect that you would extend an invitation to my home." He enunciated each word.

"Well, I didn't know that, did I?" She lit her candles, and feeble illumination fell on the neat, narrow bed, the chipped basin and pitcher, the musty draperies. "So instead of doing what you wished, which I would have done if you'd been willing to discuss it with me, I made the aunts happy by writing to Her Majesty. I included their written invitation to come to view their humble tribute to her and her reign."

Dougald withdrew a rich, ivory-colored paper from his waistcoat, and he stared at it as if it threatened to explode.

From here, Hannah could see the royal seal. Her Majesty's polite refusal.

Dougald's reaction to being the recipient of imperial correspondence surprised her. Some people stood in such awe of the Queen, they were unable to imagine having an exchange of letters with such an exalted personage, but she wouldn't have expected it of Dougald. Rather charmed by Dougald's amazement, she gently said, "Yes, Dougald, I admit it was audacious of me, but Her Majesty will not be insulted, if that is what worries you, and the aunts' invitation was charming. They truly struck the right notes of eagerness, excitement and entreaty."

The paper rattled as his fingers shook. "This was your revenge on me for not listening to you."

Ah. So perhaps he was not in awe of the letter, but annoyed with the instigator. Hannah saw the need to pick her words carefully, for while it was true his unresponsiveness had given her an excuse to write the letter, it was also true she had written the Queen while in a rage. "*Revenge* is too strong a word; however, I admit I didn't care if you were perturbed. I didn't appreciate you treating me in such a cavalier manner."

"*Cavalier?*" he roared loudly enough that she started.

When she recovered, she shook out her skirt in a display of assurance, but she kept him in her wary gaze. "Goodness, Dougald, there's no reason to take on so! You've got an answer, and that's good. Now we have something to show the aunts. They'll be disappointed, of course, but having a letter addressed to them from the Queen should soothe the sting of rejection."

Dougald lifted his head and stared at her.

Impatiently, she exclaimed, "Dougald, I don't know why you're acting this way. At least she didn't accept!"

"She did."

Impossible. Hannah opened her mouth to say so, but nothing came out.

"Yes, exactly!" he said, just as if she'd spoken. Opening the letter, he read, " 'Her Gracious Majesty, Victoria, Queen of England, accepts your courteous invitation—' "

Still mute, still numb, Hannah shook her head.

"She accepted, Hannah, accepted. She'll be here in a fortnight!" He flapped the letter at her. "Do you realize the work this castle needs done to it just to make it livable? Not to mention to make it suitable for a royal visit!"

She nodded.

"I'll have to hire every able-bodied man for miles around just to finish the projects I've already started." His voice rose. "To put up the wood panels, to finish the painting in the corridor and the great hall, to make bookcases in the library. To finish the new foyer and construct stairs so Queen Victoria doesn't have to come in through the kitchen."

"That wouldn't be impressive," she mumbled.

"The royal party will stay the night. The Queen. The royal consort. The royal children. They'll need bedchambers, sitting rooms, a nursery that's not covered in dust and cursed with rotting floorboards!"

"Oh."

"Oh." He mimicked her savagely. "Shall we talk about how many servants will be traveling with them? And where we'll put them up?"

"No."

"How shall we transport them all from the railway station to the castle when we have a limited number of vehicles, none of them less than fifty years old?"

"Alfred's cart?" She used her smallest voice, and retreated when her joke caused his glower to become a snarl.

"What were you thinking?" He paced across her tiny bedchamber. "*What* were you thinking?"

"That Her Majesty wouldn't come?"

His nostrils flared like a stallion's scenting a challenge. "Hannah, this sewing project better be bloody wonderful."

She was aghast. "You haven't even seen it?"

"No! Why should I care how four old women use their time?"

"You're truly the biggest toad in the puddle, Dougald! I thought you knew, and I suspected you were using the aunts' tapestry to get Her Majesty here for your own glory."

"Using the aunts for my glory? That's silly!"

She experienced no end of satisfaction when she retorted, "Perhaps, but I couldn't ask you because you wouldn't ever allow me to speak to you in private."

He stopped pacing. He glared. "Tell me I'm worried for nothing. Tell me the tapestry is grand."

She thought of the tapestry. The beautiful, big, richly

colored tapestry on which the four old ladies had worked for twenty-four years. She took a breath, then let it out in a long, quavering sigh. "It . . . was."

In a strictly composed voice, he asked, "What do you mean, it *was*?"

"It's a . . . um . . . tapestry. Very splendid. Very large. Very worthy."

"But?"

"But the aunts didn't quite have Prince Albert's features right, so I suggested they take that panel apart—" His low growl brought her stumbling to a halt. "I'll help them finish it?"

"You have a fortnight." He backed her into the corner between the wardrobe and the wall and leaned so close his hot breath touched her cheek. "A fortnight before Her Gracious Majesty, Victoria, Queen of England visits our little castle. Make sure this tapestry gets done."

She wanted to tell him it was impossible, but his eyes were slits of fury and . . . well, probably just fury. He used his closeness to intimidate her, and he was making a fine task of it. Certainly it was his threatening posture that made her heart pound, her knees weaken and her insides contract. She should not choose this moment to notice the scent of him— leather, soap and Dougald. And she had backed away from him because she feared he would put his hands on her in violence, not because if he touched her, she'd quiver and sigh and want more than she should want from such a cold-hearted beast.

"The tapestry," he said.

"It will get done," she promised.

Turning on his heel, he stalked out and slammed the door.

Hannah slumped into the corner and covered her eyes with her hands. What had she gotten herself into? A fortnight to reweave and sew a tapestry that had taken twenty-four years to complete—and do it better than before? It seemed an impossibility.

And sadly, the tapestry was the least of her problems. By some mad quirk of nature, she now discovered that no matter how thoroughly Dougald ignored her, no matter how aggrieved she was with him, when he came close she still trembled and yearned.

Obviously, her presence did not affect him in such a manner, or—

The door slammed open and Dougald stomped back in. "And where have you been?"

Perplexed, she repeated, "Where have I been? When?"

"Today. Tonight. Why weren't you in the castle?"

The events of the day rushed back at her. Her grandparents. She, wanting to speak to them but not having the nerve. She, staring with her nose pressed against the fence like some homeless waif. No power on earth could have made her tell him where she'd been or what she'd done. He would think himself a great success. He would laugh.

"It was my half day off, and therefore none of your business." She was proud of her inscrutable answer until she saw the flare of his red wrath.

He looked her up and down. "You're dressed up. *I* haven't seen you so dressed up. Not since you've been here." His fists clenched. "If you were out with that little pudknocker Seaton—"

"It would still be none of your business." Was he jealous? How lovely.

He leaned back over her, only this time he wasn't

angry about the Queen. This time, his fury was personal. "It bloody well is my business where you go
and what you do."

She jutted out her chin. "Why?"

"You're my wife."

Indignation came boiling up from her frustrated
self. "When? Nine years ago? Not today, that's for
sure. Not now. Not when you won't even speak to me
to instruct me as to your orders."

He stepped back and surveyed her, scrunched in her
corner. She stepped forward and glared at him, the
egotistical pompous cad who thought to control her
money and her fate.

And he swept her into his arms.

And she grabbed his hair and brought his lips down
to hers.

They kissed in a whirlwind of passion, frustration
and anger, their bodies pressed together, her feet dangling, his tongue in her mouth. Damn him! To treat her
so insolently again, still, as if she were a girl of eighteen and he the superior older man. But he wasn't superior now; he wanted her, for his arms crushed her to
him, his hands searched through the layers of her skirts
and petticoats to find her thighs and lift them around
him. And she . . . she wrapped her legs around his
waist, pressed her bodice against his waistcoat, kissed
him with her lips open and her tongue thrusting
against his, and wished the clothes that separated them
would vanish in some magical puff of smoke.

He tore his mouth from hers. "You dreadful tease."
Swinging her around, he headed toward her narrow
bed.

"Not me." She could scarcely think to answer him,

but some instinct made her reach up to bite his lower lip. "I don't tease. This isn't teasing."

"No." He tumbled her onto her back on the mattress, his body between her legs, his chest pressed to hers. "Not now. But since you've been here. Every day." He stared into her eyes. "Prancing around the castle. Up the stairs. Down the corridors."

"I did not prance, sir." She ran her fingers through his hair and decided he should never cut it. "I am not a horse!"

"Talking so that, while I work in my office, I strained to hear you speak to Charles."

"Is it your command that I not speak?"

"Laughing with that knave Seaton."

"You come from a family of knaves, and you are the worst of the lot."

"Dressing provocatively."

"Provocatively!" She squinted down at the chestnut gown.

Climbing to his knees, he wrestled her skirt and petticoats to her waist, and like a magistrate proving guilt, he pointed at her ankles. "Look at this. Lace on your pantalettes!"

"I never showed you." She kicked her leather slippers off.

"I knew about the lace. I sensed it was there." He untied the string at her waist.

"I cannot help if you have developed clairvoyant abilities."

"Only where you're concerned." He rolled her pantalettes down. "Only about you."

He was exposing her in a way she hadn't been exposed in nine years. Nine long years. Deep in her womb, she experienced that slow, warm, deep slide of desire. Nine years. Too long. She'd been ignoring her body, telling herself she didn't want, didn't need, didn't care. Now, at the first taste and touch of Dougald, she was ready. Embarrassingly ready, completely ready, and not willing to slow or stop and certainly not to think.

His mouth curved in a slow, wicked smile. "I've dreamed of you." His fingers opened her.

Her eyes shut in an excess of sweet, warm longing.

"I've dreamed of touching you here"—the slightest of caresses brought her up off the bed—"and here"— he stroked with impertinence—"and I have wanted to fill you with my fingers."

As he thrust a finger inside her, she pressed the back of her hand to her mouth, trying to stifle her groan of delight.

"You never wanted me to hear you." His thumb massaged her while his finger slid in and out, in and out. "Always you tried to deny your pleasure."

"Only"—she caught a breath—"only after you made it clear this was not love. It was only duty and—"

The compression of his palm against her pubic bone stopped her resentful speech. When he held her like this, with one finger inside her and his hand rubbing her, and rubbing her, she no longer remembered old rancors. All she could think of was . . . grabbing his lapels, she pulled him forward and glared into his eyes. "Do it now."

He chuckled. Chuckled like the high-hat, self-important ass that he was. Until she loosened her grip on one lapel and slid her hand down his chest, across his belly, and down to the satisfying obvious bulge in his groin. Then, as she shaped his length, caressed his testicles, his laughter stopped. His eyes half closed, and as he lifted his head she saw the strain of the tendons in his neck and the bright flush of desire that lit his cheeks.

"Do it now," she repeated.

This time he didn't laugh. Stepping back, he pulled her pantalettes all the way off, then opened his trousers and shoved them down past his knees.

His hurry satisfied her pride, at the least, and her desire . . . my God, he was big and bold, wanting her in the most explicit way, and if he didn't put himself into her soon . . .

"Dougald, please." She held out her arms to him.

He fell on her like a ravaging beast, bothering with none of the niceties, responding to her demand for union with a satisfying instinct that had him impetuously pushing into her.

She sucked in her breath. She had been without satisfaction for too long . . . she was too tight. Pain threatened, then became a reality. Digging her nails into his arms, she said, "No."

He glared at her, glared like a drowning man deprived of rescue. Then he took in her expression: fierce, tortured, unsatisfied. Swallowing, he slowed, and in the warm, hushed voice of her lover, commanded, "Let me fill you, darling. Just relax and let me in."

When he talked to her like that, she responded like any female creature to the claim of her mate. She relaxed, adjusting her body around him, and he slipped right in to the hilt.

She whimpered. It felt so good. This was so bad. He had her. Again. But . . .

He hadn't wanted to do this, either. Only tonight,

when his unimpeded frustration and anger had broken through, had his restraint been vanquished.

So it was all right. This was not manipulation. This was truth.

She lifted her hips. She flexed her inner muscles. And in a voice as warm and caressing as his, she said, "Please, lover. I want you."

17

$\mathcal{D}$ougald knew he shouldn't be doing this. This was not at all what he planned. He had planned to drive Hannah mad with desire while he held tight rein on his passions. Then he would dictate the conditions of their reconciliation, and she would recognize her master.

But the heat of her . . . the scent of her . . . her voice saying, "Please, lover. I want you." He was weak, but he had to take her. Every primitive instinct within demanded he fill her with his seed. She was his possession, his fief, his wife.

Without elegance, without restraint, he gave himself over to his passion. Every important drop of his blood, every important part of his body, fought to get inside her. He entered her and withdrew, entered her and withdrew. Beneath him, he could hear the mewling noises she made. Her hips rose and fell with the rhythm he set. Her arms gripped him as if she feared he would disappear. He feared it, too. Feared good sense would prevail before he had his fill of her. He was going too fast, he knew it. She wouldn't be able to come, not with him pounding at her like this, but he couldn't slow down, couldn't wait . . .

"Hurry," she urged him. Doubling up a fist, she struck him on the shoulder. "Hurry!"

He redoubled his efforts. She scratched at his back in a catlike frenzy, fighting to reach her peak, taking her frustration out on him in the most primitive way possible. Later he'd be glad he still wore his clothing. Right now it was nothing but a bloody damned nuisance. Hell, he still wore his cravat tied like a noose around his neck.

Hannah was so beautiful with her hair coming undone. It spread across the dark coverlet like a river of scented gold. Those startling brown eyes opened and shut, alternately languid and desperate, as if desire and need fought a battle for her soul. Her gown, her idiotic satin gown, was buttoned all the way to her neck.

"Dougald, Dougald, Dougald."

He heard that note in her voice. The note he hadn't heard for nine long years, yet he recognized it.

Deep in his groin, pressure grew. Instinct demanded that he thrust as hard as he could. He wanted to finish inside her. He needed to drench her with his seed. But first . . . he had to watch her. He had to.

Her eyes closed. A flush started at her collar and rose up her neck, her cheeks, her forehead. Her nose scrunched up, her lips opened in a long series of gasps. Her hips lunged at him, demanding satisfaction. Her legs clutched at him, bringing him close. Deep inside her, the spasms took her, rocking her, bringing her gratification of the most primitive type.

He exulted in this primitive outbreak, this unstoppable passion. She hadn't been able to resist him. Her body had hungered, just as his did. She was his.

Then he couldn't wait.

He pressed her down on the bed with his hips. He held her with his hands. He forced her to take him. She writhed against him, waves of ecstasy rocking her, moans of pleasure breaking from her. He invaded her, going as deep as he could. His balls tightened. Then, irrevocably, he came, filling her with himself. He plunged, wildly, blindly, branding himself on her, demanding that she acknowledge she was his, coercing her physically to overwhelm her mentally.

He succeeded. Every sound she uttered sounded capitulation, every movement she performed signaled acceptance.

He had won. She had surrendered to him.

For now.

Hannah relaxed under Dougald's weight, loving the exhaustion, the repletion . . . the lack of conscience. It wouldn't last long, she knew. In a moment she would have to open her eyes. She would be aware and ashamed, fighting to save her pride, denying that she had surrendered. But right now—

He lifted himself off of her, separating their two bodies carefully.

Shame hit her at once. She dragged her legs together, drew her mind together, prepared for battle . . . and he flipped her onto her stomach. She tried to sit up, but he held her down with one hand. She heard the rustle of clothing; she craned around, trying to see, and observed as he flung his cravat, waistcoat and jacket across the room.

"Dougald, what . . . ?"

"Do you want to talk now?" He sounded brusque.

She didn't care how he sounded. "No."

"Then *silence*."

She smiled into the counterpane.

The mattress sagged as he sat. His boots thumped to the floor one by one.

She didn't have to look to know which of his garments he removed next. His trousers were already half-off anyway. They dropped to the floor with little effort, then he sprang onto the bed. With a knee on either side of her hips, he fumbled with the buttons at the top of her gown, pulling them roughly apart. She wanted to protest, fearing damage to her dress, but she lacked the breath, the vigor, and the stylishness.

He leaned close to her neck, and his breath brushed her ear as he whispered, "You and your stupid damned clothing. You wear so much of it just to keep me from you, but that's not going to work anymore, Hannah. I want this off of you."

She found the breath to defy him. "I don't wear anything to keep you away or draw you near. I never think of you at all when I dress."

"That is your mistake." He pushed the material off her shoulders, lifted her and slid it down the front of her, jerked the sleeves off her wrists. He let her settle on the mattress again, and with lightning swift determination, he stripped her out of the garment completely. Her petticoats followed, leaving her clad in her chemise, her corset, and her best silk stockings.

He laughed, a rough and rocky chuckle, and plucked the flowered garter with his finger. "Exquisite," he said. "An indication of what resides above." One of his hands glided up her thigh to the globe of her buttocks. There he rubbed like a collector uncovering a fine diamond, and then, lightly, he slid a finger down from the base of her spine, down her cleft to that place of utter, complete sensitivity.

She rose half-off the bed, ready to turn and take him.

But with his hand on her back, he propelled her back down. Climbing atop of her again, he slipped his hands under her and, gently, tenderly cupped her breasts.

She closed her eyes and pressed her cheek against the coverlet. She didn't have to think. Not yet.

His hands worked magic, holding her with just the right pressure, circling her nipples with his thumbs, then gently squeezing them between his fingers. Her mind drew pictures; he would draw her to her knees and mount her from behind. She would mew and claw like a cat. She shuddered, ready to have him inside her, wanting to demand he do as she wished. But she didn't have any power here; he was too strong, too experienced. A woman was never a match for a man in these circumstances.

When Hannah woke in dawn's first light, Dougald stood over her, dressed in his trousers, holding his boots, and glowering. Glowering at the room, at the narrow bed . . . at her. "This bedchamber is shoddy." He kissed the top of her head.

Lifting herself on her elbow, she pushed her hair out of her eyes. "Good morning to you, too."

"I'll have Mrs. Trenchard move you to a better room."

Hannah almost leaped out of the bed in protest. Almost, but she wore not a stitch and that put her at a distinct disadvantage in any confrontation with Dougald. "You will not! We'll be fortunate if we remain unobserved anyway." Then she realized what he had said. How she had answered. In both of their minds, they had copulated. They had not reconciled. "Anyway," she said, choosing her words, knowing she would falter, "it doesn't matter whether you approve of my bedchamber. You . . . won't be in it again."

He seemed to grow taller, broader, darker. "If I choose—"

"No. You know we can't do this again. Someone *will* see us. We'll be the center of gossip and speculation, and I . . . you . . . we don't want that right now. Do we?"

During her fumbling speech, he became the stern, impassive gentleman she had come to know in her time at Raeburn Castle. "No."

She couldn't read anything from his posture or his expression. It was as if the night had never been. Intimacy might have been a figment of her imagination, and passion . . . she moved her legs and experienced the muscle-deep ache.

The passion between them had been real. She couldn't deny that.

But the passion between them always had been real, and it had been for naught in the face of their marital problems. So—

"We must not do this again," she said firmly.

"I do agree."

"In a fortnight?" Miss Minnie groped for a chair and sat down hard. "The Queen will be here in a fortnight?"

A merry buzz broke out among the servants.

"Isn't it marvelous?" Aunt Spring stood, hands clasped together, eyes shining. "Queen Victoria herself is coming to see us!"

"I don't bloody believe it," Seaton said for the fourth time. "It's bloody impossible."

Dougald stood in the great hall, his back to the gaping fireplace, in front of an incredulous assemblage made up of the aunts, his treacherous heir, Charles, Mrs. Trenchard, the castle servants—and Hannah.

Hannah, his wife. He had had such torturous plans for her. And at first he'd been a complete success. He had trapped her. He had put her in a place of his keeping, made her do what he wished, and believed he would soon bring her to heel.

Then she had proceeded to turn everything on its head.

He should have anticipated that. He should have recalled her predilection for doing the unexpected.

Aunt Isabel and Aunt Ethel held hands and danced a jig while the younger servants watched and laughed.

Mrs. Trenchard clapped her hands and the footmen and serving maids quieted, but nothing could hinder their glee at knowing their sovereign would soon arrive.

Very well. Dougald had been alerted to the danger Hannah posed, and he would respond accordingly. She would no longer send letters willy-nilly around the country. She would by God never go anywhere unescorted. And he would no longer yield to her sexual blandishments. He was a man with ice in his veins. Through solitude, hard work and desolation, he had made himself into the image of his father, dedicated to the family name and unswayed by affection of any kind. He would not let Hannah resurrect any softness in himself.

Dougald raised his voice to reach to the fringes of his audience. "This is wonderful news. We are privileged to have Her Majesty as our guest, but I don't need to tell you what we must do to prepare for a royal visit."

Charles looked Dougald up and down as if measuring him for a suit. "You need new clothing. I told you you needed new clothing."

"We shall host a grand reception." Aunt Spring's eyes narrowed. "We shall invite everyone in the district to honor Her Majesty."

"Everyone in the district?" Hannah swiveled to face Aunt Spring. "Here? At Raeburn Castle?"

The Burroughses would be here for her to meet. Dougald considered the ramifications. She was settled here at Raeburn Castle, fond of the aunts . . . involved with him. Very well. She would be allowed to meet her grandparents.

"The paneling. The entry." Mrs. Trenchard put her veined hand to her chest and looked around in dazed dismay. "The great hall. All must be cleaned."

"All must be restored," Dougald corrected.

"Extra care must be taken by the workmen, my lord," Charles said, "to prevent a disaster."

Aunt Isabel put her hand to her head. "I'm going to have to dye my hair."

Dougald noted his suspicion was verified.

"Try not to splash shoe polish all over the basin." Aunt Ethel measured her waist in her hands. "I wonder if I can get into my best silk."

"You look good in anything," Aunt Spring said comfortingly.

Seaton changed his chant. "This is a bloody disaster. A bloody disaster."

"Stop swearing, Seaton," Miss Minnie chided him. Extending a hand to Hannah, she said, "Is it really true, Miss Setterington? I never thought she would actually come."

"I knew Hannah would come through." Aunt Isabel tossed her dark head. "She's efficient. She's a modern woman."

Hannah took Miss Minnie's fingers in hers. "It *is* hard to believe, but it's true."

Aunt Spring took Hannah's other hand. "Dear, dear girl, this is our dream come true, and all because of you."

Hannah's smile blossomed like the brightest flower. "Not because of me, Aunt Spring, but because of your wonderful work. You"—she gestured to include all the aunts—"all of you have done this, and now all our dreams *are* coming true."

Hannah was good with people, Dougald had to admit. His grandmother had loved her, and Grandmama was not always an easy woman to please. Her last illness had hurried their nuptials, for she had wished to see Dougald safely wed. In the months that followed she had been satisfied only when Hannah was with her. Funny. It had taken seeing his wife handling these old women to remind him how much he appreciated Hannah's care of his grandmother. Remind him and think that maybe . . . that maybe matrimony hadn't all been so bad.

There had been moments when he and Hannah were alone, and he forgot his duties and she forgot her resentments, and they had talked. Just talked. He'd been amazed by her maturity, by the experiences that had shaped her. She had never been the typical carefree maiden, just as he was not the normal rich man's son. He had lost his mother, been isolated by a father who knew nothing of affection. Love brought only hurt.

Hannah had been showered with motherly affection, but all of her mother's love couldn't protect her from the taunts of the cruel, the proper and the bigoted.

Years separated them in age. Time separated them from their closeness. But perhaps they could capture that affinity again.

"I didn't know you knew Her Majesty, Miss Setterington." Seaton had made his way over to Hannah, and his voice had become obsequious. "You must tell me all about your acquaintance."

Dougald could almost hear his father speaking. *That's what comes of daydreaming, boy. You lose authority. You fail to keep your woman. Someone thinks they can kill you. Stop being so soft. Pay attention to business.*

His father would have been right. This was no place to contemplate Hannah and the pleasures of their marriage. Here, now, with a death threat hanging over his head and the Queen on her way, he had to be the man he had become. "We will begin at once." He leveled a stern look at Seaton. "No one here will be exempt from work. No one."

As Dougald expected, Seaton scurried away. Within an hour, Dougald got word Seaton had vacated the castle. It appeared his heir had discovered a great many calls he needed to return, and before the royal visit he would daily inflict himself elsewhere.

Now, Dougald had only to treat Hannah with the indifference she deserved.

He would never again be conquered by pleasure.

Why had Hannah ever thought she had no power? The power she wielded over Dougald grew to dazzling proportions. True, they had to be alone, he had to be naked, and she had to be kneeling between his legs, but right now he held the headboard of her bed in both his hands and writhed in quiet agony because she had told him not to touch her or she'd stop. And he would sell his soul to keep her doing what she was doing.

She smiled as she kissed her way down the left side of his abdomen, licking the sleek skin over his hip, then skittering over to his navel and pressing a kiss there. He tasted clean—he'd come to her right from his bath—and the scent of his excitement blended with the odor of his spicy soap.

He was waiting, vibrating with suspense, wondering if she would do what he thought she might. And she planned to—just as soon as she'd made him suffer. After all, she owed him some suffering, and what better way to repay that debt? So she drew out the anticipation, stroking his thighs, sliding her hands around to cup his buttocks, reveling in the firm muscularity. She caressed his ballocks, investigating the rough texture, the exuberant hairs. Had it been only two nights ago when he held her down on her bed and forced her to celebrate in her own dissipation? Well, now she could celebrate his.

"Do you like this?" She placed a low, pursed-mouth kiss on his groin just above the triangle of hair.

He didn't answer, but writhed on the bed.

"Dougald?" She lifted her head. "Shall I stop?"

"No! I love it." He took a deep breath, and his chest heaved with the effort. "Anything you want to do. Anything."

He didn't want to ask her. Probably he thought she'd be shocked. And she might have been—two nights ago. But in those two nights Dougald had taken her on sensual journeys that could only be called hedonistic.

He had licked and kissed her everywhere, reduced her to a whimpering wreck, made her beg. She knew very well what he wanted. Soon she would give it to him.

She kissed him again, this time right at the base of his penis, but still she kept her lips closed. "Is that what you like?"

"Yes. Yes, that's good. But maybe . . ."

She blew a slow, warm stream of breath over him as she listened to him struggle for words.

"But maybe if you used your tongue . . ."

"Like this?" With slow anticipation, she licked all the way up his rigid straining organ.

He gasped. The muscles on his arms bulged as he fought the instinct to take her head and show her what he wanted.

"What else?" she asked softly.

Softly, he said, "You could just imagine what I'd like."

"I could." She lifted her head and smiled at him. "But I want to hear it."

He stared at her, then a slow dawning occurred. He glowered, but he recognized defeat when it stared him in the face. He wasn't going to fight her now. In a slow, deep, desperate tone he said, "Please, Hannah. Please take me into your mouth and just . . . please . . ."

She forgave him his ineloquence and gave him what he desired.

After all, this time was absolutely the last time.

18

As Hannah stood in the small dining room, she could hear the chatter of eager voices from inside the breakfast room. She could hear the carpenters' hammers from the drawing room. And in the corridor she watched as seamstresses carried bolts of upholstery cloth up the stairs. The excitement of the Queen's visit permeated the castle on every level. Yesterday Hannah had worked far into the evening to organize the aunts' rapid completion of the tapestry. Then last night she had been awake because of . . . other matters.

As she primped in a gold-framed mirror hung on the wall, she smiled wickedly at herself.

Other matters which would not be repeated.

Her smile faded.

Because in the end, she didn't know whether Dougald's passion was false and his seduction part of some pernicious, covert plan to weaken her resistance and force her to be the wife he demanded.

Work and sleeplessness had taken their toll, and now worry added its weight. A weary reflection peered back at her from the mirror, so she pinched her cheeks to bring up some color. Everyone was involved in the excitement of the Queen's visit. No one would be looking at her anyway.

Unless Dougald did, and she didn't know if, after last night, she could meet his gaze.

She hadn't experienced this mixture of jubilation, confusion and misery since . . . since they had lived together as man and wife. She had to keep in mind he was not the man he had been.

But neither was she the same woman. She didn't know what was going to happen, but she knew that, if they were to reconcile, it would not be on only Dougald's terms. No amount of seduction or coercion would commute the misery that would ensue.

The babble of voices in the breakfast room rose to a new level. She had to go in and face them, and after all, no one within knew what had occurred in Dougald's bedchamber last night except her . . . and Dougald.

And he wouldn't say anything to compromise her. She clenched her teeth. If anything, he hated this obsessive passion more than she did.

Giving her cheeks one last pinch, she stepped through the door. She made her way past Mrs. Trenchard, who held a steaming teapot, past Dougald at the head of the breakfast table, past the aunts and Seaton.

Aunt Spring held a sheet of paper from which she read aloud, speaking loudly to made herself heard over the hammering in the drawing room. "I've written invitations for the Hendersons, the Gilmores, the earl of Nasker, they're such dears, always gracious, Mr. MacAllister and his new wife who is much too young for him, the silly old goat, Sir Preston and Lady Susan, the Howells, I hope she's still not suffering from her confinement, Sir Day and Lady . . . Good morning, Hannah, dear. You look dreadfully tired this morning."

So much for Hannah's hopes of an unnoticed entrance. "I feel fine, Aunt Spring."

Aunt Spring ignored her protestations. "Don't you think she looks tired, Dougald?"

Dougald didn't look up from his full plate. "She looks fine."

"Miss Setterington is lovely as always, Aunt." Seaton sounded shocked at Aunt Spring's frankness.

"Of course she is, dear." Undeterred by Seaton's rebuke, Aunt Spring placed her list of guests on the table and examined Hannah with interest. "Circles under her eyes don't detract from a young lady's appeal. Don't you agree, Dougald?"

Dougald grunted, apparently unperturbed by the aunts' ceaseless attempts at matchmaking.

Hannah sank into her chair, perturbed enough for the both of them.

Aunt Isabel jumped into the silence. "Yes, dear, I think circles under the eyes add an air of mystery."

"She has a *lot* of mystery about her today," Aunt Ethel observed.

Miss Minnie opened her mouth to speak, and for a moment Hannah hoped that sensible woman would turn the conversation.

Hannah was destined to be disappointed.

"Dougald appears to be weary, too," Miss Minnie observed. "We worked late last night preparing menus for the Queen's reception. Perhaps Miss Setterington worked late last night helping Dougald prepare the Queen's welcome."

Aunt Spring straightened in her seat. "Yes!"

"Absolutely!" Aunt Isabel smiled brightly.

"A lot of mystery," Aunt Ethel repeated.

Dougald chewed, swallowed and patted his lips with his napkin. Looking down the table from his position in the master's chair, he said, "I can unequivocally say Miss Setterington and I were not working together last night to prepare the Queen's welcome. Miss Setterington has her tasks, I have mine, and I have no interest in working with Miss Setterington at all."

"Dougald, that is so impolite," Aunt Spring rebuked him.

"You'll hurt the dear girl's feelings," Aunt Ethel said.

"No, he won't," Hannah hastened to assure them.

Dougald flashed a glance at her. A rather warm, angry, passionate glance that confused her, brought a blush to her cheeks and made her wish she had skipped breakfast altogether.

Dougald went back to his meal.

Seaton glared at his downturned head. "Lord Raeburn *is* impolite. Miss Setterington doesn't deserve to eat breakfast with a barbarian."

Looking up, Dougald grinned at his heir. "Or with a murderer, either."

Mrs. Trenchard gasped.

Aunt Isabel asked, "Did he just admit he murdered his wife?"

Hannah stared at her husband. When he smiled like that, all fierce mockery, she remembered the reasons she suspected him of every evil intent. Sitting there surrounded by the evidence of his wealth and ancestry, his green eyes glittered with ice, his teeth glinted white, and he looked like some vengeful medieval lord.

"No, Aunt Isabel. I didn't murder my wife." He didn't look at Hannah as he spoke. "Yet."

"Yet?" Aunt Isabel's voice boomed louder than ever. "What does he mean, yet?"

"Yet." Miss Minnie stroked her chin thoughtfully.

Putting down his fork, Dougald smiled evilly at Aunt Isabel. "You know, if you think I murdered my wife, it would seem the height of cruelty to throw Miss Setterington at my head."

It was one thing to know the matchmaking was happening, another to speak of it. Hannah could have cursed him, but instead she said, "Come, Lord Raeburn, they have done no such thing."

No one paid the slightest bit of attention to her.

Aunt Isabel's mouth opened and shut. Then she stammered, "I . . . I never thought of that." Her brow wrinkled as she thought.

Dougald waited, his gaze flicking around the table, a beastly smile curving his mouth.

"I hate to say it, but—you have a point. Very well. I will acknowledge that you didn't murder your wife." Aunt Isabel sighed. "But the notion was so mysterious and romantic."

Dougald's smile disappeared. "Murder isn't romantic. Murder is the instrument of a weak mind."

Seaton stood and rapped the table with his knuckles. "I, for one, will not change my mind. His Lordship did kill his wife."

"Seaton, you know you're only saying that because it makes such a good story," Aunt Ethel said.

"What's wrong with that? A rattlepate with no story is no rattlepate at all." Seaton pushed at his chair, and a footman rushed to pull it back for him. "I am off to visit the Sheratons. I will be gone overnight. Farewell, until tomorrow." He stalked from the room in high dudgeon.

Dougald watched him narrowly. "A weak mind," he repeated.

Aunt Spring chewed her thumbnail. "But Dougald, dear, you did have a wife. What happened to her?"

"That is the mystery." With a brief nod, he began to eat once more.

Hannah could have thumped her head on the table. Why had Dougald made such inflammatory remarks? Why did he reveal so much yet so little? Was he mocking her and her ardor?

Was he threatening her again?

She didn't know. She didn't know anything, and the truth was that, while she wanted nothing so much as to make love with him, she didn't trust him. How could she? In the six months they had lived as man and wife, he had hurt her so badly.

Hannah stood before the desk, confronting her husband of five months. "Ever since your grandmother died, I've had nothing to do."

Dougald smiled, his affection for his grandmother clear. "You did a wonderful job in her last illness. She told me how much she appreciated your care. She told me we settled on the right wife."

Like a sword to Hannah's belly, the words sliced her wide. More and more, the reality of their marriage had been laid bare. Everything she had accused him of on that train had proved true. She had been chosen to be Dougald's wife by his grandmother. Because he had done as his grandmother advised in the matter of his nuptials, he had saved himself time and worry. Thus he had been able to spend more time on his business, and the achievements and riches he coveted fell more and more his way.

"I still miss Grandmama." He looked down at the stack of papers, but not before Hannah spied the glint of sentimental tears. "I could always talk to her. She was a very wise woman."

You could talk to me now. *Hannah wanted to, but she didn't say it. She had learned the futility of making such statements. She hadn't proven herself to Dougald—mostly because he wouldn't give her a chance.*

"Did I tell you I was grateful for the time you spent in the sickroom?" Dougald asked.

"Yes." They had rushed the marriage ceremony because of his grandmother's ill health. Hannah couldn't be sorry for that. As the old woman lay dying, she had been grateful to know her grandson was settled. "Yes, you did."

"You're still pale from the strain." Opening his desk drawer, he pulled out an envelope of cash. "Take this and go shopping. That should relieve your ennui."

She put her hands behind her back, lacing her fingers, determined not to take his offering. She needed to make him understand that an application of money wouldn't cure their problems. "I don't suffer from ennui. I suffer from inactivity. When your grandmother was ill, I had her to care for, but now that she's gone, I need something to do. You promised me a dress shop."

Sternly, he said, "You are the wife of one of Liverpool's prominent businessmen. I would look like a fool if you opened a dress shop."

"You promised!"

"I didn't promise. You said you didn't want to pros-

titute yourself for a dress shop." Placing the envelope on the desk, he slid it toward her. "You said you saw no reason to compromise your principles for money."

It was true. On the train, she had said those things. Then he had seduced her, and in her infatuation and her rush to wed, she had assumed things. She had assumed he would want her to be happy. She had assumed he would trust her to know what would make her happy. She had never thought he would deliberately twist her words so she would have to dance to his tune. "I don't understand why you care what others think."

"I'm still a young man. The memory of my wild years follows me yet. If I am to be successful, I must have the respect of my colleagues." He gestured dismissively. "I don't know why I bother to try and explain. Just trust me, dear. I know what's best."

"You are successful."

"Not the most successful. Not yet." He declared his goal with an insouciance that belied his determination. "You'll be happy when you have children to raise. I need an heir, you know, and you—you want that family. A baby would be yours, and he would love you."

She hated when he did that. Used her desire for a family as a weapon against her.

He smiled at her, clearly thinking she would melt at the thought of a child. "Have you missed your monthlies yet?"

"No." No, thank God. The idea of raising a child in a household in which she had no authority and a neglectful husband terrified her.

"If I can get away early tonight, we could try to create a child."

She shook her head. "You have a meeting."

"That's right." He frowned at his calendar. "Tomorrow night, then."

Frustration roiled in her. She couldn't continue like this, cared for and disciplined like a lapdog. "If I can't have my dress shop, at least let me take over the direction of the servants. Charles ran the house while I cared for your grandmother, and now he won't relinquish responsibility!"

Dougald shuffled papers. He had lost interest in her plight. "Most women would be glad to be relieved of all responsibility for their households."

Do I look like most women? You should have married someone else.

She'd said it all before, innumerable times. He didn't listen to her. He didn't even seem to hear her. He just indulged her with endless patience, patting his little doll on the head. Now, wearily, she said, "I have nothing to do. I can't live like this. I'm warning you, Dougald, if something doesn't change soon, our marriage is going to fail."

She succeeded regaining his attention. His head whipped around, his face reddened, his eye narrowed. "Are you threatening me?"

"I'm trying to talk to you."

His voice rose to a shout. "Talk to me? You're nagging again!" He visibly controlled himself. "There's nothing to be done. We're married until death do us part. Make the best of it."

So she had made the best of it, but not as he had imagined she would. Before she could become pregnant and trapped for eternity, she had left him. Taken the money he showered on her in lieu of affection or trust, and left him.

She faced the same trap now. She looked toward the head of the table. Dougald sat there, calm, remote, unconquerable. They didn't talk. He didn't offer her any more understanding or kindness than before, and time and again he had proved that, for him, coition did not equal love. Yet she understood what so many women had found out to their dismay—love was not necessary. When two people indulged in intercourse, a child would result.

So she had to be wise. If he came to her room, she had to turn him away. And if he did not—well, that was fine.

She certainly wouldn't go to him.

"This mattress is lumpy." As Dougald shifted, trying to move the snarled mass of feathers beneath him out from under his spine, he wondered why in hell he hadn't had his bed replaced. If Hannah was going to continue to visit him in his chamber, he would have to improve conditions.

"You said it didn't matter." Hannah snuggled her head on his bare chest. "You said you didn't sleep anyway."

"I don't. But I'm in bed now, and I'm uncomfortable."

"I suppose we could do this somewhere else."

"Your bed is lumpy *and* too damned narrow."

"I didn't mean in my room. I meant in here." She lifted her head and gazed around at his dismal furnishings, then lowered her head and sighed. "Never mind. It's all awful."

Dougald looked around. She was right. It was all awful, but even if he were inclined, there was nothing to be done about it. He had hired workmen to restore the castle's beauty. He had them laboring from dawn 'til dusk and beyond to prepare for the Queen's visit. He didn't have time for the frivolity of fixing his own bedchamber, regardless of the pleasures he and his wife shared, albeit clandestinely, in the darkest part of the night.

He frowned. He hadn't yet gained the discipline he sought. When she came to him tonight, he should have turned her away. Instead he told himself that, because she had come to him, he had won a victory. Yes, that was how he would choose to view this. As a victory.

Lifting himself, he dumped her backward on his bed. Leaning over her, he said, "I can make you forget your discomfort."

She linked her hands behind his neck. "Yes, do. But tonight is positively the last time."

Hannah picked her way through the ladders and Holland cloths along the upstairs corridor on her way to the aunts' workroom. She had taken to arriving at the workroom early every morning. Then Hannah had a moment of quiet to organize the day's weaving before the laborers arrived for the day's work. A moment she didn't know if she wanted. After all, when she was busy she had no time to think of Dougald and the wretched weakness he engendered in her. When the sun was high and her lusts satisfied, she resolved to stay away from him, refuse his attentions and take what pleasure she could from her principles.

But every night for the past week she had tossed and turned, knowing he waited just down the corridor, that he expected her . . . wanted her. Most nights she clutched her pillow to her chest and stared into the dark. But some nights she rose from her narrow, cold bed and crept to his door. The dark corridor was just as lonely. The endless, empty rooms were just as frightening. But his presence drew her like a moth to the flame, and like a moth she burned in his fire. Madness, but such sweet madness.

And on the nights she didn't go to him . . . he came to her.

Doubts about his intentions still dogged her, but pleasure and affinity inexorably overlaid the old bad memories. Slowly, hope was growing in her, and she wavered between exultation and incredulity. Was she being a fool to believe they could reconcile, or was she a greater fool to think Dougald planned anything but her subjugation?

But passion was one thing.

Love was another.

Was this emotion that simmered within her love? Not the girlish, immature sentiment she had imagined nine years ago, but a deeper feeling, one that saw Dougald's fears and courage, his imperfections and his strengths, and loved him in spite of, and because of.

She scarcely dared think of what might happen if she loved him.

Stepping through the door that led to the tower, Hannah looked up the rounded turret. The narrow stairway spiraled toward the landing outside the aunts' workroom. The simple wooden steps were shallow and a rough handrail had been erected for the old women's convenience and safety.

Hannah feared Queen Victoria would wish to see where the work on the tapestry had been done. So a hasty coat of paint had been applied to the plaster walls, and the carpenters had begun the job of replacing the treads with polished oak and creating a curving banister of cherry wood. It would be handsome when finished, but for now Hannah stepped carefully, testing each board before she placed her weight on it. After all, the work was being done with undue haste, and one mistake could end in unnecessary injury.

On the landing at last, she gave a sigh of relief. When the aunts arrived for the day's work, they would be safe on the stairway.

The key was in the reticule hanging from Hannah's belt. She reached for it as she stepped up to the door—and screamed as the board cracked, and her foot went down into nothingness.

19

Dougald stood in his bedroom in his stocking feet and glared at his tardy valet. "If it is your desire that I sport a properly tied cravat, then I would suggest that you arrive in a more timely manner to assist in my dressing."

Several of Charles's sparse hairs floated about his head in a haphazard manner, his coat gaped open and his own cravat moved as he swallowed. "My lord, there's been an accident."

Dougald's focus narrowed on his man. He had never seen Charles agitated before. Nothing ruffled his tedious French composure. Certainly not an accident occurring to any of the workmen. Picking up his coat, he shrugged it on. "What kind of accident?" Then he realized—"One of the aunts?" Alarm raced through his veins, unanticipated and disagreeable. "Not one of the aunts!" And why did he care so much? They weren't really his aunts. They were nothing but a bother and a responsibility.

"No, my lord. *Madame* . . . Miss Setterington . . . she fell through the floor."

Stunned, Dougald spoke without thinking. "That's impossible. She left here only—" He caught his breath. He shouldn't say that, but it was true. She had left him less than an hour ago, not long enough to get dressed and into trouble already.

But Charles was nodding and even dabbing at his nose with a handkerchief.

Dougald strode forward and grabbed his shoulders. "Is she alive?"

"*Oui*, my lord, but I fear her leg—"

"What?"

"May be broken."

"Good." No, it wasn't good, but Hannah would recover from a broken leg. Damn her, she would recover.

"Where is she?"

"They are carrying her to her bedchamber."

Dougald started into the corridor.

"Please. My lord. Your shoes!"

"Blast my shoes." But he might need them when he kicked some arse. "No, bring them."

He met the little procession almost at once. Mrs. Trenchard was in the lead. A serving maid walked beside her, lugging a black satchel. Hannah had her arms over the shoulders of two burly footmen. She hopped along, her skirt torn, her lips tight and a militant light in her eyes. When she saw Dougald she launched into speech. "Lord Raeburn, you must make it clear to the workmen that, before they leave at night, everything relating to the aunts is to be safe and secure. If I hadn't gone up to the workroom before the aunts arrived, one of them could have been badly hurt."

Dougald's heart resumed beating. She was injured, but if she was scolding, she was unscathed.

He retained the good sense not to sweep her into his arms. "Where were you hurt?"

"On my foot," Hannah snapped.

Yes, she was going to be fine.

"I was on the landing leading to the aunts' workroom," she continued. "A board collapsed under me."

Dougald jerked his head toward Charles. Charles handed him his shoes, eased past the little group, and headed toward the scene of the accident.

"I was mindful as I climbed the stairs, but the carpenters weren't doing work on the landing."

Dougald realized with surprise that her voice was wobbling.

"My foot went right down. Then the whole board gave way and I fell through"—she blinked rapidly—"and if I hadn't grabbed the handrail I would have fallen all the way and I couldn't pull myself back because the board had splintered downward—"

To hell with good sense. His indomitable wife was *weeping*.

Dougald dropped the shoes, pushed the footmen aside and tenderly picked her up. The footmen fell back and none dared look surprised. Hannah shoved at Dougald for only a moment, then she clutched him as if he were her port in the storm. In other circumstances, he might have enjoyed her neediness. Used it. But right now, it seemed right.

Hannah whispered, "If Mrs. Trenchard hadn't found me, I don't know what I would have done."

Dougald noted that he owed his housekeeper a generous gratuity.

"My lord, bring her in here, please." Mrs. Trenchard stood on the threshold of Hannah's bedchamber.

He carried her to the bed, scowling all the time.

What had he been thinking to put her in such a place? With sunshine streaming in, the room looked even shabbier than at night. If Hannah had to spend time recovering, this was a poor place to do it. And why was she even having to recover? When he was done speaking to the carpenters, they would wish they had chosen gardening as a profession. To Mrs. Trenchard, he said, "Call the doctor."

"The doctor's a drunk." Mrs. Trenchard motioned the serving maid forward and took the satchel. "I'll care for Miss Setterington myself." She glanced at Dougald's dubious expression. "I assure ye, my lord, my mother was the midwife for most of the district as well as Miss Spring's nurse, and she taught me well. Miss Setterington is in good hands."

Dougald hesitated, but Mrs. Trenchard seemed quite sure of herself as she opened the satchel and removed a series of clay jars. With a curt nod, he gave permission. "Very well."

Mrs. Trenchard arranged the jars on the small end table beside the bed, then stopped and stared around her. In a scandalized tone, she said, "Miss Setterington, you've already burned your week's supply of candles!"

"Who cares about . . . her week's supply?" Dougald didn't know what the housekeeper was talking about.

Mrs. Trenchard removed a roll of white cotton cloth. "I allow the lesser servants eight candles a week. That's one a night and two on Sunday, but they sleep four in a room, so that's plenty. If they're wise with their light, they can take candles home to their mums. I allow the upper servants fifteen candles a week. That's two candles a night and three on Sunday. Miss Setterington has exceeded her limit."

"Yes," Hannah said. "I . . . I've been reading late."

A lie. She and Dougald had burned the candles during their nights together.

"I was afraid of this," Mrs. Trenchard said. "That's what comes of having them books. Well, I'm sorry, Miss Setterington, but you can't have any more candles until Sunday."

"Of course she can," Dougald interposed.

"Please, it doesn't matter." Surreptitiously, Hannah thumped his thigh with her fist. "I'll do better next week."

As was proper, Mrs. Trenchard ignored her and responded to the master. "As ye wish, my lord, but 'tis yer tallow I'm seeking to save, and 'twill set a bad example for the other servants."

"I can afford the tallow." He glared down at Hannah.

She glared back.

Her damp eyes spoiled the effect. Women. Their tears weakened a man. If he were truly a man like his father, he wouldn't care if his woman cried. He would stand strong against every unruly emotion she engendered and every appeal she might make. If Hannah had remained away a little longer, he could have achieved that level of detachment. As it was . . . "Miss Setterington is more than just an upper servant."

"Please, my lord, would you just leave?" It was clear Hannah didn't want him interceding on her behalf.

He handed her his handkerchief.

She used it liberally.

Mrs. Trenchard passed the roll of cloth to the serving girl, and said, "Start tearing this into bandages." She lifted Hannah's chin and examined the bloody scrape on her chin. "Pardon me, my lord, I misunderstood. Before Miss Setterington arrived, you made it clear she was to have no special privileges."

In fact, he remembered, in a moment of excessive drink he had been rather slanderous of his wife. Not that he'd spoken of the marriage to Mrs. Trenchard. That he most certainly had not done, but she had probably wondered about the reason for his vitriol. "Miss Setterington may be wakeful because of discomfort from her wounds." Recalling Mrs. Trenchard's dedication to Aunt Spring, he added, "She did, after all, save the aunts from injury."

Mrs. Trenchard nodded. "That's as may be, but I can't approve of bending the rules. Next thing ye know, ye'll be banishing the curfew."

Dougald sometimes wondered if he knew what went on in his house. "What curfew?"

"For nine o' the clock. Gets the servants in their rooms and no one gets hurt . . . in the dark."

He didn't understand this at all, but the serving girl who assisted Mrs. Trenchard was staring at him like so many of the serving maids did—with trepidation bordering on hysteria. With a jerk of his head, he indicated the girl. "Does she think I'm going to kill her?"

The silly female nodded. Actually nodded.

"For God's sake, girl, I don't care about you at all."

His impatient snarl didn't seem to reassure her. In fact, her eyes widened and she shrank from him.

"That's the way to hearten her," Hannah bit out.

Mrs. Trenchard patted the girl on the shoulder. "Go on, now. I don't need you anymore."

"Wait!" Dougald tried to plump the thin pillow beneath Hannah's head. "Go into my bedchamber and bring one of my pillows for Miss Setterington."

The girl swallowed and stared.

"No, don't." Hannah lifted herself onto her elbow. "My lord, I don't need any special privileges. What I need is to have Mrs. Trenchard look me over so I can get back to the aunts. They need my help to finish the tapestry."

Dougald pushed her down. "We'll worry about that later." She needed a dose of laudanum, and he exchanged a significant glance with Mrs. Trenchard.

Mrs. Trenchard nodded at him, then spoke to the uncertain maid, who ran to do her bidding.

"Now, my lord, if ye would just step out . . ."

"No." He planted himself on the far side of the bed. "I'm staying."

"Nonsense," Hannah said. "You cannot stay."

He motioned to Mrs. Trenchard to proceed.

20

"Considering what the results of her accident might've been, Miss Setterington is very lucky." Mrs. Trenchard hustled Dougald out of Hannah's bedchamber, leaving Hannah propped up on his pillows, sipping Mrs. Trenchard's special soothing tea while the maid watched over her. "As ye saw, she suffered scratches up her leg and slivers in her palms. She's going to hurt greatly from the sprained ankle and her torn fingernails, and she hit her chin so hard her head's going to ache something vile."

Mrs. Trenchard's labor in Hannah's bedchamber had convinced Dougald the housekeeper did indeed know how to care for the ill. He could trust her, and now he wondered what Charles had discovered in his hunt for the culprit. "Walk with me," he commanded, and strode down the corridor. "How long should she stay in bed?"

"Today at least, perhaps tomorrow. For several days she should stay seated as much as possible and keep her foot elevated."

"You will see that she does." Dougald glanced at Mrs. Trenchard as she hurried beside him. Certainly this woman had proved her worth today. "You have been here for many years."

"All my life."

He paused, picked up his forgotten shoes, and stared into her eyes. "You know Sir Onslow well." He saw the flash of wariness. Was that the reaction of a servant to interrogation, or did she know something?

"I've known him since he was a lad."

"Would you call him an admirable character?"

"He's a dear man."

Which told Dougald exactly nothing. He walked on.

She hurried after him. "Good to the servants, likes my menus, and with a comely smile."

"A flirt."

"There's no crime in that."

Except when he flirted with Hannah. "Not at all," he said. Mrs. Trenchard liked Seaton, that was clear, and perhaps that should weigh in the little pustule's favor. "I was asking only because he is my heir, and should something happen to me I wonder what kind of lord he would be."

"A good one," she said promptly.

She didn't deny that something might happen to Dougald. Was it a foregone conclusion that he would go the way of his predecessors? "But he loves London. I fear he would be an absent landlord."

"Aye, absent but not forgotten." She slowed. "He . . ."

"He what?"

She didn't answer, and he turned to see her holding her side. "What's wrong?"

She leaned against the wall, her face paper white.

"Indigestion, my lord. Sometimes it feels as if the devil is clawing at my gut." Digging in her apron pocket, she produced a vial. Uncorking it, she swallowed the contents and stood with eyes closed until her color returned. She straightened, bobbed a curtsy, and said, "Beg pardon, my lord. It comes when I work too long."

"Then stop." Although he well knew the trouble he invited, he would not have the woman dropping from exhaustion.

Mrs. Trenchard sighed. "My lord, may I speak freely?"

Dougald looked down at his housekeeper. She was tall, big-boned, and capable, the kind of servant he appreciated. She kept out of his way, did her job, and never ventured an opinion. She was going to now, and he wondered which of the unusual events of recent days had driven her to this pass. "What is it?"

"I've not said a word about the changes here, although there's been complaints from the other servants, because ye're the master and ye should do as ye like."

"Exactly."

She flagged slightly. "But when people are in danger, I can't help but speak out. There are men around all the time, tearing things down and building them up, and not a shred of proper reverence for the past. Seems to me, even with Queen Victoria coming, it would be better to do less and ponder what must be done first."

"What do you mean?"

"For instance, the great hall. Just yesterday I caught one of the carpenters hanging by the beams while the others stood below with a ladder and mocked him."

Dougald had heard the shouting and come out to see

what the commotion was about. He had considered the incident nothing more than a bit of horseplay to ease the tension of nonstop labor. But obviously Mrs. Trenchard took the matter more seriously. "I hope you took them to task," he said, without indicating his amusement. "I would hate to have one of the men fall and break his leg."

"More than that, my lord, he could have broken one of the carvings." Dolefully, she shook her head. "Done in the fourteenth century, most of them, some of the finest carvings in this district."

"I will speak to them myself."

"At least I take comfort those rough men are not tearing up the chapel, too."

Every morning after devotions, he had seen Mrs. Trenchard alone in the chapel, dusting and polishing the pews and the altar. Her religious sensibilities were obviously of the highest, and he assured her, "When the men start working in there, I will personally supervise their efforts."

She started in surprise. "But my lord, I thought ye weren't going to change the chapel."

"Change? No. The venerable atmosphere should be preserved. But clean and repair, certainly."

"Of course." Rocking back on her heels, she said, "So ye do intend to restore the chapel."

"Your piety does you credit." He awkwardly patted her arm. "I would not neglect what has long been the heart of the castle."

"How soon?"

He considered his schedule. "I don't have time before the Queen's visit to oversee the repairs, but I promise to do it as soon as possible. This is no hastily thought-out transformation. I have long known what I wished to do with Raeburn Castle. My focus was simply elsewhere." On capturing and subduing Hannah. "Now all must be done, and quickly. I assure you no other incidents with the workmen will dare occur again, nor accidents of the type that Miss Setterington suffered."

Mrs. Trenchard wrung her hands. "I don't want to see anyone hurt."

"No one will be hurt. Do not distress yourself further."

She hesitated, wanting to say more.

He lifted his eyebrows. He'd heard one opinion from her. One was more than enough.

She must have read it in his face, for she bobbed a curtsy. "I'll sit with Miss Setterington, then."

"Do that. If she needs anything, you are to give it to her. We want her well by the time Queen Victoria arrives, for it is in honor of their friendship that Her Majesty graces us with a visit."

"Yes." Mrs. Trenchard turned back toward Hannah's bedchamber. "You're right, as always, my lord."

Finding a seat, he pulled on his shoes and buttoned them. Not long ago Dougald would have believed Mrs. Trenchard. For more years than he could remember, he had thought himself always right. But Hannah and her confidence and her laughter and her—dare he say it?—her intelligence made him doubt himself. A dreadful thing for a man of his age and with his responsibilities to doubt himself in any way. He didn't like it. If not for Hannah he would not now be faltering. If not for Hannah, he would be happy.

But even he had to admit that was a lie. He hadn't been happy for more years than he could count. Since she had left him and people starting calling him a murderer. Although he couldn't remember being happy before, either. Determined, stubborn, cockily sure of himself, but not happy.

What did he want?

He knew the answer. He wanted Hannah to adore him with all her heart, just as she had done in the days before their wedding.

Nevertheless, nothing was going to take her from him before he had decided her fate. Yes, when he found the man responsible for her accident, he would punish him, and no one would dare fail again.

He proceeded down the stairs, through the great hall and the chapel to his office. Charles would have rounded up the carpenters responsible for the accident, and if he knew Charles, the men would be waiting in his office and quaking in their shoes.

But Charles was not in the anteroom, and the office was empty. Dougald frowned, then heard the approaching sound of men's voices.

"I'm tellin' ye, I don't want t' talk t' His Lordship. Frightens me into conniptions, he does."

Using his most soothing tone, Charles said, "*Oui*, I know, but he will wish to hear what you have to say."

"I don't want t' tell him."

"I promise he will not be angry at you, Fred."

"I seen him glare. That's enough t' kill a man—an' it's not like he hasn't done that, too."

For the first time in a great many years, rage roared through Dougald. He was, he discovered, tired of being unjustly accused of murder. Hannah's murder, the murder of the other lords of Raeburn . . . he had never killed anyone. Never laid hands on another soul in violence except during a fair fight. Yet he had taken the

punishment, and damn it, he was tired of being ostra-
cized.

The workman's voice turned to a whine. "Don't ye
see, man? 'Twas probably His Lordship who done
this."

Ostrasized, and by a man Dougald had rescued from
the depths of poverty, brought to Raeburn Castle, and
provided with honest work. He didn't expect gratitude,
but a little loyalty wouldn't go amiss. Stepping to the
door, he used a tone like a whiplash. "I probably did
what?"

Charles and the head carpenter stood just inside the
chapel, and Fred paled. "My lord." He pulled his cap
off his head. "I didn't mean . . . Mr. Charles here
thought ye'd not be in yet . . . that is . . ."

"Did what?" Dougald repeated.

Charles gave Fred a push. "Go! We can't talk about
this here."

Dougald stepped away from the door to give Fred
some room, but he didn't feel compassionate enough
to walk behind his desk. Instead he paced back and
forth across the study until Fred had stepped in and
Charles had closed the door. Then Dougald rounded
on Fred. "What is it you think I did?"

Fred stood twisting his cap, clearly incapable of
speech.

"The carpenters have not been working on the landing, my lord," Charles informed Dougald.

Dougald's eyes narrowed. "They've been working
on the stairs."

"Only the stairs. They had not yet done anything to
the landing."

Dougald understood immediately, and his rage

chilled. "Yet Hannah fell through the floor there." He paced away, then back. "Could it have been rotting boards?"

The carpenter worked up his nerve. "It could have been. But it wasn't."

"What was it?" Dougald asked in a soft, vehement voice.

"Someone sawed a couple of the boards here an' there. Weakened them. My lord, I swear t' ye— 'tweren't like that last night. We were going t' start work on it this morning, an' me an' Rubin looked it over good before we left."

Someone had deliberately hurt Dougald's wife. Someone who knew she always went up to the aunts' workroom first thing in the morning.

But they didn't even know she *was* his wife. "Why the hell would someone do this?" Dougald demanded.

He didn't really expect an answer, but Charles opened the door and allowed Fred to escape, then closed it behind him. "My lord, you and *Madame* have been indiscreet in your . . . connubial visits."

Dougald swung on Charles. "How did you know that we—"

"I come to dress you. She is slipping out of your room. The next day I come again to dress you. You are slipping out of her room. I hide at the end of the corridor to discourage any servants from seeing, but . . . my lord, those are the secrets which cannot be kept. There is gossip. I have heard it. The servants speculate as to why you are less forbidding. They see the tension between you and *Madame*. The glances. Her blushes. They speculate correctly."

"Damn." Dougald didn't want to hear that he had been the reason for the threat to Hannah's life.

"Yes, my lord." Charles said soberly, "I don't believe anyone could imagine that *Madame* is your wife, but I think they might believe matrimony is in the offing. If, as you suggest, it was Sir Onslow who tried to kill you so he could inherit your title—"

"You said you didn't believe it was Seaton. The detectives have seen no sign that he is guilty."

"That means only that they have not yet caught him. Me, I didn't believe he had the wit or the malice." Charles's jowls seemed to sag ever longer. "But he does have the motive, and I have seen him, my lord. He skulks about the corridors. He hides things under his greatcoat. I even caught him exiting the east wing."

"Could you find where he had been?"

"Nothing had been disturbed in your bedchamber, and at the time I thought him harmless."

"I'm not convinced he isn't. He isn't even at Raeburn Castle most of the time. He's out frolicking while we work."

"An agent working for Sir Onslow, then. That would absolve Sir Onslow of guilt when murder is declared and charges are brought." Charles's jowls drooped almost to his collar. "There is another incident which I found curious but did not call to your attention."

Dougald turned on him. "Yes?"

"One day while *Madame* was waiting on you outside your office, she wandered into the chapel. When I came in, she was on the floor. She said she hit her head." Charles looked sheepish. "At first, I did not believe her."

"What do you mean, you didn't believe her?"

"There was nothing to hit her head on." Charles lifted a shoulder in a half shrug. "And she's a *jeune fille. Jeune filles* are given to their little exaggerations, their little dramas."

With grinding exasperation, Dougald asked, "Charles, is there anything about women you like?"

"*Oui*, there is one thing I like very much. But they do not have to speak for that."

Perhaps, Dougald admitted to himself, Hannah had her reasons for detesting Charles. "But she *had* hit her head?"

"I found a heavy piece of trim nearby, broken off from somewhere. We speculated it had fallen from the rafters, but if it had, it had fallen long ago, for the broken wood was not clean, but dark with dust and smoke."

Dougald stalked to Charles and stared down at him. "What did Hannah say about that?"

"The blow stunned *Madame* and she did not notice. I asked one of the workmen where it had come from. He said it matched the trim on the rafters." Charles pointed up with his forefinger. "On the rafters in the great hall."

"So it was thrown."

Charles lifted a shoulder. "*Oui*, I suspect."

Anger swept like a chill across Dougald. "Why didn't you tell me this sooner?"

"You didn't wish to hear me say another word about *Madame*. Not a word."

Charles delivered his answer with scarcely a hint of triumph, a feat Dougald gave him credit for, for Dougald well remembered that day in his office and the mandate he had given Charles. "Very well, Charles. I deserved that."

"Yes, my lord." Charles took a quick breath. "But

that is the reason I urged that care be taken in the restorations. I feared another accident."

"Thank you." But Dougald could never forget Charles's part in driving Hannah away the first time. "Still I wonder why you do it."

"Do you wonder? Don't you see?" Charles's accent strengthened as he grew excited. "It is my dearest wish that you and *Madame* reunite. I have done everything in my power to make it so."

"Why?" Dougald asked flatly.

"She must come and be your true wife. You are unhappy while she is alive and elsewhere, but you will not consider a divorce." Charles looked down his long nose at Dougald. "Or if she will not return to you, she must die so you may be free."

Ah. Now they got to the root of the matter. "I would rather not face another murder charge."

"No! My lord, I did not mean that *you* should kill her. This accusation of murder already sets you beyond the realm of polite society. You cannot wed another, better young maiden if her father believes you will slay her." Charles smiled with obviously false cheer. "So it must be reconciliation."

"Live with me as my wife or I will kill you? There's a proposal every woman wants to hear."

"But you don't have to kill her, my lord. Someone is willing to do it for you."

Charles's blunt reminder sent Dougald to his seat. He sank down and tried once more to face the depths of this disaster. "So Hannah is in danger because of me?"

"A son born of you and *Madame* will eliminate Sir Onslow's chances of inheritance. Somehow it must be Sir Onslow."

Dougald could face danger. He felt nothing but contempt for the coward who had made an assault on his life. But to try to kill Hannah . . . No. No. "Is Seaton in the house now?"

"No, my lord, he is gone for the day to Conniff Manor."

"When he returns, I wish to speak with him."

"May I be there, my lord?"

Dougald exchanged a grim smile with his valet. "Indeed, I depend on your presence. Seaton does not currently fear me."

"This indifference on his part can change."

"Yes. I think it must. But until I speak to him, make him confess, we have to watch over Hannah."

"My lord, I have been watching every chance I get. But it's not possible. She flits here and there, up and down stairs. She speaks to everyone, she is everyone's friend." From Charles's sneer, it was clear he didn't approve. "There are workmen here, strangers. Any of them could have been hired to harm her. Or it could be someone we know—one of the servants, Mrs. Trenchard, Alfred—"

"You."

"Me?" Charles's impressive nostrils flared, and in the sarcastic tone at which the French excelled, he said, "Of course, it could be me. But if I wished to kill her, I have passed up many a chance."

Maybe not to kill her, Dougald thought. Maybe just to send her away—again. He looked at Charles, at the drooping face, the bulbous nose, the scanty hairs on his head. After that last time when Charles had worked so hard to get rid of Hannah—how could Dougald ever completely trust him again?

As if Charles read his mind, Charles said, "You must send her away, my lord."

"She won't go." And Dougald didn't trust her enough to tell her why she must. Not only would she not leave—her affection for the aunts, her duty to the Queen, even, perhaps, her passion for him would keep her here—but also the Hannah who had come into this house was different than the youthful Hannah. She decided on a course of action and performed that action with sense and determination. If she decided she could help Dougald find the culprit, she would insist on doing so. And when Dougald thought about Hannah bravely confronting that little jackass Seaton with his hidden degeneracy . . . well, she wouldn't do it, because Dougald wouldn't tell her.

In an exasperated tone, Charles said, "I cannot watch over her and you, and you know who I will favor if I am driven to make a choice."

Yes, Dougald knew, and nothing he could say would change Charles's loyalty to him.

"You can make her go." Palms on the desk, Charles leaned forward and stared with grave sincerity at Dougald. "You know how."

"Yes." Until Dougald had positively identified the guilty party, and dealt with him, he did have to send her away. With grim intent, he unlocked the bottom drawer of his desk and pulled out a packet of letters tied in a faded, pink ribbon. "But it's going to wreak hell with our reconciliation."

21

$\mathcal{T}$he aunts stood around Hannah's bed and stared at her with a curiosity that bordered on suspicion.

"Explain again, dear, how you came to trip on the stairs going up to the workroom," Aunt Isabel said. "I couldn't hear you the first time. You mumble something dreadful."

Hannah hadn't mumbled; in fact, she had mastered the art of speaking slowly and loudly so Aunt Isabel could hear her. But she could hardly challenge the older lady's truthfulness, so she said, "I was carrying a new box of yarns up the stairs and I tripped on my skirt."

"Um-hum." Aunt Ethel nodded.

"Such a *big* box," Aunt Spring said.

"Why didn't you have a footman carry it up for you?" Aunt Isabel asked.

"The footmen were all so busy with the construction and the cleaning, I hated to take one away from his duties. I know better now." Hannah tucked her striped, faded, flannel dressing gown tighter about her and gestured toward the chair. "I wasn't expecting guests, but please, won't somebody sit down?"

"No, dear, we're more comfortable standing," Miss Minnie said.

Miss Minnie meant they were more able to peer intimidatingly at her while they stood. The swelling in Hannah's ankle was less painful than this interrogation.

Sitting up straighter against the pillows, Hannah attempted to turn the conversation. "Thank you for the flowers, Aunt Ethel." The cut-glass vase rested on the bed table, and Hannah touched the delicate petals of a pink rose. "They're beautiful."

Aunt Ethel beamed, easily won over by the praise for her blossoms. "I'll bring you more tomorrow." Aunt Spring nudged her and recalled her to her duty. "Oh! Yes." Aunt Ethel fixed a frown on Hannah. "You were telling us about your fall."

"There's nothing else to tell." Hannah attempted a free and easy shrug. "How are the plans proceeding for the reception?"

Aunt Isabel patted her newly dyed, very black hair. "Lord and Lady McCarn sent their gracious assent, as did the Dempsters. Sir Stokes and Lady Gwen won't miss it, and—"

Miss Minnie interrupted, "It would be faster to say that everyone has accepted."

"Everyone?" Hannah thought of her grandparents and clasped her hands. She was going to meet them at last. The swelling in her foot was diminishing. She thought she would easily be able to wear shoes by the Queen's reception. For that she was grateful; she wanted to look perfect when she met the Burroughses.

Aunt Isabel snapped to attention. "Yes, it would be faster to say that, and of course we will be prepared with food and drink suitable for a Queen. If only you were well, Miss Setterington."

"Thank you, I am well. When Mrs. Trenchard checked on me this morning, she said I could rise tomorrow so long as I use a cane." Hannah chafed at the time in bed. "How is the work on the tapestry going?"

"We have less than five days until Her Majesty's visit. I don't know if we can finish in time." Aunt Spring shook her head dolefully. "Not without the case of yarns we need. Oh, but you said it came." She put her finger to her chin. "Where did you put it?"

Hannah pleated the folds of her skirt and wondered why she ever thought she could lie to these women. For the first time since her mother died, she faced chiding eyes and felt the sting of guilt. "I dropped it when I fell. Perhaps someone else picked it up." The yarns had been scheduled for delivery yesterday. The case had to be in the castle somewhere, didn't it? Heaven help her if it had failed to arrive.

"We'll ask Mrs. Trenchard." Miss Minnie made the simple sentence sound threatening.

But Hannah approved of that idea. Mrs. Trenchard would lie for her if necessary. Mrs. Trenchard wouldn't want the aunts worrying, either.

"Yes, I'll speak to Judy," Aunt Spring said. "She and I are like twins."

Taken aback, Hannah blinked. "Like twins . . . how?"

"My mother died, you know, so her mother was my wet nurse." Aunt Spring pointed to herself. "We're the same age."

"You . . . are?" For some reason, Hannah had thought Aunt Spring to be older than Mrs. Trenchard. Mrs. Trenchard was so sturdy and capable, able to pro-

pel a staff of fifty servants, while Aunt Spring was . . .
Aunt Spring. Vague, eccentric, eternally kind.

Aunt Spring forgot the drive for truth and perched
on the edge of Hannah's bed to gossip. "We were
raised like sisters. In my youth, dear Judy was my
constant companion. She always watched out for me,
even when I was grown. Even after she was married.
Why, if not for her, I could have never met Lawrence
in secret—"

"Miss Spring!" Mrs. Trenchard stood in the doorway. "Ye're not to say such things. We don't want yer
reputation to suffer."

"Pshaw. What matter is my reputation? Lawrence
was my true and only love." Then, in a sudden switch
to a pragmatism, Aunt Spring said, "I'm far too old to
marry, anyway."

Mrs. Trenchard edged into the tiny, crowded room.
"Now, Miss Spring, that's not true. Men are lined up
just waiting for ye to give them the nod."

"*I* haven't laid eyes on any of the old dotards," Miss
Minnie said tartly. "Spring has faced that her matrimo-
nial prospects are finished, Trenchard. Why can't
you?"

A retort clearly hovered on the tip of Mrs. Trenchard's tongue, but something—respect for Aunt
Spring or fear of Miss Minnie—stopped her. After a
silent, uncomfortable moment, she said, "Miss Setterington, I have come to examine yer foot. Lord Raeburn
wants to know if ye can rise today."

"I remember!" In a sudden return to business, Aunt
Spring put her hands on her hips. "Judy, how did Miss
Setterington get hurt?"

"I told you," Hannah said, "I tripped going up the
stairs."

"I asked Judy," Aunt Spring said irritably.

"I wasn't there when Miss Setterington fell." Mrs. Trenchard twisted her hands in her apron and refused to meet Aunt Spring's gaze.

"You found her at the bottom of the stairs?" Miss Minnie asked.

Mrs. Trenchard looked around as if she were trapped, and her Lancashire accent broadened. "Not quite at the bottom."

From the doorway, Dougald said harshly, "That's enough, aunts. I'd like to speak to Miss Setterington."

Four sets of bright eyes fixed on him.

"Go ahead, dear," Aunt Ethel invited.

"Alone," he clarified.

"I can't believe you expect us to let you do that," Miss Minnie said in her severest tone.

"It's most improper," Aunt Isabel added.

"But we will allow it!" Aunt Spring jumped to her feet. "Come on, girls. Let's leave these children alone."

With indecent haste, the aunts filed to the door. One by one they squeezed past Dougald.

Aunt Isabel was the last one out. In a piercing whisper, she said to Dougald, "By the way, dear, you might think of moving dear Hannah to a different bedchamber. This one is frightfully dilapidated." With a quick glance back at Hannah, she added, "Perhaps your bedchamber would do."

As Aunt Isabel whisked from the room, Hannah considered banging her head on the bedpost. Bad enough that Dougald should ask to see her alone, but for the aunts to agree! For Aunt Isabel to say something so salacious! And all in front of the housekeeper. Hannah didn't know how to meet the woman's gaze.

Before Dougald could step forward, Aunt Ethel returned. "Come along, Mrs. Trenchard."

"She will stay," Dougald said. When Aunt Ethel would have challenged him, he turned his dark head and looked at her.

She skittered back as if she had discovered in his face the venom of a serpent. In a frightened whisper, she said, "As you wish, my lord." With one wide-eyed glance of sympathy at Hannah, she hurried away.

As he turned back, Hannah saw why. He stood on the threshold, a solid, black-clad entity with a grim face and flat green eyes. "Lord Raeburn? Is anything wrong?"

He ignored her. "Can she rise today, Mrs. Trenchard?"

Mrs. Trenchard took Hannah's hurt foot in her hand. "Aye, my lord. That she can."

A remarkable diagnosis, Hannah thought, considering she hadn't even looked at it.

"Very good," he said. "Mrs. Trenchard, you may go."

"Wait." Hannah caught the housekeeper's hand. "Did the tapestry yarns arrive?"

Mrs. Trenchard glanced nervously at Dougald, but she answered, "This afternoon. They're up in the workroom now."

"If the aunts ask, I was carrying them yesterday when I fell."

Mrs. Trenchard nodded, then hurried out of the room as if the hounds of hell chased her.

Something was going on that Hannah didn't understand. She struggled to turn and put her feet on the floor. "Dougald. What is it?"

"Don't get up yet." He didn't move, yet he exuded menace. "Keep your foot up on the pillow as long as you can. It's a lengthy train ride back to London."

"Back to . . . London?" She didn't lie back down, didn't notice the cool floor against the soles of her feet. She didn't notice anything but Dougald, filling the doorway.

"I'm sending you back."

She blinked. "You're jesting."

"I don't jest."

"Then why are you saying such a thing?"

"Because I'm done with you."

She caught her breath. Such a short, brutal sentence. So effective.

So wrong. "Done with me? Done with me for what?"

"Come, Hannah, you're not usually so dense. I made my plans. I succeeded with my plans." He smiled, the smile of a buccaneer who delights in inflicting pain. "I'm done with *you*."

Sensations, impressions, confusion whirled in her brain.

"I admit I intended to use you longer, but look at you!"

Hannah glanced down at her bedraggled dressing gown.

"You've fallen. You're injured. You're no good to me in bed—not for any reason. You can't care for the aunts in your condition, and as for our little bouts of passion . . . well, I certainly don't desire you when you look like *that*."

Catching her lapels, she pulled them up and close to her throat. Still not comprehending, she tried for a humorous tone, "I'm not at my best, but—"

He interrupted ruthlessly. "And I'm sure you sus-pected my intentions."

"Your intentions?"

"You must have wondered if my passion for you matched yours for me."

Her chest tightened. He was speaking to her fears.

He stepped into the room and slammed the door. "Your passion was very affecting. Very moving." Like some silent-footed predator, he slipped to the end of the bed and leaned over the footboard. "Very piteous."

"Piteous!" *The swine!*

"Can you think of a better word for a woman who lusts for a man who encourages her only for revenge?"

"That's not true." She knew it wasn't true. "You're lying."

"You did suspect me of leading you on."

He waited until she admitted, "Yes."

"You'd have to have been a fool not to, and Hannah, I know you're not a fool." His hands gripped the finials with white-knuckled care. "Or at least . . . not a fool about anything but me."

"Again." She was beginning to believe what he so enjoyed telling her.

"Yes. Again. But the first time I seduced you, it was for marriage. This time, it is for divorce."

She wanted to slap his smug face. To straighten her shoulders and spit defiance. But he shattered her with his malevolence. "You made no false promises this time."

"Absolutely not! You do remember how very careful I was not to talk to you any more than necessary dur-ing our nights."

"Because . . . because we busied ourselves with other things."

"Because I know how very much you hate when I make promises that I don't keep." He shook the bed frame, and it rattled. "It's almost as bad as making wedding vows and abandoning them."

He still didn't understand. Refused to understand. "I didn't abandon them. You drove me to leave you."

"You could have been stronger. You could have been tougher. You could have forced Charles to bend to you." His voice grew lower, deeper, more intense with each accusation. "You could have made me listen to you."

She felt like he'd slapped her. "But—"

"You gave up. In six months, you gave up."

"I didn't want to." She hadn't wanted to. "It wasn't right, I knew it, but I could never win against you and Charles."

"Win! It wasn't a bloody war, it was a marriage, and you had power you never tried to use."

Stung, she bounced up. "What power? I had no power. I tried everything."

"Did you try feminine wiles?"

She was disdainful. "They're not honest."

"Honest, hell!" He pointed a blunt finger at her. "Six months, Hannah, to abandon the most sacred vows a man and a woman can make to each other. You slept in my bed. I was in thrall to your body. If you'd spoken to me in the dark of night after you'd made me the happiest man in the world, I would have done anything for you."

"And you would have cried manipulation."

"Probably. I was young. I was stupid. I was stubborn." He sneered at his younger self. "But I would have listened, and you would have got the right to run your household, own your dress shop, become the woman you wanted to be and the wife I dreamed of. But you . . . you were too proud to used the weapons you wielded so well. You just whined. Whining is so much more honorable than feminine wiles."

"I didn't whine! I tried to make you listen—"

"To words. And when words didn't work, what did you do?"

She had to swallow around an upswelling of tears. "You're twisting everything. It wasn't my fault!"

"You abandoned me. You left me alone. You left me to face misery and injustice and charges of murder."

He meant it. She could see pain in him, pain such as she'd never imagined this cold, cynical man could feel. He hated her. He *blamed* her.

"I have waited years for this moment, my dear." His voice got softer, deeper, more menacing. "Years for the moment I would stand in front of you and watch you break into little pieces."

She couldn't comprehend a Dougald who reeked of complicity and cruelty. Yes, she had doubted him the night she arrived at Raeburn Castle. Yes, she had occasionally wondered if he meant his threats of mayhem and abuse. But somewhere in her soul she still cherished the image of Dougald, undressing on the train, joking about his own intense desire, at pains to put her at ease. Always she had thought of that Dougald as the real Dougald. Not the man she had left. Not the man who was lord today. "Did you plan this?"

"Every bit of it," he answered steadily.

"Except for my fall through the landing."

He looked away. "Are you sure about that?"

She sucked in a single, shocked breath. "Dougald," she whispered. "You didn't really try to hurt me?"

When he returned his gaze to hers, only a tiny rim of

green showed in his eyes. The rest was black, a fathomless, cruel, black hole that opened, not onto his soul, but onto pain, bitterness, nothingness. "I told you before. I already stand accused of your murder. I've already served my time in hell. Why should I not kill you? As long as I don't get caught, I'll be no more notorious than before."

She stood up. The agony in her ankle caught her by surprise. She fell back on the bed in pain and in shock.

He came around the foot of the bed so quickly he looked like he would pounce.

Shrinking from him, she scrambled backward toward the head of the bed.

He smiled, a quick, insincere, upward motion of the lips. "Put like that, divorce sounds like quite the bargain, eh?"

"Get out," she ordered. "Get away from me."

Stepping back, he bowed. "As you wish, Miss Setterington. I won't see you again before you leave."

There would be no farewell from him, just as she had not said farewell that first time, so many years ago, when she had left for London.

A much younger Hannah stood in the yard of Liverpool's Knight Arms Inn and watched as the hostlers and the stableboys scrambled over and around the coach, changing the horses for the next stage of the turnpike. It had been a long time since she'd ridden in a public conveyance—since before her mother died. Since before they'd come to Dougald's house.

Dougald's house. The place where the child Hannah had thought she could live forever and be safe. The place the girl Hannah had come as a blushing bride, full of hope that she would at last be part of a family. Now, that cold gray-stone mansion reminded her of nothing but ruined dreams.

Even on the train with Dougald, she'd had her doubts. Even before they had married, she had wondered if she was making a mistake. After all, her mother hadn't married because her father had been too weak to defy his family. In a way, Dougald had married for exactly that reason.

Deep in her heart, she had always expected that Dougald wouldn't love her. She had wanted it. She had hoped for it. But she hadn't fought for it. In her youth, she'd been wounded too many times by friends who turned away from the homeless bastard she had been.

So this morning she had packed her most serviceable clothing, her mementos of her mother, and the money Dougald had given her. Money he pushed at her as a pacifier, and that she had taken these last weeks for just this reason—to leave him. She was running away to London in the quickest way possible. London, where she could disappear and never be found. London, a place of exile.

As soon as the stableboys had finished their job, Hannah walked up to the coachman. "I have my ticket. My bag is there." She pointed. "Please load it on the coach. How much longer until we leave?"

The coachman looked her over, and she knew what he saw. A young lady dressed in the finest of mourning clothes, veil pinned to her hat, blond hair glinting through the gaps. She didn't have a maid, and that was a mark against her, but apparently her appearance branded her as quality, for the coachman tipped his hat and in a voice of respect, said, "We're ready t' go, Miss."

"Thank the Lord," Hannah whispered. She didn't want to be caught. Probably she wouldn't be, for Dougald had traveled to Manchester. Charles was with him, but she never knew about Charles. The sly Frenchman had a way of knowing everything about his household, and it had taken all of Hannah's cunning to escape undetected.

"Aye, Miss, we'll get ye t' Lunnon in time fer th' funeral," the coachman said.

"Thank you." She pressed a coin into his hand. "You're very kind."

Opening the door of the coach, the coachman bawled at the passengers, "You gents move t' ride backwards. We've got a lady comin' in."

A foppish gentleman stuck his head out the door. "A lady? What do I care if a lady joins us? I was here first."

The coachman pulled him onto the ground in one easy motion. "Ye'll do as I say, or ye'll ride on th' roof."

The gentleman straightened up to roar an insult, when he caught sight of Hannah.

She stared at him without expression.

He stepped forward and offered his hand. "May I assist you in entering, Miss . . ."

Mrs., she almost corrected him. Mrs. Pippard. But she caught herself, and in a moment of quick thinking said, "Miss Setterington. Thank you, sir." She stepped into the coach. On the seat facing front sat a plump older woman and a seedy-looking girl, clutching her valise in her lap. She summed them up in a glance— the lady was trustworthy, the girl was a country miss on her way to the city to make her fortune. "May I?"

she asked. They made room, and she squeezed in between them.

The foppish gentleman settled directly opposite her, and with a smile, he said, "So you're going to London, are you? What a coincidence. So am I."

Hannah knew she was going to have to fend him off. She also knew she could do it. She wasn't the wealthy, innocent young lady he imagined. She was a jobless bastard, used to traveling the roads, to judging people in a moment, to living by her wits.

It would take all her wits to hide from Dougald, and hide so well he would never find her. But somehow she would. She was now Miss Hannah Setterington, independent spinster.

The coach door shut, the whip cracked and, with a jerk, the coach started. Hannah bent forward for one last look at Liverpool, then leaned back and shut her eyes. After only six months of marriage, everything she longed for was gone. She was leaving her dreams of marriage and family and love behind, and she would never think of them—of him—*again.*

A sound at the door abruptly brought Hannah back from her black memories to the painful present.

Mrs. Trenchard stood there, holding a cane. "Lord Raeburn sent me up to help you pack."

"Pack?" Hannah still could scarcely believe Dougald would be so brutal.

"Pack to go back to London."

Last time Hannah had left Dougald, it had hurt, yes, but she'd been willing to leave to preserve her self-esteem, her will, her independence. If she left this time, what would she have but broken pride, a crushed spirit, and dreams of a family that could never come true?

Dreams of a family with Dougald. Dougald, who had proved himself to be cruel and mean-spirited with every word he spoke. Dougald, who had read her mind and all of her fears and taunted her with each one.

Hannah frowned.

He accused her of abandoning him. Of abandoning their marriage without really trying to make it work.

But she had tried. She had! And just to show him he was wrong . . . "I'm not going," she said.

Consternation filled Mrs. Trenchard's face. "Miss Setterington?"

Carefully Hannah swung her feet onto the floor.

Dougald *wasn't* cruel or mean-spirited. He was cold. He was difficult. He was driven by demons she didn't understand. But he would never set a trap for her to fall through! The idea was ludicrous. "I'm not going. He can't make me."

Mrs. Trenchard licked her lips. "Miss Setterington, while I hesitate to disagree with you . . . yes, he can."

Ignoring her, Hannah stood, testing the strength of her ankle. Testing the strength of her resolve.

Mrs. Trenchard showed her a letter. "I wrote this for you. A letter of recommendation. The highest praise for your skills."

Hannah took the letter, glanced at it, tossed it on the bed. Something was going on. Something she didn't understand, but she wasn't leaving the aunts before the Queen's visit. She wasn't leaving before she had met her grandparents. "Thank you, Mrs. Trenchard. But I'm not going."

With desperation in her tone, Mrs. Trenchard said, "The master is adept at getting his way."

Hannah hobbled a short step forward. Satisfied that

her ankle would not collapse, she held out her hand for the crutch.

Dougald was chasing her away for some reason. Perhaps because he was finished with her. But perhaps something more was occurring. Something concerning her grandparents, or the aunts, or Hannah herself. Perhaps Dougald had found a lover he desired more than he desired Hannah. But whatever the reason, Hannah wasn't leaving Dougald until he was suffering as she suffered.

When Mrs. Trenchard brought it, Hannah looked straight at her. "Nothing and nobody is chasing me away from Raeburn Castle until I am ready to leave."

22

Dougald stood behind his desk and stared, slack-jawed, at the impassive Mrs. Trenchard. "Miss Setterington dared defy me?"

"Do you wish me to have the footmen carry her to the carriage and from there onto the train, my lord?" Mrs. Trenchard used the same tone she might have used to offer him a warm cognac.

He grimaced, uneasily aware he had mishandled the task of ejecting Hannah.

He had said more than he planned and fiercely meant what he said.

He had reproached her for abandoning their marriage. He hadn't proposed to say that, or even realized how deeply he resented her desertion. But once he'd started talking, his condemnation had been both damning and truthful, revealing to both her—and him.

"Miss Setterington is not so tall that two hefty footmen can't remove her on my order," Mrs. Trenchard said.

"No doubt, but I have no wish to see her dragged

away while the aunts cry and wring their hands." He ran his hands through his hair. "Where is she now?"

"She dressed in her work clothes and made her way to the butler's pantry. She said her foot hurt and she couldn't go any farther, so she stopped there to count the silver." Mrs. Trenchard shook her head. "It needs counting, but I didn't want to let her, my lord. It's a risky business, putting the Raeburn silver in the hands of a disgruntled domestic. Still, I thought you'd want to be notified about her defiance at once."

"I doubt Miss Setterington will develop any great attachment to the Raeburn silver, no matter how disgruntled she is. Thank you, Mrs. Trenchard." He tugged his jacket into proper position. "I'll deal with the matter." When he had left Hannah in her bedchamber, he would have sworn she was leaving, that he had succeeded, as he always did.

Except he seldom won with Hannah. Hannah repeatedly thwarted him—but not this time. Her life was at stake. He had to send her away. It was for her own good. Someday she would appreciate his consideration and understand that he hurt her to help her.

She *had* to understand, because for the sake of his family name, *he* needed a wife.

Yet as he strode down the corridor, he worried. Yes, he needed a wife. He needed an heir. He already had Hannah; in the last few days they had sufficiently, repeatedly and amazingly proved that they functioned well in bed together. They would produce an heir, one hoped, in short order.

He stopped outside the open pantry door. The small room was used as storage for crockery, livery, napkins, a few extra chairs, anything the servers might need. Shelves lined one wall, a table stood against the other.

If he had upset Hannah so much she would never again welcome him into her bed, he faced several options, none of them attractive.

He could divorce her and marry a new wife.

He could employ the full force of the law and compel her to return to him.

Or he could woo her.

Wooing Hannah would be an inefficient use of his time. She was already his. But the other two options repulsed him, and he knew without a doubt he would never find another woman to grace his bed like Hannah. When he and Hannah mated, they consumed each other with fire and pleasure. He had to have Hannah, and he had to have her willing.

To have her and have her willing, he could, of course, use the logical method. When he had dispatched the gallowsbait who tried to murder her, then he could find her in London or Surrey or—heavens, he hoped he hadn't chased her out of England completely—and explain that he had rejected her for her own good.

No doubt she would slam her door in his face—or preferably on his fingers.

She sat on a stool, her back to him, facing the sideboard. Her crutch leaned in the corner. Silverware covered the narrow surface of the sideboard in a glittering array, and as he watched, she sorted spoons, stacked them together, and placed them next to the stacks of forks already neatly arranged on one end. A few tendrils of hair had escaped from her chignon and touched the nape of her neck where he longed to touch, and his gaze bored into her with heated intensity.

For now, to get rid of her, he knew what to say. In

his diatribe in her bedchamber he had, after all, forgotten one very important and insulting issue.

With one hand he pushed the door back so hard it slammed against the wall.

She didn't jump. She did pause.

In a contemptuous, infuriating drawl, he said, "I suppose this is about your piddling little stash of money."

Her shoulders stiffened. Deliberately, she turned to face him. She wore a plain, brown wool gown and, as an accessory, held a fine silver meat knife in her hand.

"My lord Raeburn," she said, "what are you talking about?"

"You." He stepped inside. "Still here. That's what I'm talking about."

"That surprises you?" She swiveled on the stool until she fully faced him and, twirling the knife, she leaned her elbows negligently back against the sideboard. "But why, my lord? When have I ever done what you told me to?"

He had come in here determined to play the game he had begun so well in her bedchamber, and thus save his wife from the threat of death. But she sat there so insolently, like a hooligan of the streets, uncaring of him, his authority, his sacrifice. Stepping inside, he shut the door. "You will this time."

She smiled, if he could call that a smile. "But Dougald, I'm your wife. I'm back with you after *abandoning* you for so many years. Surely you're glad I took your message to heart and am refusing to leave."

Blast. He *had* said the wrong thing. This was what came of allowing oneself to experience disorderly emotion.

Worse, he felt the rise of more emotion in his gut and in his heart. "I don't want you here."

"Let me try my feminine wiles on you." She batted her eyelashes and in a croon, said, "Darling, let me stay with you forever." The picture was spoiled by exaggeration—and her continued spinning of the knife.

He took a step toward her. "Hannah, if I have to send Mrs. Trenchard and some footmen up to your room to pack your bags, you're going to be humiliated."

"You'll have a difficult time explaining your action to the aunts." She slid off the stool. "You will admit, the aunts' tears could make you very uncomfortable. There—is that manipulative enough for you?"

"The time when you could manipulate me is past." Not true, but she was better off not knowing that.

"The aunts need me."

"They have Mrs. Trenchard."

"With all due respect to Mrs. Trenchard, she has too many duties already." She took a limping step toward him. "Without me, the aunts haven't a hope of finishing the tapestry in time. And Her Majesty expects me to be here. After all, I did send the invitation."

He wanted to take Hannah by the shoulders and shake her the insolence right out of her. "Her Majesty will scarcely notice your absence. We're having a tremendous reception with the entire neighborhood attending."

"There we have it." She leaned her free hand on the shelf and glared at him. "You can stop pretending, Dougald. I know what you're doing. You're removing me so you can monopolize the Queen's attention."

Her accusation surprised him so much, he didn't even have to think to be insulting. "Don't be ludicrous. I don't need the Queen's patronage for prestige."

"Then what is it? You're sending me away for *some* purpose."

He barely restrained a gasp. How did she know? *What* did she know? "I told you my purpose. I'm done with you."

"Because you've found my replacement?"

What was she babbling about? "Your replacement?"

"The girl you want to marry."

"I'm . . . married." And confused.

"A small obstacle for a tactician such as you. Did Charles find her for you? A pretty young girl who knows her place, right?" Hannah waved her arm in a grandly scornful gesture. "That's the plan, isn't it? You get rid of me, obtain a divorce and marry your little hussy."

"Contrary to what you seem to believe, divorces are not easy to obtain, nor are they cheap." He realized this was not the subject to discuss right now with the wife he was trying to save and ultimately planned to keep.

"Did Charles advise you on how to get rid of me? Did he tell you what to say?"

"Why would I need Charles to do that?" He concentrated on wounding her once more, on chasing her from Raeburn Castle. "You're a simple woman."

Hannah appeared unscathed by his derision. "So you're trading the simple woman you have for a simpleton you can command."

"This is a stupid conversation," he snapped. "I am not going to remarry."

"Then it's the other." She glanced away, her lips trembling. "The final revenge, the greatest of all, the opportunity to crush Hannah into the ground and know she will never rise again."

They stood three feet apart, and the air between

them quivered with heat and hostility. "You have lost your mind."

"My grandparents are coming to that reception, and you are not going to cheat me out of meeting my family."

He'd forgotten about her grandparents. He knew she looked forward to and dreaded the moment she would meet that family. They were the anchor in his scheme to keep Hannah tied to this place, and in a brief moment of insight, he wondered if he had forgotten the Burroughses on purpose.

Did he, after all, hate so much to think she might belong somewhere but with him?

"You are more cruel than even I realized," she said.

"Then leave."

"I'm not leaving."

He took another step. The small distance between them was closing fast. "You are trying my patience."

She laughed caustically. "Piffle. You have no feelings; therefore, you have no patience."

"I have feelings," he ground out.

"No. A man who would seduce a woman to use and humiliate her has no feelings." The hand with the knife lowered, and her grasp changed to a fighting grip.

He looked at the blade. "Where did you learn to hold a knife like that?"

"Some of the girls I taught at the Distinguished Academy of Governesses had skills I thought it best not to question." She limped up to him, so close her bosom almost brushed his chest, and pressed it against his ribs. "I hope it doesn't make you uncomfortable."

"No." It made him furious, and he caught her wrist in his fingers before she could even lunge. "Your student didn't teach you well at all, if she didn't teach you not to threaten unless you mean to follow through."

"You know me." She twisted her wrist and in as sarcastic a tone as he'd ever heard her use, she said, "I'm a quitter."

"Not just a quitter," he taunted. "A whiner, too. You whine until a man can't hear himself think."

She tried to lunge at him with the knife, a futile endeavor, but while he was distracted by her effort, she managed to place a solid fist in his stomach. The breath gushed out of him.

It seemed she'd learned a few other defenses from the girls in her Academy. With practice, she could be lethal. Luckily, she hadn't had practice, and he wanted to subdue her in the quickest way possible. Plucking the knife out of her fingers, he threw it against the sideboard. It stuck, quivering, in the wood.

"There," he said. "Now we can talk like reasonable people." Gathering her into his arms, he kissed her.

She didn't want to be kissed. She tried to jerk her head away. He pulled her closer, bent her over his arm, forced his kisses on her while savoring the sensation of her body against his.

Rather distantly he wondered at himself. He had thought that, after years of loneliness and isolation, he had learned discipline. He had thought of himself as relentless, scheming, destitute of passion, warmth and humanity. It would seem he had been wrong. He was passionate, warm enough to forge steel, and all too human.

Then she bit him, right on the lower lip.

He lurched back and glared at the woman he still held.

She glared back at him, bosom heaving with the effort to get her breath. Her lips, reddened and cherished by his, were firm. Her steady chin was lifted. Her eyes were a mix of chestnut color and turbulent passions. He could have sworn she watched him, judged him and made a decision.

In the inflexible tone of the world's sternest governess, she said, "Dougald, let me go this minute, or I'll never be able to get you out of your clothes."

In a scorching flash of truth, Dougald realized he loved her. All this time, all these years, he'd been telling himself the plotting and the intriguing had been to get even with Hannah for making a fool of him, when in fact he'd been in love with her all the time. He didn't want to subdue her. He wanted to make her his.

But . . . why was she doing this now? Why wasn't she scratching his eyes out?

Why did he care? If she was going to undress him and seduce him, even if it was to distract him so she could plunge a knife in his heart—well, there were worse ways to die.

Shedding his jacket as he went, he grabbed one of the spare dining chairs and stuck it under the door handle. Returning to her, he stood quiescent as she unbuttoned his waistcoat. He helped her peel it away. He tried to tear the cravat off his neck.

She stopped him by the simple expedient of putting her hands over his. "I want to undress you."

The most beautiful words in the English language, spoken by his wife. *I want to undress you.* Was she giving him another chance? Was she in love with him as he was with her? He didn't know, but somehow it felt impossible that he should love so strongly that each breath, each heartbeat, each thought was dedicated to Hannah, and she did not return his regard. He loved her. She wanted him. Therefore, she loved him.

She untied the intricate bow and unpinned his starched collar. "There's something so tantalizing about the first glimpse of indecorous male skin. It's so soft right here"—she stroked the curve above his breastbone—"and gets to be deliciously wicked almost immediately." Her hand spread his shirt and burrowed down into the hair on his chest.

What maggot was in his brain that he thought he could send away a woman like this? Even for her own good?

She stroked him with her palm, with her fingertips, finding the sensitive places he knew of, and a few he didn't.

He eased the buttons free on his trousers.

She pulled his shirt over his head, then kissed the length of his collarbone—and lightly bit his nipple.

He grabbed her waist. "Woman, I ought to—"

She turned her back to him. "Unbutton me?"

He did, and with complete efficiency. After all, anything worth doing was worth doing well. "This is the ugliest dress you own," he said conversationally.

"I'm glad you hate it." It fell to her feet. "I picked it out for just that reason."

Their battle still raged, and the reminder renewed his disquiet. He had started it; he'd kissed her. But she had readily joined him; she had demanded his clothing. So she wasn't going to change her mind . . . was she? She wasn't going to slip away and leave him wanting, and justify her actions by telling him he deserved it . . . was she? He needed to unlace her corset and untie her petticoats, and that would take time. Time for her to think. To remember what he'd done since she'd been here. To remember what he'd said in her bedchamber.

He didn't want that.

A pile of folded white linen napkins caught his gaze. They stood stacked on a shelf, pristine and orderly, and an idea sprang into his mind full blown. Without considering the wisdom, he seized the corner of a napkin.

Hannah tried to twist around. "What are you doing?"

He caught her shoulders and faced her forward again, then with a flip of the wrist twirled the napkin into a long band and laid it over her eyes.

"Dougald!" Her hands went up to push the blindfold away.

But he was ready for that. With one hand he fended her off, with the other he held the ends together. "You'll like it," he said.

Actually he had no idea whether she'd like it. He only knew if she couldn't see she couldn't leave, and he needed her naked and in his arms.

"You must be mad." But she stood still while he tied it at the back.

"I have begun to think so," he acknowledged. What other explanation could account for his actions now?

With cautious hands she explored the band across her eyes. "I can't see at all."

She was, he realized, going along with his odd, guiltily pleasurable scheme. "Are all your other senses working?" He slid a fingertip down her neck and along her shoulder.

She shivered. "Yes . . ."

In a race against good sense—her good sense—he loosened her corset and petticoats. As he worked, her chemise slipped off one shoulder and he realized—she had been doing her part. She had untied her chemise and now he could lean over and look down. A breast from this angle looked different than a breast straight on, and the contrast made him want to do experiments. Look from the side, touch from the top, lick . . .

Even considering the care he took of her hurt foot, he had her out of all her clothes in record time.

But where to place her? The table was hard and cluttered, the sideboard was high and stacked with silverware, the floor . . . no. In the corner. In one of the master dining chairs with its shining wood, upright back, and softly curved arms.

He supported her as he led her, making sure she stepped softly on her injured foot. "Sit here."

She groped, then slowly lowered herself onto the chair as he watched. He saw the shiver she gave as her bottom met the cool wooden seat. With ever-increasing haste, he divested himself of his remaining clothing, and watched the sensual exploration of her fingertips across every polished surface. Everything about her charmed him, enticed him. He wanted her so much he would gladly spend the rest of his days in this pantry, giving her pleasure. He loved her so much, he wanted to shout her praises up and down the corridors of Raeburn Castle.

And he couldn't keep her, or say a word, because someone wanted to kill her.

23

*W*ithout her sight, Hannah's world shrank, became a place confined by touch, scent, sound and odor. The chair where Dougald placed her was a craftman's pride, with curlicues and posts smooth to the touch and scented with beeswax. Her nakedness loved the lustrous wood, glossy as silk, supporting her limbs. The floor was cool beneath her soles, easing the ache in her foot. The chair sat in the corner; she investigated with her hands, finding the walls stretching out in either direction. Dougald stood near; she could hear the soft pant of his breath and the rustle of his clothes. He watched her; she could feel the heat of his gaze and sensed the gratification he got from seeing her so helpless.

Not that she was. Like their marriage, her subjugation was an illusion. She could discard the blindfold at any time. She could stand up, put on her clothes, and leave him if she wished.

She didn't wish. This was farewell. All those times they had said, *Never again*, and met again in furtive desire. This time, she meant it. She loved partaking of pleasure with Dougald. The taste of him, the scent of him, the demand of his body moving on and in her. He had imprinted himself on her, and she would never want another man.

But his cruelty had no end. His vindictiveness ate at her soul. And while she was willing to give herself wholeheartedly to her husband Dougald now, after this last good-bye she would ruthlessly end the love affair with the man Lord Raeburn. For the rest of her life, she would try to remember the passion and forget the pain.

Conscious that Dougald must be almost nude, she arranged herself in the seat. Head up, back straight, hands on the chair arms, knees and feet together.

If he wished for her, he would woo her.

"Darling, let me serve you." Dougald knelt before her, a supplicant mortal before his goddess. His belly pressed against her knees, his palms stroked her thighs. He wanted her to spread her legs. He urged her subtly, using his body to guide her.

She didn't wish to take his guidance. Instead, she leaned back against the chair, allowing the slats to cool her back. She lifted one arm, turned her head to the wall, and tucked her hand under her cheek. "Make it good for me," she commanded.

He chuckled, quiet and deep. "As you direct, my dearest." Taking her free hand, he lifted it to his lips and kissed each finger until he reached the little one. He slipped his mouth around the knuckle, sucking it in a manner that suggested . . . well, suggested a motion she much enjoyed. Then he nipped the end. She jumped, and tried to retreat, but he said, "No. Sit still. If I'm to make it good for you, you must sit still."

So she settled back as he kissed her palm, and

trailed that kiss up the inside of her wrist, up the inside of her elbow, over each sensitive freckle and mole. His hands held her shoulders. In her darkness, the caress and texture of his callused fingertips enthralled her. When she realized that her turned head had bared her neck to his exploration, she began to wonder at the wisdom of her decree.

He loved to kiss her neck. Normally when he ran his lips over that tender skin, her toes curled, her breath hurried and she tried to push him away. Now, because of her command, he had carte blanche. But he must have sensed her wariness, for he whispered in her ear, "Trust me, dear heart." With one hand on her shoulder, one on her head, he kissed so lightly she almost didn't know he was there. Almost . . . except for his scent, that combination of spice and leather, so close to her. The way the fine hairs all over her body rose toward him. The tightening in her womb. The lift of her breasts. She wanted to turn toward him, to hold his head in her hands and open her mouth over his. She wanted to do to him what he did to her, and more.

Mates. They were lifelong mates, and this was their last time.

Sorrow filled her, but he couldn't see her eyes. He didn't know. That was best. She didn't want him to realize how very much she would miss him. Today she would hide her sorrow. Someday perhaps the pain of loss would fade.

He toyed with a fallen tendril of her hair. "When I see a single lock loose, I want to take it all down, to spread it across a pillow, to bury my face in your hair and breathe your scent." His fingers cruised along her cheekbones. They caressed her lips. They followed the curve of her chin downward to her chest, then separated to support her breasts. "I love these. When I see the curve of them hiding in your gown, I want to come to you and open your bodice, and view again the mystery of your body."

His praise made her smile in her grief. His touch made her forget everything but desire. In a voice husky with pathos, she said, "There's no mystery. It's a woman's body."

"You're wrong. It's your body. It's my mystery to try and puzzle out. And when I do, I always think—I understand her now. She'll be mine forever. And you stand up and clothe yourself, and I don't know you at all."

Ardent, vibrant, earnest, his voice wove a spell that held her as surely as the darkness. To hear him, he worshiped her—and perhaps he did. Perhaps that unwilling worship spurred his pride and made vengeance a necessity for this imperious man.

"You'll never know me," she whispered.

"No." Something grazed her nipple: breath, and soft lips. "Never all of you. I will come back again and again until I do."

"No." She shook her head and tried to confront him.

"Not yet." He turned her face again, tucked her hand back under her cheek, put the other on the arm of the chair.

Then . . . nothing. He was still there, but unmoving, barely breathing.

Looking at her. She knew it, and without self-consciousness knew the sight moved him.

"I should have you painted like this," he said.

"No."

"Taut, regal, glorious."

Her hands went up to the blindfold. "No."

He caught them. "Wait." He kissed the curl of her fingers, then each palm. "I've barely begun." With renewed fervor, he kissed her nipple, then with slow relish drew it into his mouth. He tasted it as if he savored the flavor. His hands settled on her hips, his thumbs brushing her belly. Pleasure prodded her again, a little more intensely, bringing a warmth between her legs. She began to want his hands proceeding with explicit intent along her skin, his mouth kissing more than tasting, his body stroking against hers. She wanted to move restlessly. Soon she would. Soon this would all be too much . . . a tiny moan escaped her. For now, she would let the craving build.

He kissed her belly, and in a moment of madness she let him part her thighs. His lips slid lower. She knew what he intended. Would she let him? Then his fingers brushed her curliest hair. He opened her and settled his mouth in precisely the right spot. Melancholy disappeared, thought scattered, coherence ended. Ecstasy conquered with chills, with delight so irresistible it was almost agony.

His tongue swirled against her, delved inside her. She whimpered with the rapture. His lips drank at her. Her head fell back. One foot rose. She braced it against the seat of the chair. Unable to stop herself, she arched her back. "Dougald." She groped for his head. She caught handfuls of hair, slid her fingers along his scalp. The scent of his excitement acted as an aphrodisiac. "Dougald."

He slid his hands beneath her and lifted her higher. Relentlessly, he followed the movement of her hips, giving no quarter, demanding nothing less than surrender.

At last, with a cry, she gave him what he required.

Instinct triumphed. Dimly she was aware her hands clasped the chair arms. Her back braced against the spindles and her thighs spread. But mostly she knew the pure bliss of release, of a luxurious climax dedicated to her. Only to her.

She finished, finished at last, and as she began to collapse, Dougald invaded. Her bottom rested at the edge of the seat, and he entered her urgently, filling her with his need—and dragging her back to ecstasy. Immediately her body spasmed in his arms, her inner muscles clasping him, requiring that he give everything in him.

"Embrace me." His voice was ragged, commanding.

Her arms rose and enfolded his back. Her legs clamped around his thighs. His hands clamped on the chair, he plunged at her so hard the chair rocked and thumped on the wall. They didn't care; hearing the rhythm of their debauchery increased their vigor. Her blindfold fell away, the knot unbound by their impetus.

His gaze met hers. She saw his beloved face. The beautiful green eyes shot with gold. The blunt, short nose. The high cheekbones. That stubborn jaw, and the long, shining black hair with its streaks of white. And she realized she was crying. She didn't know why. Too much pleasure. Too much pain. Too much bliss. Too much, and never again.

"Darling," he said powerfully. He didn't look away. He claimed everything in her. "Darling."

She was his. Forever his.

He was hers. Forever hers.

This time they climaxed together, pressed together, giving each other everything. She welcomed the surge of his seed, the warmth, the wetness inside her. She had this, at least.

At least he had given her the possibility of his child.

"Darling," he said again. Gradually he came to rest on her. He nuzzled her neck, wiped the tears off of her cheek. "Darling." His voice was fainter, but no less vibrant.

They cleaved together, not wanting to separate, but at last he slipped from her body and knelt before her. "Hannah, I forgot."

He cupped her injured foot and pressed a soft kiss on the curl of her little toe. "Poor foot." He stroked the swollen part with gentle fingers. "So bruised." Surprising her, his palm flattened against her chest. "Poor Hannah. So brave."

She clenched her teeth against the sudden, urgent compulsion to sob aloud. Did his admiration mean so much to her?

No, she was just prone to the weakness pain brought.

She swallowed, hard, and said, "I forgot about my sprain, so I suppose it's not that bad."

He looked down at the foot he held.

He was thinking. Oh, God, she could almost hear his thoughts. She almost knew what he was going to say, and nothing could help her brace for the grief.

Squaring his shoulders, he scrutinized her, nude, exhausted, debauched beyond sense. And he said, "I'll leave the money in your account if you will just go away."

Her tears dried. She was able to speak, and in a steady tone. "You've nothing to worry about, my lord. After Queen Victoria has gone, you can suffer my abandonment again. And this time when I leave, I will never come back."

24

Dougald sat at his desk, hands folded, and listened as they came through the chapel.

"You can't force me to do this! What are you doing, putting your hands on me, you filthy frog? I'm going to have you flogged!"

Dougald recognized the shrill note of panic in Seaton's voice. Charles had properly frightened Seaton.

Now Charles would play his part. "Sir Onslow, I'm sorry. I have no choice. My lord commanded that I bring you, and when I fail him, he . . . ." Charles allowed his voice to trail off. "My lord is a harsh master, Sir Onslow. I dare not disobey."

"It's almost morning light!"

"He commanded your presence the instant you returned from Conniff Manor." Charles kicked the office door open and used a gesture that both released Seaton from his grip and shoved him into the room. "My lord, here is Sir Onslow."

Dougald didn't rise. He didn't move. He knew very

well what he looked like. Night's last darkness had settled in his office, except for the candles that had been carefully placed around him. Each flame illuminated his dark and silver hair, his black jacket, his black cravat, his fixed expression and glittering eyes. If Seaton remembered Dougald's reputation for murder, that was good. If Seaton thought he was facing the devil himself, so much the better.

Because Seaton had tried to kill Hannah. Seaton was going to confess. Seaton was going to pay.

"Sit down." In a slow gesture that set the light sparkling in the gems of his ringed fingers, Dougald indicated a straight-backed chair placed in the middle of the room.

Seaton wore a well-tailored dark jacket, a plaid waistcoat and matching plaid trousers, shining boots and the diamond collar pin which looked so much like Dougald's. Only his rumpled hair showed the rigors of carriage travel, with the usually precisely arranged stands disarrayed by the wind. Such an undistinguished brute; no wonder he had gone undetected for so long and through so many murders.

Now he stared at Dougald's impressive array, and with his lips quivering and his nose in the air, he said, "Is this display of power supposed to impress me?"

Dougald didn't know whether to give him points for audacity or demerits for stupidity. By the time this meeting was over, he would know. "Charles, help Sir Onslow sit down."

"I'll sit!" Seaton had learned respect for Charles's fighting hold.

Too late. Charles twisted Seaton's arm behind his back and pushed him toward the chair.

Seaton walked on his tiptoes to relieve the pressure,

and whimpered, "Ow, ow, ow." Then, as soon as Charles released him, he straightened his cuffs, and said, "That was not necessary."

"I beg your pardon, sir." Charles leaned over and rubbed his hands together, over and over. "Since rumor of the killing got whispered about, I do what my master tells me."

Seaton straightened with a snap. Staring at Dougald, he asked, "Is that what this is about? That I mentioned the tale of your murderous marital tendencies here and there? Because I assure you, I might have added a few details, but most people had already heard the account."

"Of course not, Seaton." Once again, Dougald sat absolutely still. "You're not significant enough for me to care what you say."

"Well, I would hope not!" Realizing the insult too late, Seaton glowered. "Then what am I doing here?"

"It's your other activities which have attracted my attention."

"O . . . other activities?"

Dougald realized how close he was to violence when he had to concentrate on remaining in his chair. He wanted to pummel Seaton until he lost that snippy attitude and a few teeth and confessed everything. Then Dougald would finish removing Seaton's teeth . . .

Dougald took a slow, calming breath. This wasn't about revenge. It was about prevention, and keeping Hannah safe. Because he loved her. Even if he couldn't have her, he loved her. "Seaton, you can't have thought your activities would remain unnoticed forever."

Seaton squirmed, then lifted his snub nose into the

air again. "I . . . I don't know what you're talking about."

Dougald exchanged a glance with Charles. That squirm was as good as a confession of guilt. But Dougald wanted that confession. He wanted the details. He wanted to catch the conspirators and hear what Seaton had planned. Since Hannah had insisted on staying until after the Queen's visit, Dougald had to know everything.

After a lengthy and silent pause, during which Dougald observed Seaton squirm twice more, Dougald said, "It's quite late. I'm tired. Charles says I get disagreeable when I'm tired. I hope you don't keep me at this for very long, or my patience will run out."

Leaning closer to Seaton, Charles in an obsequious tone, said, "It's best to confess to the master before he grows irate."

Seaton's gaze slid back and forth between his two interrogators, and he did a little interrogating of his own. "Is that what made him kill his wife? A jealous rage?"

Rubbing his hands again, Charles said, "No, sir. He wasn't jealous at all."

Dougald barely maintained his gravity. Charles was enjoying this a little too much. As Dougald would be, if the situation were not so serious. "Charles, you overstep your bounds."

Charles cowered back to the far wall.

After a long, hard stare, Dougald turned his attention back to Seaton. "Now, I want your confession, and I want it now. What foolish little action have you been taking?"

Seaton glanced at Charles, then at Dougald. "Nothing. I haven't been . . ."

Dougald began to stand.

Charles whimpered.

Seaton changed his tone and his intent. "That is . . . I . . . I didn't think that you knew . . ."

Dougald reseated himself. "Confess."

Squaring his padded shoulders, Seaton said, "I'll return it all."

Dougald didn't have to feign confusion. "Return . . . it . . . all."

Seaton clasped his forehead. "It was that necklace that gave me away, wasn't it? The one I took from Mrs. Grizzle?"

Still not comprehending, Dougald stared at Seaton, his distant cousin, the man who was confessing . . . to the wrong crime.

Charles took over the interrogation. "You took a necklace from Mrs. Grizzle?"

Seaton glanced around and realized he had guessed wrong. He tried again. "Not the necklace? Then it was vases. Lady McCarn's prize Ming vases. They were too big, but such a challenge I don't know how anyone could expect I wouldn't be tempted."

Dougald recovered enough to string words, and thoughts, together. "You took Lady McCarn's prize Ming vases. You *stole*—"

"Not *stole*. *Stole* is such an ugly word. I . . . gathered the vases. They look quite lovely in my bedchamber." Clearly, Seaton didn't know what to make of Dougald's dumbfounded expression, and in a typically Seaton diversion, he shifted the blame. "It's your fault, Lord Raeburn, that I needed to decorate my own bedchamber. You can't expect a man of delicacy to reside in that disgrace of a room, and you wouldn't spend the blunt to make my habitation worthy of me."

"I felt that the family rooms should be done first . . ." Dougald realized he was excusing himself to a thief, and snapped, "Redecorating your bedchamber doesn't explain a stolen necklace. I assume you're selling the jewelry for cash."

Seaton placed his hand on his chest. "*I* am a gentleman. I don't sell the things I gather!"

Baffled, Dougald tried to clarify. "You . . . keep them?"

"Of course."

"What do you do with them?"

"I look at them." As Seaton realized Dougald would allow him to live, he relaxed. He leaned back in his chair and in a chatty tone related, "I have quite an extensive collection. You can come and gaze on it sometime."

If Seaton was seeking to distract Dougald, he was doing a dazzling job. "You still have everything."

"Indeed."

"Then I will take you up on your offer. You will return it all."

Seaton's eyes widened. He sat up straight. His hands clenched. "Not really? To whom?"

"The owners."

Panic filled Seaton's voice. "People will not understand. They will think badly of me."

Charles used his most soothing tone. "A master such as you will be able to replace the items so that the owners will believe them simply misplaced."

"But *I* won't have them."

"You can do it, or I'll do it for you."

At Dougald's less-than-subtle threat, Seaton gave a sob. "The jewelry? The ceramics? The paintings?"

"Paintings?" Dougald could imagine Seaton taking a large painting off the wall, hiding it under his coat and slipping out.

"Did I say paintings?" Seaton dabbed at his eyes with a lace-trimmed handkerchief. "I meant . . ."

"The paintings, too." Dougald didn't know whether to laugh or join Seaton in tears.

"This is an outrage!"

"I couldn't agree more." Obviously the servants had to know about Seaton's little idiosyncrasy.

"I don't have to submit to such an indignity."

"You do if you want to continue living here." At least one of Dougald's neighbors must have noticed the losses associated with Seaton's visits.

Seaton pulled his gloves out of his pocket and slapped them against his palm. "Such cruelty and lack of refinement would cause yet another stain on your reputation."

"If I have survived the rumors of murder, which you have taken such care to spread, I believe I could survive the ignominy of turning out my brigand heir." Dougald couldn't imagine what kind of rumors followed in *Seaton's* wake.

Seaton stood. "Such an ugly word—*brigand*. Very well. I shall do as you wish. But may the results be on your head!"

Charles opened the door, and Seaton stalked out.

As Charles shut the door, Dougald leaned his head into his hands. He was tired. He was worried. For the first time in years, he didn't know what to do next. "Charles, do you think Seaton pulled the wool over our eyes?"

Enigmatically, Charles replied, "I will speak to the detectives again."

Dougald lifted his head and stared at his valet, silently demanding a better answer.

Charles yielded. "No, my lord, I suspect Sir Onslow is just as you accused—merely a petty thief."

"We have no other suspects."

"Not at this moment, my lord."

"You must continue to watch over *Madame*."

"As always," Charles proclaimed.

Another, lesser suspicion struck Dougald. "I suppose that diamond collar pin Seaton wears that looks so much like mine—is mine."

"I thought I had misplaced it."

Dougald met his valet's cynically amused gaze. "I never liked it anyway."

25

$\mathcal{S}$he would never be pleasured again. Morosely, Hannah sat in the afternoon sun in the aunts' workroom and stitched the pieces of Prince Albert's face together. The weight of a man, the press of his chest against hers, the sounds, the smells, the friction, the closeness . . . never again.

"That's Prince Albert's eyebrow, not his chin!" Miss Minnie plucked the weaving out of Hannah's hand.

Miss Minnie was certainly cantankerous today.

Hannah moved to sit next to Aunt Spring.

"Would you thread me a needle, dear?" Aunt Spring suggested.

The first time Hannah had left Dougald and his lovemaking behind, she had been stoic—because, she now realized, she'd been too much of a looby to realize what she was giving up. Now she knew. The scrape of a morning beard across her breasts when he suckled her. The texture of rough hair against her palms when she stroked his chest. Silken strands of his mane falling around her face when he kissed her. And he'd allowed Charles to cut his hair!

To put in a proper appearance before Her Majesty, Charles had said.

To spite her, Hannah thought.

"Not that color, dear." Aunt Spring pointed at the gold thread. "That color. Wherever is your mind?"

Hannah blinked at her.

"Never mind." Aunt Spring gave her a gentle push. "I'll get one of the serving maids to thread my needle."

Hannah made her way to the looms.

Although if Dougald had been happy these last four days, Hannah had seen confounded little evidence of it. Rather he looked haggard, as if he'd been getting little peace and less sleep.

Hannah hoped so. She hoped he was miserable. She hoped every time he saw her at the breakfast table, every time he heard her call to the aunts, every time he thought of her, he felt guilty, distressed, angry . . . but she couldn't lie to herself. Actually, what she wanted him to feel was the torments of the flesh. She hoped he looked at her and his cock rose and crowed.

Heaven knew she'd been dressing to encourage his refractory instincts. Every night she stayed awake late, stitching on her gowns—lowering the necklines, tightening the waists, adding a ruffle of lace on her petticoats or her pantalettes. Every day she made sure he viewed her cleavage, her ankle . . . her smile. He would never know she suffered when she gazed at him, imagining how empty her flesh would always be, how she would wither and grow old alone, without the comfort of a husband. A lover. Dougald.

The treadles thumped and the shuttles flew as Aunt

Isabel and Aunt Ethel wove the last bits of the Queen's tapestry.

The old women's shoulders sagged, their eyes were bloodshot, but their lips were set in firm determination. Two days hence, just before noon, Queen Victoria would arrive in her royally outfitted train car. With the help of the maids, who fetched and carried anything the aunts might need, and Hannah, who organized and lent a hand, the tapestry would be complete and hanging on the wall in the great hall, majestic in its splendor.

Hannah was satisfied she had done her part—in between imagining, with the faintest of smiles, how she could further torment Dougald. She had to move quickly; she had little time, after all, before she would leave Raeburn Castle. She had little time before she saw the Queen again, before she was introduced to the Burroughses and told them who she was.

Her eyes narrowed. Dougald had better be willing to produce the packet of love letters as proof of her parentage, or she would be forced to . . . to . . . stay here until he did.

She laughed bitterly.

Aunt Ethel's loom slowed. "What's so funny, dear?"

Hannah stared at her. "What?"

Aunt Ethel handed her a piece of the weaving that would soon be placed within the tapestry. "Dear, your needlework is so delicate. Minnie outlined a crown there to be stitched. Would you like to work on it?"

"Of course, ma'am, to help you is what I'm here for." Hannah took the tapestry and dipped the already threaded needle into the weaving

Dougald would produce her father's love letters to

her mother, because he had made it clear he would do anything to get rid of her.

She had abandoned him.

She hadn't really tried to make their marriage work.

Which just showed that man had rats in his garret. She'd done everything she could to make their marriage work, and nothing he had said had caused her the slightest doubt that her efforts had been of the highest order. No doubt. Not the slightest.

He'd been the one at fault. For everything!

"Dear, what are you doing? It's supposed to be a crown of beaten gold, not a raw nugget."

Aunt Ethel snatched the tapestry away from Hannah while Hannah blinked in astonishment. A quick glance showed the needlework to be slightly less than perfect, yes, but she considered the aunts to have been remarkably unappreciative of her efforts to help them. Oh, perhaps she had been a little distracted, but surely—

Aunt Isabel's shuttle slowed. "Miss Setterington, dear, would you please go elsewhere? It irritates me when you sit there in a brown study. Brace up, girl! The Queen is coming!"

Hannah dragged her attention to Aunt Isabel. "I irritate you?"

Something about her expression must have alarmed the two old ladies, because Aunt Ethel muttered, "Now you've done it."

Aunt Isabel waved her hands. "No, no, not irritate. Only when I'm peckish, then everything irritates me."

"And Isabel must be hungry, for she's been as cross as the colonel's cat," Aunt Ethel said. "You'd be doing me a favor, Miss Setterington, if you would seek out Mrs. Trenchard and see if tea is on its way up."

"One of the maids—"

"No, not one of the maids!" Aunt Isabel caught herself. "I mean . . . I swear the maids wander off, their minds on their shattered love affairs, and they never deliver the message, and we're up here famished. Please, Miss Setterington, we trust you."

That made sense to Hannah.

Miss Minnie and Aunt Spring came to stand by the looms and watch her as she drifted out of the chamber in search of Mrs. Trenchard.

"She's walking well," Aunt Ethel said. "Her ankle has healed nicely."

"Yes, but she's brooding." Aunt Spring held her needle, gold thread dangling. "Now we have Dougald *and* Hannah brooding."

"I've had to take out every piece of work she's done for the last two days, and there's no time for this." Exasperation sounded plain in Miss Minnie's voice.

"I vow, when she hurt her foot she lost her mind," Aunt Ethel said.

Aunt Isabel's chin set. "Perhaps we should sit them both down and give them a good lecture."

Aunt Spring patted Aunt Isabel's shoulder. "Now, dear, we shouldn't interfere."

"But we will," Miss Minnie said. "If they don't work it out on their own soon, we will definitely interfere." She swept them all with a leveling glance. "Please do remember my conviction."

"Minnie, I told you, that's the balmiest thing I've ever heard," Aunt Ethel said.

"I never wager unless I'm sure I'm right." Miss Minnie cracked a rarely used and utterly complacent smile. "Now, back to work, ladies. We have the Queen's tapestry to finish."

* * *

Charles caught Hannah as she descended the stairs. "*Mademoiselle* Setterington, I was given a message for you from His Lordship."

Hannah stared down at Dougald's valet. He stood a step below her, allowing her an exceptional view of his bald spot. He had been hanging about a lot lately. She'd glimpsed him watching her as she walked the corridors, she'd seen him peering at her when she spoke to Seaton, she had even had him escort her from her bedchamber to the breakfast room.

If she'd been in the mood to care, his obsessive gawking and his constant presence would have annoyed her. But what did it matter if her old enemy hated her for not leaving as his master demanded? She would be gone soon enough, and Charles could find Dougald a real wife, one who was dewy and meek and deferential. And stupid. And ugly. And infertile. With a hidden mean streak.

Cheered by the thought, Hannah said, "I thought His Lordship was out inspecting the gardens." Then she wished she had kept her mouth shut, because if she didn't care she wouldn't have remembered Dougald's schedule.

"*Oui, Mademoiselle* Setterington, but one of the maids brought me this and asked that I give it to you." He offered the folded paper. "As you know, I live to serve you and the master."

Hannah wondered if wild laughter was inappropriate, then decided it was too much effort. "Very well." She accepted the note with ill grace and stuffed it into her apron pocket.

"Aren't you going to read it?"

"It's not sealed, so I'm sure you read it. What does it say?"

Charles snapped to attention. "I do not read the master's letters to his beloved wife."

"Sh." Hannah glanced around. A maid knelt on one of the upper steps, scrubbing and waxing. In the corridor, a footman balanced on a ladder, dusting the cornice. If they had heard Charles identify her as Dougald's wife, they gave no notice.

"*Madame*, we cannot keep your title a secret. Everyone must know soon."

"Not until I'm gone."

"You're not leaving."

"Indeed I am."

Charles stepped closer and lowered his voice. "His Lordship cannot wed another woman because of the shameful rumors of your murder. If you divorce, it will be expensive and disgraceful, and again he will not be able to wed. So one way or another, you must stay."

Hannah watched his expressive nostrils quiver. Charles wanted her to stay? How unlikely. Yet . . . why would he say it if it were not true?

She knew the answer to that. She wanted to leave, and Charles made it his policy to want the opposite.

Hannah snorted.

"Completely unladylike," Charles scolded.

"I have to find Mrs. Trenchard." Turning her back on the pompous little gump, she hurried down the stairs.

"In his note, His Lordship might be expressing his desire to see you immediately," Charles called.

She walked backward down the corridor. "He doesn't always get what he desires."

"If I can help it . . ."

She turned the corner into the sparkling clean great hall and Charles's voice faded. Did he always have to have the last word?

Yet . . . she slowed. Curiosity nibbled at her. Why
had Dougald sent her a note? She drew it from her
pocket. He had scarcely spoken to her these last days,
and now he had taken the time to write a note and send
it in from the gardens. What did it mean? Was this a
drastic attempt to get rid of her before Her Majesty arrived? Or did he yearn to beg her pardon, to beg her to
stay?

Moving as cautiously as if the note contained an ambush, she spread the sheet and read the simple message.

*Hannah, come to the tower room in the east wing. I
have an idea for the Queen's visit, and I wish to consult with you.*

Not an insult. Not a plea. She stared at the thin,
black handwriting. Just a request that she attend him.
Consult with him . . . *consult with you*. He never
wished to consult with her, so what did this mean?
Was it some kind of apology? Did he want to get her
alone and beg her forgiveness?

Outrageous. Absurd.

She liked the notion.

She started back.

Of course, she wouldn't forgive Dougald. He didn't
deserve forgiveness—stupid man who thought she was
responsible for part of their breakup. It wasn't true. It
just wasn't.

As she approached the stairway, she looked for
Charles, but he had disappeared. She breathed a sigh
of relief; she didn't want him to know she had given in
and read Dougald's note. Stopping, she read it again.
Why in the east wing tower?

Hannah passed the maid on the stairway.

Perhaps Dougald thought of taking Queen Victoria
to the top to show her the view.

As she trod the corridors to the east wing, Hannah saw only one footman, carrying a bucket of sudsy water.

Perhaps Dougald had heard how Queen Victoria liked to hear local legends. Perhaps he had some fanciful notion of telling her the tale of Lord Raeburn's bride and how that wife had loved unwisely, been imprisoned by her husband, and jumped to her death. It wasn't a bad idea; the picturesque tale would probably enthrall Her Majesty.

Hannah had never been in the tower; the tale of old Lord Raeburn's rage with his young wife was too close to her own story, and Hannah had taken care to busy herself elsewhere. But now the door to the tower stairway stood open, and when she walked through it, she found herself transported back to the fifteenth century.

Romantic nonsense, of course, but the west wing's tower had been used for years by the aunts, making it look well tended in contrast to this east tower. The west tower had plaster on the walls and a wooden stairway no older than Aunt Spring herself. In this tower, the only illumination came through the narrow, long slits in the stone, remnants of the days when archers repelled a siege. In the dim half-light, the winding stairway clung to rough stone walls. The steps themselves looked as if they might had seen Lord Raeburn drag his French bride into her prison. And that prison was reached, not by a new and civilized landing and stairway, but by a trapdoor and a wooden ladder. The whole structure seemed steeped in a hoary chill. The light from the chamber above shone only faintly, and inside, Lady Raeburn's ghost probably still wept for her lost lover.

Hannah shivered. Romantic nonsense, indeed, but she didn't like this place.

Whatever Dougald wanted to consult about, the answer was *no*. Queen Victoria wouldn't want to see the view, she wouldn't want to hear the tale of the Raeburn bride, and most important, she wouldn't want to climb that ladder. *Hannah* didn't want to climb the ladder, but curiosity drove her.

Was Dougald already up there?

The memory of her accident proceeded with her as she tested every step. Her ankle still ached faintly; her wariness increased as she climbed.

If Dougald was in the tower, wouldn't he have already acknowledged her presence? She wasn't being quiet. As she got closer to the top, she called his name. "Lord Raeburn?" Then, as she put her hand on the ladder, she said, "Dougald?"

No answer, but the note hadn't said he would be there when she arrived. Should she have waited at the bottom and gone up with him? Cautiously she clung to the railings as she took each creaking rung. When she popped her head into the tower room, she realized the chamber was a twin to the aunts' workroom in size, but in every other way it was neglected, unused, sad—and empty of Dougald.

She climbed the last few steps. A few old, broken pieces of furniture had found their way up here. The floorboards were bare of everything, even dust. The windows gaped without glass or draperies, and had only shutters to keep out the weather. The thatched roof thinned in places; sunlight trickled through carrying motes that drifted without aim. Hannah thought of herself as a sensible, no-nonsense woman, but the age and emptiness fed a soul-deep sorrow.

The gaping maw of the trapdoor made her ankle

ache, and prudently she closed it. Moving with the stealth of a mourner at a funeral, she moved across to the south-facing window and unlatched the shutters. They swung wide, opening the room to sunshine. The sense of abandonment deepened. The view faced the empty side of the castle where no gardens grew and no people wandered. This tower had paid the price for its notoriety.

She wanted to look beyond, to see the panorama beyond this room. Yet she well remembered how the wall dropped from her bedroom window, and this would be worse, much worse. So she leaned back, then lifted her gaze toward the horizon. There she could see the bluish haze of the sky over the ocean, then the waves on the beach, then the undulating hills, and in the valleys the fields bright with the earliest spring growth. She could have made Lancashire her home. She could have loved this combination of land and sea. She could have . . . she did.

She did love this place, and she would come back— if all went well and her grandparents would have her. And Dougald would be here, at Raeburn Castle, perhaps married to another woman, perhaps steeping in his own bitterness. Hannah couldn't save him. She couldn't even save herself.

Leaning against the casement, she crossed her arms across her chest and stared fixedly at the vista. How she hated to admit it! Yet what good did it do to lie to herself? The truth was, and the irony was—the lies she had told herself at eighteen were true. At eighteen, she had given herself to Dougald because she loved him. And here, in Raeburn Castle, she had given herself to Dougald because she loved him still. No matter how angry she was, no matter how he'd hurt her, no matter who was responsible for the ruin of their marriage—she would always love him.

The metallic squawk of a hinge had her whirling around. Dougald stood there, holding a piece of paper out to her. With knit brow and wary gaze, he asked, "Hannah? What did you want?"

26

"*H*annah? What's wrong? You look odd." Dougald strode toward her, then stopped short. He straightened to stand stiffly, and when he spoke, he used his most pretentious tone. "Whatever it is you had to tell me, it better be important. I haven't a lot of time if we're to get the drive prepared before Her Majesty arrives."

"I thought you were supervising in the garden," she said, then cursed herself for her inanity. It was only that—he had looked as if he'd been about to embrace her. He'd spoken to her without being forced by the demands of society. He'd come at her summons. Except . . . "I didn't ask you to come here. You asked me."

"I assure you, I did not." Spreading his note wide, he showed it to her.

She glanced at it. *Dougald, Meet me in the east wing tower. I have something of great importance to tell you.* "That's not my handwriting."

"It isn't?" He frowned and inspected it. "If you say so, but how was I to know? It's not as if you wrote me every week while you were abroad."

She contained her impulse to throttle him and pulled his note from her pocket. "Here's yours."

He looked it over. "Not my handwriting," he said in a clipped tone. "But how would you know? I couldn't write you. I didn't know where you were."

How he provoked her! "I came up here because I thought you wanted to consult me about some detail in regard to the Queen's visit. I should have known you wouldn't be so logical as to ask my opinion just because Her Majesty and I are acquainted and I might know something about her preferences."

"And don't you love to remind me of that." He crumpled the note he held and dropped it to the floor. "You left me and did so well for yourself you're now a woman of independent means who has friends of the highest caliber. Whilst I have remained in northern England and garnered a reputation as a murderer." He placed his hands on the wall on either side of her. "*Your* murderer."

She crumpled her note, too, and tossed it at his chest in a telling and, she freely admitted, petty gesture that relieved a great deal of her aggravation. "I am not boasting"—maybe a little—"and it's not my fault you didn't deny that you'd killed me."

"For all the good that would have done me. No one would have believed, except for those few who took the occasion to laugh at me because I couldn't even keep my wife at home. I ought to take this occasion to fling you out this window . . ." His voice trailed off. His brow knit.

"Go ahead, bully. Try and throw me to my death. Another Raeburn wife destroyed. Another tale added to the legend of the earl of Raeburn's lousy—" A thought occurred to her, and she stopped. "Dougald, if you didn't write and I didn't write, why are we up here?"

"Blast!" He leaped for the trapdoor and stopped short. "It's closed."

She approached slowly. "Closed. Who closed it?"

Kneeling, he tugged at the handle. "There's the question, isn't it?"

She didn't care for his tone. He acted as if he knew something. Something he hesitated to disclose. "Dougald, what are you talking about? What's going on?"

He braced himself and pulled without replying.

"Dougald, who sent the notes?"

Stepping on the trapdoor, he looked first at a large, scratched hutch, then at a smaller cupboard, then glanced at the lighter furniture in the tower. "The same someone who is trying to kill the earl of Raeburn and his wife."

She lifted her hand, then let it drop. "That's you and me." Suddenly she made sense of this last ghastly week. "That's you and me."

"Exactly." He pointed. "Please, would you hand me that table?"

She stared at the simple wooden end table with the broken leg. "What are you going to do with a table? Decorate?"

"I will hit whoever sticks his head through this trapdoor."

"Oh." The table was small and light, and Dougald was clever to think of it.

"In the meantime, I'm using my weight to thwart any attempts to enter."

She picked up the table and carried it to him. "But nobody knows that I'm your wife. Except—"

"It's not Charles." He positioned the table beside the trapdoor and cautiously stepped off. "I wish you would get over your unhealthy prejudice against him."

"Unhealthy? Charles gave me that note. He had to have known it wasn't from you."

He barely glanced at her. "We'll ask when we see him, but I'm sure there's a logical explanation."

He might have been a parent using his most strained and patient voice, but she recognized his tactic. He was trying to distract her. "Someone is trying to kill the earl of Raeburn—and you were beat to a pulp. Someone has already tried to kill you?"

"Um . . . yes." He hefted the table in one hand. "I don't know why he locked us in, though."

Horror and fury mixed in her mind. "To give me time to get to the bottom of this!"

Keeping his gaze on the trapdoor, he said, "You know everything now."

"Do I? Have there been any other attempts on you?"

"No, but I've been very careful." He flashed her a smile. "Thanks to you, I haven't been riding out at night."

The smile was an effort at distraction, too, but nothing could keep her from the truth. "After I fell through the landing, you realized someone was after me, too, and you didn't want me to be hurt so you tried to send me away."

"Yes!" He was obviously relieved she understood. "That's exactly right."

She sucker punched him in the ribs and followed that up with a stiff clip to the cheek.

He dropped the chair and staggered backward.

"You beast. You put me through hell!"

"With good intentions!"

"So I wouldn't be a target and you would be." She heard herself. She was yelling.

Dabbing at his face, he spoke in an absently superior tone. "I knew I wouldn't get hurt and feared for *you*."

"Not get hurt?" She stalked him. "Like you didn't get hurt when those men beat you up?"

"They shot at me first."

His confession jerked her to a halt. "They shot at you?"

Dougald stared at the trapdoor to avoid her gaze. "Yes, and I let us get trapped in here—"

Fury returned with a roar. She rained blows on him, not good, solid punches now, but girlish, rhythmic thumping on his chest, his arms, anywhere she could reach.

He flinched and tried to avoid her.

"You stupid jackass," she railed. "You tiresome cad. You worthless—"

Finally, he caught her wrists. "It's not so bad."

"That's why you said those things to me. You were trying to send me away so I wouldn't get hurt."

He had the good sense to look apologetic. "Yes . . ."

Apologetic wasn't enough. Apologetic didn't repair the damage he'd done to her soul, to her heart. "Who do you think I am? Some kind of quivering limp piece of flotsam who washes out at the first sign of danger?"

"That's not at all what I think." He glanced at the trapdoor.

"You think I'm a coward." She struggled to be free so she could hit him again. "You think I'd leave you to face an assassin while I run away to the city."

"Hannah." Still holding her wrists, he turned her in his arms so she faced into the room, her back to his front, her arms crossed across her waist and her wrists in his hands. "The last thing I think is that you're a coward. I think you're too brave for your own good. I was afraid you would do something foolish like hunt out the villain, or stand between me and a pistol."

"Don't flatter yourself." Tears sprang to her eyes. Tears of frustration and scorn she told herself. Not tears of hurt. "You said those things to me . . . you destroyed me . . . and you think that doing it for my safety is excuse enough?"

"An assassin could have captured you and threatened you."

She understood in a heartbeat. "And you would have had to sacrifice me for the good of the Pippard name."

He dropped her wrists. "Is *that* what you think?"

Blinking to clear the tears from her eyes, she faced him. "When have you ever given me any reason to think differently?"

They faced each other, adversaries still and forever. Perhaps her skepticism hurt him; she didn't know. All she knew was that they were caught in a legendary tower haunted by the ghosts of all the previous Lord Raeburns' accursed marriages, and unless a miracle occurred they would join the infamous and unbroken line. "Dougald, you said you had lured me to Raeburn Castle to use me and since you had succeeded, you didn't want me anymore."

"I didn't . . ." He held his hands as if he wanted to grab her. "That wasn't quite the truth."

"The truth would be nice for a change."

"You won't think so when I tell you." His laughter contained a sharp blade of amusement, although who it was directed at, she couldn't tell. "I found you in London and trapped you here for one reason—to be my wife. But first, I planned to compel you to fall in love with me. Then I would suitably subjugate you."

"Think well of yourself, don't you?" The trouble was, he could possibly have succeeded. But she would not tell him that. "What made you change your mind?"

"I still wanted you." He sounded gruff and rushed. "I didn't mean to. I thought nothing could lay waste to the discipline I had so carefully cultivated, but you did. Right from the first moment, I hated the way you made me . . ."

He couldn't even say the word. "Feel?"

He shook his head. Not in denial, but at his own vulnerability. His green eyes glowed, and abruptly he said, "I still want you."

She expected to feel gratification. Instead she discovered she had never truly doubted his desire.

As for love . . . even in the first flush of their marriage, she had distrusted his love, and with good reason. He had wed her expediently. While fond of her, he had loved money, wealth and power more. Now time and loneliness had left their scars on a belligerent soul, turning his defiance to bitterness—and injustice. "But do you still blame me for leaving you?"

The glow in his eyes dimmed. His elegant lips thinned. Once again he looked like the cold, emotionless lord who had welcomed her to his castle and threatened her with murder—and worse.

When he didn't reply, that was answer enough for her. In a low voice, she protested, "It wasn't my fault our marriage ended. How can you believe it was my fault?"

Still he gave no explanation. He refused to admit he was wrong.

Another glance at his cold expression changed her mind. He refused to *accept* he was wrong.

The creak of a hinge sounded loud in the telling silence.

Annoyed, distracted, she glanced around. She looked once. Twice.

The trapdoor lurched upward.

She pointed. "Dougald? Who—"

Dougald pushed her aside. She landed on her weak ankle. With a cry, she went down on one knee. Pain burned through the abused muscles and tendons, but she caught herself before she fell. She clutched the windowsill, and dragged herself back up in time to see the chair shattering on the trapdoor.

Alfred. Alfred, big, healthy, dirty. He ducked, then he was back, a pistol cocked and in his grip.

In a swift gesture Dougald grabbed him by the hair and the collar and dragged him into the tower chamber. Like a troll caught in a trap, Alfred howled, a mad light in his pale blue eyes. The pistol spit fire; the thunder rolled around the stone walls. A flurry of black thread and red blood exploded into the air above Dougald's shoulder. "Damn you!" Dougald recoiled.

The single-shot pistol was useless now, so Alfred struggled, hitting Dougald with the smoking barrel. Still Dougald dragged Alfred with him.

Toward the open window.

Hannah wanted to scream with fear, but drops of blood spattered the floor. Dougald had been hit. Alfred landed a blow on the side of Dougald's head. Dougald staggered like a man in distress and Alfred slithered from his grasp.

Dougald needed help.

Hannah sprang toward them. She struck Alfred from the side, knocking him into the wall.

Reaching into the pocket of his grubby jacket, Alfred pulled forth another pistol.

"Don't!" With both hands extended, Hannah shoved at him.

The pistol wildly wavered. "She's goin' t' kill me," Alfred said. The barrel straightened and pointed at her.

As Alfred's finger tightened on the trigger, Dougald shoved him out the window. The shot echoed up, bringing a flurry of thatch raining down on their heads.

But Dougald and Hannah watched in horror as Alfred fell silently, all the way to the ground.

Hannah turned away before he landed. "God rest his soul."

"I don't know that God will even see him." Dougald pulled his head in. "For the murder of two lords and the attempted murder of you and I, I imagine he will receive damnation."

Hannah thought about the events of the last minutes. "It wasn't Alfred who committed those murders," she said with conviction.

"No. Not on his own." Pale and sweating, Dougald leaned against the wall. "I fear there'll be no rescue for us. No one saw him fall."

"Dougald!" Hannah wrapped her arms around her husband. He hugged her back, and the sensation of his arms around her gave her a warmth she had not experienced for two days. For too long, and now he was shot. "Sit down."

"Yes." Slowly his eyes closed, and he folded over onto the floor. "I think I must."

Frantic, she tried to hold him up, but his weight and the revived throbbing in her ankle dragged her down with him. Cradling his head in her lap, she moaned. "Are you dead?" She groped for the pulse in his neck.

It raced beneath her fingers.

"You're *not* dead." Stating the obvious gave her a bizarre kind of comfort.

His head lolled sideways into her torso.

In a frantic bargain with the Almighty, she said, "If You will just allow Dougald to live, I'll be just the kind of wife he always wanted." She ran her hands over his shoulders, but she couldn't find the bullet hole. Yet she had seen that spray of thread and those drops of blood, so she searched again. "I'll do whatever he says, if you'll allow him to keep"—she found the place where the bullet had struck him—"breathing,"

She looked into his face.

He watched her through those marvelously piercing eyes. "Would you repeat that, please, with your hand on a Bible?"

The bullet had sliced through the fleshy part of his shoulder above his collarbone and exited within an inch of its penetration. She knew it hurt him; it most certainly had not killed him. "You . . . you're barely injured!"

He shifted, trying to make himself comfortable. "It burns like hell."

"Don't you try and bamboozle me, Lord Raeburn. That beating you suffered was worse." She tried to push his head away.

He wrapped his arm around her waist.

After a moment of halfhearted struggle, she yielded. Because he was bleeding, although the wound was already clotting. Because the struggle with Alfred had frightened her out of what few wits she had left. Because he was Dougald, and she loved him.

Foolish Hannah, in love for years with a man who wanted her and hated wanting her, then blamed her because she found such an arrangement unfair and left. "You don't deserve a good wife."

He tucked his head closer to her bosom. "I don't want a good wife. I want you."

"Is that supposed to flatter me?"

"Doesn't it?"

Sadly enough, it did. To hear him say he wanted her for his wife, regardless of her lack of skill at living the traditional wedded life, or even sticking with it . . . well, she wanted to smile at him.

But she kept her head. They had been fighting before Alfred made his appearance, and what had just happened amply illustrated his idiocy. As his wife, it was her job to point that out. "You stepped between me and a pistol."

"Of course." Painfully he lifted himself onto his elbow. Her eyes were at his level, and he stared into them with soulful solemnity. "No matter what you think, Hannah, I wouldn't sacrifice you for the Pippard name."

She ignored the soulfulness and the solemnity, and concentrated on making her point. "Yet you didn't want me to step between you and a pistol. How is what you did any better?"

"I'm a man."

She lashed him with scorn. "People with dangly parts are better equipped to stop a bullet?"

His long, dark lashes lowered, and in a tone of absolute sincerity, he said, "I assure you, at this moment none of my parts are dangly."

She tried to speak. Took a breath and tried again. Scorn and a burning sense of justice was not proof against the realization that neither a quarrel nor a shooting could stop him from wanting her.

And when he smiled at her, she wondered crazily if desire would be, could be enough.

At last she managed to stammer, "You shouldn't have taken a chance with your life."

"I'm not going to argue with you about this, Hannah." He took her hand and kissed it. "You are wrong. Just accept that. But in this case, honor demanded I save you from a bullet. I'm the reason you are in danger."

"Were in danger."

He sighed. "I wish that were true, but Seaton is still at large. He's the one who told me to come to the tower. He must be the killer."

"You think that, and you weren't suspicious?"

His cheeks colored faintly. "I had decided it wasn't him, and then I thought you had asked to see me, I . . . well, I was foolish."

She liked seeing his flush, knowing he had come running for her. "And you're wrong. It's not Seaton." She stared out the window where Alfred had disappeared. "But I know who it is."

27

$\mathcal{D}$ougald's arm felt slightly numb and his fingertips throbbed, although he thought the problem with his fingertips was more of a desire to grab Hannah and steal her away than any reaction to his wound. "Don't be ridiculous," he stated flatly.

She argued with him. Of course. "Why ridiculous? Don't you remember what Alfred said before he fell out of the window? '*She's* goin' t' kill me.' He was more afraid of *her* than that fall."

As they descended the tower stairway, Dougald kept his good arm firmly locked with Hannah's. She was, after all, still limping, and after the scuffle in the tower, she moved with deliberate care and leaned against the handrail. "I agree it might be a *she* who gave him his orders," he said.

"Also, why close the trapdoor and lock us in? Once we noticed that, we had time to work on our strategy."

"We?" He loved that she took credit for his planning. "*I* was decorating with a table."

Disgruntled, she frowned at him. "Are you through being superior, my lord Peacock?"

"Watch your step," he advised. "The handrail is shaky here." He cast a glance below. The spiral stairway hid much of the floor from view. Someone could be lurking below in the late-afternoon shadows, although he had neither seen nor heard anything.

He noted, also, that the door to the tower had been closed. Had Alfred done so when he came up? Or had someone else with the intention of shooting them when they came through?

If Hannah was aware of the danger, she hid her concern with the fiery desire to convince him she was right. In her most persuasive tone, she said, "If it was a woman who followed us up the stairs, then she would have shut the trapdoor and fetched her conspirator to kill us."

"Why? A pistol functions as well in the hand of a woman."

"That wouldn't have worked with her plan."

"How do you know her plan?"

Hannah shrugged. "Because I would do the same."

He never meant anything so much as when he said, "Hannah, sometimes you frighten me."

Stopping, she looked at him. "As you frighten me. But after the scene above, I no longer wonder if you are going to kill me."

"Not today."

She smiled and started down again. "That woman was going to make it look as if ours was one of the cursed noble Raeburn marriages. Alfred was going to shoot you first. Then he was going to throw me out the window."

"He couldn't throw you out the window. He was not a young man. He would have used that second pistol on you."

"No, that was for a spare. Which he needed, I might add. And he was large enough to take me on and win."

Dougald recalled Alfred's build. Broad and tall.

Alfred's involvement had surprised Dougald. He hadn't thought the shiftless yeoman with his rheumy eyes and shaking hands could be part of an ongoing plot to kill the lords of Raeburn Castle. Yet the prospect that Alfred might have got his hands on Hannah made Dougald shudder.

Hannah didn't seem to expect a response. She just clung more tightly to him. "After he'd shot you and thrown me out, he was going to put the pistol in your hand. When it was discovered who I was, everyone would say you tossed me out and shot yourself."

Dougald was appalled. "Hannah, you have a criminal mind."

She seemed to ponder that. "I suppose. I prefer to think of it as analytical."

"What about the fact that Seaton handed me the note that sent me to the top of the tower? That is proof that *he* instigated the plan to rid Raeburn Castle of us."

Hannah did not accept his skepticism with any amount of grace. "Well, *Charles* gave *me* the note, so ha!" She stuck out her tongue at him.

He wanted to retaliate by taking her tongue in his mouth, but the woman insisted they behave with logical caution and seek out the true assassin. She wanted to be involved in the search, which proved he was right in keeping the truth from her as long as possible.

But damn, the matter had waited this long. It could

wait a little longer while he took Hannah up to his bed-chamber and indulged in all the fantasies he'd been unable to fulfill these last days.

"Charles must be a dupe." If he was not, then Dougald had been a bigger one. "We'll find him and ask the name of the maid who gave him the note."

"And find Seaton and ask who gave him the note," Hannah retorted.

"If we must."

"I don't know how you could have *ever* thought it was Seaton."

"He is the heir."

"He doesn't want the title." She shook her head at Dougald's lack of perception. "He's a fribble. He wants to gossip and play. He doesn't want the responsibility that comes with the legacy."

Dougald didn't answer because he didn't want to tell her that, for the most part, all evidence agreed. The three gentleman detectives had followed Seaton on his visits. His only suspicious activity had been that he "found" Mrs. Grizzle's lost necklace between the cushions of a sofa and been hailed as a hero.

Dougald and Hannah reached the floor without incident, and he examined the area for hiding places and weapons. There was nothing; no place to hide and nothing for him to take for defense. Easing his arm from around Hannah, he quietly instructed, "Stay here," and moved toward the door.

She mumbled something; he couldn't hear what.

Just as quietly, he came back to her and shook his finger in her face. "You are not to try and help me. You are not to get shot."

"*I* didn't get shot," she said in a fierce whisper.

"*I* saved you," he answered. He waited until the mulish expression had settled on her face, then shook his finger at her again.

She gave a short, grudging nod, then murmured, "She's not there. What could she do to us in the corridors of the castle? She hopes to wait and try another day."

"You may be right." He pressed a brief, hard kiss on her lips. "But let me take precautions anyway."

Taking the handle, he jerked the door open—and the empty corridor of the east wing stretched before him. Doors opened off into vacant rooms, but Dougald surmised that Hannah was right.

After all, why should Hannah's suspect put herself in jeopardy by killing them in full daylight in the castle? She had no idea she had betrayed herself to Hannah.

With that thought, Dougald realized Hannah had convinced him. "You're right," he said. "Mrs. Trenchard is the killer."

"Yes," Hannah said, seemingly unaware of the munificence of his concession, "and I've been thinking. The evidence is in the chapel."

"In the chapel? Why in the chapel?"

"I had the headache to prove the whole plot centers around the chapel."

With a start, Dougald recalled what Charles had said. Hannah had been struck down in the chapel. "Of course."

"Besides, if I'm correct in my sad theory, where else could the evidence be?"

He remembered how protective Mrs. Trenchard had been of the chapel, doing all the cleaning herself, and how she had spoken to him of his renovations. She had been interested in his plans. Very interested.

"I have a plan," Hannah said.

Taking her arm, he led her down the corridor. "Tell me."

By the time she had finished, he was shaking his head. "No. There has to be a better way."

"Perhaps so, but I can't think of one right now, and we haven't a lot of time before the Queen's visit. It would show a decided lack of etiquette if one of us was killed before her arrival."

"I can't argue with that, but I must tell you I still doubt your deductions. I've observed that Mrs. Trenchard is quite fond of Seaton."

"Most women are."

Dougald didn't like that one bit. "Why? He's nothing but the runt of the litter."

"He's charming, he always has the best gossip and he likes women."

"I like women."

"And you used to be charming. Perhaps you can cultivate that trait again." She gave him a saucy smile. "But a gossip? I think not. You can glower, or you can gossip, and in the past nine years, you have perfected the glower."

He glowered. "I liked you better when you worried I would kill you."

Her smile disappeared. "I still worry, but about something entirely different."

About what? He wanted to ask what put that pensive expression on her face, but not now. Not until they'd settled this other matter.

"So you think Mrs. Trenchard targeted the lords to get the title for Seaton," Hannah said.

"Yes."

"Is a crime of property and possession more likely than a crime of honor and loyalty?"

"It's more logical."

In a mocking tone, she said, "Because you can *see* land and money, and honor and loyalty are ephemeral."

He knew she was about to spring a trap, but he couldn't quite see where the teeth would bite. "Such honor and loyalty are rare."

"Yet for honor and loyalty you stepped in front of a bullet."

And for love. He ought to say it. Make his confession and let her laugh or weep or whatever she wished. But he couldn't. The realization was too new. The time wasn't right. There were too many half-truths and past hurts between them. And perhaps, just perhaps, she would not laugh or weep, but she would be embarrassed for him. After all, she had loved him once. How pitiful to try and revive an old tenderness. So he said only, "You're my wife."

"Honor and loyalty," she said triumphantly.

"And vows which I respect," he couldn't resist saying.

With that she got very quiet.

She hadn't forgiven him for accusing her of abandoning him. Just as he hadn't forgiven her for doing it.

He glanced sideways at her. With strands of her fair hair falling around her face and those slanted brown eyes solemn, she still looked magnificent. He loved her height. He loved that she looked him in the eye even when he was in a rage. He loved her sarcasm. He loved her kindness to the aunts. He loved her breasts, especially the cleavage she showed right now. He loved her so much, and unmindful of past hurts and a bleak future, he had to save her.

He, who had taught himself confidence and iron determination—he was afraid he might fail. He had made mistakes, intolerable errors of character-reading and motivation.

As they approached the broad stairway that descended to the main level, Hannah said softly, "There. There is our quarry."

"Seaton," Dougald breathed. He could scarcely stand to look at Seaton in his blue plaid trousers, matching waistcoat, and stolen diamond collar pin.

Seaton spotted them, too, for he cried out, "I see you found each other." He observed the way Dougald held Hannah's arm and bathed them in a fond smile. "There's quite a bit of blather about you two turtle-doves in the district."

With slow, bitter emphasis, Dougald said, "I know where the blather came from."

Still wary from their midnight encounter, Seaton skittered sideways. "I'm not the only newsmonger to be invited to a party, you know!"

Hannah petted Dougald's arm as if he was a dog to be tamed. "Of course you're not, Seaton. But you're the best."

Seaton looked sideways at Dougald and murmured, "Well . . . yes."

Hannah continued, "Lord Raeburn was wondering—who gave you the note I wrote him?"

"One of the maids," Seaton answered.

"Where did she get it?"

Seaton's eyes widened. "From you, I would suppose."

Dougald took up the interrogation. "Why didn't the *maid* give it to me?"

"She said Mrs. Trenchard wanted her to work inside, and you were outside . . ."

"You were willing to carry it for a chance to read it," Dougald bluntly interpolated.

Seaton wasn't the slightest bit offended. "A man has to learn what's going on about him."

Dougald hated to do this, but he had no plan other than this. Seaton had produced a cue, and Dougald would respond. He had to find the killer before Queen Victoria arrived on the morrow.

In his roughest, most disgruntled voice, he said, "You want to know what's going on? I'll tell you what's going on. I'm not satisfied with the way Mrs. Trenchard has prepared the chapel."

"Oh, Dougald." Hannah squeezed his arm.

"The . . . chapel?" Seaton wagged his head.

"Yes, the chapel," Dougald repeated. "It has to be perfect for Her Majesty's visit tomorrow."

"As you know, Sir Onslow, I personally know Her Majesty." This time Hannah was definitely bragging, but with a purpose. "Queen Victoria will want to say a prayer, and we mustn't be embarrassed by our house of worship."

"Dear, dear." Seaton tsked sadly. "I feared old Trenchard was failing. You know she has those spells."

"Has she suffered from them long?" Hannah asked.

"Years, but they're getting worse." Seaton tapped

his chest. "Heart, I suspect, but she won't slow down. Except that she no longer tends the aunts." He lavished a smile on Hannah. "She must be so grateful to you, Miss Setterington."

"I've never had gratitude expressed in quite such a manner," Hannah replied.

Dougald hurried into speech. "Mrs. Trenchard has done all the cleaning herself, but first thing tomorrow morning I am ordering the workmen in to replace the rotting wall panels. Then all the maids and footmen will polish every pew, every step, every sconce." Dougald gave Hannah a gentle push to start her toward the aunts' workroom. "But Seaton, I depend on your discretion. Don't let Mrs. Trenchard know what I have planned."

"I wouldn't dream of it!"

Dougald and Hannah watched as Seaton tripped off down the stairway.

"I wonder how long it will take him to find her," Hannah mused.

"If I were a wagering man, I would say within the hour."

For over an hour, they sat in the darkness waiting. Dougald and Hannah. The aunts. Charles. And Seaton, who had heard about the discovery of Alfred's body at the foot of the tower and, when he came to confront Dougald, realized he had the front-row seat to the greatest scandal since the marquess of Bersham discovered his wife was a bigamist.

Dougald allowed him to come—he was afraid of what Seaton might do if left on his own—but Dougald had also threatened Seaton with dismemberment if he so much as peeped.

Everyone sat on the far right of the chapel, away from the wall with the stained-glass windows. The pew was hard beneath Dougald's behind, and although his wound had been bandaged, his shoulder stung like the blazes. Hannah moved restlessly beside him. He wondered what the aunts thought of Hannah's request that they remain here without speaking until something—she wouldn't tell them what—happened.

He also wondered why he had let Hannah talk him into inviting the aunts. He would rather have done this alone, but she seemed adamant that the old ladies accompany them. The whole arrangement reeked of calamity, but he had taken the precaution of arming Charles.

Dougald himself remained alert, a motionless warrior waiting for battle. "What do you think we're going to find?" he murmured close to Hannah's ear.

She answered him just as quietly. "Papers of some kind. Keepsakes. Possibly even a marriage certificate."

Perhaps she was right. After all, *he* had no other answers.

Eventually Hannah dozed, her head on his shoulder. One of the aunts snored softly.

The clock in the great hall had struck nine. The servants' curfew was in effect when Dougald saw the faint light of a single candle and heard a woman's faltering footsteps.

He shook Hannah awake. Someone must have done the same with the snorer, for she ceased with a snuffle.

Mrs. Trenchard entered. The single flame lit her

face, and Dougald realized gauntness painted the formerly plump hollows of her cheeks. She wore a black gown and an apron, and she moved like a woman with a mission, a woman who knew the chapel in both daytime and darkness.

With a shock, Dougald realized his wife must be right. Mrs. Trenchard had come to remove the evidence. But what? What paper or keepsake could be so important that she would kill so many of her lords?

Everyone remained perfectly still. The lone candle did little to lighten the gloom. Mrs. Trenchard didn't seem to notice the onlookers at all. All her attention was focused on a single location, on the left wall close to the altar. The place where Hannah had been struck down.

Mrs. Trenchard knelt. She placed the candlestick on the floor beside her knees. Taking a small pry bar from one pocket, she worked it under the deteriorating panel of wood and lifted it free. Raising the candle, she shined it into the recesses of the wall, and inside Dougald spied a small wooden box.

He had seen enough. The woman must be insane. It was time to capture the criminal and end the series of murders which had so shadowed Raeburn Castle.

Standing, he said in a slow, patient voice, "Mrs. Trenchard, what are you doing?"

The woman gasped, then turned so quickly Dougald blinked in astonishment. She held her candle high. In her other hand, she held a pistol. She aimed it at him— and Hannah.

Seaton dived for cover.

The aunts gasped.

Hannah tried to step between Dougald and the barrel.

He pushed her behind him.

And in a quavering voice, Aunt Spring asked, "Judy, is that where you buried my baby?"

28

*T*he candle started to shake and the pistol drooped.

Dougald relaxed his painfully tense muscles. He'd been shot once today. That was enough.

Aunt Spring stood and walked toward Mrs. Trenchard. Kneeling beside the wall, she touched the brown box. "Is my baby inside?"

As Hannah sank back into her seat, she whispered, "Oh, dear heavens."

At a gesture from Dougald, Charles hastened to bring more light from the office, and illumination sprang from the two candelabras he fetched.

Seaton stood, back pressed to the far wall as if he realized he didn't wish to witness this scene after all. Aunt Isabel sat, eyes fixed on the sad scene, her handkerchief over her mouth. Aunt Ethel wept softly. Miss Minnie moved closer to Aunt Spring as if trying to lend her strength to the tiny old lady.

"M . . . Miss Spring?" Mrs. Trenchard stammered. "What are ye doing here?"

"I came because Hannah asked me to, Judy. The dear girl wanted me here, and now I know why." Aunt Spring smiled sweetly at her. "I always longed to know what had happened to my baby. I'm so glad she's here in the family chapel. Judy, did you put her here?"

Mrs. Trenchard looked around at the pitying, accusing, horrified faces, then fixed her gaze on Aunt Spring. "I did it. Yes, I did it."

Aunt Spring took the pistol out of Mrs. Trenchard's hand and without looking, passed it to Miss Minnie. "You were always so good to me."

Dougald took the pistol from Miss Minnie and carefully unloaded it.

"I didn't want to be good to ye," Mrs. Trenchard said to Aunt Spring. "I didn't like ye at all."

"I know." Aunt Spring rescued the candle from Mrs. Trenchard's shaking grip and set it on the pew. "But you were good to me anyway."

Mrs. Trenchard twisted her apron in her large, work-roughened hands. "My mother made me be good to ye."

"Your mother was a lovely woman."

"Of course ye would think so." Mrs. Trenchard seemed sunken, cowering before the smaller Aunt Spring. "She loved ye better than she loved me."

"This is horrible." Hannah moved forward to stop Mrs. Trenchard.

Aunt Spring waved her away. "Sit down, Hannah." Her voice was firm, not at all like the Aunt Spring Dougald had come to know.

Hannah sat.

Miss Minnie nodded at her and gave a rueful smile.

"Your mother coddled me because I wasn't clever like

you." Aunt Spring stroked Mrs. Trenchard's shoulder. "How I used to envy your height and your strength!"

Dougald realized that, while Aunt Spring might be vague, she understood more than he had realized. He sat beside Hannah.

"No, Miss Spring, ye shouldn't have. Ye shouldn't ever have envied me anything." Mrs. Trenchard breathed heavily through her mouth. "All the time I was growing, all I heard was *Help Miss Spring. Give it to Miss Spring. Don't upset Miss Spring.*"

In a soothing voice, Aunt Spring said, "How tiresome for you."

"Then I got old enough to get away, so I got married."

"Mr. Trenchard seemed like a pleasant man." Aunt Spring lifted her brows in inquiry.

"He was a disappointment," Mrs. Trenchard said flatly. "He didn't take me away. He just lolled around on his arse and said, *Make Miss Spring happy. Then I won't have to work.* So I had them both at me all the time. Mother and Trenchard, using me and adoring ye. Ye got older. Ye were thirty-two and couldn't find a man. I comforted myself that ye were on the shelf. I had a man, for what he was worth. Then ye . . . ye met Mr. Lawrence. He was handsome and strong and brave."

Aunt Spring smiled at the memory. "Oh, he was."

"Everything I didn't have. I resented ye so much, it ate at my guts. I was glad to arrange yer secret meetings."

"I appreciated your help."

"I know ye did. Ye saw nothing but goodness in me."

"Dear . . ."

"No. I wasn't being good. I was hoping yer brother would catch ye and throw ye from the castle. Instead, ye know what happened? Mr. Lawrence got ye with child." Mrs. Trenchard put her hand over her eyes and gave a sob. "I couldn't have any babies. In all those years of marriage, my body never quickened. But ye . . . ye were increasing. His Lordship, yer brother, sent Mr. Lawrence away to the wars, but ye were still happy, hugging yer secret to yer bosom. Ye glowed, and not even the prospect of yer disgrace could make up for my unhappiness."

Tears trickled down Aunt Spring's rosy, wrinkled cheeks. "Judy, you're not responsible for what happened."

"I ill-wished ye. I wanted all yer happiness to die."

Hannah's icy fingers convulsively clutched at Dougald's, and he took her hands and warmed them between his.

"If ill-wishing could end a pregnancy, Trenchard, there'd be many a woman who would be childless," Miss Minnie pointed out.

Mrs. Trenchard didn't seem to hear. She spoke to, listened to, only Aunt Spring. " 'Twas my fault. I just hated and hated. I imagined yer death, and the babe's death . . . instead, the word came about Mr. Lawrence. I didn't mean to hurt him. I tried to take it all back. I truly did, but the news shocked ye so much. Ye lost the babe."

"Judy, dear, it wasn't your fault." Aunt Spring tried to embrace Mrs. Trenchard.

Mrs. Trenchard shrank back. "I helped Mother deliver it. A sweet infant girl, perfectly formed, too tiny to live."

"I remember." Aunt Spring's voice shook.

"Mother gave it to me to bury. She said to bury it in holy ground so it could be blessed, but hide it so no one would ever discover its existence. She said if we managed this right, no one need ever know about the disgrace, and ye could marry and be happy."

"But I couldn't marry another." Aunt Spring wiped tears away with her trembling fingers. "I loved Lawrence, and he was dead."

"I failed. I swaddled the babe and put it in my sewing box and brought it here. I thought it would be safe. I protected the babe from everyone who tried to find it. I protected ye, Miss Spring." Mrs. Trenchard lifted her gaze from Aunt Spring at last to toss Hannah a contemptuous glance. "But that nosy bastard found the place—"

Hannah lunged toward Mrs. Trenchard.

Dougald caught her arm.

As if nothing had happened, Mrs. Trenchard finished, "—And now because of *her*, ye'll never marry. Ye'll never be happy."

Hannah settled in her seat, but she trembled in little spurts, like someone who'd been gut-shot.

Dougald had never seen her react with such vehemence, but then, he'd never heard anyone call her a bastard before. "She's crazy," he murmured to Hannah. "No one cares what she called you."

"I care." Hannah glared at him, then turned her face away. "Crazy or not, I care."

Aunt Spring took Mrs. Trenchard's hands in hers and stared her in the eye. "Judy, dear, did you kill all the earls of Raeburn?"

"So she does understand," Dougald murmured to Hannah.

"Poor dear Aunt Spring," Hannah whispered back. "To face this, now."

Mrs. Trenchard answered Aunt Spring without hesitation. "I didn't kill *all* of them. Not yer brother, or his sons. But the other two, aye. They were going to tear apart the chapel to fix it. I couldn't allow that."

"Judy, killing people is a bad, bad thing," Aunt Spring said.

"I know." Mrs. Trenchard sounded impatient with Aunt Spring's gentle instruction. "But I was already damned for murdering Lawrence and the babe. What did the others matter?"

Aunt Spring shook Mrs. Trenchard's fingers. "You must promise never to kill again, not even for my sake."

Mrs. Trenchard nodded. "I won't, Miss Spring."

"Now, Judy, I think you should go rest."

"Yes. I need to rest." Moving with the weary lethargy of an aged crone, Mrs. Trenchard hefted herself off the floor and left.

A stunned, grieving silence settled on the chapel.

Finally, Hannah murmured, "I shouldn't have meddled."

"You had no choice." Dougald turned her to face him. "I object to being murdered for whatever the reason."

The candlelight changed Hannah's hair to molten gold, gave her eyes the curve of mystery and blessed her with a ethereal glow. But Hannah was not ethereal, and the problems between them wouldn't be solved on some heavenly plain.

They had to talk.

He didn't want to. While it was easy to blurt out

truths in a rage, this conversation involved painful truths, confessions and possibly even emotion.

But if they didn't communicate, they would separate again. He couldn't bear that.

Hannah tilted her head, her eyes wide with alarm. "Dougald, what's wrong?"

"We need to—"

In a loud, nervous voice, Seaton asked, "Lord Raeburn, shouldn't you send someone to arrest Mrs. Trenchard?"

Dougald wanted to snap at Seaton. Tonight, he wanted to be free of the duties of lordship. For a few hours, he would like to be alone with his wife to talk, and then, if everything went well, he would pleasure her until he had imprinted himself onto her forever.

"That woman killed two earls of Raeburn," Seaton insisted. "You have to arrest her."

Dougald gazed at the aunts. Miss Minnie, Aunt Ethel and Aunt Isabel sat on the floor beside Aunt Spring. Aunt Spring, who had been the catalyst for so many dreadful events, and who cried now for her baby, her lost love and an old friend. He glanced at Charles, still holding two full candelabra and looking as aghast by the emotional events as only Charles could look. He watched Hannah, whose tears still trembled on the tips of her lashes. And he thought about the broken old woman who even now made her way down the stone steps to the kitchen.

Dougald was the lord. The babe needed to be removed and placed in a proper coffin. The chaplain would have to be called to minister to Aunt Spring. Mrs. Trenchard . . . he would have to decide what to do with Mrs. Trenchard. Dougald couldn't escape his duties tonight.

His talk with Hannah would have to wait.

"Charles, will you follow Mrs. Trenchard?"

Charles placed the candelabra on a table and hurried out of the chapel.

To Seaton, Dougald said, "You don't need to worry. Mrs. Trenchard wouldn't hurt you, and I doubt she is going to run before morning."

29

The funerals were over. The mourners were gone. Only the flowers remained with drooping stems and faded scent. The flowers, and Dougald and Hannah.

They sat side by side, alone in the chapel, not touching, while the awkward silence stretched so long Hannah wondered if she should pretend an emergency and escape out the door.

Finally, Dougald commented, "A grim day."

Grateful that he'd spoken at last, Hannah said, "I don't know. More than Mrs. Trenchard and Aunt Spring's baby were buried today."

He turned to her, black brows raised, complexion pale. "What else?"

Hannah realized that, after last night's events—the discovery of the tiny coffin, Mrs. Trenchard's confession, the fainting spell she had suffered, her fatal fall down the stairs—he might well be alarmed to hear anything had been buried without his knowledge. "I just meant a weight has been lifted from Aunt Spring and all of the Raeburn lands. The mystery is solved, the stain dissolved, and tomorrow is a new day." She smiled at him in the hope he would smile back. "Tomorrow we will welcome the Queen of England."

"Because of you, my dear." He didn't smile, and his formal praise chilled her. "Because you listened when Aunt Spring spoke of her lost love."

He wore a black suit and an implacable expression. Yesterday's ease between them had vanished. She didn't know why. She had seen his transformation occur here in the chapel the night before. He had been staring, intent, focused only on her. Then Seaton had spoken, and the Dougald who held her hand, who listened when she spoke, who respected her opinion, vanished. In his place was the old, remote, responsible Dougald, lord of the manor and master of organization.

Did he regret the things he'd said yesterday? The truths he had revealed? Had she said something which made him realize how deeply he rued their marriage?

Did he intend to tell her to leave today?

For her part, Hannah behaved like any wife who was about to be cast off. She sat serenely, her back straight and her hands at rest, and worked to retain a pleasant expression. In short, she behaved with dignity and grace. "Aunt Spring is just vague, not crazy. She cried last night over both bodies, she buried them in the family plot today, and soon she'll be upstairs with the other aunts putting the finishing touches on the tapestry."

"So you like my Aunt Spring?" Dougald asked.

"Very much." Hannah watched as the afternoon sun radiated through the stained-glass windows and striped Dougald's black suit and beloved features with azure and scarlet and gold. "The aunts are lovely, and none of them seemed particularly surprised by the tale of Aunt Spring's baby."

"She had told them."

"That's not the kind of tale a woman will tell. It's hard to talk about something so painful, but the truth was there if you listened."

"Are you saying I don't listen?" he asked abruptly.

His defensiveness startled her. "Not at all."

"Because it's probably true. My father never listened, and I have worked to be like him. Until recently, I succeeded rather well." He leaned forward, elbows on his thighs, and stared at the altar. "Did my grandmother ever tell you the tales about my father and me?"

Hannah's breath caught. Dougald was going to talk about himself. About the past. To *her*. Striving for a faintly humorous tone, she said, "No, in fact when I asked, she said your father was a saint and as a child you were a saintlet."

He chuckled, as he was supposed to, but he still didn't look at her. "She would. Grandmama perceived her function in the family as peacemaker and developer of the icons, and if she had to lie to fulfill her duty, it was a lie well told."

Hannah noticed Dougald's hands. They were clasped, and his knuckles were white with tension. This was difficult for him; so difficult, she wanted to pat his hand and tell him *never mind*. But she didn't. He wanted to tell her something. He actually sought a conversation not precipitated by a fight or a bullet wound. "I had suspected you weren't the saintlet she claimed," she said.

"Not to speak ill of the dead, but I had my reasons." His mouth set in its usual stern line. "I don't remember my mother. My grandmother gave me affection. But my father was a tyrant, without love for me or interest in my doings except as they advanced the family name."

"So you rebelled."

"You've heard the rumors."

"A few," she admitted. "Years ago, and more recently from Seaton."

"Seaton." Dougald smiled, but not pleasantly. "If he knew the details, he could dine out on them for years."

"Are the details so dreadful?"

"My father insisted on hard work and abstinence. I scorned him. My grandmother blathered on and on about the family honor and tradition. I hated it. Everything they said seemed so old-fashioned and restrictive. I knew what I wanted, and it wasn't the life of a businessman, dressed in a black suit and hung by the cravat around his neck." Flinty-eyed, Dougald touched his formally tied cravat. "No, my family was rich, so I lived the good life. By the time I was fifteen, I nightly drank myself into oblivion, I smoked cigars until I reeked and visited the finest whores. I was *tough*. I was a *man*."

Hannah couldn't imagine Dougald behaving with such abandon.

He glanced up to see her incredulous gaze fixed on him, and added, "Until my father cut off my allowance."

She winced.

"I couldn't believe it. I couldn't believe he would do that to me. I hated him so much."

"I understand that."

He stared at her. "You?"

"I had a father, too," she explained. "He didn't marry my mother."

"Perhaps he wanted to, but couldn't defy his parents."

"The grandparents I will meet tomorrow." She almost wished she could put that encounter off until she had developed more confidence, or a tougher spirit, or at least the worst of this emotional tumult had passed.

In his most pessimistic tone, he said, "We are a pair."

"Don't sound so cheerful."

He didn't in any way respond to her jocularity.

With a sigh, she asked, "So you went home?"

"Me? Not me. Father was trying to bring me to heel. I was determined he would not succeed."

She could imagine the younger Dougald, choking on his pride. "Did you live with friends?"

"When the family money was gone, I didn't have any friends."

He didn't sound bitter, but his friends' desertion must have taught the youth a savage lesson. "What did you do?"

He sliced a glance at her. "I sank to the depths. I was a blackguard of the first water. I led a coterie of thugs. We fought other thugs, attacked any dandies foolish enough to be out after dark, and stole whatever happened to be at hand, and when I was caught . . ." His voice faded away.

Her heart leaped into her throat. They hanged thieves. "You were caught?"

"The magistrate had to show me the gibbet before I gave in and sent a message to my father." He straightened up without expression, said, "My father died of the shock. Clutched his heart and keeled right over."

Hannah sat, stunned, and tried to imagine what the guilt had done to the impressionable lad.

"Charles paid the magistrate a hefty bribe and got me out of the gaol. He took me home to see my father—and there he lay, in his coffin."

"How dreadful," she whispered.

Dougald stared at the flowers, drooping in their vases. "Funerals always make me think of my father."

Comprehension dawned. "You blamed yourself for his death."

"With some justification."

She bristled with indignation. "Of course with *some* justification, but it's not all your fault! You were only a boy. He should have taught you values, and if at first he failed, he should have tried again. He should have hunted for you and persuaded you to come back. He was a successful businessman. His pride could have taken the blow. Instead he died without ever seeing you."

Dougald watched her, his mouth curled in a crooked grin.

"Is that why you always supported the orphans' home, and found decent jobs for the men on the streets and the women in the workhouses?"

"I have a lot of reparation to make."

"And here I just thought you hid a kind streak." She pressed her head to his shoulder, then straightened up. "Yet you were always such an uncompromising businessman."

"Because I wanted to be better than Father, yes. But also, I was sixteen when I took the reins of the business. If I hadn't been ruthless, I would have been wiped out by Father's 'friends.'"

Hannah tried to speak. She *needed* to speak, to tell him what she had discovered these last few days.

But he misinterpreted her attempt. With harsh honesty, he said, "Don't try and tell me you would have stayed if you'd known. You wouldn't have. I was determined to beat my father in every way possible, including as a merciless bruiser. Eventually I would have chased you away."

She tried to speak again.

But he waved her to silence. "You were too young to handle me. You had no mother, no friends, no one to tell you what to do when a man was stubborn and stupid. I shouldn't have married you so young. That was my mistake."

Finally, she snapped, "More than lying to me about my dress shop?"

He stared at her, and when he saw her impatience, he put his hand on his shoulder and leaned back against the pew. "My wound is starting to hurt . . ."

"So is mine."

He straightened. "Your ankle?"

"No." This time it was her turn to face the front and speak toward the flowers. "The wound you inflicted when you said I abandoned you without trying."

"Oh." Dougald tried to brush her pain away and take responsibility for everything. "That was part of my scheme to drive you away."

"The real part." She faced him again. "Don't lie to me, Dougald. I recognized the truth immediately. I've spent too many years trying to justify my escape to myself. I knew I had done wrong."

"You were young."

"Other women have said their wedding vows at

eighteen and meant them. I left because I wanted to go before I began to swell with your child."

He jerked, almost as if he'd been stuck by another bullet. "Sound reasoning."

"Yes. Yes, it was. But the truth is, beneath my original starry-eyed wonder, there lurked the ghosts of my past. Always they whispered to me." With a shaky sigh, she admitted, "I never expected our marriage to last."

His face stilled into the cold mask of the businessman and lord. "I see."

"No, you don't. You and I could not have been more mismatched. You, with so much to prove. Me, knowing that no man would ever want me forever."

His mask dropped away, leaving a man confused. "Not want you? I wanted you all the time. So much I was embarrassed. I feared I was out of control. Didn't you know that?"

"No, and if I had, it wouldn't have mattered. From what I had seen, there was no home in this world that lasted. Not for me, anyway."

"I allowed Charles to run our home, so it was never your home."

"But you were right when you said I could have fought him and won. I had the weapons. I just . . . thought it was no use." Hannah had heard Dougald's tale, been touched by his trust, and wanted to give him her trust in return. But this was hard. This hurt with the lingering pain of ancient memories. Still she spoke, ignoring the quaver in her voice. "My mother . . . you knew my mother."

"A good woman."

"Yes, and she raised me the best way she could. She

enfolded me in her love. She tried to make me proud and strong, but she had to leave me while she worked." She tried to smile at him. "Do you know, the first words I remember hearing are, 'Hey, bastard, stop that?' My nursemaid couldn't remember my name. Neither could her children. So I was, 'Hey, bastard.' "

He gripped the pew in front of them. "Did your mother know about this?"

"Of course not, and I didn't tell her." She remembered the times she'd wanted to speak, but she had recognized the burden her mother carried. "What choice did she have?"

"None." He frowned. "But I don't understand what this has to do with our marriage. I never worried about your legitimacy. *I* never reproached you. I would have killed anyone who did."

"For my sake?" Stiffening her spine, she asked the difficult question. "Or because no one should slander *your* wife?"

"For you . . . because . . . it was never . . ." He stammered to a halt. "I . . . don't know, Hannah. Even at that time, even when I was a selfish youth, it wasn't all for the sake of my pride. Now . . . now I don't give a damn what anyone else thinks of you. All I care about is what I think, and I think you're a remarkable woman."

She chuckled, just a little. "Now *that* I believe."

"That you're a remarkable woman?"

"That you don't care what anyone else thinks."

"Then believe this—nothing less than a remarkable woman could have turned me from my well-planned revenge."

A fine declaration, and one she would treasure. Sincerity shone from Dougald, brighter than the colors of the stained-glass window. He was proud of her, and if she wished, she could stop talking now. They had said so much. She didn't have to tell him everything. Didn't have to expose every shameful reminiscence. "I know who I am," she said. "I know what I've done. I've founded and run a successful business in a man's world. I realize how I've grown from the girl who left you and our marriage."

Dougald had been so brave; could she do any less? He wouldn't turn away if she showed him the ugly secrets chained in the dungeon of her soul . . . would he?

She wanted to laugh, but contained herself. Perhaps her ugly secrets didn't reside in her soul, but in her gut, for her stomach twisted with protest when she imagined telling him the truth. "If you say I'm remarkable, then I would not disagree with you."

"That's my Hannah," he approved.

When he found out who she really was, he would probably turn away. Wetting her suddenly dry lips, she finished, "Most of the days."

"I knew there had to be a catch."

"Sometimes, somebody says something, and all the fear and guilt comes flooding back. When I was a child, I would make friends tentatively. They'd like me. We'd laugh together. We'd eat together. I'd think, 'This time will be different,' and then they would turn on me when they found out." Hannah tried to look at him, but although she'd been as intimate with this man as any woman could be, her gaze skittered away. Physical intimacy, she realized, could not compare to the sharing of thoughts, memories, feelings. "You can't beat a dog every day without it sooner or later attacking."

He leaned back, watching her through that enigmatic, knowing gaze. "Last night, I thought you were going to jump at Mrs. Trenchard."

She had hoped he wouldn't notice. Foolish Hannah, Dougald noticed everything. "I haven't heard it for so long. *Bastard.* She called me a bastard." She touched her forehead, her lips, her throat. Her gestures betrayed her agitation, but she couldn't stop. She had to move, had to shake off the pain, or all the old rage would rise in her. She feared it would take possession, and she'd be the young Hannah once more—desperate to please, afraid of rebuff, always searching for a home and a family of her own. "I thought I had come so far." Dropping her hands into her lap, she said in a low, intense voice, "But when Mrs. Trenchard said that, I just wanted to make her stop before everyone knew . . . before they all turned on me . . ."

"They all . . . the aunts wouldn't turn on you. They adore you."

"I know. I know! But I didn't think, I just wanted to fight or to run away."

"Oh." He understood now. "Like you did with me."

"I expected you to hurt me. As I got deeper and deeper in love with you, I realized that when you turned on me, my pain would be devastating." It hurt now to tell him how vulnerable and frightened she had been. And to know that, with him, she still was. "You almost did me a favor when you refused me my dress shop. My dream wasn't really destroyed. You gave me the excuse I was looking for. The excuse to leave."

He stood up, then sat back down. "My God, we could never have stayed together."

"No." She was glad he realized the truth, and knew that she realized it, too. It had taken both of them to end their marriage. "Before we could ever succeed, I had to learn I could make friends, that I was not just the poor little bastard the world despised. You . . . you had to learn that you didn't want to be your father."

"I didn't *learn* I didn't want to be like my father. I just learned that because of you, I *failed* to be like him. How could I be cold, indifferent, unloving, when I had you to snap at me and nag at me and take me to the heights of passion?" Carefully, he picked up her hands and rubbed them between his own. "There is a wise adage that says you can never cross the same river twice. You can go to the same spot on the bank, but the water that was there before has flowed on to the sea. We're standing on the bank of a river, and we've been here before. But it's not the same river."

"We're not same people." She returned the clasp of his hand. "I would like to cross the river with you again."

A smile broke across Dougald's face. An open smile, one that united the old, charming Dougald and the new, taciturn Dougald. "Are you asking me to marry you?"

She stilled. For one moment, she remembered how he had plotted his revenge on her. The recollection of his searing diatribe rose from her memory and romped like a drama across the stage of her mind.

If she surrendered to him now, he would have succeeded. She would be his forever, to hurt as he wished.

But the Dougald who held her hands had had faith in her beliefs. He had showed her his past. He listened when she spoke. Although she didn't approve, he had even taken a bullet for her. She had to return that faith. Perhaps it wasn't love or anything more than passion, but it was Dougald, and he was what she wanted.

So she took a breath and she said, "Remember when you told me you wanted to make me fall in love so you could subjugate me to your marital demands?"

He shifted warily. "Yes."

"Well . . . you've succeeded in half your plan."

He understood at once. Gathering her into his arms, he held her tight, his cheek on her hair. "You have made me happier than I have been in my whole life. I wish that I could . . . wait." He stood up and dragged her with him. "Come on." He pulled her out of the pew and to the front of the chapel. He positioned her directly in front of the altar, then took his place beside her.

She had stood in front of a church with him one other time. Then the pews had been filled with the best families in Liverpool, her gown had been of the finest blue velvet, and a minister had stood in the pulpit.

This time the chapel was empty of witnesses, she wore her black mourning gown, and only the two of them would know what they said this day, yet she understood what he proposed.

This time, the vows would be real.

Taking her hands again, he faced her and stared into her face for a long moment. "There have been times this week when I thought I would never know love again. I woke with the hope of seeing you. I bathed with the memory of your smile. I walked the corridors while imagining you walked with me. My soul bled every time I glimpsed you—the froth of lace, the satin of your cleavage, the narrowness of your waist. I told myself that I only wanted you in my bed, but every day I moved closer to the truth. I wanted you for my wife."

She should have been triumphant. She had tried to make him suffer, and she had succeeded. But he had suffered enough in his life, and she would never be the cause of his suffering again.

Dougald's eyes were solemn, his voice deep and vibrant. "I want to talk to you. I want to listen to you. I want to walk with you and, yes, I want you in my bed. That's what I want today. That's what I'll want in a hundred years. If you will promise to be my wife forever, I will pledge myself to your happiness. Please, Hannah, will you be mine?"

She wanted to tell him. That he had been everything to her—guardian, lover, husband. For years he was the man whose memory she fled. For years he had been the man she remembered. Since she had come to Raeburn Castle, he had been her nemesis, her defender, and nothing more and nothing less than her man.

Yet she could barely speak. All she could do was take his face between her palms, look at him with tear-filled eyes, and whisper, "Forever. I am yours forever."

30

The train had arrived. Queen Victoria was on her way in the carriage he had had brought in from his home in Liverpool, and Hannah paced into the newly constructed foyer on the main floor of the castle. "It's raining. How dare it rain today of all days?"

"This is England," Dougald replied. "Her Majesty has been damp before."

Hannah gave him a look that plainly told him what she thought of his good sense, and waited while the aunts came in and lined up.

Dougald didn't know which made Hannah more coltish, the prospect of presenting Her Majesty with the tapestry or knowing her grandparents would be present at the reception following. Certainly she marched up and down the line of aunts, giving them an oration that would have made Nelson proud and examining each for appropriateness of dress.

The aunts, bless them, were so nervous they let her.

Dougald followed Hannah as she tweaked and

straightened and generally frightened them to death, and as he passed, he smiled at each of the aunts. "The crimson velvet much complements your coloring, Aunt Isabel. The blue brings out the color of your eyes, Aunt Ethel. Aunt Spring." He took her hands and spread them wide. "The little pink flowers on the white material are so cheerful."

"I like it," Aunt Spring answered. "You don't think it's too soon after the funerals, do you?"

To have had two funerals one day and a celebration the next did seem a little peculiar, but Dougald said, "I think the funerals were extraordinary circumstances, and the Queen's visit is a special moment. Her Majesty would not wish to think she was intruding on our mourning, and we would not wish to make her uncomfortable by unnecessary lamentation."

"So I told Spring, my lord," Miss Minnie said.

"You are very wise," Dougald answered. "And may I say, you look lovely in that gray silk."

Miss Minnie smoothed the skirt. "I haven't worn it in years. It lacks élan."

"But with your dignity, you carry off the older styles." Dougald watched as the aunts got into a little group where they tittered and talked, then he walked to the archway where Hannah stood with her fists on her hips.

"How did you do that?" she demanded.

"What?" He smiled at her.

"Make them relax. I've been telling them to, but they don't listen to me."

"I don't understand it." He stroked a strand of golden hair. "Did I tell you how beautiful you look today?"

Her fists unclenched.

"Your gown is perfect for an afternoon visit from Her Majesty. I would never have thought that color of gold would so perfectly match your hair."

A faint smiled touched her lips, and she glanced down. "I do like it."

"The shimmer of the silk gives just the right touch of elegance to the severe fashion."

"I'm tall. Furbelows look ridiculous on me."

"You have a wonderful sense of style." Taking her hand, he led her to the outside door, a new double wooden affair with a window above and on either side. After a clap on the shoulder of the footmen who watched the road, Dougald told Hannah, "Pretend you are Her Majesty and you have just stepped into Raeburn Castle. What do you think?"

She looked around, and he looked with her. The meticulous work by the carpenters, plasterers and stonemasons exhibited no signs of haste. The rose-marble floor stretched smoothly through the foyer to the hardwood in the main corridor. The carved wood casements shone with polish, and the cream paint was smooth on the walls.

"It's lovely," she said.

"I think we should have some gold leaf done on the soffit—when we have time, of course."

She looked up. "Yes."

"I'm especially pleased with marble detail on the new outside stairs. Too bad Her Majesty won't get to see much in the rain."

Hannah drew her fringed shawl a little closer around her shoulders. "Dougald, are you deliberately soothing me?"

He'd always known she was too clever by half. "Is it working?"

For a moment, she seemed torn between laughter and ire, but her sense of humor won the hard-fought battle. She chuckled reluctantly. "You're a scoundrel."

"An adoring scoundrel."

"You have to stop smiling." She glanced around. "Everyone's going to know what we were doing last night."

"Let them."

"They don't know we're married yet."

"I rather like that. I haven't done anything illicit for . . . well, since the last time we were illicit."

"Last week." She thought the man deserved to languish for manipulating her, even for a good cause, so as she left him she cast a flirtatious glance over her shoulder.

She hadn't had occasion to practice flirtatious glances, but this one seemed effective for he straightened, lost his smile, and stalked after her.

Joining the aunts, she said with considerably less formality, "I'm so excited."

"Are you sure Her Majesty will like the tapestry?" Aunt Ethel asked for at least the fifth time.

"It is the most magnificent tapestry I have ever seen," Hannah said. "Only a fool would fail to like the tapestry, and Queen Victoria is no fool."

The aunts exchanged glances, and chorused, "We're excited, too!"

Seaton skidded around the corner at a run. "Am I late?"

"Not at all." Hannah stood in amazement of Seaton's garb. Where other men wore proper, somber colors to greet their sovereign, Seaton strutted like a peacock in a combination of emerald, yellow and dark blue.

Making Hannah his best bow, he begged, "Dear Miss Setterington, would you introduce me to Her Majesty?"

"When protocol allows it, certainly." Protocol being the moment when Queen Victoria needed some amusement. "But possibly you should wait in the great hall."

Eyes shining, he straightened his plaid, satin waistcoat. "As you wish, Miss Setterington!"

Hannah smiled after him. "He's a dear," she said.

"He's a cretin," Dougald replied.

The watching footman almost tripped over his feet as he arrived to announce, "My lord, they're here. A dozen carriages, all full."

A flurry of activity broke out among the serving folk; they each had been assigned a station and they guarded their duty fiercely, anxious to see their Queen. The butler opened the door. The footmen with their umbrellas rushed outside and down the stairs, each dressed in his finest livery and knowing he would be soaked for the glory of escorting any one of the Royal Party. One very lucky young man had been chosen to lift the largest umbrella over Her Majesty, and he trembled with the honor done him.

Hannah reflected that the excitement could only be a release for the family and the staff. The Queen's visit had inadvertently distracted attention from the death of Mrs. Trenchard and the discovery of Aunt Spring's child. For the next fortnight, the gossip would be about Her Majesty, the Royal Family, and the reception.

The aunts hurried to get in line once more, and Hannah took her place at the front of that line. Dougald had never met Her Majesty, so Hannah would greet the Queen first and introduce them.

Dougald stood alone by the open door, a tall, spare, handsome man of unusual dignity and an impressive physique.

Hannah knew. The night before she had explored every muscle, every sinew, every inch of skin. She really should have gotten more sleep, but of what value was sleep when she was in love?

"Your Majesty." Dougald's words, his low bow brought Hannah's mind back to the foyer, from whence it should never have strayed.

The Queen discarded her coat into the butler's hands. A petite young woman with dark hair and pale skin, she had been queen only six years, yet already she had made her mark on the nation. She adored her husband, who adored his two children, and they lived an exemplary family life. Indeed, Hannah realized with a shock Her Majesty was increasing again.

Hannah looked hungrily at the Queen's swollen belly. For some reason, pregnancy seemed a condition to be highly desired.

Stepping forward, she curtsied. "Your Majesty."

"Miss Setterington." With a warm smile, Queen Victoria extended her hand. "How good to see you again."

Prince Albert stood behind her, and beyond him extended a line of the royal children held by their nursemaids, ladies-in-waiting, and gentlemen of the royal chamber all wrapped in coats, trudging up the stairs, crowding into the foyer, and dripping on the floor.

"Your Majesty, it is good to see you again." Conscious of the need to hurry, to get all these people inside, Hannah turned to Dougald. "Your Majesty, may I introduce Dougald Pippard, earl of Raeburn?"

"Lord Raeburn, how good to meet you." Queen Victoria walked toward the aunts.

He accompanied her. "A pleasure to meet you, also, and may I introduce the ladies whose work brought you here."

Hannah stepped out of the way, but watched with pride as the aunts charmed the Queen and Prince Albert. The guests continued to stream in, the aunts led Queen Victoria toward the great hall where the finished tapestry hung behind its curtain, and Hannah directed the guests and the servants as unobtrusively as possible.

At last, she noticed that four of the guests stood still beside her. She turned to them, prepared to show them the way to the great hall when she saw—

"Charlotte!"

The former Lady Charlotte Dalrumple, cofounder of the Distinguished Academy of Governesses, smiled with brilliant delight. And—

"Pamela!"

The former Miss Pamela Lockhart, another cofounder of the Distinguished Academy of Governesses, threw her arms around Hannah. "Her Majesty asked us to come along to surprise you! Are you surprised?"

"I'm . . . stunned." Hannah could scarcely speak for excitement. These women were her friends, the two out of all the world with whom she had shared trials and tribulations, joys and triumphs. As Hannah went into Charlotte's more restrained embrace, her heart overflowed with pleasure.

Over Charlotte's shoulder she saw Viscount Ruskin looking delighted and smug as only Charlotte's husband could look.

Pamela's husband, Lord Kerrich, chuckled as the three women stared at each other, embraced again, and drew back.

"I can't believe you're here." Hannah tried to curtsy to both gentlemen while keeping her arms around her friends. "I'm so excited. So pleased. Everything has come out so well. Oh, Charlotte! Pamela!"

Ruskin folded his arms over his massive chest. "It is good to view women's excitement."

"Indeed." Kerrich lifted his monocle and surveyed the little group. "Such dear friends are seldom seen."

Hannah ignored them. Both were handsome men, but arrogant and given to bombastic self-assurance and incredible impertinence. The only trait that saved them, in her opinion, was their unceasing devotion to their wives. That, and the fact that Charlotte, with her quiet assurance, and Pamela, with her blunt outspokenness, directed their husbands when the men got too obnoxious.

From down the corridor, Hannah heard Dougald's warm tones speaking, delivering his speech of welcome.

In fact, if one were inclined, one might say both Charlotte's and Pamela's husbands were cut from the same cloth as Dougald.

Hannah examined her friends more closely. "Charlotte, Pamela . . . pardon my curiosity, but are you two also increasing?"

Her friends exchanged glances.

"We are," Pamela said.

"We think our babies will come at the same time." Charlotte patted her slightly expanded abdomen.

Increasing . . . for just one moment, Hannah wondered if she should confess her own suspicion.

She discarded the idea. To try and explain here in the foyer . . . and after all, Dougald should hear the news first. Instead she said, "This is prime news, indeed. Many, many congratulations."

"When Her Majesty received your invitation, she invited us to accompany her at once," Charlotte said.

Pamela leaned close to Hannah and whispered, "We accepted, of course, but not just for the pleasure of your company. I confess, we were curious about your fate after discovering that you had been married for so many years."

Hannah opened her mouth, but she didn't know what to say. She and Dougald hadn't discussed when or where they would announce their marriage. Indeed, last night they hadn't discussed anything at all. The whole night had been one long, tender consummation not of their passion, but of their love.

Although it hadn't escaped Hannah's notice that Dougald had never quite said the words. He had said everything else, and she was an ungrateful wretch to expect more, but a bit of uncertainty lingered.

She began to try to clarify a situation which she could not easily explain, when Aunt Isabel stuck her head around the corner from the great hall, and cried, "Miss Setterington, we are all waiting for you."

"We have to go in." Hannah ducked away.

"Saved," she heard Pamela mutter.

Inside the great hall, a new, magnificent purple-velvet drapery covered the wall. Dougald stood before it with the Queen and Prince Albert. The aunts were lined up, hands folded at their waists, eyes sparkling.

Miss Minnie gestured for Hannah to come to them. "We must have Miss Setterington with us. She is our dearest girl."

Hannah hadn't thought the aunts could make her blush anymore, but Miss Minnie's praise and the others' fond smiles brought color to her cheeks. She made her way through the impatient crowd to stand with the aunts.

As they had arranged, Aunt Spring stepped forth and curtsied to Queen Victoria. In her happiest voice, she said, "Dear Majesty—"

Hannah sliced a glance at Dougald, who managed to look serious. Neither one of them had thought to tell Aunt Spring one didn't call one's Queen, "dear."

"—When you were born, my companions and I were so excited by the appearance of our own Princess Royal that we determined to do something to honor you. As the years have passed, we have followed your life with delight and interest. You were crowned, you married, you had the dear little princess and prince, and through all that time we have worked on a gift for you. We, all of us, would like to present that gift to you now."

"I would be honored," Queen Victoria said.

Dougald nodded to the two footmen, who drew back the drapes to reveal the tapestry.

The lords and ladies gasped, then the great hall fell absolutely silent.

The great work stretched across the wall, a dazzling display of artistry in a chamber large enough and steeped with enough history to do it justice. The royal blue was sprinkled with yellow stars, a silver moon and a golden sun. The jewels spilled forth from the chest in radiant emerald, sapphire and ruby. Roses of red and white and pink intertwined with the border, and at the very center was Queen Victoria herself, resplendent in her coronation robes, with Albert and his newly woven and even features at her side.

Even Hannah, who had seen the tapestry, worked on the tapestry, worried about the tapestry, could not help but be impressed.

The aunts stood staring at the Queen.

The Queen stood staring at the tapestry

And Her Majesty was silent for so long, Hannah began to worry.

At last she stirred and turned to the aunts. In a voice that trembled, she said, "You ladies have worked on this for twenty-four years?"

"Give or take a few months," Aunt Spring said. "I must confess, we wouldn't have been nearly as excited if you'd been a prince."

Her pronouncement brought a few coughs from the onlookers, and Hannah had to smother a smile.

Queen Victoria extended her hands. "I'm touched by your kindness, your generosity. Your inventiveness, your skill has no compare. On behalf of myself and the generations of English who will treasure this tapestry, I am delighted to accept this gift."

Prince Albert said, "The tapestry will have a place of honor in Buckingham Palace."

At a nod from Hannah, the aunts gathered around

the Queen to take her hands and, inevitably, all called her "dear."

In her clearest voice, Aunt Isabel announced to Dougald, "Miss Setterington was right. Her Majesty is no fool."

31

*A*unt Isabel had been making stentorian pronouncements all day, and she didn't fail Dougald now. "Dear, it would seem your neighbors aren't *that* worried about your reputation as a murderer." She gestured around at the crowd that spilled out of the great hall and into every chamber in Raeburn Castle. "They all came."

Aware that a few of those neighbors, at least, were listening, Dougald said only, "I welcome them."

"Yes, this is a triumph for all of us." Aunt Isabel hadn't stopped smiling all day. Leaning closer to Dougald, she actually lowered her voice to ask, "Do you think they've heard the rumors about Spring's baby?"

"I'm sure they have."

"But it doesn't matter, does it? Look at the dear girl, chatting with our own monarch. Her Majesty loves Spring. The neighbors won't ever dare snub her." Aunt Isabel took a swig of her cup. "Shallow bastards."

Aunt Isabel, Dougald realized, had had a bit too much of the mulled wine.

Aunt Ethel came to them and locked her arm through Aunt Isabel's. "Minnie sent me to get you. Her Majesty wants to speak to us again."

Aunt Isabel flashed a grin at Dougald. "Her Majesty likes *me,* too."

Dougald plucked the cup from her hand. "Yes, I'm sure she does." He suspected Queen Victoria did enjoy being called "dear" and being treated to the innocently blunt comments from these meddling women he called his aunts.

"Dougald, dear," Aunt Ethel said, "dear Hannah is standing alone. Perhaps she's shy. Why don't you go rescue her?"

Aunt Ethel didn't think Hannah was shy, Dougald knew. She was matchmaking again—or still.

He also knew that Hannah wasn't shy, she was worried. As the guests for the reception came streaming in, she stared into the face of each one, looking for her grandparents. So far they had not arrived, but it was early yet, and the rain made the roads difficult.

Yet he had welcomed a chance to be with Hannah, and so he replied, "I'll do that, Aunt Ethel." Taking a glass of champagne from a passing footman, he walked to Hannah's side and offered it, a lowly gift for his goddess.

Hannah stood in the midst of the most successful reception ever seen in Lancashire and wrung her hands. "They're late. Why are they late?"

"The roads are muddy and difficult." Dougald pried Hannah's fingers loose and placed the glass within.

She stared at it as if she'd never seen champagne before. "What if they don't come?"

"They'll come." Dougald knew that without a doubt. They would walk if they had to. He had taken care of the matter. He glanced up and saw the butler signaling him, and said, "In fact, I believe they must be here."

She stood petrified, staring at nothing.

"They're going to love you." He now pried the glass from her frozen grip and placed her hand on his arm. "As we all love you."

Without moving her head, Hannah looked at him. "Do we love me?"

"Yes, we do." He put his hand over hers. "All of us love you."

Aunt Spring must have been watching for the Burroughses, for she excused herself from the Queen and hurried to Dougald and Hannah. "Come on, dears," she instructed, and led them toward the older couple who stood poised in the doorway. "Alice, Harold, how nice to see you again." She pressed her cheek to Mrs. Burroughs's, and gave Mr. Burroughs a swift hug. "I have two very important people here I want you to meet. Dougald Pippard, our dear earl of Raeburn, and Miss Hannah Setterington, my dear companion."

The Burroughses dismissed Dougald with a glance, then stared searchingly at Hannah.

Hannah stared mutely back.

Dougald recognized fear when he saw it. His darling was paralyzed, afraid to be once more rejected by the people she most needed to embrace her. He could take credit for at least a little of her apprehension, so he would correct matters. With a bow, he said, "If I might add—Miss Setterington is Miss Carola Tomlinson's daughter."

Mrs. Burroughs shook with a violent tremor, then stepped closer to Hannah and gazed up into her face.

"It *is* you. I knew it was. I see my boy in your face."
She wrapped her arms around her much taller granddaughter. "Oh, my cherished girl, welcome home."

For one more moment, Hannah stood still. She met
Dougald's gaze with her own wide, shocked gaze.
Then with a choked laugh, she said, "Thank you.
Thank you."

Tall, white-haired, dignified, Mr. Burroughs enfolded them both in his embrace.

Dougald and Aunt Spring watched for a moment,
then Aunt Spring plucked at Dougald's coat sleeve.
"The Burroughses certainly seem taken with Miss
Setterington."

"They certainly do." Dougald waited. Aunt Spring
might be vague about some things, but when it came to
people, Dougald had come to realize she was shrewd
to the bone.

"You said she's Miss Carola Tomlinson's daughter,"
Aunt Spring said.

"That's right."

"I seem to remember that was the name of the
young lady who was involved with their son."

"Yes."

"How lovely." Aunt Spring watched the reunion
with hands clasped before her heart. "Wait until I tell
the girls." She hurried off, back toward the group surrounding Her Majesty.

The little scene attracted some gaping attention
from the neighbors, so after the first few, emotional
moments, Mr. Burroughs withdrew from the embrace.
Directing a piercing glance toward Dougald, he said,
"You have our appreciation for the packet of letters
you sent. Not that we needed proof of Hannah's her-

itage. She has my height and resembles our son in a startling manner."

"You sent the letters to them?" Hannah still had her arms around her grandmother, but the smile she sent Dougald left him in no doubt of her gratitude.

It left Mr. Burroughs in no doubt, either, for in a gruff voice, he said, "You will wish to return to your guests. Our granddaughter will show us this famous tapestry everyone's talking about."

Dougald recognized the banishment. With a lift of the brows, he checked with Hannah, and at her nod, he bowed, excused himself, and went back to speak with Lord Kerrich and Viscount Ruskin. He liked them. The two men showed remarkable good sense in their dealings with their wives who, from what Dougald could tell, were just as quick-witted and clever as Hannah. Only men of their exceptional character could manage women like these.

Hannah watched Dougald walk away then, proud and awkward, she gestured into the great hall. "The Queen's tapestry is here." She walked with her grandparents toward the long wall where it was displayed.

"It's beautiful!" Mrs. Burroughs exclaimed.

Mr. Burroughs blinked in amazement. "Good God, I always thought Spring and her coven were nothing but mad old women, except for that Miss Minnie, and I thought she was mad *and* cantankerous. But I see they were actually sewing something in their upstairs den."

Hannah stiffened. Slowly, she rotated to face Mr. Burroughs, and in her most frigid tone, she said, "Sir, I would not allow anyone to make rude statements about you, and you are only my grandfather. Aunt Spring and her companions have, for no reason other than kindness, taken me to their bosoms, and I will not allow anyone to disparage them within my hearing."

"Well . . . well . . ." Mr. Burroughs sputtered. "Young lady, you . . . you . . ."

Mrs. Burroughs stepped up beside Hannah. "She's a proper young lady with admirable sentiments, Harold, and you know it. What are you going to do about it?"

Mr. Burroughs glared at his wife.

She glared back.

He looked at both of them. "I see a resemblance between you two, also, Alice." He bowed with the upright posture of a general. "I beg your pardon, Hannah. I should never have been so blunt."

"Rude," Hannah corrected.

"Harold, you *were* rude," Mrs. Burroughs insisted.

"Yes. Rude. Beg pardon." He bowed again. "Won't do it again."

"I'm sure you won't," Hannah answered. "I appreciate that."

Mrs. Burroughs hugged Hannah's arm in hers. "You and Harold are just alike! I can't wait to hear the fights you two will have."

Aunt Ethel drifted by. "Good to see you, Mr. and Mrs. Burroughs." With a significant glance at Mr. Burroughs, she said, "The Queen likes her tapestry." She drifted away, but not too far.

"Not mad, eh?" Mr. Burroughs asked the ether.

"Perceptive would be a better word." Hannah changed the subject. "Perhaps you might like a glass of champagne after your journey?"

"Yes, I would. Thank you, dear." Mrs. Burroughs smiled.

"Champagne. Pah!" Mr. Burroughs's mustache quivered with disdain. "Silly stuff. Don't know why anyone would want bubbles in their wine. Give me a good English ale every time."

Hannah led them toward the table of refreshments. "An ale for Mr. Burroughs," she instructed the footman, and handed Mrs. Burroughs a glass of champagne.

Seaton bounded up, a smile curling his lips. He bowed to the Burroughses, then clasped Hannah's hand. "Thank you for the introduction. Her Majesty was most gracious, and she admired my ensemble most emphatically. Thank you, Miss Setterington. Thank you, thank you."

Hannah smiled her first real smile for the day. "You are indeed welcome, Seaton."

He bounded away again, alive with the pleasure of the day.

The crowd had ebbed around the refreshment table, but Hannah suspected Mr. Burroughs would have spoken regardless of their audience. He seemed a man unimpressed by subtlety.

He said, "Hannah, I know you're wondering why we have ignored you all these years."

"Not at all," Hannah said politely. *All the time.*

"Nonsense. Of course you wonder. You're our granddaughter."

Which meant she should answer honestly, or at least for as long as it suited him. "Yes, sir, I have wondered."

"When we got the packet of letters from Lord Raeburn, we were surprised." He accepted the tankard from the footman.

Mrs. Burroughs hugged Hannah's arm again. "We had no idea that our dear boy wrote Miss Tomlinson after she left the district."

"Have you read those letters?" Mr. Burroughs asked.

"No, sir, I haven't had the pleasure." Although Hannah didn't know if it would truly be a pleasure, or the greatest agony of her life.

"According to the letters, Henry planned to come to your mother and marry her."

Hannah released a painfully held breath.

"But until we read his own words, we didn't suspect Miss Tomlinson was expecting a child." Mr. Burroughs stared at the brown foam on the top of his ale. "I thought I had stopped them before . . . well, obviously, I didn't. Wish the boy had told me. Thought he would get over his infatuation. Despondent. Drank too much. Died so suddenly." He took a drink, then glanced at his wife. Pulling a white ironed linen square out of his pocket, he said, "Alice, I *wish* you would remember to carry a handkerchief."

"Yes, dear." Mrs. Burroughs dabbed at her cheeks.

Mr. Burroughs stared Hannah in the eyes. "If we had known about you, we would have found you and your mother and brought you home at once."

Hannah looked right back at him. "Thank you, sir, for that." For announcing that they wanted her. For saying they would have taken her mother into their home, also.

Miss Minnie patted Hannah on the shoulder. "I see you've met our dear girl," she said to Mr. and Mrs. Burroughs. "She is the finest young woman of our acquaintance."

"Yes, of course she is." Mr. Burroughs glared at Miss Minnie. "She's our granddaughter."

Miss Minnie glared back at him. "No thanks to you!"

Placidly, Hannah moved to stand between them. "Miss Minnie, do you or any of the aunts need me?"

Miss Minnie transferred her scowl to Hannah, then her brow smoothed. "No, dear. Her Majesty is circulating through the neighbors, being so gracious and kind, and we thought we would stand near in case you needed us." With an innocent smile at Mr. Burroughs, she walked toward the other aunts.

"She wants to hear what we're saying," Mr. Burroughs said impatiently. "May I call them busybodies without incurring your wrath, Hannah?"

"No," Hannah answered. "I will not let them call you a crusty old top, either."

Mrs. Burroughs intervened. "That's fair."

Lifting his voice so that it carried to the aunts, Mr. Burroughs said, "As our granddaughter, you will of course move into our home with us."

"Oh, no!" Aunt Ethel exclaimed.

Hannah was startled. "What . . . why?"

"It's not decent for our granddaughter to be out in service."

Hannah tried to think of what to say. Mr. Burroughs obviously considered her career a disgrace. She didn't feel that way. The work she had done in the last years had taught her self-reliance, efficiency, and confidence.

In her soft, ladylike voice, Mrs. Burroughs said, "Besides, Hannah, you are unmarried. You shouldn't be living under the roof of a bachelor. It's scandalous."

Now Hannah was truly disconcerted. She had thought only of the time she would meet her grandparents. She never considered having to explain the events of her life to them.

However, Mr. Burroughs seemed to find nothing unusual in her silence. In a brusque gesture of affection, he hugged her shoulders, then released her. "So you will remove with us at once."

Mrs. Burroughs took Hannah's hand and patted it. "Yes, granddaughter, you don't have to make your own way in the world anymore."

For the first time, Hannah comprehended the pressures her father faced. If he loved his parents, as he undoubtedly did, he would have been torn between that love and his love for her mother. And while Hannah despised the choice he had made, she well understood the contest between the love of a woman and the concern of family. "I'm afraid it's not possible for me to go and live with you. Someone needs to be here to care for the aunts, and . . . there are other factors."

"I didn't want to tell you this. It will upset your delicate constitution." Her grandfather frowned and combed his mustache with his fingers. "But that fellow, that new Lord Raeburn—he's not a good influence." Mr. Burroughs's voice boomed out. "I remember gossip about him when he was young. He's dissipated, he's from common stock, and they say he killed his wife."

Hannah realized how tired she was of hearing that when her temper snapped. "He didn't kill his wife."

"Now, Hannah"— Her grandmother gazed sweetly into her eyes. "You must trust your grandfather to know what's best. He always does. And you can't know that Lord Raeburn didn't kill his wife."

"Yes . . . I . . . can." Hannah enunciated clearly so her grandfather could hear. "I'm his wife."

Wide-eyed and with dropped jaws, the Burroughses stared at her.

Miss Minnie crowed.

The other aunts groaned.

Hannah drew herself up. "We've been married for almost ten years. He didn't kill me, I ran away. We've been very foolish, but we are reconciled now, and I will stay here at Raeburn Castle with him and start a family."

Her grandfather harrumphed. Harrumphed again.

Her grandmother's hands fluttered, then came to rest on Mr. Burroughs's arm.

Both of their gazes lifted from her face to a place just above her shoulder.

A hand came to rest on her waist. It was Dougald. She didn't have to turn to know it was he. She recognized his scent, his heat, his presence. She breathed with him. Her heart beat with his. They were truly one.

"Mr. Burroughs, it's too late for me to ask you for Hannah's hand in marriage, but I do promise I will honor her all of our days." Dougald's sincerity flowed like balm over Mr. Burroughs's offense and Mrs. Burroughs's distress. "I lost her once, and I will never do anything to lose her again. I love her."

"You do?" Hannah faced him. "You do?"

"What do you mean"—Dougald looked taken aback—"*you do?*"

"You've never said it."

"What do you think that was all about in the chapel yesterday?"

"It was lovely." She petted his cheek, admiring its high-boned structure and faint burr of whiskers. "I will cherish that memory forever."

"But you want the plain words." He wrapped his arms around her waist. "I love you, Hannah."

Whispering, Hannah confessed, "I love you, too."

"I suppose . . ." Mr. Burroughs was rumbling. "Damned shock . . . the whole day . . ."

"But good shocks," Mrs. Burroughs added to Mr. Burroughs's stammering.

"Yes. Good. Not every day one finds that one has a granddaughter, happily married—" his eyebrows bristled menacingly as he bent his gaze on Hannah—"you are happy?"

"Very much, sir."

He nodded. "And to the local earl. Boy, you have a gem here. Treat her well, or you'll have to answer to me."

The sudden onrush of tears startled Hannah and sent her searching for her handkerchief. She'd never, ever, not even in the early days of her marriage, had anyone to stand behind her. Now she had her grandparents, and they were everything she'd ever dreamed of.

Her grandmother saw her tears, and her own tears sprang forth. "Oh, my sweet girl!" She opened her arms, and they embraced spontaneously, weeping and laughing at the same time.

"Silly women." Mr. Burroughs's voice sounded a little raspier than normal. "Always crying about the most baffling things. Ladies, you're supposed to be happy!" He shook Dougald's hand.

"We are." Mrs. Burroughs used her lace handkerchief to mop her eyes. "See?" She beamed a smile at her irascible husband.

"Now I'm afraid you're going to have to excuse us." Dougald used his own handkerchief to blot Hannah's face. "Her Majesty, Queen Victoria, is asking to speak to my wife."

As she and Dougald walked away, Hannah reflected that the royal favor certainly wouldn't hurt her standing with her grandparents, and might indeed smooth familial relations between the Burroughs and her black sheep of a husband.

Charlotte and Ruskin, Pamela and Kerrich stood

with Prince Albert and Queen Victoria, and they shared pleased smiles between them as they watched Dougald and Hannah walk toward them, together and in love.

But heads turned as Aunt Isabel's voice sounded clearly through the sitting chamber. "Minnie, I'll give you your due. They *are* married. You've won your wager. But nobody likes a gloater."